# The Irish Midwife at War

Seána Tinley is an Irish author of saga historical romance. She also writes regency romance as Catherine Tinley.

After a career encompassing speech and language therapy, Sure Start, being president of a charity, and managing a maternity service, she now works as NI Country Director for a leading UK charity.

Seána was appointed as chair of the Romantic Novelists' Association in August 2024.

Also by Seána Tinley

*The Irish Midwife*

# The Irish Midwife at War

## Seána Tinley

HODDER &
STOUGHTON

First published in Great Britain in 2026 by Hodder & Stoughton Limited
An Hachette UK company

The authorised representative in the EEA is Hachette Ireland,
8 Castlecourt Centre, Dublin 15, D15 XTP3, Ireland (email: info@hbgi.ie)

1

Copyright © Seána Talbot 2026

The right of Seána Tinley to be identified as the Author of the Work has been asserted by her in accordance with the Copyright, Designs and Patents Act 1988.

All rights reserved. No part of this publication may be reproduced, stored in a retrieval system, or transmitted, in any form or by any means without the prior written permission of the publisher, nor be otherwise circulated in any form of binding or cover other than that in which it is published and without a similar condition being imposed on the subsequent purchaser.

All characters in this publication are fictitious and any resemblance to real persons, living or dead, is purely coincidental.

A CIP catalogue record for this title is available from the British Library

Paperback ISBN 978 1 399 74771 4
ebook ISBN 978 1 399 74772 1

Typeset in Plantin Light by Manipal Technologies Limited

Printed and bound in Great Britain by Clays Ltd, Elcograf S.p.A.

Hodder & Stoughton policy is to use papers that are natural, renewable and recyclable products and made from wood grown in sustainable forests. The logging and manufacturing processes are expected to conform to the environmental regulations of the country of origin.

Hodder & Stoughton Limited
Carmelite House
50 Victoria Embankment
London EC4Y 0DZ

www.hodder.co.uk

*To my husband Andrew, with love*

# PART I

# I

*Belfast, New Year's Eve, 1936*

'Ladies and gentlemen!' The voice rang out around the hall. 'Welcome to the New Year's Eve gala party, as we prepare to greet the year nineteen hundred and thirty-seven!'

Sometimes, change comes as a surprise – a lightning bolt with no warning. On other occasions, you can almost *feel* it in the air before it arrives; a rumbling sense of tension, of occasion, of transformation. All day, Kathleen Gallagher had had a strange feeling inside: a delicious mix of excitement, and nerves, and anticipation. If asked, she could not have said precisely what it was that was making her pulse thrum and her senses hum that day, and would have muttered about the fact it was New Year's Eve, she was going to her first dance, and everyone in Belfast was excited and ready to usher in 1937.

Yet there was more to it. Kathleen knew there was. She just did not – yet – know what the *more* was.

*I am sixteen now.* Perhaps that was it. The number had a magical ring to it, for everyone knew that respectable girls were allowed to walk out with boys once they turned sixteen. Kathleen and her best friend Therese Flynn had been speculating for months about what it would be like to walk out with a boy, to hold a boy's hand. To kiss a boy.

Sixteen meant excitement. New freedoms, maybe. At least it would be a change from dreary ordinariness. At the age of twelve Kathleen had started as a half-timer in the Broadway Damask Works – a fancy name for a bog-standard mill – with three days in school, three days in the mill, and Sundays off. At fourteen she had left school along with most of her classmates to become a full-time milly, and since then she had known only the humdrum of life as a mill-hand: up at five winter or summer, standing at the hackling machines or looms all day long, with a couple of breaks and a dinner hour at one. There were two hundred hands employed there, and thousands more across Belfast. Some of Kathleen's school friends and their families were in the match factory or the brickworks, but most were in the mills, and would be for life.

Belfast was famous for its fine linen and intricate damask, all created on the back of heavy labour from its poorest citizens working six days a week. Thank God for God, for without religion no doubt the mill owners would have them working seven days a week. Yeah, and Christmas and New Year, too, if they could get away with it.

For now, more important matters were claiming Kathleen's attention. She and Therese had just arrived for the dance in the parish hall – the first time Kathleen had ever been allowed to go to a proper grown-up dance. How different the place looked, festooned with greenery for Christmas, and with only half the lights on! The hall was rapidly filling up, though the dancing had not yet begun. Kathleen and Therese had timed their arrival perfectly, for judging by the announcement things might get underway very soon.

A team of volunteers were looking after the drinks: tea for anyone who wanted it, club orange or lemonade for under twenty-ones, but Kathleen also saw some of her friends' parents and older brothers drinking alcohol, the men supping bottles of beer and the women with glasses containing an interesting-looking liquid which, she deduced, must be sherry.

Mammy would always have a wee couple of sherries at Christmas, despite generally disapproving of alcohol. Mammy disapproved of quite a lot of things – including dances. And since Kathleen was the youngest, she always seemed to come in for more attention from Mammy than the others had, or so she suspected. Kathleen's older brothers John and Dominic were married and away, as was her sister Jane. Kathleen already had half a dozen nieces and nephews, the older ones being only a few years younger than herself. Though Mammy was very loving, she was also very . . . protective. She was certainly a lot stricter than Therese's mammy.

The only ones left in the Gallagher home now with Mammy and Daddy were the eldest, Bronagh, who had never married, and Kathleen, the youngest, and Mammy was strict with both of them. Even though Kathleen had turned sixteen and was feeling like a proper young lady, she suspected Mammy would continue to treat her as though she was a child.

Maybe it was *because* she was the last child in the house. Was that why Mammy always seemed to come down so hard on her? Mammy seemed to expect much more of Kathleen than Therese's mother expected of Therese. To be fair, Therese had plenty of work to do, being the oldest girl in a house with six children and a mammy but no daddy. Poor Mrs Flynn hardly got a minute from one end of the day to the other.

But no, for Kathleen's mother was equally strict with Bronagh, who was long past sixteen. Maybe it was just Mammy's way.

Despite having all that worry on her, Therese's mammy Mrs Flynn was here tonight making tea, Kathleen saw. Therese's older brother Liam was probably here too somewhere, though Kathleen hadn't yet seen him, and their younger sister Christine would be minding the two wee ones at home along with the other brother, Seány. Their Granny Flynn lived with them, but was too old to help much now. Kathleen was so close to them all that she called Granny Flynn 'Granny' as well.

Six children in that house, five in her own. Most families around here were even bigger; nine and ten childer wasn't uncommon, some families had eighteen or twenty children, and most homes were beautifully chaotic.

Her mind flicked briefly to her own house, which was the opposite of chaotic now that there were so few of them living there. Kathleen could clearly picture the current scene. Mammy and Bronagh would be knitting or darning quietly, Daddy reading the paper, and the radio would be on in the background. *Like every night.* She shuddered. If they had stopped her from coming here tonight she might have gone pure mad.

Why Mammy and Daddy wouldn't even come to a dance at the parish hall, and why Bronagh hadn't even *asked* to go, Kathleen simply couldn't fathom. She'd had to do some serious persuasion even to be allowed to come herself, and Mammy had only agreed because Mrs Flynn had put her on the spot.

*Still, I'm here*, Kathleen thought, a thrill of excitement running through her. The band was already up on the low stage, fiddles being tuned along with a banjo, while she also saw a bodhrán and a couple of tin whistles on the wee table on the stage.

'Let's walk about the hall,' Therese suggested, and Kathleen, her heart pounding, agreed. Exactly as Therese had told her would happen, all the girls were sitting along the left-hand side of the hall, or standing chatting in groups on that side, while the boys were doing the same on the right-hand side. Therese had turned sixteen in September – a full three months before Kathleen – and had managed to get to two dances before the pause for Advent had begun.

Running a critical eye over the lads, Kathleen spotted quite a few that seemed to be about sixteen or seventeen. There was an unwritten rule that you were supposed to stick to lads that were within a year of your own age. While there was many a boy at the far side of the hall, Kathleen wasn't at all sure how long it would take to find one of the right age that she liked, and then to get a kiss. It could be months – years, even! Yet she was also quite ready to be fussy. Boys generally were unattractive creatures who used to pull your hair at school. It was odd that they had become strangely fascinating all of a sudden. The thought of even having to speak to boys now made her feel nervous.

After folding their shawls and placing them on two chairs near the third window, Kathleen and Therese ambled about, keeping to the female side of the invisible line that bisected the space, which was only currently being crossed by those helping with the event. Naturally, both girls were in their Sunday best, Kathleen having received her new dress as a combined Christmas and birthday gift a few days ago. It was a gorgeous shade of blue with a full skirt and tiny flowers embroidered along the edge of the bodice, and Kathleen knew she had never worn anything so pretty. The wardrobe in Mammy and Daddy's room had a mirror in the door, and Kathleen had twisted and turned in front of it, loving how the dress swished and had seemed to shimmer in the electric light.

Her curls could be hard to tame, but tonight she had persisted and with the aid of some hairpins she had managed a semblance of the fashionable styles she had seen other girls wear. Fair hair, blue eyes, and a tall, willowy shape, enhanced by her new dress. She was lucky, she knew, to be reasonable looking. Life was hard enough at fourteen and fifteen without worrying about bad teeth or a nose that was too big for your face. Therese was dark-haired and good-looking like all the Flynns, and Kathleen knew the two of them were attracting exactly the right sort of attention from the boys on the other side of the hall.

Surreptitiously they tried to work out which boys they knew, recognising quite a few of them from Beechmount – their part of Belfast's Falls Road. These were boys Kathleen and Therese had played with in the streets before they were all old enough to take up their places in the various mills. Tonight, though, the lads had taken on something of an exotic character, as Kathleen assessed each one with fresh eyes – the eyes of a sixteen-year-old looking for an adventure.

'God, Jimmy McKeown is looking fine!' Therese hissed. 'Just look at the shoulders on him!'

'And he's good-looking too,' Kathleen agreed.

'Flip! He's seen us looking at him!' Quickly they turned as if entirely focused on the noticeboard to their left. Since this contained only boring hand-drawn posters about meetings of various prayer groups, Jimmy may not have been convinced.

Thankfully, distraction came from an unexpected source. 'Therese! Kathleen!' Mrs Flynn was beckoning them, and so they made their way to the tea table. 'You remember Mrs Clarke, don't you?'

Mrs Clarke was well known in West Belfast. Along with Mrs Kennedy and Mrs Quinn, she was one of the leading handywomen in the area, supporting women who were having babies, and helping families where someone was dying.

'Hello, Mrs Clarke,' they said politely.

'This here's my Therese, and this is her great friend Kathleen Gallagher. As I was saying, they're both sixteen – Therese since September, Kathleen a few days ago.'

'Are yous now?' Mrs Clarke cast a keen eye over them, and Kathleen felt suddenly alert. *Why is this happening?* This was no casual conversation, she was certain of it.

'Your mother was saying you're both working in the mills. Is that so?'

'It is.'

'Aye.'

'How do yous like it?'

What a question! You weren't supposed to *like* the mills. Nobody *liked* it. It was your work, that was all. Everybody worked, and everybody was glad of it. With the world in a Great Depression they were lucky to have work at all. It wasn't that long since a million Irish people had died in the famine. Work was work, rent was rent, and food was food. But *oh*! How Kathleen dreamed of something more!

The truth was, she hated the mill. Hated the smells, the heat, the sheer physical toil of it all. Not being blessed with sturdiness she found the lifting and pushing and pulling difficult. Nobody even *talked* about work in this part of Belfast because there was literally nothing to say. Nearly everybody worked in the mills or the factories, and everybody hated it. There was no point looking at it, for it would only get you down. Which was why Mrs Clarke's question was so odd. And significant.

Therese shrugged. 'It's all right, I suppose.'

Kathleen swallowed, and didn't answer.

'Did you ever fancy doing something else alongside your work?'

Mrs Clarke's meaning was obvious. *Become a handywoman?* Suddenly there was a roaring in Kathleen's ears. This was the solution! This was what she had been waiting for!

Of the hundred or so people in the hall tonight, Kathleen was willing to bet that nearly ninety of them worked in the mills and factories and brickworks. The only ones who didn't were mothers, the old or infirm, or those lucky enough to have found an escape route – another type of work. For the lucky girls, that usually meant working in a shop or as a servant in a big house. The luckiest of boys got an apprenticeship for a trade.

Here, suddenly, unexpectedly, and wonderfully, was another option. Being a handywoman. While laying out the dead and sitting with the dying would be hard, surely helping women with wee babies would be interesting? Anything would be better than mill work from the age of twelve until the day you were crushed by a machine or took tuberculosis.

'What do you mean, Mrs Clarke?' Therese asked cautiously.

'We're a bit short of handywomen these days. I took over training Peggy Cassidy after her aunt Mrs Devine died near two years ago, Lord rest her, but that still leaves only a handful of us for this whole area. Mrs Quinn and Mrs Kennedy have apprentices, but now that Peggy is a qualified midwife I want to start again with a new girl.'

'Oh.' Therese looked dubious.

'What would it involve? You know, the training?' Kathleen's heart was thumping with nerves, but in even asking the question she was opening up the possibility of a whole new life.

Mrs Flynn was smiling. 'Aye, I reckon you'd be well-suited for it, Kathleen.'

Mrs Clarke's attention focused on her. Kathleen could see it all in her gaze: the intelligence, the compassion, how special she was. Handywomen were special. *Could I become special like that?* 'Is that so? And why would you think that, Mrs Flynn?'

'They're both great workers – no laziness in them. But our Therese would be a bit of a panicker, wouldn't you, Therese?'

Therese shrugged. 'Aye. Can't cope with blood or anything.'

'And what about you, Kathleen?'

Kathleen felt as though her entire life was at a turning point. Here was another path – if she was brave enough to take it. 'I-I don't mind it.' God, why could she not say what she really thought? *Please take me on, Mrs Clarke!*

'Kathleen's a wee star, so she is. When somebody's annoyed or injured or not well, she's always the one looking after them.'

'Is that right?' Mrs Clarke's gaze returned to Kathleen. 'When are you back to work?'

'Not till Monday.'

'Right so. Come and see me tomorrow. My house is on the corner of the Falls and St James's Park. About ten?'

'I'll have to ask my mammy.'

'You do that.'

Mammies were the bosses at home. Men always got the better jobs, or were paid more money for the same job, but women were in charge really. Everyone knew that.

Someone else came for tea then, and Mrs Clarke went to serve them. As they walked away, Therese slipped her hand into Kathleen's arm. 'God, I wouldn't wanna be a handywoman – not for a hundred pound! Imagine having to wash and dress dead bodies!' She shuddered. 'Would you do it, Kathleen?'

'I think so.' The dead bodies were, naturally, the least appealing aspect. 'Wee babies and all.'

Therese rolled her eyes. 'That's cos you've never had to mind them. Our Maria and Rita-Anne are well up now, but I still remember how foul the nappies were!'

'What age were you when your ones were born?' Kathleen asked curiously.

'Liam, Therese, Seány, Christine, Maria, Rita-Anne,' Therese recited in a singsong voice, 'and wee Alfie who died. He was between Christine and Maria.' Kathleen squeezed her friend's arm. Most mothers around here had lost at least one child to miscarriage, stillbirth, or death in infancy. No one really talked about it, but everybody knew. 'Let's see,' Therese continued. 'Our Liam's nearly eighteen now . . .'

'Aye.' Kathleen tried *not* to think too much about Liam Flynn – the way his blue, blue eyes smiled when he was in good form, the way he had stepped up to be the man of the house, helping his mammy after his daddy was killed. The way he never *saw* her. Not really.

Therese was still talking, her brow furrowed in concentration. 'Our Seány is fourteen so I would have been two when he was born. Christine is twelve so I was four. Maria is nine so I was seven. And Rita-Anne is seven so I was . . . nine!'

Kathleen sighed. 'You're so lucky. Being the youngest is horrible.'

'Being the eldest girl isn't the best of craic!' Therese retorted dryly. 'Oh, the music is starting!'

Sure enough, the band was now ready and playing a few bars of a jig to get everyone's attention. The dance was of course to be a céilí, with Irish music, Irish dances, and later on no doubt there'd be a couple of locals getting up to sing a song or say a poem. West Belfast had found itself again in the expression of Irishness through music, dance, and song. The English might enjoy their Charlestons and quicksteps: in this part of Belfast people were quite content with a céilí.

The *fear an tí* – the host – then took up his position again. With a great deal of flourish he called them to the floor, and there was a murmur and a rustle as the crowd all moved into the centre of the dancefloor. 'The Siege of Ennis!' the man called, repeating the name of the dance in Irish. '*Ionsaí na hInse*! Four facing four! Find a partner!'

*Find a partner.* If only it was that easy! Still, Kathleen and Therese moved with the rest, arm in arm to make it clear they would be part of the same set. Abruptly, Therese pulled Kathleen to the right – and there was Jimmy McKeown and another lad, keenly eyeing all the girls as they moved forward.

Therese planted them straight in front of the lads, while Kathleen died a little inside.

'Well, Jimmy, what about ye?'

'Jayz, Therese, you're lookin' well. Dance?' Jimmy held out a hand and Therese took it, leaving Kathleen bereft.

'Aye.' Therese and Jimmy both looked at Jimmy's friend, who shrugged, then held out a hand to Kathleen.

Feeling decidedly second-best, Kathleen took it, and the four of them moved into the line. A minute later the music began properly, and Kathleen went through the steps they had learned in school, while the *fear an tí* called them out. *Advance* . . . they moved towards the four dancers facing them. *Retire* . . . they went backwards again. *Advance . . . retire . . .* They repeated the opening step then split into couples, Kathleen and her partner weaving behind Therese and Jimmy, then returning to their places for the next move. Kathleen then swung with the lad facing her, afterwards returning to their line of four to move forward to the next set.

The simple sequence was repeated a dozen times, and Kathleen got to swing with a dozen different lads as their line progressed up the hall. Some lads were better looking than others. Some were better dancers than others. A couple of them even made conversation, asking her for her name and telling her theirs. Throughout, Jimmy's friend didn't speak. Not one word. At the end they all thanked each other politely, then walked away.

'How did you do that?' Kathleen asked, as they retreated to the girls' side of the hall.

'Do what?'

'Just like – walk right up to him.'

Therese tossed her head. 'If you know what you want, why not go for it?' Her eyes narrowed. 'Now I need to completely ignore him for the rest of the night.'

Kathleen's jaw dropped. 'Why would you do that? I thought you liked him?'

'That's exactly why.'

Reaching the chairs where they had left their shawls, they sat, retrieving their narrow bottles of club orange from underneath.

'I don't get it,' said Kathleen, sucking her paper straw. The drink was delicious: orangey and sweet and very fizzy. 'Why can you not let him see that you like him?'

'Because,' Therese said, an air of mystery about her, 'you have to not seem too keen.'

Kathleen thought about this. Boys could be strange creatures. 'Is it . . .' She thought for a minute, trying to articulate the thought. 'Is it that they have to feel they're *winning* something or someone?'

'Yeah. Like we're a prize heifer at the cattle market. You know, the more bids that are made, the more bidders join in!' They laughed, but there was something deeper there, Kathleen knew. She did not want to be a heifer. Ever.

And so when the next dance was called she let Therese find them partners again, and once again she kept herself to herself, not encouraging any of the boys. Thank God for Therese's confidence, or Kathleen might have been left sitting some of the dances out, like the girls who had not managed to find a partner by the time the music began.

There was a fine line here. While she couldn't bring herself to actually flirt, Kathleen didn't want to be a wallflower either. *God, this is complicated!*

About halfway through the evening the *fear an tí* called everyone to gather for 'tunny horry', causing a buzz of excitement around the hall. The Waves of Tory (or *Tonnaí*

*Thoraí* in Irish) had been the most popular dance in school when they had been taught it by the nuns, and that excitement had clearly persisted for everybody here tonight.

This time everyone took part, for there was no need to find a partner before it began. Instead the boys stood in a single long line, facing the girls. Kathleen knew that as the dance progressed she would end up partnered with a boy from roughly the same part of the line as herself, so cast a critical eye over the boys opposite.

Boys? Some were *men*, for the dance included people of all ages. Running her eye along the line, she caught her breath. *Liam Flynn!*

Lord above, he was something special. Like all the men he was sporting his Sunday trousers and a crisp white shirt, but very few of the males opposite had Liam's good looks. Or his physique.

Gulping, Kathleen drew her gaze away from his strong shoulders and arms, focusing on his face – a face she knew well. Thick dark hair, those blue, blue Flynn eyes, a strong jaw. God, how she wished she was the same age as him! He put every lad in the place to shame.

After the jig part of the dance the march began, and they all followed the leader down the hall to where the top dancers had made an arch for couples to pass under. Kathleen ended up with a grinning, perspiring middle-aged man, missing the chance to dance with Liam by only three dancers. The girl who got him had a gorgeous pink dress and as Kathleen watched, the girl literally fluttered her eyelashes at him!

Kathleen shuddered. Maybe it was a good thing she and Liam hadn't ended up partnered, for she'd never have managed to behave like that! Mammy's strictness had rubbed off on all her girls, for both Bronagh and Jane were reservedly polite in company – exactly like Kathleen herself.

Despite this, Jane had somehow managed to acquire a boyfriend (Pat George, who was now her husband), but Bronagh had not. Kathleen knew she would somehow have to break through the Gallagher reserve if she was to have any chance. The thought of being condemned to a life like Bronagh's filled her with horror. Imagine still living with your mammy and daddy when you were over thirty!

Kathleen and her partner were now in the waves part of the dance, working their way up the hall as other couples worked their way down, alternating making an arch for them to pass through, then bending to go under the next pair of lifted arms. Under and over, under and over, the effect that of waves in the sea. Liam and his partner were always three couples ahead, and Kathleen couldn't help but look every time she could. Reaching the top, they stopped and turned, lifting their joined hands to the next couple, even as Kathleen and her partner made their way closer.

Recognition flared in Liam's eyes as he lifted to allow Kathleen and her partner to go under his arch. 'Well, Kathleen!' He grinned.

'Liam!' she managed, feigning surprise.

And that was that. The dance moved on, and he was gone.

# 2

'So, what did you think?'

The girls were standing under the streetlight outside Therese's house on Clowney Street, where they usually parted. What wasn't usual was the fact it was twelve thirty in the morning – half past midnight on the first day of 1937. Kathleen had never been outside so late before. It was cold, the sky leaden and not a star to be seen. Yet Kathleen didn't give a damn. She felt *alive*, for the first time since the heady freedoms of childhood – freedoms she had taken for granted, not being able to understand what working in a mill would actually mean.

All around them people were making their way home after the dance, being joined by men pouring out of the Rock Bar in various stages of inebriation. The Falls Road and Beechmount Avenue were as busy as they would usually be at dinner time on a work day! The whole thing was wonderfully odd.

'It was class, Therese. Honestly, it was!'

Therese grinned. 'Did ya see any boy you might fancy?'

'Not a one! Jimmy McKeown is the best-lookin' of the boys our age, and he only has eyes for you!' She tightened her shawl around her. It was getting colder by the minute.

Therese snorted. 'Not so sure about that – although he's danced with me at all three of the céilís I've been to.'

'Well that can't be a coincidence, surely? He must be after you?'

'I think . . .' she said slowly, 'that he's getting there. But he's not there yet. Here—'

'What?'

Therese shook her head then deliberately changed the subject. 'What did you make of Mrs Clarke? Are you actually gonna go and see her the morra?'

'Honest to God, I'd love to. If Mammy lets me.' She made a face. 'And I can never predict what way Mammy will go. She could stop this in its tracks, or push me to do it.'

'Therese.'

*I know that voice!* Kathleen's heart skipped a beat as they spun around to where Liam was approaching, his brow furrowed.

'You may go on in, Therese,' he said, jerking his head towards their house. 'Drunks everywhere, and I'm after seein' a fight outside the Rock.'

Therese grimaced. 'Aye, s'pose you're right. See ya the morra, Kathleen.'

'See you!' Daringly, Kathleen sent a saucy look in Liam's direction. 'Goodnight, Liam.'

'Wait. I'll walk you round.'

'Ach, you don't need to do that, Liam. I'll be grand.' *Oh, please walk me home!*

Therese was rolling her eyes. 'You may take his company, Kathleen. Once he gets a big brother notion into his head, there's no diverting him.'

*Big brother. Right.*

'She's right, you know. And sure you're only in Locan Street.'

Kathleen fell into step beside him. 'Aye, it's two streets away. I'm perfectly capable—'

'I don't doubt it, Kathleen. It's not *your* intentions I'm worried about.' He sent a meaningful glance to the far side of the road, where two men were staggering along the edge of the street.

Kathleen grimaced. 'Fair enough.'

They made small talk then: the céilí, the crowds there tonight, speculation as to what 1937 might bring. Throughout, Kathleen's spirit was floating about five feet above the footpath. This was the most conversation she'd had with Liam in years.

Impulsively, she told him about Mrs Clarke's invitation, and his eyes widened. 'A great opportunity – though it would never do for our Therese. She's far too fond of drama. The thing about the handywomen is that they have a sort of *quietness* about them, you know? They're strong, but quietly strong.' He eyed her appraisingly. 'Like you, Kathleen.' He shook his head then, laughing lightly. 'Jaysus, listen to me! Getting all soft!'

Storing away his compliment – for it *was* a compliment, she could tell – Kathleen jumped straight in to reassure him. 'No, I think you're right about the handywomen.' She could picture Mrs Clarke, and Mrs Quinn, whom she knew slightly. And Peggy Cassidy, who had been ahead of her at school. They all had a *stillness* about them. 'That's really well observed.' She sent him a sideways glance. 'Do you often notice things that other people don't?'

He shrugged. 'Sometimes. Not that it's of any use to me. I'm still stuck in a mill pulling loom beams about or sorting flax once it's hackled.'

'I know exactly what you mean. They don't need our brains at all, only our bodies.' She shuddered. 'We're just part of the machine to the mill owners.'

'Aye. And supposed to show gratitude for having work at all.'

'Exactly.'

'Kathleen, go and see Mrs Clarke,' he said suddenly, his tone harsh. 'You have the sniff of freedom. Take it!'

She nodded. He was right. His vehemence touched her, though. 'What about you, Liam? How do you get freedom?'

He shook his head sadly. 'I keep looking, searching, thinking . . . but there's nothing. We don't have the money to buy me an apprenticeship. I have to keep bringing my full mill wage in – my family needs me.'

*Trapped.* The word, unspoken, resonated in the air between them. She nodded, and their eyes met. Somehow, they had reached Kathleen's street, and had stopped walking. Kathleen's heart was thumping like the noise of a hundred looms, and her knees felt strangely soft. His eyes were on hers, and the world had stopped. Then slowly, allowing her every opportunity to turn away, he bent his head to hers.

Not in a thousand lifetimes would she have turned away. Ignoring the cold which was now seeping through her thin shoes and her sturdy shawl, Kathleen's attention was focused entirely on Liam. His lips brushed hers lightly, sending delicious sparks shooting through her. He brushed her lips again, then settled his mouth on hers. Kathleen's eyes fluttered closed, even as she felt his arms gently sweep around her, drawing her closer. And now his mouth was moving ever so slightly, creating the most wonderful friction. He kissed her bottom lip, then her top lip, once again angling his mouth to hers. Instinctively she tilted her head, gasping at the wonder of it all. Instantly his tongue darted out, brushing her lips briefly and making her gasp again.

An apt pupil, she followed his lead, touching his lips with her own tongue and thrilling at the deep groan he made in his throat. His arms were wrapped around her, and hers were on his back as their tongues danced and her body swirled inwardly.

The kiss lasted for a lifetime – or maybe a minute. He stepped back then, taking her two hands and bringing them to his lips. 'You're freezin', Kathleen.'

'Am I?' Something feather-light was tickling her face. She blinked. 'It's snowing!'

All around them, silent flakes were falling thickly, enveloping them in a white world. Only Liam was real. Liam, and the magic.

She tilted her face to the sky, joy coursing through her. 'It's beautiful!' He didn't respond, and when she looked at him he had a strange expression on his face.

'Beautiful, yes.' His voice was almost a whisper. Then, as if awakening from a dream, he shook his head vigorously, dropping her hands. 'I'm sorry, Kathleen, I shouldn't have done that.'

Instantly, the magic vanished. The dance had ended. *Advance, retire.* She stood there eyeing him blankly as he spoke on. Something about her being only sixteen, and Therese's friend. 'Goodnight.'

Then he was gone, and in a haze Kathleen walked the ten or so steps to her own front door.

And there was Mammy, rapidly descending the stairs. 'Where the hell were you till this time?'

# 3

Mrs Clarke lived in a Big House. Oh, not a stately home like Beechmount House up the hill. That one used to be owned by a wealthy Protestant family by the name of Riddel, but it was now a convent and a home for the elderly. People always said that old Mr Riddel had decreed the house was never to fall into the hands of papists. If that was true then surely the old bigot was rolling in his grave at the fact his daughters had sold it to the bishop and it was now overrun with nuns.

No, the Clarke house was not on that scale. But it was detached, with gardens in front and behind, four chimney pots, and bay windows either side of the front door. It was built in the same red brick as most of the houses in this part of Belfast, but was easily three times the width of the Gallaghers' two-up-two-down in Locan Street. The snow had stopped before dawn, and already the roads and pavements had lost their serene white carpet, now stained by countless footsteps, cartwheels, hooves, and motor-cars. A transient, momentary beauty.

Kathleen and Mammy trudged through the slush, pausing to greet acquaintances every few yards. In between, Kathleen was getting lectured, Mammy having continued unabated since giving Kathleen a clip on the ear last night.

'Out gallivanting till all hours! Chasin' boys, no doubt. You needn't think this is what you're gonna be at now, Kathleen.

It was quarter to one when you came in! Quarter to one, and me distracted with the worry!'

'I'm sorry, Mammy. I wouldn't want you to be worrying.' After apologising for the dozenth time, Kathleen was beginning to think she'd never drop the issue. And she couldn't even robustly defend herself against the accusation she had been 'chasin' boys' – not after the magical way in which the night had ended.

'Well I was. That dance finished at twelve! Where in God's name were you?'

'It didn't actually finish at twelve. After the bells they did Auld Lang Syne and "The Parting Glass", and everybody was hugging. It was actually lovely. You know, the New Year and all.'

'And who were you with?'

Kathleen suppressed a sigh, having already been over this. Did Mammy really think she'd catch her out in a lie if she asked again? To be fair she hadn't mentioned Liam at all, knowing instinctively Mammy would not approve of Kathleen being walked home by a lad – especially a lad nearly two years older than herself. *Thank God she didn't see anything!*

'Therese Flynn. Mrs Flynn stayed behind to tidy up.'

'Shush now.' In a very different tone Mammy hailed the lady approaching them on the footpath. 'Hello, Mrs Martin. How are ya?' They stopped, and Kathleen welcomed the respite from her interrogation as Mammy and Mrs Martin conversed, polite as you like.

'This your girl, Mrs Gallagher?' Mrs Martin sent a curious glance in her direction.

'Aye. My youngest. Kathleen.'

'Och, yes, your wee late baby, Mrs Gallagher! My God, she's shot up. You're a quare young woman now, aren't you?'

To answer would be walking into a trap. Mrs Martin was only being polite, but the last thing Kathleen should be doing was to remind Mammy she was now sixteen. Mammy definitely didn't want Kathleen thinking of herself as a 'young woman'. That was abundantly clear.

Thankfully Mrs Martin walked on soon afterwards, and Mammy's attention was now back to the handywoman.

'Tell me again what Mrs Clarke said,' she demanded, as they were going through the gate. The Clarke garden still had a blanket of snow, Kathleen noticed, as though it was capable of holding magic for longer than everywhere else.

'She said they were short of handywomen, and would me or Therese be interested.'

'Well, at least we're here early.' Mammy rang the doorbell. 'If there's only one apprenticeship going, you need to get it.'

'Oh, but I don't think Therese—'

The door opened, an unfamiliar lady standing there.

'Ach hello, Mrs Gallagher!' she declared in a friendly way. 'Mrs Clarke said your daughter might be calling. Come in, come in!'

'Aye. This is our Kathleen. Kathleen, this is Mrs Savage.'

Kathleen responded politely, realising that Mrs Savage worked for the Clarkes. *Wow. They must be quare and rich to be able to employ a housekeeper.*

Mrs Savage led them to the first door on the right, knocking and awaiting a response. When it came she opened the door and announced them. Kathleen had never in her life been announced before.

Mrs Clarke was all smiles. 'Mrs Gallagher, good to see you. And Kathleen! Come, have a wee seat there. Happy New Year to yous.'

Kathleen murmured a response and sat, noting the thick carpet, the bookshelves, the massive fireplace, and the fact that the framed paintings on the wall were not in any way religious. *So fancy!* In most houses round here the only pictures on the walls were saints, popes, or Irish rebels.

The conversation began as it usually did, with the two grown-ups asking after each other's health and enquiring after their families.

'And have you only Kathleen at home now, Mrs Gallagher?'

'No, our Bronagh never married, so she's still with us too. The other three are all up and married.'

'Ach, right.' She turned her gaze to Kathleen, and once again Kathleen felt the effect of her character – keenness, sharpness, and kindness all at once. 'And would you be interested in training with me, Kathleen?'

'She would,' Mammy confirmed.

*It's a good thing I do want this, for Mammy has already decided I'm doing it.*

Mammy was still talking. 'It's hard for girls to get anything outside the mills, so it is.'

'You're right there. But I should make it clear that being a handywoman isn't easy. Nor does it pay well. This' –she waved vaguely at her fancy room –'is because I happened to marry a lawyer. Most handywomen don't earn more than they would if they were full-time in the mills.'

'Aye, but it's the *respect*,' Mammy said. 'Handywomen are well respected. They're . . .' She paused as if seeking the right words. 'They're well thought of.' Her eyes narrowed. 'How much would she earn, by the way?'

Mrs Clarke grimaced. 'Nothing as an apprentice – well, maybe something now and again, but nothing you can rely on. Once a handywoman starts doing births by herself around here she gets about ten shillings from each woman. *But*' – she emphasised, as Kathleen's jaw dropped at the notion of such riches – 'that includes ten days of help after the birth. And some women can't afford the fee, but we help them anyway.'

'Aye, I thought that,' said Mammy. 'Still, you'll always have work, even if the mills ever lay people off.'

Mrs Clarke nodded. 'What do *you* think, Kathleen? Do you want to be a handywoman?'

Finally she was allowed to speak. 'I do.' It sounded like a vow.

'And why is that?'

'I like helping people. And I think I'm – you know – not bad at it.' She couldn't bring herself to say she was *good*. 'I don't panic when people are hurt, like, and I can be . . .' In her mind she searched for the right word. When it came to her, it was in Liam's voice. 'I can be *quiet*. And still. And patient. I think that's important for a handywoman.'

Mrs Clarke nodded approvingly. 'You're exactly right, Kathleen. Well said.'

'But I don't know anything about women having babies, or people dying.' She bit her lip. Life with Mammy and Daddy and Bronagh had left her sheltered from such things.

'Aye, well that's where the training comes in.'

'What would it involve?' This was what she had asked last night. This was what she really wanted to know, so she could picture it.

Mrs Clarke explained. Kathleen would work alongside her, mainly unpaid, until she picked up the skills. It would take a few years to be fully independent, and like any apprentice she would earn very little while training. Once she started doing births by herself the women would pay her. The work was unpredictable, but involved many hours of sitting with the dying, or sitting with women about to give birth. As she spoke, Kathleen developed images in her head of how it would be: supporting, caring, learning how to handle different situations that might arise. Instead of spinning rooms and weaving sheds, she would be in people's houses. Instead of working only with her body, she would be working with her mind. And her heart.

It sounded wonderful.

'So what do you think? Would you be interested?'

Kathleen nodded and went to speak, but Mammy had another question. 'What about the polis? I heard what happened to poor Mrs Devine.'

'Aye, that was a bad business.' Mrs Clarke shook her head. 'But the fact she died that night will stop them from doing anything similar – at least for a few years.'

'What's this?' Kathleen had found her voice. 'What happened to Mrs Devine?' Mammy never told her anything controversial, and conversations were often hurriedly ended when Kathleen entered the room. *Can't have the chile of the house learning anything about real life, can we?*

'Being a handywoman has been made illegal,' Mrs Clarke declared. 'It's important you know what you're getting yourself into, Kathleen. They're saying only qualified midwives should be sitting with the women.' She sniffed. 'As if midwife isn't just a fancy name for handywoman anyway. Do you think Our Lady cared whether the handywomen that helped her were *qualified* or not when she was having baby Jesus?' She dipped her head on the last word, as you were supposed to when you said 'Jesus'. 'Mrs Devine was lifted by the police the day she died,' she continued. 'They held her for hours and she took a stroke when she got home, Lord rest her.'

Kathleen's hand flew to her mouth. She had been reared on stories of violence and discrimination from the Royal Ulster Constabulary. 'What did they do to her?'

Mrs Clarke shrugged. 'She said they didn't lay a finger on her. But she must have been terrified.'

'That's desprit!'

'Aye. So we do try to stay out of their way, you know? What we do is none of their business. It's *our* business.'

*Women's business.* The business of West Belfast, of the nationalist community, of the Irish. 'What about Protestant handywomen?'

'A good question, Kathleen. Aye, there are handywomen in the Protestant areas too. Strangely it wasn't one of them that got lifted.' She raised a cynical eyebrow and Kathleen nodded slowly.

'So, Kathleen, knowing what you know, would you like to be an apprentice handywoman?' Mrs Clarke's tone was firm, and she looked Kathleen in the eye.

'She would, aye,' said Mammy, but Mrs Clarke's gaze didn't so much as flicker.

'I want her to answer for herself.'

For the first time in her life, Kathleen was being asked to make an important decision. Her insides were churning with nerves, and excitement, and something she recognised as determination. Feeling the weight and significance of the moment, she shivered, then said firmly, 'I would love to.'

# 4

Everything had changed, yet on the surface Kathleen's life continued exactly as it had for years. She went to the mill every workday, to Mass on Sunday and confession every fortnight. She did her housework and called round for Therese and occasionally went to dances in the parish hall.

Yet inside, all was different. The magic of Liam's kiss had melted away like snow off a rope, but always it shone within her. She had wished him a happy birthday in January, knowing that him being eighteen while she was sixteen meant there would definitely be no more kisses. They had managed to connect on New Year's Eve, during the tiny window created by their birthdays where there was numerically only a year between them.

That window had now closed. Might it open again, next year? Kathleen had no way of knowing.

Going by Liam's behaviour towards her, it was likely a *No*. He was friendly but distant, treating her like his sister's best friend, as he always had. As if their kiss had never happened. And Kathleen had no idea how to change that. He had said he regretted it immediately afterwards. Perhaps he had kissed so many girls that he had succumbed to a momentary impulse. An impulse that had been to him meaningless.

The thought sat uncomfortably with her. Perhaps the magic had been only in her own head, created from the night and the snowflakes and the pounding of her own heart.

'Kathleen! I'm asking you a question!' Mammy sounded cross.

'What? Sorry.' They were just finishing supper. Bronagh was sipping tea, and Daddy was still eating his bread-and-dripping. It was a world away from magical snow-touched kisses.

'How did you get on with Mrs Clarke today?'

Kathleen shrugged. 'It was interesting. She told me all about early labour and how a woman might know she's starting.'

'Yes, well,' Mammy said primly, glancing towards Daddy, who seemed oblivious, 'we'll talk about all of that some other time.'

Kathleen's eyes met Bronagh's. *Classic Mammy!* Wants to know everything, but doesn't allow you to talk about women's topics in front of Daddy.

Bronagh rolled her eyes, then set her teacup down. 'Right! Is everybody finished?' Daddy had finally cleared his plate. She stood, picking up the uneaten bread which would do for the morra, while Kathleen gathered the other plates and the cutlery.

Safely in the kitchen away from Mammy, Bronagh started scraping the plates. 'Mammy's a laugh, isn't she?'

'I dunno. She does my head in at times. Am I supposed to answer her questions or not?'

'Ah, but, Kathleen, do you not know you're supposed to magically figure out what to do each time?'

'It's so unfair!'

Bronagh shrugged. 'She's a good woman, our mammy. She cares, you know?'

Kathleen could still feel indignation burning within her. 'Aye, she cares, but she's so . . . *controlling*!' Lifting the kettle from the stove, she poured hot water into the sink bowl.

'Mammies are meant to be. It'd be worse if she just let us do what we wanted, wouldn't it?'

'No!' Kathleen sent her a wry look. 'Think about what you're after sayin'.' She added some cold water from the tap along with washing soda, swirling it about to get the soda well mixed in.

Bronagh laughed. 'You're right of course. But I'm contented enough.'

'Are you, though?' She sent her sister a curious look. 'Do you never wish for more? To get out of here?'

'There was a time when I did.' A wistfulness came across her expression. 'I wanted to get married, be a mother . . . all those things. But there's no point in wishing for things that might have been.' She frowned. 'Or do you mean get out of Belfast?'

Kathleen thought about it. 'I didn't mean that, though now you come to mention it, I'd love to visit somewhere else. Dublin, maybe.' She frowned as she began washing the plates, a vague memory coming to her. 'Haven't you been to Dublin?'

'I have. Me and Ma were there for a few months – a long time ago, when there wasn't enough work here.' She shrugged. 'Dublin's basically like here, only bigger.'

'Still, I'd like to see it some day.'

'Well, you may start saving up for a train ticket, then!'

Kathleen grinned at her. Bronagh hadn't said she couldn't, or that she was foolish for having such notions. Bronagh wasn't like Mammy. In fact, if it wasn't for Bronagh, Kathleen would have cracked up a long time ago. When Kathleen had found blood in her underwear not long before her fourteenth birthday, it had been Bronagh who had explained things, Bronagh who had told her how to use rags, Bronagh who had fetched her a hot-water bottle when she had pains. Mammy – clearly uncomfortable – had simply muttered generalities about a monthly curse that she had to endure because Our Lady had had to endure it too.

When Kathleen had questions about how her body worked, she had always gone to Bronagh with them. She now had new questions – mostly about babies and how they were made – but could hardly bring those to her unmarried, childless sister. Mrs Clarke though was quite another matter. While she barely knew the woman, she sensed that the handywoman was forthright –or at least, that she could be, given the right circumstances.

Yes, becoming a handywoman might prove liberating in more ways than one. She only hoped she'd be allowed to help at a birth soon.

# 5

On Holy Saturday, it finally happened. Kathleen was called to the home of Mrs Thompson, who was having her third child. Mrs Thompson's younger sister was in the same class as Kathleen's niece, and so she vaguely knew the family. Mrs Thompson's own mother was in the house in St James's when Kathleen arrived, tagging uncertainly behind Mrs Clarke.

'Come in, come in, Mrs Clarke! She's in the kitchen peelin' spuds.'

'Ah, good stuff,' Mrs Clarke replied. 'And how are you these days?'

The woman replied at length while Kathleen hovered with one arm as long as the other, trying to look interested. She should be used to this, for Mammy did it all the time. Grown-ups would talk to each other for as long as they wanted to, and you were expected to stand still even if you were bored.

To be fair, today Kathleen was anything but bored. Today she would see a baby born. From what Mrs Clarke had already told her, the baby would come out from between the woman's legs – via the same exit that period blood came out of. The notion was astounding. How could a whole baby come out of somewhere so small? It seemed impossible.

The lady had come to the end of her saga, and now glanced towards Kathleen.

'This is Kathleen Gallagher, my new apprentice.'

'Ach, right.' Her eyes narrowed with curiosity. 'Gallagher? Now which Gallagher would you be?'

'I'm from Locan Street. Near the bottom.'

'Ach, sure, I know you now! I know your mammy, and your big sister Bronagh.'

Kathleen nodded.

'Bronagh's a great help at the St Vincent de Paul group, so she is. Great girl, your Bronagh.'

Kathleen was unsure what to say to this. Bronagh did indeed help with the St Vincent de Paul group and she was indeed a great girl.

'So how are things progressing?' Mrs Clarke jerked her head towards the kitchen.

'Aye, goin' rightly. Sure, you know yourself. Third baby.'

'Aye.' They exchanged a look of shared understanding – one that meant absolutely nothing to Kathleen. What was so significant about a third baby?

'Right. I'll go and say hello and check she's all right for me to have Kathleen here.'

'And I'll go and round up the rest of them. They're all staying at my house tonight.'

'A great treat for them all.'

'Aye, though my Vincy won't be impressed. He's had his fill of childer, he says. But sure it's only for the one night.'

'Men!' They both rolled their eyes, then Mrs Thompson's mother went outside and began yelling her grandchildren's names, while Mrs Clarke made for the wee back kitchen.

Kathleen looked around curiously. The house was identical to her own in layout: two rooms downstairs, two above, and an outhouse with a pull-chain toilet in the yard. Scullery houses, they were sometimes called, though Kathleen was unsure why, for scullery was simply another word for kitchen, and all the houses had kitchens.

Mrs Thompson's furniture looked rather old and battered, but the pictures on the walls were familiar: the Pope above the fireplace and St Therese the Little Flower on the wall opposite the window. That was the saint Therese Flynn was named after. Therese still thought she was mad in the head for agreeing to apprentice with Mrs Clarke, and Kathleen had a fear she might be right.

Mrs Clarke had explained that being in labour was not, as Kathleen had always assumed, something to do with a woman having worked too hard. Instead, it was the name for the hard work of giving birth. Period pains happened, she had explained, because the womb was tightening to expel the period blood, and the same thing happened in childbirth – only the pains were bigger and stronger, for the womb had grown to accommodate a baby and was now working to expel the child. The whole thing could take quite some time apparently, and the handywoman's job was to be there supporting the woman.

The notion was fascinating, if rather terrifying. And today, if Mrs Thompson agreed, she would witness it for the first time.

'All good!' Mrs Clarke poked her head through from the kitchen. 'Come on in, Kathleen!'

Tentatively, Kathleen made her way the few steps to the tiny kitchen, where Mrs Clarke introduced her to Mrs Thompson.

'Hello. Thank you for letting me help,' she offered diffidently, feeling a hundred miles away from the girl who had lifted her head to gentle snowfall. That girl had felt as though she could do anything. This girl, not so much.

'Ach, you're grand, love,' said Mrs Thompson. 'Everybody has to start somewhere.' She winked at her. 'You'll always remember me and my baby, because we'll be your first birth.'

This made Kathleen smile. 'That's true!'

'And don't you be worrying that you'll have to do anything complicated,' Mrs Clarke added, going to the sink. 'As you'll see, a lot of it is just ordinary housework followed by a lot of waiting.' She scraped the potato skins into the wee metal bin then began washing the chopping board and knife. Mrs Thompson had already placed the pot full of peeled spuds onto the stove, covering it with the lid.

'Right, that's tomorrow's spuds ready. My husband will be getting his dinner at my ma's house the day, along with the children.'

'Kathleen, can you make a start on the living room?' Mrs Clarke handed her a damp cloth. 'Do the woodwork first and then the polishing.'

'Polish and duster is in that cupboard.' Mrs Thompson pointed to one of the doors under the sink. 'Thanks, Kathleen.' Strangely, she then stopped, leaning over the edge of the wooden board beside the sink, and breathing in a very controlled, careful way. Instantly, Mrs Clarke abandoned the dishes, dried her hands and went to Mrs Thompson. 'Good, good,' she said, her tone low and soothing.

With a start, Kathleen realised Mrs Thompson must be having a pain. Standing very still, she watched as the woman stood there, her eyes closed and her breathing slow. After a minute or so she straightened, shaking her head. 'Getting a bit stronger now.' She laughed lightly. 'Never gets any easier, does it?'

'That's for sure.'

Things seemed to be back to normal now, so Kathleen went to the living room to begin cleaning, thinking about what she had just seen. Period pains could be very sore, and if Mrs Thompson was after experiencing something worse, then fair play to her.

The fire had already been cleaned out and a new one set for this evening, so she wiped the windowsill, the narrow mantelpiece, and the skirtings, then picked up the circular metal tin of Johnson's Wax Polish. Half a shilling for this small tin, so it should be used sparingly. Carefully she swiped some of the soft wax onto her duster, then dusted and polished Mrs Thompson's wooden table, chairs, and sideboard. By that time Mrs Clarke had finished cleaning the kitchen, and together they brushed and mopped the floors, cleaned the windows – drying them off with old newspaper – and scrubbed the step at the front door. All the while Kathleen was keeping a subtle eye on Mrs Thompson. Mrs Clarke had suggested she sit and rest if she wished, but instead, the woman was pacing up and down her tiny living room, pausing at times to lean over the table.

If each time was a pain, there were a lot of them. Maybe one every quarter of an hour. And was it Kathleen's imagination, or were they coming more frequently? When they had first arrived it was more like every twenty minutes or so. As she and Mrs Clarke went upstairs to start cleaning up there, Kathleen asked, and Mrs Clarke beamed at her.

'Yes! Well observed, Kathleen! They'll gradually get closer together and last for longer, until they're on top of one another, and that's when we'll be focusing fully on Mrs Thompson. In the meantime, let's get her housework finished. Some women can't ease properly into labour until they know their children are all minded and their jobs are done.'

That made sense. Mrs Thompson was barely speaking now, and Kathleen noticed that Mrs Clarke wasn't asking her any questions or bothering her. Upstairs they cleaned everywhere, then brought two kitchen chairs up and moved the big bed in the front bedroom out from the wall. 'We'll need to get round both sides of it later,' Mrs Clarke explained. 'Now, can you get the fire ready? Bring the coal bucket and the extra bucket from the yard.'

'Up here?' Kathleen was aghast. While the front bedrooms of the scullery houses all had small fireplaces, they were never used. *Ever.* Such extravagance would be so wasteful.

'Aye. When the baby's born we'll need the room to be warm.'

*Oh.* Her mind buzzing, Kathleen descended to fetch newspaper, sticks, and coal from the yard. Expertly, she then made up the fire; a task that had been one of her own jobs at home since she was about ten. She set the box of matches on the tiny mantel – Maguire and Patterson of course, for the factory was on Broadway close to the damask mill, and most locals knew someone who could buy them matches at factory rates. Setting the coal bucket by the hearth, she put the second bucket in the corner, having no idea what it was for.

Mrs Thompson wasn't talking at all now, but when Mrs Clarke quietly went and made tea and toast for them all, she took some. It had been morning time when Kathleen had arrived at the house, and now it was late afternoon, and would soon be dark. Spring was slow to come this year.

Tomorrow would be Easter Sunday, yet the weather was still damp and dreary.

Their jobs done, the women sat with tea – Mrs Thompson rocking rhythmically from side to side – and Kathleen sat with them feeling both privileged and daunted. Here she was, only sixteen, witnessing one of the secrets of womanhood.

Once darkness came Mrs Thompson's pains seemed to become more intense. She began moaning softly with each one, although her face looked calm throughout. Mrs Clarke gave her quiet encouragement, sometimes with words, other times with touch. Quietness was everywhere – in Mrs Clarke, in Mrs Thompson, in the house itself. It wasn't silence, for the clock was ticking and the fire crackling and the women's voices sounded regularly. But it was quietness, nevertheless. Liam's words came to her: *The handywomen have a quietness about them*, he had said. He had told her that she had it too.

She did. She knew it. Being still and patient and yet focused and alert was what was required right now, and it was coming easily to her. Therese would never cope; she was too impatient, had too much energy for something like this.

There was a rap on the door, and Mrs Clarke tutted. Rising, she answered it, taking a leaflet from someone and setting it on the side table. Kathleen's gaze flicked to it curiously, then away again. It was only another of those boring things about gas masks. Why should they need gas masks in Belfast? Everybody said there was no way war would come again, that it would be utter stupidity given how awful the Great War had been. *Ridiculous*.

'Ooooww!' Mrs Thompson's face was screwed up, and Mrs Clarke quickly moved to crouch beside her, murmuring praise and reassurance. Had the interruption at the front door unsettled her? Perhaps so, for after the pain had passed Mrs Clarke asked her if she wanted to go upstairs. Mrs Thompson nodded vehemently. *Privacy*, Kathleen realised dimly. Privacy was important, and no distractions.

Together they accompanied Mrs Thompson upstairs between pains, walking behind her on the stairs. They helped her undress and don a soft cotton nightdress, Kathleen scarlet at seeing the woman naked. Her abdomen was huge and distended, and there seemed to be a brown line in the middle extending from her belly button downwards.

'Can I check what way the baby's lying?' Mrs Clarke asked.

Fascinated, Kathleen watched as Mrs Thompson lay down and the handywoman placed her hands on her stomach. First the sides, then the middle, then the top and bottom.

'Right!' she declared briskly. 'All good. Baby is head down and facing the back – exactly how we like it.'

Kathleen gaped. How on earth had Mrs Clarke figured that out?

'Do you want to feel it too?' Mrs Thompson was looking directly at Kathleen.

'Me?' Her voice was almost a squeak.

'Hang on.' Mrs Thompson shifted on to her side, puffing out air as another pain took her. When it was over she shuffled back round. 'Quick, now.'

Mrs Clarke guided her as she placed her hands on Mrs Thompson's sides. 'Now press gently,' she instructed, putting her own hands over Kathleen's to demonstrate the amount of pressure, which did not seem gentle at all! 'No baby here – only the bag of waters. See?'

Kathleen didn't see. She was barely coping with the fact she had her hands on a woman's belly. But when Mrs Clarke got her to gently press in the middle, the contrast was obvious. 'It's hard!'

'That's the baby, and the fact that you can feel baby up and down the middle, and not at the two sides, means it's not lying crosswise.' She ran her hand swiftly down Mrs Thompson's belly. 'So *this* is either the baby's backbone or its stomach. Next job is to figure out which it is.'

'Is it important to know?'

'Aye. You don't want spine against spine. A back-to-back baby can be awful slow to come out, and can give the mammy desprit back pain.' She pressed again. 'Feels like backbone to me. Good.'

Kathleen felt pressing carefully, but had no idea how Mrs Clarke knew the baby's backbone was there.

'Now we want to know if the baby's breech or not.'

'What's breech?'

'Breech is when the head is at the top so the bum or the legs end up coming out first.' Mrs Clarke shrugged. 'It's grand like, but head down is better.'

'So how can you tell?'

'It's easier to tell from the top. Feel up here. You all right, Mrs Thompson?'

'Aye. Keep goin'. It's good to hear this stuff.'

Mrs Clarke got Kathleen to feel the hard, hard lump at the top of Mrs Thompson's bump. 'Could be either, right? Could be a head. Could be a backside. But if I keep one hand here on the spine, and I move this hard lump a wee bit, sometimes the back moves too and sometimes it doesn't. I always think when the back moves it's more likely to be the backside up here.'

'Because it's nearly part of the spine! They move together!'

'Aye. Whereas the head—'

'Can move on its own because the neck is movable!'

'Exactly! Well worked out, Kathleen. It's sometimes wrong, but it's probably better than fifty-fifty. Now, are you wanting to walk about a bit more?' The last was addressed to Mrs Thompson, as they were helping her sit up again.

'I'd rather sit on the bed,' the woman managed, just as the next pain came.

So she sat, and knelt, and walked, and sat again. All talking stopped then, allowing Mrs Thompson to concentrate on each moment, each pain. Kathleen lit the bedroom fire when the evening began to get cold – it was March in Ireland, after all – and Mrs Clarke got her knitting out.

Mrs Clarke continued to quietly give Kathleen lots of jobs to do, like boiling water and finding as many clean towels as she could. They both washed their hands frequently, Mrs Clarke being a stickler for avoiding germs, and so Kathleen became well acquainted with Mrs Thompson's kitchen.

Between contractions, Kathleen mopped Mrs Thompson's face and held a cup of cold water to her so she could drink. This was thirsty work, clearly! Mrs Thompson then expressed a wish to use the chamber pot and did so. After she had done a wee, Kathleen took the pot downstairs to empty it in the outhouse and wash it, pausing for a moment to rest her hands on the edge of the sink and just breathe. What was happening upstairs was so intense. Could she handle it?

The answer came immediately. *Yes.* For whatever she was feeling was as nothing to what Mrs Thompson was going through, and Mrs Thompson needed their help. Straightening, she washed out the sink, picked up the clean chamber pot, and headed back upstairs. There she put it back under the bed, then washed her hands once more.

Something changed, then. Mrs Thompson, who had been softly moaning and only occasionally seeming distressed, abruptly began emitting a strange noise. It was loud, yet strangled – a restrained roar. Startled, Kathleen looked to Mrs Clarke, who was carefully wrapping her knitting and putting it in her little cloth bag.

'Good, good,' she said for what seemed like the hundredth time that day. So this was normal, then? Kathleen didn't know what to make of it.

Mrs Thompson was sitting on the edge of the bed again, but something had changed. Her whole body seemed tight, her face now red with effort. *Is she pushing? Is this what pushing looks like?*

# 6

Mrs Clarke had told Kathleen that once the womb had opened up fully, the woman would push the baby out. She had not, however, mentioned the noise.

Mrs Thompson took a breath then pushed again, and once again the noise came from her throat. *Like a demented cow*, Kathleen thought, a bubble of hysteria rising within her. Ruthlessly she suppressed it, by the simple action of trying to understand what Mrs Thompson must be feeling right now. After hours of pain, her body had now been taken over by this compulsion – a compulsion that looked all-consuming. *God, rather her than me!* It looked truly awful. And yet between pains Mrs Thompson looked serene, if exhausted.

Mrs Clarke washed her hands yet again, nodding at Kathleen to do the same. As she was drying them, Mrs Thompson let out another loud, intense groan-roar, and she turned back to see that Mrs Clarke was kneeling on the floor, peering under the woman's nightie.

'I can see the head,' she announced. 'You're doing a great job, so you are.'

Shock rippled through Kathleen. The head was visible! Strangely she had almost forgotten there would be a baby, so long it had all been going on. Mrs Thompson's groans subsided again.

'Water,' she muttered, and Kathleen sprang into action, bringing the cup to her. There were no thank-yous. Well how could there be, when every ounce of energy the woman had was going into her labour?

'Is it all right if I show Kathleen?' Mrs Clarke asked, and Mrs Thompson nodded. With a fair amount of trepidation Kathleen dropped to her knees, bending to look under Mrs Thompson's nightdress. And there, where there had only been normal female parts before, was a glimpse of something else.

'That's the head,' Mrs Clarke said, as though Kathleen needed to be told. How odd it was, to see it! The groaning began again, and as Kathleen watched the head moved, bulging further.

*My God!* It seemed impossible to Kathleen that the woman's skin wouldn't just tear under the incredible pressure. Yet somehow it didn't, and three groans later the head emerged fully – turning to reveal a perfect little squashed face. It surely had to be the most bizarre and amazing thing Kathleen had ever seen; a woman with a baby's head attached to her. But there was barely time to think. Mrs Clarke was putting pillows and towels on the floor between Mrs Thompson's feet. *Might the baby fall out and hit its head?* Kathleen wondered, fresh fear coming over her at the notion.

Mrs Thompson groaned again, bearing down with her whole self, and Mrs Clarke held her hands in readiness. Sure enough a shoulder emerged, followed by the second shoulder along with the entire baby in a single wet slither.

In a single movement – or so it seemed to Kathleen – Mrs Clarke caught the baby, picked up a towel, and wrapped the child up. It was wet, and pale pink, and its skin seemed to be covered with some sort of white wax. There was a long purple cord too, linking the baby to its mother. Stunned, Kathleen could only rest on her heels and watch as Mrs Clarke passed the baby up to its mother, who crooned and cried and made exclamations of wonder.

'A wee boy!' she said, smiling despite the tears running down her cheeks. 'He'll be called Francis.'

Kathleen was also watching Mrs Clarke. She was bending again, and beckoned Kathleen to look as well. 'See there?' She pointed. 'A tiny tear, but nothing major.'

*I see it!* A small wound, bleeding a little. Amazingly, Mrs Thompson's body had stretched and stretched to allow the baby out, and without serious harm to his mother.

'A quarter to nine,' Mrs Clarke pronounced, glancing at the clock they had brought up from Mrs Thompson's living room. Kathleen gaped. The whole thing had taken less than ten hours from when she and Mrs Clarke had arrived. 'Need to warm the room up more, Kathleen.'

Kathleen jumped to add more coal to the fire, afterwards washing her hands yet again. She watched with a smile as Mrs Thompson cuddled her baby. He was rooting around for the breast and his mother expertly positioned him for his first feed.

All the while, the cord attaching him to his mother remained, beating with her pulse. Mrs Clarke noticed her eyeing it curiously.

'Can you see how the cord is changing colour, Kathleen?'

She looked more closely at the colour. 'Yes! It's paler, isn't it?'

'It will be pure white in a wee while, and we'll cut it then – once it's done its work.'

'What's it doing?' Kathleen asked curiously.

'Nature knows what it's at,' Mrs Clarke explained. 'Remember I told you how babies breathe in the womb?'

'Yes. They don't use their lungs, they get their air through the cord.'

'Aye, well that baby is still getting air that way, while he's learning to breathe. Sometimes they don't breathe straight away, so this helps them. Usually lasts about twenty minutes or half an hour.'

'Like nature's back-up plan?'

'Exactly! Also, what do you notice about the colour of the baby?'

She eyed Mrs Thompson's son dubiously. 'Err, he's pinker? Is that not because he's warming up?'

'Not exactly. They do be warm when they're first born; it's like a bath in there, inside their mother's belly. But they can get cold very quickly once they come out soakin', which is why we have to warm the room up and make sure they're well happed up and dried.'

Baby Francis was indeed well happed up, being covered now by three soft towels, his belly against his mother's.

Mrs Clarke's question was like a riddle, and Kathleen had always had a good brain. The baby was definitely pinker than it had been when it first came out, while at the same time the purple cord was getting paler and paler, yet still pulsating . . .

Her eyes flew to Mrs Clarke's. 'Is there extra blood going into the baby? From the cord?'

The handywoman nodded, smiling. 'I reckon so. It's the only explanation for why these two things happen at the same time. Just look at how white that cord is getting!'

'Amazing!'

A little later, Mrs Clarke tied the cord – which by now was flaccid, limp, and white – in two places with twine that had been boiled in water. 'Why have you tied it twice?' Kathleen asked.

'Once I cut it a wee bit of blood might leak out, and we don't want a mess,' she explained, taking the scissors which she had just cleaned in the same hot water. Bringing them to the cord, she paused. 'Come here, Kathleen.'

Kathleen moved closer, sitting beside the handywoman on the edge of the bed. Mrs Clarke handed her the scissors. 'Now, cut between the two ties,' she instructed.

Holding her breath, Kathleen did so, and the cord came apart neatly.

'Well done!' Mrs Clarke turned back to Mrs Thompson. 'You done a great job, Mrs Thompson! He's a wee dote!'

'It was bloody hard, I tell ya!' the woman declared, her hand gently cupping her wee baby's head. 'I was never so relieved as when this head came out!'

'I'm sure!'

'Ooohhh!' Mrs Thompson was groaning in pain yet again, startling Kathleen. What on earth was happening?

'Ah!' There was an air of satisfaction in Mrs Clarke's tone. 'Time for the afterbirth!' declared Mrs Clarke. 'Kathleen, take the baby.'

And so Kathleen Gallagher, at the grand old age of sixteen, gathered up a baby who was less than half an hour old, taking him and holding him while his mother expelled the afterbirth from her body. He was so tiny, and so perfect, and he smelled amazing. She sniffed his head, drawing in the essence of baby, then sighed happily.

It was good to have the distraction of the baby's squirms and snuffles, for the thing Mrs Thompson was after pushing out looked like it was part of her innards. Kathleen was used to preparing raw meat for dinner, and this thing – the afterbirth – looked like meat; liver, perhaps. It was broadly circular, and had thick blood vessels on its surface. Mrs Clarke inspected it carefully, then placed it in the bucket. *Ah, so that's what the extra bucket was for!*

Mrs Thompson was ready to take her baby back and so Kathleen relinquished him. While she and Mrs Clarke cleaned up, the new mother simply rested, speaking to her baby in soft tones. Standing by the stove waiting on the kettle boiling yet again, Kathleen took a moment to marvel at the miracle she had witnessed today. None of her friends, she knew, had ever been privileged to see such a thing – apart from Mary McArdle, who had apparently helped when her older sister gave birth last year. It was a rare thing though, and Kathleen was grateful for the opportunity.

She said as much to Mrs Clarke when she returned upstairs with tea and toast for the new mother. 'Aye, you done well, Kathleen. You're a good worker, and you know how to be quiet. We'll make a fine handywoman out of ya!'

Kathleen felt her colour rising, and muttered something about not being afraid of hard work. It was hard to know how to take a compliment, for they were rarely given round here.

A little later they helped Mrs Thompson to leave her bed and use the chamber pot, then they washed her with facecloths dipped in warm soapy water, while her wee one was briefly placed in a sturdy cradle that Mrs Thompson's husband had apparently made when she was expecting her first. They changed the sheets too, and Mrs Thompson expressed her delight as she slid into the freshly-made bed in a clean nightdress, a thick band of rags in her underwear and two towels on the bed beneath her. Kathleen and Mrs Clarke then left her in peace, her wee baby tucked in beside her.

Their work was not yet done. Downstairs they washed the sheets, towels, and soiled nightdress, hanging them out in the tiny yard behind the house. It was after midnight when they finally sat down to their own supper – tea and toast – and it was the most delicious thing Kathleen had ever tasted.

'Happy Easter, Kathleen,' said Mrs Clarke quietly.

Of course! It was now Easter Sunday. 'Happy Easter.'

'I'm gonna stay the night here with Mrs Thompson in case she needs anything. Away you on though, for you need your sleep. No doubt you'll be at the big Easter céilí tomorrow night – *tonight*, that is.'

'Aye, probably – if I'm not needed.'

'Call back in the morning. And on your way home can you check if there's a light on in her mammy's house? If they're still up, you can give them the good news.'

'Will do.'

Ten minutes later Kathleen had done exactly that, having seen the candle in the window of the house fluttering dimly against the electric light behind it. Mr Thompson and his wife's parents were delighted to know there was a baby boy, and that both mother and baby were doing well.

Walking home to Locan Street, Kathleen felt tired, but quietly satisfied. If this was what it meant to be a handywoman, then she would be perfectly content to be a handywoman her whole life.

# 7

The parish hall was full to bursting, this being the first dance in six weeks. No dances were allowed during Lent, which made it all the sweeter to hear the jigs and reels ring out across the hall tonight. Kathleen and Therese danced every dance, and once again Jimmy McKeown and his quiet friend came to claim them, this time for the Haymaker's Jig.

Once it finished Jimmy asked Therese to stay on – a significant development, and one that Therese had been hoping for. It meant she and Jimmy would dance together for the rest of the evening. He might even ask to walk her home. Naturally, Therese agreed and both she and Jimmy looked delighted with themselves, while Jimmy's dour friend simply stood there silently. What was Kathleen supposed to do? Mortified, she went to walk away but Therese stopped her. 'I'm only staying on if Kathleen stays with me,' she declared, in a reassuring demonstration of loyalty.

Jimmy was undeterred. 'Aye, sure Mugsy here will dance with your friend. Won't you, Mugsy?'

Mugsy nodded, and Kathleen wished herself a hundred miles away. But Therese really liked Jimmy, and Kathleen had to support her, so she stood on silently waiting for the next dance, while Therese and Jimmy bantered like they were a comedy act in a pantomime.

At least there was the dancing. While the laconic Mugsy wasn't the best dancer, he managed reasonably well, and Kathleen allowed herself to enjoy the moves and patterns of the various dances, all the while surreptitiously keeping an eye on Liam Flynn. During 'The Walls of Limerick' she saw that Liam's line and theirs were gradually getting closer. Praying that the music wouldn't end too soon, Kathleen kept an eye on his progress, until finally he was facing her. His gaze briefly lit on her dance partner, and he frowned. *Does he not like Mugsy?* Or maybe it was Jimmy he didn't approve of. Big brothers were often very protective of their sisters. But there was no time to think, for they were advancing and retiring, and his eyes were on her, and her heart was pounding.

His eyes were smiling. 'What about ye, Kathleen?'

'All good,' she managed before they stepped backwards, away from each other. Advancing again, she offered, 'I worked with Mrs Clarke last night.'

His eyes widened. 'Good for you!' His expression changed, becoming sweetly sad – almost as if he was yearning for something. 'You have a great chance there, Kathleen. You go for it.'

'Oh, I will.'

The dance then required Kathleen to swap places with Liam's partner and she did so, noticing that he never seemed to dance with the same girl twice. The realisation gave her a satisfaction that was entirely disproportionate. He was her best friend's brother, that was all. The fact that she had had her first kiss with him was neither here nor there, for he had made no moves since to suggest he wanted her to be his girl. And besides, she was too young for him. Standing by his side briefly, she wondered what it would feel like to be his actual dance partner – to be a girl that he liked enough to dance with. He and Mugsy then changed places, each returning to their own partners.

But the set wasn't done. Liam held out his right hand to her, and she placed hers within it. Mugsy was doing the same, and the two couples then split, going out to the side then back in again. Liam's eyes remained fixed on hers through the full eight bars of music, and it was as if the rest of the hall was not even there.

And that was that. Kathleen and Mugsy met for the swing, manoeuvring past Liam and his girl to meet a new couple.

All too soon the night was over, and after the anthem she made her way back to the chairs where she and Therese had left their shawls earlier. Jimmy was by Therese's side, and Mugsy was hovering around them all.

'He's walking me home!' Therese muttered in Kathleen's ear, her words quick with excitement. 'You and Mugsy walk ahead of us!'

'Right.'

Mugsy wasn't the worst. He was probably just shy. So on the way to Beechmount, Kathleen tried to draw him out. He worked in the match factory, had ten brothers and sisters, and lived in the Rock Streets. He didn't reciprocate with similar questions, but Kathleen told him the basics about herself anyway. As she was speaking his arm crept around her waist, and she allowed it.

It was a strange feeling, but she had to be brave. Liam's kiss had been magical, but she needed to understand if the magic had been in the kiss, or in Liam. If Mugsy wanted to kiss her, then she would allow that too, and then she would know. She sent him a sideways glance. While he could never be described as handsome, his features were pleasant, his clothes and hair clean.

A laugh from behind her reminded her that Therese and Jimmy were following; still getting on great, clearly. At the corner of Therese's street Kathleen glanced back. Therese and Jimmy had arms around each other's waists like herself and Mugsy, except they didn't look in any way awkward.

'See you tomorrow, Therese!' she called gaily.

'Aye! See ya!' She and Jimmy had now stopped, and Kathleen knew exactly what would be happening next. Suddenly nervous, she walked in step with Mugsy around the corner and on to the bottom of her own street.

'Thanks,' she said, stopping and turning to face him. 'That's my house.'

'Oh.' He leaned in, and she didn't pull away, and then his lips were on hers, hard and pressing and almost painful. She shrank back but he followed, his teeth pressing into her lower lip.

'Oi!' A shout from behind him made Mugsy stop, and as he lifted his head Kathleen stepped back, relief flooding through her.

'Ach well, Liam.' Mugsy sounded pleased with himself, and Kathleen shuddered. *Why in God's name did it have to be Liam Flynn?*

She looked up. Liam was alone, and walking back in the direction of his own street. He must have just walked his own girl home. A pang went through her at the knowledge that some other girl had been on the receiving end of Liam's magical kisses, while she—

She stepped back. 'Goodnight!' Her tone sounded bright, belying the sinking feeling within her. As she made her way to her front door she saw the living-room curtain fall back into place, and a new dread came over her. Sure enough, there was Mammy, and her expression was one that Kathleen knew well.

'Kathleen Gallagher!'

Kathleen stopped in the doorway, wondering if she was about to get slapped.

'Get you in here past me!'

Bracing herself, she stepped inside, and sure enough received a slap to the ear that made a ringing sound in her head. Knowing her best chance was to brazen it out, she said 'Ow! What was that for?'

'For kissin' boys in the street! What the hell are you at? I didn't rear you to be at that nonsense at sixteen! Who is he?' Her head jerked towards the street.

'Mugsy,' Kathleen mumbled. *Feck! What's his real name?*

'Mugsy, is it?' Mammy's tone was scathing. 'Mugsy who?'

'Mugsy Mulligan,' Kathleen managed, knowing it sounded ridiculous. 'From the Rock Streets.'

'Get you up to your bed, and no more céilís for you!'

'That's not fair!'

'Not fair? I'll "not fair" you with a wooden spoon! Now, get out of my sight!'

Feeling wretched, Kathleen made her way to the tiny back bedroom she shared with Bronagh. Stepping inside, she left the door ajar so she could undress by the landing light. Thankfully, her sister was still awake in their big bed.

'It's all right,' she murmured, 'you can turn on the big light.'

Relieved, for Mammy was on her way up and would no doubt have more to say if she saw her, Kathleen closed the door and turned on the main bedroom light.

'What was Mammy giving off about?'

'She saw me kissing a boy.'

Suddenly Bronagh looked wide awake. 'Oops. Did you get a clout for that?'

'Aye. I've a warm ear,' Kathleen said, rubbing it.

'Who's the boy? Anybody special?'

Kathleen shuddered. 'No. I definitely won't be letting him walk me home again!'

'Fair enough.'

'Mammy says I'm not allowed to go to the céilís any more.'

'Ach, don't be worrying about that. She'll come round. She'll keep you away from one or two dances, but I'll work on her for you.' There was a pause while Kathleen hung her precious blue dress carefully in the wardrobe. She ran a loving hand over it before closing the door. Hopefully any last traces of Liam's magic hadn't been taken away by Mugsy.

'Thanks, Bronagh. Why is she so . . . so . . .?'

'So controlling?' Bronagh shrugged. 'It's my fault I think – or at least partly my fault. I was probably a bit wild when I was sixteen, though I didn't see it that way at the time. I had a boyfriend and she didn't approve.'

Kathleen's jaw dropped. 'You had a boyfriend? I never knew that! Who was he?'

'He was called Michael. He was from Dublin, and was only up here staying with his cousins for a few months. The War of Independence was goin' on and they didn't want him getting sucked into it.'

'What happened?'

'Mammy wasn't a bit impressed when she heard I had a boyfriend. I missed two céilís. Or maybe three.'

'No, I mean what happened to Michael?'

She shrugged. 'I never saw him again after he went back home.' The big light was unforgiving, and Kathleen saw in Bronagh's eyes remembered pain. 'Mammy didn't even know who he was, only that I had a boyfriend.' She grinned. 'Just like you, I was caught kissing him in the street one night.'

'No way!'

'Aye! I got a warm ear too, that night, but I didn't care. I was stupid and thought I was in love!' She gave a twisted smile. 'I soon found out better. For all his fine words, he soon forgot about me.'

'Ach, I'm sorry, Bronagh. What an eejit!'

'Who, me or him?'

'Him! You're class, and if he was too dopey to see that, then it's his loss!'

'True. He's lost plenty.' Her eyes softened. 'But I have a good life, despite him. We both do.'

'I suppose so.' Taking a breath, she drew on the memory of what it had felt like, leaving Mrs Thompson's house knowing she had helped the woman in some small way. 'I like working with Mrs Clarke.'

'Aye, she's a good one. And I'm so proud of you for training as a handywoman!'

Kathleen squared her shoulders. 'I am too. I actually think I'll be able to do it.'

'You can do anything, my Kath-a-leen!' Kathleen grinned at Bronagh's old pet name for her. 'Now turn out that feckin' light and let's get some sleep!'

Lying in the dark, Kathleen lay awake a while, thinking about many things. Becoming a handywoman. Michael, who had kissed Bronagh and run away. And Liam Flynn, who had in a sense done the same to her.

*Feckin' lads. Not worth the grief!* Turning on her side, she allowed her eyes to close.

# 8

Boys, thought Kathleen, were more trouble than they were worth. Take Mugsy Mulligan. Take him and throw him in the River Farset, for all she cared. His kiss had been horrible, and now she was banned from going to céilís. Plus Mammy had been ranting at her for two days about boys, and being sixteen, and being careful . . . she was going to crack up if Mammy didn't give over soon. But Mammy was Mammy, and would never change. She had obviously given Bronagh the same grief years ago.

Thankfully they were all back at work, so Mammy's giving off was limited to mealtimes and evenings. Tonight though, Kathleen had a means of escape.

'And where do you think you're going?' Mammy asked, as Kathleen put on her shoes and wrapped her shawl around her.

'Mrs Clarke's. I told you earlier. More training.'

'Hmm. Are all them dishes done?'

'Yep.'

'And did you brush and mop the floor?'

'I brushed it. Bronagh's finishing the moppin' now.'

'Make sure you go straight there and straight back! D'ye hear me?' *Don't be meeting Mugsy Mulligan for any more kisses.*

'Oh, I will. See ya, Bronagh. Right, Daddy.'

He looked up from his paper. 'You enjoy yourself, love.'

Mammy sent him a dirty look and Kathleen stifled a grin. A minute later she was out in the street, and heading for Mrs Clarke's.

She could almost feel the tension draining out of her as she walked through Beechmount towards the Falls. By the time she had reached Mrs Clarke's house, Mammy's chuntering was entirely in the past and she was eager to get stuck in to more learning about birth.

There was tea, and calmness, and Mrs Clarke, and Peggy – the other trainee handywoman, who was only a couple of years older than Kathleen. *This is the world I want.* Not one where you were treated like a ten-year-old and nagged at for hours on end. They talked about Mrs Thompson's birth, and Kathleen had her questions answered, and Mrs Clarke told Peggy that Kathleen was doing well. The praise was such a contrast to what she got from Mammy that she couldn't help a feeling of pride inside. You weren't supposed to feel proud – it was one of the seven deadly sins – but Kathleen couldn't help it.

'Right. Kathleen, I want you to come with me for the Sunday calls next week. Come over here after nine Mass.'

'I will, aye. Erm . . . who will we be calling on?'

'Pregnant women who need to get to know us properly before the birth, and new mothers who might need a hand.'

'Oh, all right.' That made sense.

Mrs Clarke was referring to a written list. 'We've two new ones who've said they want us to be with them when their time comes.' She frowned. 'Mrs O'Neill from Violet Street is due again, and her youngest one isn't even ten months old yet. Probably nine and a half months. God love her.'

'Irish twins!' said Kathleen. She knew of quite a few families who had children born less than a year apart.

'Aye. It's not right, though. Bloody men!'

This was confusing. While Kathleen could see it would be hard on the mother to have two wee ones to look after at the same time, why was Mrs Clarke blaming the father? Did Mrs Clarke mean that the men in those houses wanted more babies, but it was the woman who had to birth them and look after them?

Peggy raised a cynical eyebrow. 'Happens far too often. Eleven or twelve months of a gap might be all right, but *ten*? *Nine and a half?*' She shuddered. 'We know it takes women's bodies time to heal. Two weeks after a birth is far, far too soon for marital relations.'

*Marital relations!* Kathleen had long been trying to figure out how babies were made, and here was another clue.

'Some women might be all right with it. If she had a straightforward birth and no tear, she might be up for it fairly quickly – though two weeks is highly unlikely. And it's not our place to interfere or judge anybody. But if it's just him taking his due, that can't be right.'

'Thank God for Lent!' Peggy's tone held knowing humour. 'I've heard so many women say they're delighted to be having a baby round Ash Wednesday, knowing her man can't go near her till Easter.'

'Aye. You know the hymn – "Jesus Christ Is Risen Today"? Aye, and half of Ireland along with him!'

They laughed together, and Kathleen had a sense of being part of something secret, hitherto unsuspected, and *important*. Being a handywoman was bringing more benefits than she could ever have anticipated.

'Anyway,' said Mrs Clarke primly, 'as I say, we judge no woman. We're privileged to be in women's homes, and we respect that.'

*They judge the men, though.* Or at least, some of the men.

Mrs Clarke was called away shortly afterwards, but told them to sit on and finish their tea. Kathleen was happy to do so, realising that part of the reason she felt so contented in the handywoman's drawing room was because it was so airy and bright. Big fancy windows. Kathleen wasn't in any way ashamed of her family or her home, and she loved how cosy the dark living room was in winter, but now that spring was here there was something energising about the daylight in Mrs Clarke's front room.

Feeling brave, she waited until Mrs Clarke was safely away, then said, 'Peggy, can I ask you something?'

'Of course!' Peggy sent her a look. 'Would it be about marital relations by any chance?'

'It would!' Kathleen sighed in relief. This whole conversation was so awkward, but thankfully Peggy was smart.

'What do you want to know? Now, I should say I'm not married myself, so I don't know all of the details obviously, but I know the *theory*. Or at least, I think I do.'

Kathleen took a breath. 'Right. The main question is like, how does the baby get in there? I mean, how does it – you know – how does it *work*?'

There was a furrow on Peggy's brow. 'Has your mammy not told you *anything*?'

Kathleen shook her head. 'My big sister Bronagh could probably tell me some things – it was her who helped me when I started my monthlies – but she's not married either *and* she's not a handywoman.'

'And you sixteen! Right. Well, I'm going to tell you what I know, which isn't much, but when you work with women like we do, you need to know.'

And so Peggy told her about eggs, and sperm, and how they came together to make a baby. 'So the baby literally gets made from part of her and part of him!'

'Which is why you get family resemblances and stuff.'

'Aye. People always say me and Bronagh both look more like my daddy's side of the family. But . . .' She thought for a moment, 'How does it actually get in there?'

Peggy took a breath, then explained. The 'birth canal' was situated between the other two exits. Period blood came out that way, and babies, which Kathleen already knew, but Peggy then told her that was also the place where sperm got in.

This was astounding information, yet entirely confusing at the same time. 'But how? Like, how can it get in?'

'Ah, *that* is where the marital relations bit comes in. I don't know *exactly*, but the sperm comes out of the man's – you know . . .' She gestured, and Kathleen's jaw dropped.

'His *willy?*'

'Uh-huh. So the willy needs to somehow get close to the woman's private parts, and then the sperm can get in. Somehow.' She shrugged. 'I suppose we'll work it out when we get married. The number of babies isn't exactly falling, so . . .'

'That's true.' Fleetingly, she thought about the fact that Mugsy Mulligan had a willy, and shuddered. 'It sounds horrible.'

Peggy's eyes were dancing. 'Apparently it's not horrible at all. It's supposed to be really enjoyable – or so some of the women have said.' She giggled. 'They often say things about how labour and birth is like paying in pain for the pleasure they had before. One in, one out – that's what one of the women said recently, which made me laugh. Something about the "one out" experience being very different to the "one in"!'

'Well the "one out" looks horrendous!'

'Seriously, Kathleen, don't let it put you off. It's hard, yes. But women are *strong*. Try and notice how the women feel about it afterwards.'

Kathleen reflected on this. 'Mrs Thompson seemed to be in the best of form.'

Peggy nodded. 'They usually are. Oh, now and again something goes wrong – an infection maybe, or a need to go to the hospital. But most women just get on with it. Our job is to create a wee cave around them that lets them do what they need to, and to call the doctor when he's needed.'

Suddenly Kathleen felt a bit overwhelmed. 'God, how will I ever know something as complicated as that?'

'Now, don't you be worrying about that. You'll pick it up, like I did. Just do a good job every day – the best you can – and before you know it two years will have gone by and you'll be going to births on your own!'

Kathleen nodded thoughtfully, feeling as though she was blossoming in the other girl's company. Peggy had been a couple of years ahead of her in school and so had been someone that Kathleen had always looked up to. *Will I ever be as confident as that?*

'How long have you been training, Peggy?'

'Since I was fourteen – earlier, even. I used to help my Aunty Bridget after school, and didn't even realise I was training. You'll be the same, once you get the hang of it.'

*The Irish Midwife at War*

Kathleen couldn't imagine it. She really couldn't. But she had to have faith. She had to believe that, some day, she could be almost as good as Peggy. And by the time she was old, she might be almost as good as Mrs Clarke.

And maybe, some day, she might have her own baby – once she was married, of course. The idea of marital relations was odd, and while she shuddered at the thought of doing it with Mugsy, she might like to explore it with Liam Flynn . . .

# PART II

# 9

*Three years later*

> *The Bristol Blitz started at 6.30 p.m. on Sunday, 24 November 1940 and lasted over six hours. Around 150 Luftwaffe planes dropped over twelve thousand incendiaries and more than fifteen hundred tons of high explosives. Over two hundred people were killed.*

Liam Flynn trudged down the Falls Road towards Dunville, feeling as though he was decades older than his twenty-one years. War had come, and everything had changed. The mills had laid off hundreds of workers, and he and his brother Seány were lucky to be still getting part-time hours. Loads of women had been let go too, including Christine and Therese. Thankfully, Ma still had her job, but they struggled at times to put enough food on the table. Again and again he went over it in his head: Ma's wages, plus half-wages from him and Seány, meant the equivalent of two full wages coming in, to cover seven of them: Ma, Liam, Therese, Christine, Seány, Maria, Rita-Anne, and Granny. Still, it meant that both Maria and Rita-Anne could stay at school full-time – something that would have seemed like a dream come true to a younger Liam, who had stepped up to be the man of the house more than seven years ago.

His girlfriend Sadie was waiting for him at the corner of her street. There was a wee park over the road from the Royal Hospital, and they usually walked there on Sundays if the weather was decent. Today was dull, overcast, and cold, but at least it wasn't raining.

'Well? 'Bout ye?' Her smile lifted his spirits, and the hand she slipped into his was warm.

'Aye, dead on. What's the craic?'

'Ach sure, no craic really. I got a new dress yesterday, for the dance tonight.' Sadie's family had a few pound, and even though she had lost her job at the same time as Christine, she didn't seem to be looking too hard for another one.

'I'm not sure I'll be able to go.'

'Now, don't start that again! It's only a few shillings, Liam, and it's the last one before Advent starts. Don't be shit craic, now.'

He squirmed a little. It *was* only a few shillings, and might take his mind off his money worries for a few hours . . . but the few shillings spent would add to those money worries. 'I can't, Sadie. Sorry.'

He had been walking out with Sadie since the *Céilídhe mhór* in August, and while it was nice to have a girlfriend – someone to hold his hand and kiss him and have nice walks with – he wasn't yet convinced he could actually *afford* a girlfriend. Girlfriends wanted you to go to *all* the dances, and buy them minerals when you were there. Even going for walks cost money, for Sadie enjoyed treats and sweets.

Dimly he recalled one of the first Sundays he and Sadie had come to Dunville Park. An ice-cream seller had been ringing the bell on his bicycle contraption and shouting, 'Pokes and wafers!' Liam had bought two pokes, handing one cone to Sadie and keeping the other for himself. As they had meandered through the park enjoying the delicious ice cream, he recalled feeling good.

Whether or not he could afford a girlfriend, one thing was clear: he absolutely could not afford a wife. Well, how could he abandon his family to start one of his own? And the notion of Sadie or anyone else coming to live in the tiny Flynn house was unthinkable. Liam and Seány slept on mattresses in the living room every night. Nope. *Not happening.*

And what if the war got worse? He turned to Sadie. 'Did you hear on the news—'

'Don't talk to me about the bloody news!' Sadie's vehemence made him recoil briefly, before asking her why.

'Because it's stupid, and too hard to understand, and has nothing to do with me anyway!'

'But it might. Would you like me to explain any of it?' Uncharitably, he recalled a couple of other occasions where Sadie had not grasped something that she found too complicated. He wasn't her teacher – honestly, he would never go on like that – but Sadie could be sensitive about things that she didn't understand. And, like everybody else, she was probably terrified by the events in Europe, and the notion that it might spread to their wee island. *Thank God we're surrounded by water!*

She shuddered. 'Definitely not! *So* boring!' Tilting her head to one side, she added, 'You and Kathleen Gallagher, discussing all the latest, and never caring about what the rest of us are thinking.'

'What do you mean?' He and Kathleen often had good chats about the news from Europe, even when Sadie was there, but what in God's name was wrong with that?

'I dunno why she's in your house all the time anyway. She's not even related to yiz!'

'She's Therese's best friend,' he pointed out. 'Besides, you're not related to me either. And you've been in my house a few times.'

'Aye, but I'm your girlfriend. And she practically *lives* there.'

He considered this. 'I suppose she does, but . . .' He shrugged. It was hard to put into words why Kathleen belonged there. She just did.

Sadie was now wearing a definite pout. 'You can be really *dreary* at times, Liam Flynn, you know that?'

'Dreary, am I?' He gathered her into his arms, kissing her soundly.

Now she was smiling again. 'Not all the time, to be fair.'

The sound of bells from the nearby convent reminded him it was time to go. 'Don't forget to call round on Tuesday!'

She frowned. 'Tuesday?'

'Aye, my granny's birthday.'

'Oh aye, right.' Her attitude towards his family was a bit odd. She wanted them to like her, but often seemed reluctant to actually visit the Flynn house. Maybe she found it *boring*. Stifling a sigh, he headed for home.

\* \* \*

Kathleen sipped her tea in Therese's house, noticing again how much more at ease she felt there. Things at home had been tense since both she and Bronagh had been laid off, and only Mammy and Daddy were now working. Their jobs too felt precarious, and all around West Belfast families were struggling.

Kathleen had always known that as a family they were luckier than most, but now she was truly realising what some families had to do to survive. Many had given up their homes to share with relatives, with the result that overcrowding was now commonplace, while some houses were boarded up. Two wages was enough to pay rent on one house, with generally enough to spare for food, but many homes now only had one wage-earner. Kathleen and the other handywomen had begun to notice signs of hunger and poor nutrition in the homes they visited. There were children now with bandy legs and missing teeth – much more so than before – and distended bellies had even started to appear in the hungriest of children. The oldest members of their community had survived the famine – the Great Hunger as it was more properly called, for in fact there had been plenty of food exported from Ireland while its people starved. Now hunger had returned, and its bite was both sharp and lethal.

With so many people living so tightly packed together, disease inevitably ran through families like water. Deaths had risen sharply from what Doctor Gaffney the local general practitioner called 'infectious diarrhoea' and what most people called a stomach bug. Doctor Gaffney had advised the handywomen not to enter such homes to care for the dying, which was awful.

Peggy – who had spent a year training as a proper midwife in Dublin, and who was now working in the Royal Maternity Hospital alongside her new husband – had been giving the handywomen lessons in what she called 'infection control', which built on the high hygiene standards the West Belfast handywomen had already been applying. Peggy, now Mrs Sheridan since her wedding in the summer, had even provided them with a couple of boxes of the special rubber gloves they used in the hospital. Carbolic soap was also recommended, and Mrs Clarke had paid for a large box of pungent pink blocks of soap to be delivered to her home for the use of the handywomen when they went out to births.

For, despite everything – or perhaps *because* of everything – the babies continued to arrive. Kathleen's understanding of how babies were conceived remained incomplete, yet she now had a fair idea of the basics; even seeing how dogs and horses mated had helped. Apparently humans did it face to face, but apart from that the basic principles of mammalian reproduction were now clearer.

It was all theoretical, of course, and since Kathleen rarely accepted boys' offers to walk her home after a céilí, the chances of her finding a mate were minimal. While she had tried walking out with a couple of other lads around the time she had turned eighteen, she had struggled to *like* them in the way that Therese liked Jimmy, and so had politely declined their requests to see her again. The truth was that, in very different ways, Liam Flynn and Mugsy Mulligan had put an end to all of that when she was sixteen. At nearly twenty, and with the world on fire, finding a boyfriend was the least of her worries.

Their entire community was struggling, and knowing that the same and worse was happening all over Europe and beyond was no consolation. The south had so far managed to remain neutral and although they had rationing like in the north, at least they didn't have to live with the constant threat of German bombs falling from the skies. Thankfully, the sectarian violence at home had settled a bit. There were houses that still hadn't been rebuilt after the riots of summer 1935, but with so many families sharing a house now, the housing shortage wasn't quite as noticeable. If you had the money, you could find a house to rent. If you had the money . . .

While some of the mills had turned to making war-related products like rope, twine, and tents – Mammy and Daddy were busy every day making blackout sheets – the best jobs, as always, were for Protestants, in the likes of the shipyard and Mackies and Shorts. All were supporting the British war effort; Harland and Wolff had launched a warship called HMS *Belfast* last year, and the city was full of talk about the Sunderland flying boat and the Stirling bomber aircraft being made in Belfast. Tanks too were being manufactured locally, and the town and country knew about it.

It would be only a matter of time, some people said, before the Nazis struck their wee city. The air raid sirens had even sounded one night in October. Although it had turned out to be a false alarm, it had scared the bejaysus out of many.

It was the worst of times for West Belfast; all the hardship and fears of war without any of the benefits of work. Worry was constant, and stress, and people hardly knew which was worse, the notion that bombs might rain down on them at any time, or the anxiety about keeping up with the rent and putting food on the table.

Being a handywoman had been a godsend for Kathleen. Having completed her apprenticeship – despite worrying at the start she would never manage it – she was now out and about on a regular basis supporting women, and occasionally supporting bereaved families or sitting with the dying. It gave her purpose, and focus, and a feeling of being useful. It was still bringing in money too – although the numbers of women who could not afford the handywomen's modest fee were increasing. From working flat out every day, many of the young women now had unexpected time on their hands. Today at Mass the priest had said their local civil defence group needed more volunteers, and Kathleen and Bronagh were planning to attend the meeting next Saturday.

'What about it, Therese? Do you want to come with us?'

Kathleen was in her usual spot at the edge of the settee in Therese's living room – some things never changed. And yet, there were differences. These days Kathleen always politely declined to stay for supper, knowing that every ha'penny and every ration was tight. And Therese wasn't always there in the evenings, for she spent much of her time with Jimmy McKeown, planning their wedding. Luckily, Jimmy had recently completed his apprenticeship as a brickie, and so they would easily be able to afford rent. Two wages and no children meant that they'd be rich newlyweds – for a while at least.

The bigger worry for Therese, Kathleen knew, was how her family would manage without her wage coming in. Mrs Flynn still had her mill job, thank God, but Liam and Seány had been put on half hours, Christine had been laid off completely, and the two wee ones had no work at all. They were both still at school, but Maria would normally be a half-timer by now. No work. *Like me.*

Despite the income from her handywoman work dwindling, Kathleen had discovered in herself a passion for learning more and more about pregnancy and childbirth. Peggy had loaned her an astonishing book called *A Handbook of Midwifery* (Tenth Edition) by someone called Comyns Berkeley. Inside was an entire world of scientific information which Kathleen devoured over and over again. There were labelled diagrams showing the inside of the female body, and Kathleen was fascinated to visualise how the womb grew, pressing everything else out of its way, then shrinking back to hide within the safety of the pelvic bones following birth.

'Sorry, what?' Her mind had drifted, and Therese was giving her a wry look.

'I said that our Liam is going. To the civil defence thing. Better for me to be concentrating on the house, and lookin' after Granny.'

Granny Flynn's head swivelled round from where she had been gazing into the fire, seemingly oblivious. 'Lookin' after me?' She chuckled. 'I don't need no lookin' after. I can see to meself, so I can!'

Kathleen suppressed a smile. Granny Flynn was redoubtable – a fierce spirit held within a frail, thin body.

'Nearly ninety, I am,' Granny Flynn added proudly. 'How long is it to my birthday now, Therese?'

'Day after tomorrow, Granny. Today's Sunday, and you'll be ninety on Tuesday.'

Granny nodded, satisfied. 'And where is it that our Liam's goin'?'

Therese shook her head, laughing. 'You don't miss nothin', do you, Granny? He's goin' to a meetin' in the parish hall. About air raid defence.'

'Them bliddy Germans. As if we didn't get it hard enough with the English all these years.' She sent Therese a sharp look. 'You tell our Liam if I forget that he's to keep himself safe. You hear me?'

'Course I will, Granny. The whole idea of the meetin' is to work out how to keep people safe.'

Granny was only half-listening. 'He's a good lad, our Liam. Stood up to be the man of the house when his daddy died.' She sighed. 'Still, I'll see him soon.'

'Yes, you can tell him yourself, Granny. He'll be in soon.'
'Not him. The other fella. Where is Liam anyway?'
'He's out with Sadie.'
Swallowing, Kathleen glanced casually at her nails.
'Sadie? Who's Sadie?'
'She's his girl, Granny.' Therese's tone was patient. Granny had been repeatedly told about Sadie since she had become Liam's girl a few months ago. She had even met Sadie a number of times.

'Sounds like a Protestant name to me. Why'd he not get a good Catholic girl?' She glanced towards Kathleen, who felt heat coming into her face. Old people were a nightmare sometimes. And Granny Flynn was sharp as a tack.

Therese maintained her patience. 'She's Catholic, Granny. Sadie O'Kane, from up Dunville.'

'Hmmm. I must remember to have a word with him. Walkin' out with Protestants.' She tutted. 'He'll be in the Orange Order next.'

'No, Granny, she's not Protestant. She's Catholic.'
'She's no good for him. Shifty, I tell ya.'
Therese grimaced, then said brightly, 'So what do you want to do for your birthday, Granny?'

Granny sent her a knowing look, then shrugged. 'Same as every day. Take me to Morning Mass, then one of yiz can read me the paper.'

'What about dinner? We can try and get something special for you, maybe. What would you like, Granny?'

'Well, I'm bloody sick of rabbit, that's for sure.' Rabbit was one of the few meats not rationed, and it had become a Sunday dinner staple for families in the past year. 'It's like chicken, but far too strong for me. I tell ye what, though,

I fancy a bitta bacon. Haven't had bacon this long time.' She sent the girls a wistful look. 'I used to love me bacon and spuds and cabbage.'

'I don't know, Granny. But I'll try.'

'You're a good girl, Therese. Two good girls.' She sent a keen look towards Kathleen. 'And have you a young man you're walkin' out with, Kathleen?'

*Uh-oh.* Kathleen suspected she knew where this was going. 'No, I haven't, Mrs Flynn.' She leaned forwards conspiratorially. 'I'm very fussy, you see.'

Granny gave a bark of laughter. 'Quite right too. He'd be a lucky fella to get you, for you're a great girl. Now don't you be blushin' like that. I've known you all your life – well, ever since you were a wee baby brought back from away, that is. There's things I've often wondered about you, Kathleen Gallagher. Things it's better not to ask about, so I'll say no more.'

This was odd, but Granny was frequently getting mixed up these days, so Kathleen put it out of her mind. So long as Granny Flynn said no more about her having a young man, she was content.

Rising, Therese went to the foot of the stairs. 'Have yous two finished your homework yet?' She paused, listening. 'Well, get it done, and then bring it down to me so I can check it.' Returning to the settee, she grimaced. 'They're carryin' on up there. Not too much homework being done at all.'

'It's good you keep at them,' said Granny firmly. 'Nobody ever taught me to read or write – we'd enough to be thinkin' about, gettin' through the Hunger. But I can figure in my head no bother.' She tapped the side of her head, and Kathleen smiled. Many times over the years she had seen evidence of Granny Flynn's impressive mental arithmetic abilities. 'Nobody ever diddled me out of money, that's for sure!'

'It'd be a brave one would even try it!' As she spoke, Kathleen heard the sound of a firm step outside. She rose, picking up her shawl. 'Well, I better be gettin' back. Our ones will be wondering what's happened me.'

The door opened, and Liam stepped in. 'Ach, well, Kathleen,' he said easily, and she managed a reasonable response. After all, she'd had plenty of practice at keeping her mask in place.

'Well.' She bent to kiss Granny's wizened cheek. 'I'll try and call round on Tuesday. See yous!'

Then she was outside and could breathe again. Jesus, the man had a girlfriend, for God's sake! It was well past time she got over him.

As she walked down Clowney Street and into Beechmount Avenue she diverted her mind by trying to remember some of the things she'd learned in the midwifery book – important things. There was an entire chapter devoted to bacterial infection, and reading about how bacteria grew and spread helped Kathleen understand the importance of hygiene, of Carbolic soap and Dettol – the things Mrs Clarke and Peggy were always going on about. Kathleen felt a little better, knowing they were doing all they could.

# 10

*Monday, 25 November 1940*

> *IRISH NEUTRALITY CONFIRMED*
> *The Irish leader, Eamon De Valera, says there is no question of the British being given access to Irish ports while Ireland is partitioned.*
>
> *A secret report from the British Ministry of Information on Ireland highlights 'apprehension' in the south of Ireland about the possibility of invasion by Britain or Germany.*

No amount of Dettol could have solved the problem of the tiny house inhabited by the McGowan family.

'Mrs McGowan,' Mrs Clarke had said in her summary, 'Fourteen children, eight living. She won't be able to pay us anything.'

Kathleen had nodded. Mammy wouldn't be happy – which was fair enough, since money was so tight. Bronagh was already volunteering with the medical team who were setting up an old bus as some sort of field hospital in case the Nazis decided to bomb Belfast, but Mammy asked them both every single evening whether either of them had found any paid work. Every evening, the answer was no.

Daddy, who had always been a quiet man, had now retreated so far into himself that some days he barely spoke at all. They still bought the newspaper every day, as Mammy said it was the highlight of Daddy's day and he shouldn't be deprived of it, and sure enough he read the *Irish News and Belfast Morning News* from cover to cover – sometimes twice. Once the main news came on the radio at nine o'clock every evening, he would abandon his paper, and sometimes Bronagh or Kathleen would pick it up. Mammy never did, saying that things were bad enough already and she didn't want to know what else might be in store.

They were meticulous in ensuring their curtains were tightly closed at dusk, and tried not to venture outside at night at all. Of course, labour often got going once a woman's older children were settled for the night, and so Kathleen frequently found herself scurrying along the maze of streets around the Falls Road by the light of a weak lamp – the only light permitted under the new regulations, enforced by the local civil defence group – and even then it had to be mainly shuttered, the beam angled down so you could take careful steps along the road.

She arrived at the McGowans' house north of the Falls around ten in the evening, and the first thing that struck her was the stench of unwashed bodies, musty furniture, and damp. Bracing herself, she stepped inside, being careful to keep her face expressionless. Mrs McGowan's eight living children, ranging in age from three to sixteen, were all in the tiny living room, their mother engaged in separating two small boys currently attempting to thump one another, while in the corner, a small girl cried.

'That's enough!' Kathleen declared, in her best teacherish voice, and the boys stopped to look at her. 'Hello, Mrs McGowan,' she added in a different tone.

## The Irish Midwife at War

'Well, Kathleen-love,' said Mrs McGowan. She looked exhausted. 'It's happening, but I can't get into it. Too much to do. I'm sorry about this place. Didn't get the chance to red up. Cora, lift Alice there!'

The eldest girl – Cora, presumably – picked up the crying child. Alice was a cute wee thing with blonde curls, and Kathleen saw immediately that she was probably over-tired. Mrs McGowan, dealing with early labour pains, had been unable to get her children to bed tonight, so that would have to be Kathleen's first job.

Ignoring the fact the house had probably not been cleaned in weeks, Kathleen assured her it was fine, and advised her to go upstairs and settle herself. The house was cold, the hearth empty; they probably couldn't afford coal. Once the woman had gone, Kathleen got stuck in. The room was fairly bare: a settee, a single cupboard, and a faded mat on the floor. A mattress had been stuck behind the settee – that would be the parents' bed. Kathleen remembered a time before her brothers were married when they had had the front bedroom and her own mammy and daddy had slept downstairs. The walls were unadorned save for a dog-eared picture of Saint Gerard Majella. As he was the patron saint of motherhood and safe childbirth, Kathleen took it as a good sign.

With the help of the eldest two – including the boy who had been sent to fetch her earlier – she got the youngest ones ready for bed. There was not a scrap of food in the kitchen apart from tea, a small amount of milk, some porridge oats, two slices of bread, and a bottle of the free blackcurrant juice issued by the government. The children had a hungry look about them, but they would need their porridge in the morning, and Kathleen could do nothing more about it at this minute. Once the wee ones had been to the outhouse Kathleen took them upstairs to settle them for bed, instructing the older ones to put things away downstairs.

When she was sure the youngest two – both girls – would soon be asleep (it was after half-ten at night, and they were wrecked), she returned downstairs. 'Da' was at the pub apparently, and would stay at his sister's tonight. Trying not to show what she thought of Da wasting money on a pint when his children had no food, Kathleen went back to cleaning, giving the children small jobs only, poor wee things.

Within the hour the place was in reasonable shape, and Kathleen sent the three older girls up to bed. All five McGowan girls would sleep in the big bed in the front bedroom; three at the top and two at the bottom. Their mother was currently pacing up and down in the back room, where the three boys usually slept.

Following the girls upstairs, she knocked quietly on the door to the back bedroom. The house was the same shape as her own, and this bedroom was the equivalent of where she and Bronagh normally slept.

'All right?' she asked softly.

'Aye. Pains are coming stronger now.'

'Good.' They would be, now that the woman had let go of some of her burdens of worry. 'Come on downstairs when you're ready, and I'll get the boys to bed.'

'I'll come now, before the next pain.'

'Great.' Kathleen made sure to go down the steep stairs ahead of Mrs McGowan, who put hands on both dampish walls to steady herself as she descended.

'Right, boys, say night-night to your mammy!'

They did, the younger two giving her a kiss and a hug. Seeing the warmth between them made Kathleen's heart swell. *Poverty can't kill love.*

Once they were gone, things began to progress. Mrs McGowan paced, and sat rocking, and paced again. She leaned on the mantelpiece, and on the torn settee, and on the kitchen table. She moaned, and breathed, then finally began effortful groaning. Throughout, Kathleen was there with words of encouragement, with a clean cool facecloth, with hot tea or cold water when she was thirsty, with the chamber pot when she needed it. She had already established that the baby was in a good position – a memory flashing through her at the thought of herself putting hands on a woman's belly for the first time. *Mrs Thompson.* Wee Francis was now a sturdy three-year-old, and Kathleen was a fully competent handywoman.

And very few could afford to pay her. And war was upon them. And poverty was everywhere.

Shaking her head, Kathleen brought herself back to the present. Mrs McGowan needed her attention. The rest, she could do nothing about.

Before long, Mrs McGowan was sitting on the settee and pushing in earnest, and Kathleen busied herself preparing for the birth. There were towels in the kitchen cupboard that were clean, though thin and threadbare in places, and in the living-room drawer she found vests and nappies. There was no cradle of any kind in the house, as far as she could see.

Mrs McGowan was pushing again, and so Kathleen knelt on the mat to see what was happening. The woman had shed her underwear a little while ago, but was still in her dress. Kathleen reckoned she probably didn't possess a nightgown.

The head was right there, and so Kathleen reached for some of the towels she had placed on the settee by Mrs McGowan's side. The house was still cold, and Kathleen knew it would be vital to keep the baby warm once it emerged. Unusually, the baby came out all at once – head, shoulders, and body all in a single push. Catching it, Kathleen realised it was fairly small. Small babies, she knew, were not always cooperative and sometimes got themselves into odd positions making birth tricky, but thankfully this one – a wee girl – had emerged handy enough.

'Oh, thank God!' Mrs McGowan's tone was one of relief, and Kathleen smiled as she passed the baby up to her mammy, wrapped in a towel.

'A wee girl for you, Mrs McGowan.'

'Ah, good! I'll be calling her Mary after one of the ones that died.'

'That's lovely.'

The baby cried then, and they both fussed over her. Kathleen had wondered if Mrs McGowan had been too worn down by life to take to another wee one, but thankfully she was doing all the usual motherly things, and seemed delighted with her new daughter.

There was no clock, but Kathleen guessed it was sometime between two and three in the morning. Within the hour she had laid out the mattress on the floor – first lifting the mat, which Mrs McGowan said was their blanket – and mother and baby were tucked in together between a set of clean sheets, the mat over the top of them providing extra warmth. The baby was feeding rightly, and Mrs McGowan was looking contented. Kathleen had also emptied the drawer, stacking the remaining baby clothes on top of the cupboard and carefully lining the drawer with two soft towels. People round here often used drawers as cradles.

Taking the bucket with the afterbirth in it out to the yard, Kathleen stood for a moment, gazing up at the silent sky. The blackout had one advantage: you could see the stars at night. Hundreds of them. Thousands.

Offering up a prayer of thanks for the safe birth of baby Mary, Kathleen went back inside to finish her jobs. By the time she had cleaned up, made tea and toast for the new mother, checked that she wasn't bleeding heavily, and made a pot of porridge which could be easily heated up for breakfast, it was nearing morning.

Promising to call back later she made her way home, passing people walking to the mills. So it must be after half five already. The newspaper sellers were out too, and their headlines gave her pause.

Everyone was up: Mammy and Daddy getting ready for work, and Bronagh seeing to the breakfast. Grabbing a soda farl from the plate and biting into it, she announced, 'Lord Craigavon is dead.'

'What?' Daddy, normally quiet, was all interested. 'I knew he was sick, but nobody said he was dying.' He frowned. 'Maybe now we'll get a decent leader. Them shower' – he jerked his head toward the street, presumably indicating the entire government of Northern Ireland – 'are useless!' He went on a rant then, detailing all the failings of the Stormont government, including the fact they had built only a couple of hundred air raid shelters. 'We have the highest population density – higher than anywhere in Britain – but we have the *lowest* proportion of air raid shelters. I'm tellin' ya, they don't give a fuck for the people, any of them!'

'You're right, Daddy!' said Bronagh with feeling, while Mammy was throwing dirty looks at both girls for encouraging him. Mammy didn't like it when Daddy talked about the war: he was altogether too worked up about it, she would say.

Thankfully, both parents left then, for if you arrived after the six o'clock whistle you'd be shut out and your pay docked. Before heading upstairs to bed Kathleen told Bronagh about the McGowan family and how poor they were, asking if the St Vincent de Paul group could help.

Bronagh, outraged on behalf of Mrs McGowan and her children, promised to see what she could do, and Kathleen reminded her to wake her up before Mammy and Daddy came home for dinner at about twenty past twelve. Mammy didn't take kindly to anybody still being in bed at noon, even if they had been up all night.

So when Mammy arrived for her dinner – spuds mashed with raw egg today – Kathleen was up, her head still a bit groggy and feeling on edge. That pot of porridge wouldn't keep all the wee McGowans fed for long. And Mammy was going to give off; she just knew it.

It didn't take long. 'Have either of yiz done anything about gettin' a job yet? Two big lumps bringin' in not a ha'penny between you!'

Unable to help herself, Kathleen answered back, pointing out that there were no feckin' jobs anywhere for Catholics.

'Don't you be usin' that tone with me, miss! And I'll have no bad talk in this house!'

*Yeah, of course she'd go for my tone.* Ignoring the warning looks Bronagh was sending her, Kathleen got stuck in. 'Well then, you tell me where I'm supposed to find a job?

The shipyard? City Hall? Why don't you get me a job in the Damask, instead of givin' off all the time and tellin' me what to do?'

Mammy wagged a finger, and Kathleen tried not to flinch. 'I'm your mother and till the day I die I'll be tellin' you what to do. So you may get used to it. Now instead of the two of yiz runnin' about, helpin' the town and country for free, yiz should be out there every day lookin' for a job!'

'What happened to the good Christian that says we help those in need?' Kathleen's voice dripped with sarcasm. Oh, she knew she should stop, but somehow she couldn't. It was all too much: the stress at home, Mammy's endless badgering, Daddy's despondency, having no work, Sadie O'Kane, the McGowans . . .

Mammy blessed herself. 'You wash your mouth out with soap, Kathleen Gallagher! Of course we help others – but not at this cost!'

Bronagh intervened quietly, setting Mammy's dinner in her usual spot. 'There are no jobs, Mammy. You know that.'

Mammy turned on her. 'You keep out of this, Bronagh! God knows I've done enough for you over the years!'

Kathleen bristled at this. Mammy was their mammy, and had done plenty for all of them. They all did plenty for each other. That was how it worked.

'Doesn't change the fact that Kathleen's right.' Bronagh was quietly steadfast. Turning away, she began filling a second plate with lovely egg-champ.

'I might have known you'd take her side.' Mammy looked furious. 'Well met, the two of yous. And yes, you know rightly what I'm sayin', Bronagh Gallagher! Runnin' about with boys. Not bringin' a wage in. Not even lookin' for work!'

*Running about with boys?* That was so unfair. Kathleen hadn't been with a boy in about a year, and the only boy Mammy actually knew about was the disaster that was Mugsy Mulligan. And as for Bronagh, she hadn't been with one since she was sixteen – for Kathleen now knew about Bronagh's one and only boyfriend, the boul' Michael, who had told her he loved her then fecked off to Dublin, never to be seen or heard from again.

'So where should we look for work, Mammy?' Bronagh asked, her tone entirely reasonable. Setting a plate of dinner before Kathleen, she turned away again.

'I dunno, do I?' Abruptly Mammy sat, looking deflated. 'I dunno.'

The anger drained out of Kathleen as she recognised Mammy's frustration and despair. She exhaled, shaking her head. 'I'm sorry, Mammy. I shouldn't have said them things. I know you're worryin' about all of us.'

Mammy nodded in acknowledgement, and patted Kathleen's hand. 'Your Daddy won't give over about the war. It's all he thinks about. The only thing he talks about. It's not good for his head.'

So that was Mammy's biggest worry right now. Fair enough – Daddy was very morose about it all. 'Is he not right to be thinkin' about it, though? In the paper it says the risk of the Nazis bombing Belfast is high.'

'But we can do nahin' about it! If they bomb they bomb.' Mammy's expression showed a sort of stubborn bewilderment. Lifting her fork, she began to eat.

Kathleen ate too, Bronagh following her. 'In London and all the other English cities, they're building shelters. Very few here, but I think Daddy's right. I think we need shelters.'

'And we have our gas masks,' Bronagh added.

Mammy shuddered. 'Horrible things!'

'We might be glad of them if the Nazis try and gas us.'

Footsteps approached the front door. 'Give over now, here's your daddy,' Mammy hissed, even as they heard the front door opening and Bronagh rose to plate up Daddy's dinner.

The conversation that ensued was cordial, Mammy showing no signs of the frustration she had displayed just moments ago. Trying to be conciliatory – and to show Mammy she was genuinely sorry for answering back – Kathleen mentioned she was going to ask Mrs Clarke if she knew of any paid work.

'That's a good idea, Kathleen. You do that.'

Half an hour later both parents were away, headed back to work. Twelve hours a day they worked; six till six Monday to Friday. Saturdays were a bit easier, for they only did a half day. But they worked hard. Kathleen knew they did, for her memories of the mill were recent, and ran deep.

'I do feel guilty about not bringing money in,' she said to Bronagh, as they cleared up after the dinner.

'Aye, me too. I didn't wanna say, but apparently the Blackstaff Mill at the top of the Springfield Road is gonna be takin' on girls for as-and-when days.'

Kathleen stopped. 'Brilliant! How do we put our names down?'

'I'm goin' this afternoon so I'll find out the craic. It hasn't even been announced yet, but I know a girl who works in the payroll office and she told me on the quiet. They're gonna work off a list.'

'Wow, so hopefully we have a good chance. Here, put Therese and Christine down too, if you can. But why did you not mention it to Mammy?'

'Because I'm not even sure it's true. Don't wanna build her hopes up, you know?'

'Aye, makes sense. Right, I'm gonna call on Mrs McGowan, then go and see Mrs Clarke. I'll call round to the Flynns' as well if I have time before it gets dark.'

'Oh, that reminds me. I've a few bits for you from the St Vincent de Paul.' Opening one of the kitchen cupboards she took out two large bags. 'They're brilliant. Look what they got in for her in only a morning.'

Kathleen peered inside. The first bag contained flour, oats, carrots, potatoes, and a large head of cabbage, while the second—

'Oh, wow!' Kathleen held up a baby vest that looked fairly new. There was a pile of them, as well as nappies and even a wee knitted blanket. 'People are so good!'

'They've paid for a bag of coal too. I've arranged for it to be delivered later. Here, make sure she knows we never gave her name.'

'Of course.' Pride meant people never wanted to accept handouts, so keeping it anonymous always helped.

Mrs McGowan was in the house with her younger children – the big ones still at school – and the baby was feeding well. Once Kathleen had finished with the housework Alice, the littlest girl, who had been the youngest in the family until now, climbed onto her knee.

'Now, don't be annoying Kathleen, Alice!' Mrs McGowan admonished, but Kathleen settled the child more comfortably on her lap, saying, 'Ach, sure she's no bother.'

Mrs McGowan nodded, before saying again how delighted she was to receive the gifts from the St Vincent de Paul.

'Sure in a few years you'll be givin' it back for somebody else to benefit from,' Kathleen told her. 'Every house in this area is eligible, they said.'

Thankfully Mrs McGowan seemed more relieved than proud, and promised her children a feast of spuds and vegetables later. She had received her new ration book too and assured Kathleen she'd be dead on.

Kathleen wasn't convinced, but promised to call back the next day. As she walked down the street she realised school had finished for the day, for the older McGowan children were on their way up the street, a couple of them giving her a shy 'Hello'. A little further along a group of girls were skipping, their song a new one since Kathleen's day.

'Underneath the spreadin' chestnut tree,' they intoned, 'Mr Chamberlain says to me, if you wanna get your gas mask free, go and see the ARP.'

Kathleen shook her head. Their childhood had been infected by war, by fear, and by added poverty. West Belfast had always had more than its share of trouble, but this foreign war had made everything harder. ARP referred to 'Air Raid Precautions' – something that wee ones shouldn't even have to know about, never mind bring into their games. *God, what a world!*

# 11

*Tuesday, 26 November 1940*

> *In England, children continue to be evacuated from major cities as the aerial attacks continue. Some of these children are sent to Belfast, as the city is thought to be safe from Luftwaffe bombing raids.*

Trying not to think what the war might be doing to the innocent minds of the children, Kathleen walked along the Falls until she reached Mrs Clarke's house, where she discussed Mrs McGowan's birth and circumstances with her mentor.

'You did well, Kathleen,' Mrs Clarke said quietly, Kathleen noticing idly that Mrs Clarke said 'did' not 'done', unlike most people around here. *That's because she's married to a fancy lawyer and lives in a fancy house.* The good thing about Mrs Clarke though, was that she genuinely didn't see herself as better than others, just luckier.

As she made her way to the Flynns' house Kathleen braced herself; not something she would once have had to do. Going straight in without knocking – for she was like family, never a visitor – she went straight to Granny, who was sitting in her usual chair, beaming with joy. Liam, Therese, and Seány were there too, but there was no sign of the younger girls. Liam was reading the paper, but he looked up when she came in.

'Happy birthday, Granny! Ninety today!'

'Ah, thanks, Kathleen-love. Ninety! Who would ever have thought it?'

Kathleen perched on the arm of the settee, beside Seány. 'Are you having a good day?'

'I am. I had me bacon and cabbage at dinner time – great it was. Our Therese is a fine cook, aren't you, Therese?'

'I learned from the best!' Therese answered with a wink, not pausing in her mopping.

'I'm blessed with all of yiz,' Granny Flynn continued. 'Havin' only the one chile before my man died, I wondered if I'd even have grandchildren. But here yiz all are, and a fine bunch of childer too. I married late in life and so did my boy. Your poor daddy, Lord rest him. Killed in that bliddy mill. That was a bad, bad day.'

'I know, Granny.' Liam's voice cracked a little, and Kathleen had to look away. 'But we've had good days too.'

'The wee days is the good days. Never you forget that, Liam. Days when everything is just plain, and right, and routine. D'ye hear me?'

'I do, Granny.'

'Tea, Kathleen?' Therese set down the mop.

'Sure I'll make it.' Heading to the kitchen, she filled the kettle with water and set it to boil, then got the cups ready. Therese joined her for a wee chat, mostly about the wedding plans. Kathleen couldn't talk about Mrs McGowan as handywomen didn't do so unless needed, and she didn't want to tell Therese about the row with Mammy earlier. Mammy was bad with her nerves at times, and who could blame her? She looked after the money in the house – she always had – but now it must be so hard to make it stretch to cover their needs.

'They're gonna be hiring in the Blackstaff Mill, apparently.'

'No way!'

'Casual days only. You put your name on a list.'

'God, I hope me and our Liam and our Seány can get in! Christine too!'

Kathleen shook her head. 'Girls only. I asked Bronagh to try and put your name down, and Christine as well.'

'Thanks.' She made a face. 'The town and country will be on that list.'

'Aye, I know.'

'Hello, hello!' A trilling voice indicated someone had just arrived, and Kathleen knew exactly who it was. After exchanging a level look with Therese she went to the cupboard and took out an extra cup. 'Happy, happy birthday, Mrs Flynn!'

As high-pitched enthusiasm continued to emerge from the living room, she and Therese made the tea with silent efficiency, then carried two cups each into the living room. Therese gave one to Liam and kept the other herself, while Kathleen handed one to Seány and one to Granny.

'Here you go, Granny! Well, Sadie, how are you?'

'Kathleen.' Now there was a decided lack of enthusiasm.

Stifling a smile, Kathleen asked, 'What way do you take your tea?'

'Oh, Liam knows. Don't you, Liam?'

Liam looked startled. 'Errr . . .'

'Milk, no sugar.' She gave a smile that did not reach her eyes. 'I'm sweet enough.'

'Right.'

Once Sadie had her tea in her hand there was no stopping her. She rabbited on about everything and nothing, and every story she told featured herself as the starlet.

'Liam!' Granny interrupted Sadie mid-story, and Kathleen couldn't resist glancing at Therese.

'Aye?'

'Will you go and get me my knitted socks? It's gettin' cold in here.'

'We can light the fire if you like, Granny.'

'Jaysus, no. It's not even dark yet!' She sounded outraged.

By the time Liam had come back with the socks and put them on Granny – joking with her as he knelt to his task – Sadie had subsided. She left soon afterwards, once the girls came in. *Does she not like the girls?* They were noisy, it was true, but Kathleen loved their exuberance. She chatted to thirteen-year-old Maria about her schoolwork, and then wee Rita-Anne (who was now eleven) told her all about a poor wee dog that had been hit by a motor-car on the Falls Road but was luckily all right. Along with her nieces, the girls were the nearest thing Kathleen had to younger sisters, and she tried to be good to them the way Bronagh had always been good to her.

'You make sure and do your homework, girls,' said Granny. 'It's your best chance of doin' well for yourselves. I never—' Granny stopped, placing a hand on her breastbone.

'Are you all right, Granny?' Kathleen, attuned to watching for subtle signs of discomfort in the women she supported, couldn't ignore something as obvious as this.

'Probably only heartburn from me dinner.' Granny's tone was dismissive, but Kathleen wasn't convinced.

'Did you feel it earlier?'

'No, it's only after startin'. Granny seemed to be in significant pain, and as Kathleen watched her colour changed, her face gradually taking on a greyish tinge.

'Seány.' Kathleen's tone was low, intent.

'Aye?' They were all looking at her, alarm clearly apparent in their expressions.

'Go and get Doctor Gaffney.'

'Indeed and you will not get the . . . doctor for a wee— bit of— indigestion! It'll probably go— away in— a wee minute.' Granny's outrage was all too clear, but her words were punctuated by sharp, short intakes of breath. Kathleen saw the old lady's chest rising and falling rapidly, which might be from sudden fear, but might be to do with her heart.

Liam intervened. 'Now, Granny. Kathleen's like a nurse, as you well know, so if she says you need the doctor then we're gettin' the doctor.' They exchanged a worried look, but for once Kathleen's racing heart and rapid pulse had a source other than Liam's blue eyes.

She turned back to Seány. 'You may go quick. Tell him Granny has sudden chest pain and shortness of breath, and she's very pale.' As Seány left, Kathleen knelt on the mat, taking the old lady's hand even as Therese came to sit on the arm of her chair, half-hugging her from behind.

By the time Doctor Gaffney came – remarkably quickly – Kathleen knew it was bad. Far from easing, the pain had persisted and Granny had closed her eyes, her face twisted in agony. Liam had carried her upstairs to the big bed in the front room that she shared with Therese and Christine, and Therese had lit the fire up there – an unheard of extravagance which Granny had not even the energy to object to. Maria brought a hot-water bottle as well.

Once Doctor Gaffney came the two wee ones were sent downstairs to do their homework, though Kathleen knew no homework would be done. Doctor Gaffney listened to

Granny's heart and checked her pulse, then told her in a kind voice to rest as best she could. Once she closed her eyes again he jerked his head to say he wanted to speak to Liam outside on the landing. When he returned, Liam looked grim, his mouth a thin line of unhappiness.

'Is the doctor away, Liam?' Granny asked without opening her eyes.

'He is, aye.' Liam's voice was soft, and sent a pang through Kathleen. She gave him an inquiring look and he shook his head sadly.

'What did he say, Liam?' Therese's voice trembled, making Liam frown.

'He said Granny isn't well and needs to rest.' He went to the door, signalling to Seány and Therese to accompany him.

He looked at Kathleen, who nodded. No words had been exchanged, yet they had understood one another perfectly: Liam would update Seány and Therese downstairs, and Kathleen would stay with Granny.

Kathleen bent to see to the fire, humming softly as she did so. When people were unwell it was important not to add to any fear they might be feeling. Opening the door, she turned on the landing light then turned off the big light in the bedroom. *There.* That was better.

A few minutes later she heard the front door open and close, and guessed someone had left to go and get Christine, who was at her friend's house. Mrs Flynn herself would be due back from work shortly, as would Kathleen's parents. No doubt Therese would be starting to get the tea ready in preparation, but Kathleen knew Granny Flynn wouldn't be eating tonight. In fact that feast of bacon, cabbage, and spuds might turn out to be her last proper meal. Much as she

*The Irish Midwife at War*

hated to admit it, Granny Flynn was ninety, had clearly had a heart attack, and was still unwell. Her chances of surviving the night were slim, if she could read anything from Doctor Gaffney's demeanour.

Sure enough, about twenty minutes later Christine appeared, her eyes red as if she had been crying. 'How is she?' she asked in a hushed tone.

'She's more comfortable, I think. I reckon the pain must have eased a good bit, for she looks like she's sleeping comfortably.'

Christine sat on the side of the bed, a bit further down from Kathleen, and gently stroked Granny's thin hand. 'Wee Granny,' she said quietly, then fished for a handkerchief in her pocket. 'Liam says you're to come downstairs.'

Kathleen rose. 'You sure you're all right here? Call me if anything changes.'

A minute later she was in the living room.

'How is she?' Seány asked.

'Much the same. Comfortable.'

They had all been crying, she saw, and the atmosphere was tense. Therese was in the kitchen making soda farls on the griddle, Liam by her side. Kathleen hugged her fiercely.

'Is Granny dying?' she asked baldly, and Liam nodded, his face twisting as emotion surged within him. Kathleen felt it too. Granny Flynn had always been part of her life.

'Right. Right.' She turned the farls over. 'What do we do, Kathleen? What are we supposed to do?'

The handywoman within Kathleen took over. 'Make sure she's comfortable. Sit with her so she's never alone. Get people home who need to say goodbye to her. Get her the Last Rites. Listen to whatever she has to say if she wakes up.' *And start planning the wake and funeral,* she added silently. It was too soon to say that part out loud.

Therese nodded, then sent her a curious look. 'Do people say like really important things?'

'Sometimes. Mostly though it's practical things about pillows or being thirsty or whatever. Once they start refusing even tea or water you're generally near the end.'

'But Granny had a big dinner. And a cuppa tea!'

'She did. And we can offer her something when she wakes. See how she is.'

'Right.'

'I'm gonna head home for my own tea and to see our ones. But I'll be back later.'

'Thanks, Kathleen. Appreciate it.'

'No bother.'

As she put on her shawl, Liam moved to the front door, lighting the wick of the family's gas lamp. 'I'll walk you home,' he said. 'You've no lamp with you.'

'Thanks. I thought I'd be home before dark.' Her voice was surprisingly steady, given the fact her mind had instantly gone to the last time Liam had walked her home. An entirely inappropriate thought in the circumstances.

Once they were out in the pitch-black street they walked slowly and carefully, Liam holding the lamp low to illuminate the ground directly in front of them.

'Here, take my arm,' he said, as she almost stumbled on a loose stone as they crossed Clowney Street. She did so, her heart thumping at his nearness.

'So I listened carefully to what you told our Therese there now,' he offered. 'Poor Granny.'

'I know.'

'I'm gonna call for the priest once I've left you home.'

She nodded, then realised he wouldn't see. 'Yes. Good idea.' Turning left, they walked up Beechmount Avenue, past the entrance to Amcomri Street and on towards Locan Street, talking seriously about Granny and the coming hours.

'I'll be back once I've had my tea and spoken to my ones. It'll be strange being a handywoman for Granny Flynn. I've never sat with somebody I know this well. I think of her as my own granny, you know.'

'She'd say the same. You're family, Kathleen.' There was a pause, as Kathleen's heart filled with the sweetest pain. 'How do you like being a handywoman, then?' he continued.

'I love it. It's a privilege to be round families at special times in their lives.'

'Like somebody dyin'. You're so well suited for it. I'm glad you're with us right now.'

'I just hope I can help.'

'You're helpin' already.' They stopped, having reached her door. 'Right. See you later.'

'Yeah, see you later, Liam.' Was it her imagination, or was there a slight pause before he turned away. Had he wanted to say something else?

No, she must be imagining things. Opening her door she stepped inside, putting it from her mind.

# 12

*Commissioned to report on Belfast's readiness for a Luftwaffe raid in late 1940, a Home Office inspector severely criticised the fire service, stating that 'drastic action' was needed to remedy inadequate numbers, poor leadership, and a separation between the main and auxiliary forces.*

*Jesus!* Liam stomped down Beechmount Avenue, telling himself off inwardly. He thought he'd put Kathleen out of his mind, but just now . . . Just now he had been almost overwhelmed with need. A need to connect with her, as he had one snowy New Year's Eve. To say something about how much he liked her, or to find out what she thought of him. To kiss her.

But he could not. Should not even be thinking such things. He had a girlfriend, for God's sake! His thoughts shied away from Sadie, from the doubts that had been plaguing him. She was a perfectly nice girl. Just not . . .

The what-ifs began then, flooding his mind with wishes, feelings . . . things he had been trying to banish from his mind for almost four years. Like what if he'd asked Kathleen to be his girl back then, when she was sixteen? He shook his head. Impossible. He had been due to turn eighteen only weeks later. *Cradle-snatcher*, they'd have said. *Pervert*. Everybody knew girls were better sticking to lads their own age.

Where the age gap was too big a girl could be too easily influenced. Pressured, even.

He used to worry about Therese and Jimmy. Although there were only a few months between them, and Therese was as strong-willed as any woman and as Catholic as most girls, still he suspected they got up to plenty when they went on their walks. Yes, the sooner his sister was safely married, the better.

The truth was that if Kathleen Gallagher had been his own girlfriend, he would seriously have doubted his own ability *not* to put her under pressure. There was something special about her, something he had discovered that night he had walked her home. If she was his girl, he would be far, far too keen on her. And that wouldn't do. He was much better with a girl like Sadie; she was good-looking, and lively, and easy to keep at a distance. Never had he been tempted to take risks with her that might lead to a pregnancy, and he also liked the fact he could compartmentalise his life, with Sadie safely contained in her own space, separate from work and family and football.

His life was lived in a few square miles, stretching from the mill to the church to the football field, with home nicely centred among them. He knew every street, every entry, every turn in the road. In the spring and summer they sometimes went up Sliabh Dubh, the black mountain that loomed protectively over West Belfast, and occasionally the St John's Gaelic football team travelled to other parts of the county for away games, but mostly he stayed within his own area.

Occasionally when he was younger he used to complain inwardly about his fate – that awful day when his daddy had been crushed to death by a malfunctioning loom. That was the day he had grown up, had become the man of the house at fourteen. And soon there would be another funeral – this time, Granny. At twenty-one, he felt three times as old.

He rapped the door of the priest's house, waiting in the fancy hallway while the housekeeper alerted him to the caller. The place smelled of beeswax and luxury. Once he heard about Granny, Father MacLaverty came straight away, bringing his own lamp along with his holy oils. Granny was awake when Father Mac went in, and agreed to receive the sacrament with a calmness that Liam found humbling. *I hope I'm as accepting when my time comes.*

Mammy was sitting with her, and had rearranged the furniture so that people could sit on both sides of the bed. She had also brought up two kitchen chairs and placed them in the corner between the window and the small fireplace. After giving Granny the Last Rites, Father MacLaverty stayed to lead a decade of the rosary, which Liam joined in. The familiar rhythm and cadence of the prayers was strangely comforting. Granny had fallen asleep again, but seemed decidedly serene.

Liam sat on when they brought the priest downstairs for tea, but Father MacLaverty made a point of calling back up to see him again to say goodnight, treating him like the man of the house. *Which I am, and have been since just after my fourteenth birthday.*

Soon afterwards the callers started arriving, as the word spread that old Mrs Flynn was on her way out. Neighbours and friends called to show they cared, to offer comfort, and to tell them to make sure and let them know if there was anything they could do for them. Which was code for helping with the wake and the funeral, Liam knew.

Then Kathleen was there, and the tightness in Liam's shoulders eased a wee bit. She was everywhere – calm, unflappable, and discreet. She drew no attention to herself, yet Liam saw her washing dishes, making tea, going up to check on Granny and Therese occasionally. The wee ones were now asleep, thank God.

Eventually, sometime around midnight, everything quietened down. Mammy told them all to get some sleep and thanked Kathleen, then made her way upstairs. Therese and Christine were in bed alongside Granny as usual. She wouldn't be alone as she slept.

As Seány got the two thin mattresses out from the big cupboard under the stairs – the mattresses that he and Liam used every night – Kathleen picked up her shawl.

'I'll be back in the morning,' she said, unnecessarily, for Liam already knew she would be. As she arranged her shawl around her shoulders he couldn't help looking at her face, a perfect oval, her eyes blue as summer skies and her fair hair giving her an ethereal look.

'I'll walk you home,' he said gruffly.

'Oh no, you're all right. I have my lamp this time!'

'I need the fresh air,' he returned, shrugging into his donkey jacket.

The night was clear, a hundred thousand stars above them. Stopping at the corner of Kathleen's street, they stood for a few minutes gazing up at them.

'That's the Plough,' he said, pointing. 'My da taught me to spot it, because he was a great man for James Connolly.'

'Workers' rights,' she murmured, her breath visible in the cold air. 'A pity we hadn't a few more of them. Which bit is the Plough?'

He explained, until she got it. 'Like a saucepan with a crooked handle!' she declared, making him laugh.

'That's it.' He rarely laughed these days. 'But just look how beautiful it all is. How . . . immense. Makes our wee worries seem small. And yet, today's all about Granny. And losing her is . . .'

'Immense,' she provided, her voice soft.

'Yes. The end of an era. She was born not long after the famine, you know.'

'The Hunger,' she corrected him. 'There was no famine, remember?'

'Quite right. The British use that word to try and hide the fact they were exporting most of the food, while the Irish starved.'

'Your granny is a formidable woman.'

'She's kinda your granny too, you know.'

'Thank you. I do feel that. But we're not blood relatives, remember.'

'Oh, I remember that,' he declared fervently. 'All the time.' Feeling as though he had said too much, he immediately backtracked. 'Right. I'll head back. You all right from here?'

'Aye. Thanks. See you in the morning.'

'Goodnight, Kathleen.'

'Goodnight, Liam.' Had he imagined it, or was there a softness in her voice as she said his name? It didn't even matter. In the midst of grief and sorrow and worry, he had found something that lightened his steps all the way home.

★ ★ ★

It was dinnertime on Wednesday, and Granny Flynn was still hanging on. She had slept quietly and peacefully, had used the chamber pot early in the morning with Therese's assistance, but had declined all offers of food and drink. She had been sleeping most of the time since, and seemed calm in herself. When she awoke she was alternating between humour – 'Why all the long faces? D'yiz think I'm dyin' or something?' – to sincere litanies about how good they all were, and how she was gonna tell her husband and son all about every one of them.

By early afternoon, things were fairly settled. Kathleen had visited the McGowans and was now back in the Flynns'. Liam was home from work, and the younger girls still at school. Kathleen, Therese, and Christine had done a major clean in preparation for the wake, though no one had admitted out loud that's what was happening. The other two were now washing china, and Kathleen had come upstairs to do a stint by Granny's bedside. She was sitting in a kitchen chair by the window, quietly sewing, when she heard a familiar voice downstairs. Bracing herself as footsteps sounded on the stairs, she eyed the door as Sadie entered noisily, closely followed by Liam.

Seeing Kathleen, the girl looked taken aback then furious, but her voice was sweet as she addressed the drowsy elderly lady in the bed. 'What's this I hear about wee Mrs Flynn not being well? And you in such great form for your birthday yesterday?'

Granny opened her eyes, her expression one of confusion then something else, quickly masked. 'And who would you be?' she asked, her voice thready and frail.

Kathleen sent her a sharp glance, not having heard that tone before. Was Granny becoming confused?

'I'm Sadie, Mrs Flynn.'

'Sadie. Sounds like a Protestant name.'

Sadie blinked, then pasted a smile on her face. 'No, I'm a good Catholic, Mrs Flynn.'

'Are ye?'

Liam, it seemed, had had enough. 'We'll leave you to rest now, Granny. I'll be up in a wee while.' He signalled to Sadie to go, his face like thunder.

To be fair, it wasn't Sadie's fault that Granny didn't like her. Or maybe it was. Regardless, Granny chuckled when they left. 'Got rid of her, sharpish, didn't I?'

'Granny!' Kathleen feigned shock, but couldn't help chuckling. 'You're awful bold.'

'Ah, you stick around me, Kathleen. You'll learn something, love.' Her eyes were already closing. 'Think I'll have another wee sleep.'

'Aye, you do that.' Kathleen's voice was thick with emotion, as affection for the elderly lady rose within her once again.

A little later the front door went again, then Liam returned. He sat beside her and they talked in low voices, neither mentioning the Sadie incident. Eventually, as the light began to dim, Granny stirred, opening her eyes again.

'Liam! Good boy.' She reached and he moved forward to take her hand, perching on the side of the bed.

'And Kathleen. C'mere, love.'

Kathleen went to the other side, taking Granny's other hand.

'Now, I've never been a sentimental woman and I'm not gonna start now. But my Liam needs a good woman to look after him, and it seems to me that you'd be perfect for the job, Kathleen.'

Kathleen's jaw dropped in shock. *She's incorrigible!* Avoiding Liam's eyes, she said lightly, 'Now, don't you think you can start matchmaking! I'm perfectly capable of picking my own man. And I'm not interested in being a good woman who looks after a man, thank you very much!'

Granny chuckled. 'Aye, under that quiet exterior you're full of fire, Kathleen. Unlike some girls that are all sparkle and nothin' below it. Grand. You pick your own man. Liam, you're gonna have to earn this one!'

He was laughing. 'Ah, Granny, d'ye not know the days of the matchmakers is done?'

She snorted. 'You might think so. There's many's a man can't see what's goin' on around him till it's too late. Don't you make that mistake, son.'

'I won't, Granny.' Liam sounded firm, but Kathleen could see that his expression was confused. *God, I hope Granny gives over soon.* This was mortifying.

Thankfully Therese arrived not long after and Kathleen made her escape, once again avoiding Liam's eye. She kissed Granny's cheek as she left, muttering, 'You're a divil, you are!' and Granny chuckled in reply.

She was carefully stacking china cups and saucers on the kitchen table when she heard a shout from Therese. 'Kathleen! Kathleen!'

Her heart pounding, she ran upstairs. Sure enough, Granny had stopped breathing, her eyes closed and her expression relaxed. Liam and Therese were on either side of the bed, looking distressed and agitated. Kathleen picked up Granny's wrist but could find no pulse, so she checked at the neck as she had been taught. Nothing.

'She's gone. I'm so sorry.'

Therese burst into tears and Kathleen put her arms around her. A moment later she felt Liam's strong arms wrap around both of them. They stood like that for ages, until Therese's sobs became hiccups. Kathleen, too, had cried. Such a formidable woman, never to be seen again in this life.

Liam shifted slightly, resting his chin on Kathleen's head, and she closed her eyes to feel the beautiful sadness of it all. Granny was gone, and the world would never be the same.

# 13

*Saturday, 30 November 1940*

> *Late November 1940: Luftwaffe dossiers cataloguing the location of key strategic and industrial targets in Belfast were being circulated in Berlin. The dossiers included clear aerial photographs, ordnance survey grid references, and a report detailing the lack of defences around the city.*

'Welcome to this meeting of Belfast Civil Defence District B. My name is Seymour and I am coordinating across the District.' The speaker, a stout man in a dark uniform, had a loud voice and an arresting manner. Kathleen, sitting beside Bronagh in the sixth row of seats, was immediately fascinated by him. He was like a character from a play; every gesture, every sentence exaggerated.

'Our agenda this evening,' he continued, 'is as follows. First, an overview of the Belfast districts. Second, a description of the roles to be filled. And third, you will have the opportunity to sign up for your preferred role.'

He pointed to a large map hanging behind him – a map of Belfast, Kathleen realised. 'The civil defence districts are as follows.' Picking up a large wooden stick, he indicated different sections of the map. 'District A, city centre. District B, West Belfast including the Falls and the Shankill . . .'

Kathleen stifled a gasp. Why would they put the Catholic Falls and the Protestant Shankill into one district? The answer came to her immediately. It was because the Shankill was essentially surrounded by Catholic areas, and had to be put somewhere. Sure enough, the northern side beyond the Shankill was in District C – with both C and D covering North Belfast. E was the east of the city, with F the south.

'Districts G and H,' the man continued, 'cover from York Road to the docks' – he tapped the map – 'and the entire harbour area including the shipyard.' There was a murmur from the crowd. If anywhere got bombed, surely it would be the shipyard? Idly, Kathleen noticed that his pronunciation of the letter H was the English style 'aitch' rather than the way Catholics said it, which was 'haitch'. If she hadn't already guessed from his surname, she now knew for sure that he was Protestant and unionist. *I wonder how he feels holding this meeting in a Catholic parish hall?*

As he spoke on – about roles, and training, and equipment – Kathleen began to feel a little frightened. Suddenly the prospect of being bombed by the Nazis seemed a bit more real. Sure why wouldn't they bomb the shipyard and the nearby aircraft factory? Liverpool port in England had been bombed again on Thursday night, with reports coming in hinting of terrible loss of life. Apparently over a hundred and fifty people had died when a single bomb hit an air raid shelter. It didn't bear thinking about.

So far the air raid precautions had involved the issuing of gas masks, leaflets on how to build shelters, and the recruitment of ARWs (air raid wardens) within each community. The initial recruitment had happened even before war was formally declared, but Kathleen had no idea who their local ARWs were.

Mr Seymour then highlighted that across the city most volunteers had opted for the rescue, ambulance, and auxiliary fire service. However there was a shortage of air raid wardens – a role which he described as decidedly lacking in glamour, but vitally important. He hoped that some of the people here tonight would give serious consideration to volunteering for that role in particular.

Glancing surreptitiously to her right, she saw Liam and Seány Flynn sitting in the row in front. Granny's wake had been tremendous: sad, comforting, and supportive all at once. Granny Flynn had been both celebrated and mourned, and given a great send-off, with hundreds of people calling at the house between her death on Wednesday and her funeral on Friday. *Yesterday.*

The days were a bit of a blur, but Kathleen knew she could catch up on sleep any time. It had been a privilege to be part of the Flynn family during the wake. The community had rallied round, and despite the rationing they had never once run out of soda farls or tea.

Liam and Therese's mammy had wanted her to sit in the front row at the funeral Mass yesterday, as one of the chief mourners, but Kathleen had declined, sitting two rows behind with her own family. Sadie hopefully wouldn't find out about that conversation, for she already disliked Kathleen quite enough, though Kathleen was unsure exactly why the other girl had taken against her. In any event, Sadie had spent hours at the wake house – though she had stayed in the living room talking, rather than in the kitchen helping.

Bringing her attention back to the present, Kathleen realised Mr Seymour had moved on to the allocation of roles. There were about thirty people in the hall, a small enough number given the hundreds of houses nearby. Some locals would be still in denial, Kathleen knew, for she had heard the conversations as she went about the area; how it was all being exaggerated, how the south was neutral, how the planes could never reach the length of Belfast. For others, it was a reluctance to be seen to be supporting the British in any way.

The counterargument was simple, and had been rehearsed here tonight by a few people. It might not happen, but surely it was better to be prepared?

'Themmuns do nahin' for us,' she had heard one man say. 'We're gonna have to look after ourselves.'

That was accurate. If there was to be any organisation, any chance of a structured approach to a potential air raid, then the community would have to do it themselves. 'Them ones' – in other words, the authorities – could have no interest in protecting Catholic West Belfast.

It was true that Mr Seymour was here, and him a Protestant. But then, she presumed he was from the Shankill, and was probably motivated to protect his own area by cooperating with Catholics. He had finished describing the various roles, and now directed them to the sign-up tables. 'You will see tables around the edge of the hall, clearly labelled with the various options. Please now register for your preferred role.'

There was a scrape of chairs as people rose, making for their chosen table. Kathleen had already spotted the two tables marked Rescue, Ambulance, and Auxiliary Fire Service, and there was a bit of a queue when she got there. The woman seated behind the table was officious, with perfectly groomed hair and a posh South Belfast accent. Finally she reached the front.

'Which service, please?'

'Sorry, what?'

'Fire, rescue, or ambulance?'

'Oh, ambulance, please.' It was the obvious choice for a journeyman handywoman. *Journey-handy-woman.*

The woman lifted one of the three books in front of her, writing down Kathleen's name and address. She then asked for proof of her identity for some sort of special authority card they would make for volunteers.

'What sort of proof?' Kathleen asked dubiously, never having encountered this before. Everyone around here knew who she was.

'Birth or baptism certificate. You'll need to bring it the first night of training next week.'

'Oh, all right.' Kathleen had never seen either document, but she assumed they were in the locked metal box marked 'Important Documents' in the living-room cupboard. It all seemed very official, and fairly daunting. *You're a handywoman,* she reminded herself. *You have skills that very few have.* This was the litany that Mrs Clarke had told her to repeat any time she doubted herself.

While handywoman skills may not be the most obvious set of skills needed for someone signing up for an ambulance or rescue role, she lifted her chin when the woman filling in the form asked about qualifications, saying, 'I'm a handywoman.'

The woman raised an eyebrow. 'Ah, I don't think we'll be calling on you for that, dear. If needed, we'll be calling upon the properly qualified doctors in the Royal and the Mater.'

*A handywoman isn't a doctor.* The words were on the tip of her tongue, but she suppressed them. No point in arguing with someone so sure of herself. If the woman had compared handywomen to midwives she might have had a point, for despite the extra knowledge Peggy had gained while training in Dublin, she had told Kathleen that there was very little difference in the two roles. In essence, a midwife was a *properly qualified* handywoman.

Still, as a civil defence volunteer, Kathleen would get first aid training, which would help her in her role as handywoman. Not that that was the reason for doing it. No, it was more a sense of duty.

Seány Flynn was in the queue a few behind her, and she stopped briefly to chat to him after being dismissed by the official. 'Well,' he said, 'what did you go for?'

'Ambulance. What are you gonna say?'

He shrugged. 'Fire or rescue. Either.'

'Where's Liam?'

He rolled his eyes. 'You know our Liam. Has to be different.' He looked to his right, and Kathleen followed his gaze. There, talking to Mr Seymour at a different table, was Liam, all alone.

★ ★ ★

Liam had come to the meeting assuming he would volunteer for the fire and rescue type roles. If the worst were to happen, he wanted to be in the thick of the action. However after hearing Mr Seymour's appeal, and noting the rush to the two tables marked Rescue, Ambulance, and Auxiliary Fire Service, he hesitated.

Air raid wardens were a pain. All they seemed to do was to tell people off for curtains not being closed properly or lamps being too bright. The role was a source of ridicule among the men at the mill. It held no glamour, no prestige, no particular honour. And yet . . . What if the Nazis were to bomb Belfast, and some eejit with his living-room light on drew their fire to the Falls . . .? According to the newspaper there had been over five thousand convictions for blackout violations in Belfast this year. People were simply not taking it seriously.

If the Blitz did come to Belfast, Liam now knew that instead of simply running directly to the places affected to get the wounded into ambulances or rescue victims trapped beneath rubble, the ARWs would also report, coordinate, and guide people to any shelters. And part of the problem, Liam knew, was the lack of shelters in West Belfast.

'You not comin'?' Seány asked, amid the general rush to tables.

'You go on.' Slowly he rose, making his way to the table marked Air Raid Wardens. The woman took his details; he hadn't known to bring his birth certificate but promised to provide this at the next meeting.

Mr Seymour was approaching. 'Are you one of my new ARWs?' he asked, fixing Liam with a keen look.

'I am.'

'Good, good.' He indicated the bustle of the other tables. 'I don't know why it's always so unpopular. It's a crucial role.'

Liam shrugged, not knowing what to say to this. He certainly wasn't going to tell Mr Seymour the role was seen as unmanly by many.

'What's your name?'

'Liam. Liam Flynn.'

'George Seymour.' He stuck out a hand and Liam took it, fleetingly noticing it was the first time a Protestant had ever treated him as an equal. *It's only because he needs ARWs.* Over the next half hour, as most people signed up at the busy tables, only two other men made their way to the ARW table. Each time, Mr Seymour shook their hands and asked for their names.

'Well, Liam.' It was John O'Toole, a man Liam knew slightly from the football. 'ARW?'

'Aye.'

'Me too. There's a lot to be said for organisation.'

'I agree.' They were joined then by Matt Darcy, an older man who used to work in the match factory.

'Right. Three new ARWs. Splendid.' Mr Seymour's tone was clipped. Liam wondered if he had hoped for more. 'We already have four others, so I propose we get everyone together in advance of your training.' He went on to propose they meet in an upstairs room in the Falls Road Baths, a building owned by the Corporation and used by both Catholics and Protestants. Liam had gone there occasionally to bathe when younger, and knew the building well. They then agreed that Tuesday evening would suit, Mr Seymour thanked them again, and they all went on their way.

Kathleen was gone. Liam had hoped to speak with her but had missed his opportunity, something that bothered him much more than it should have done. These past few days with Granny's wake and funeral had been really strange – grief over Granny's death, exhaustion from nights and days of only sleeping in snatches, the constant, draining effort of having to speak to the next visitor, and the next. He felt like a motor-car that had run out of petrol from having had its engine on too long.

Kathleen had been there the whole time – or almost the whole time. Quietly unassuming, working steadily on the teas and the washing up, supporting the whole family. She was a gem, and he wanted to thank her properly. He was also wary of getting too close to her; not simply because he had a girlfriend, but because of . . . something else. He didn't know *exactly* what it was, but it was partly the knowledge that, if they walked out and then split up, his whole family would lose Kathleen as a friend. *And why would we split up?* He shook his head. Somewhere deep inside was a feeling that Kathleen was too good for him, and that he'd be better with someone like Sadie.

Sadie hadn't come tonight, even though everyone in their community had heard the appeal, for it had been read out at every Mass in the diocese last Sunday. Resisting the urge to judge, he reminded himself that Therese hadn't come either. Some women were panickers, or squeamish. Some men too. Those best suited to this work had come forward, and that was the right way to do it.

Seány was next in line, and he watched idly as his brother gave his details to the woman at the table. *He's a good lad, our Seány.* The Flynns had been reared with a strong sense of community, and he was proud that, at only eighteen, Seány had decided to volunteer. As they walked home in the darkness, their lamp properly dimmed, Liam realised he was quite looking forward to his new role. It was already giving him a sense of purpose, which had to be better than simply sitting around waiting for the bombs to fall.

★ ★ ★

'Well? How did yiz get on?'

Daddy seemed genuinely interested. He had mused about volunteering, but Mammy had persuaded him that, as one of the lucky ones who still had full-time work, he shouldn't risk it. Sighing, he had agreed, but now Kathleen could see something that looked suspiciously like pride in his eyes.

'Yeah, good,' said Bronagh. 'We're both on the list for the auxiliary ambulance service. First training session is this Wednesday evening.'

'We have to remember to bring our birth certificates that night,' Kathleen commented, hoping saying it out loud would make it more likely that *someone* would remember.

Mammy lifted her head from her sewing, her expression indicating she was not impressed. 'The two of yiz should get a bloody job. It would suit yiz better, instead of helpin' the town and country and us broke.'

'That's not fair, Mammy,' Bronagh returned in a low tone. 'We're hoping to get some hours in the Blackstaff Mill, remember?'

'Aye, part-time!' She shook her head, her expression relaxing. 'Still, I suppose it would be better than nothin'. And we're better off than many, with only adults in the house.'

'And everybody has a bed to sleep in,' Kathleen added. Poor Mammy worried so much about money, while Daddy didn't deal with it at all. It was Mammy who managed the household ration books, Mammy who knew the price of everything and where to go for the best value. She was burdened by it, Kathleen knew. 'Would it help if I did some of the shopping?'

'No. Thanks, love, but no. I need to keep a handle on it.'

'Right. I'll start the supper.' Heading to the kitchen, Kathleen began filling the kettle. When she turned off the tap it was suddenly quieter, and she was surprised to hear Mammy and Bronagh muttering in low voices in the living room. *What are they talking about?* It was clearly something she wasn't supposed to hear.

Having grown up as the youngest, Kathleen had often been excluded from conversations, and her eavesdropping skills had been well-honed as a result. Briefly, the handywoman within her queried confidentiality and privacy, but she rejected this. These were her own family, and they may be talking about her. A notion came to her. Was Mammy trying to stop her from joining the ambulance service, and trying to get Bronagh on side with the idea? The tone of their conversation certainly sounded tense.

Deliberately making a noise at the far side of the kitchen, Kathleen then swiftly went to stand beside the half-open door.

'No! It's time! It's well past time!' Bronagh sounded frustrated.

'Not yet. And mebbe it will never be time. Just leave it, and make sure you're the one to bring them.' Mammy's tone was flat.

'But—'

'But nothin'.'

'When are you going to stop managing my whole life and telling me what to do?'

Kathleen's heart wrenched at the desperation in Bronagh's tone. Her poor sister was still being treated as a child even though she had recently turned thirty-seven. They both felt the same frustration.

'I told you before, Bronagh Gallagher. I'll be tellin' you what to do till the day I die, so you may get used to it!'

It was too much: Kathleen had to intervene. Stepping into the living room, she enquired innocently, 'Is everything all right?'

'Everything is fine,' Mammy said firmly. 'Bronagh, go and help our Kathleen with the supper.'

With a choked sound of exasperation, Bronagh marched into the kitchen, slamming down knives and teaspoons on the worktop with great force.

Kathleen winced. 'What was that all about?'

'She drives me bloody mad, so she does.'

'Aye.' Mammy was exasperating. 'Me too, sometimes.'

Bronagh gave her a twisted smile. 'If it wasn't for you, I don't know how I'd cope. You've kept me sane all these years.'

'Same for me.' She and Bronagh had always been close; Kathleen had idolised her as a child. 'Would you not think about, like, getting away from here?'

'Every bloody day. But I can't.'

Marriage was the usual escape from the family home for most girls, especially now there was war and no jobs. 'What about marriage? Children? Did you never want those things?' Vaguely, she remembered asking Bronagh about this before, and so she half-anticipated her sister's answer.

'I did, aye.' There was sadness in her eyes. 'I wanted a husband, children . . . all of it.' She shrugged. 'But that door is closed now. No point even thinking about it.'

Kathleen snorted. 'You're not even forty yet. You'd think you were eighty, the way you're goin' on.' She nudged her with an elbow. 'Surely there's a few bachelors about the place that would love to walk out with somebody like you!'

'What? An old maid?'

*The Irish Midwife at War*

'No! A proper grown-up woman, with a pretty face, a quick mind, and a kind heart.'

'Aww! What a lovely thing to say!' She gave Kathleen a quick hug. 'Like I say, you keep me sane.'

'Mammy can't help it. She worries about everything, and her only way of coping . . .'

'Is to try and control everyone around her. I know.' She sighed. 'God love her. I gave her plenty of grey hairs in my time, and she's been so good to me. Many's a mother wouldn't have done what she did.'

'So are we both still going to ambulance training?'

'We are.' She nodded firmly. 'Just let Mammy try and stop us!'

# 14

*Tuesday, 3 December 1940*

> *The Luftwaffe raid on Birmingham lasted a full thirteen hours. The Kent Street Baths and the tram station were both hit, causing significant loss of life.*

'We're in! We got work at the Blackstaff from tomorrow!'

It was after midday, Bronagh was late for her dinner, and Kathleen had already served herself and her parents by the time her sister arrived.

Mammy blessed herself. 'Thank God for that! How much work?'

Bronagh was grinning. 'It's only as-and-when days, but apparently they're hoping for a big order from the army, so there could be more regular work if that happens.'

There were hugs all round, and tears of relief on Mammy's part. Bronagh confirmed that Therese and Christine would also start the next day, and others they knew – including Sadie O'Kane – would work their first shift on Thursday. Kathleen kept her face perfectly still when she heard this, then diverted the conversation.

She had just finished dinner when John Joe, one of Mrs Clarke's grandsons, arrived at the door.

'Could Kathleen please go to Eithne O'Reilly's house,' he recited carefully, his wee face screwed up with concentration.

She gave him a smile. 'I'll go straight away. And thank you for bringing that message and telling me it so well.'

He beamed then sped off, presumably heading back to school for afternoon lessons.

'Another birth? Don't leave yourself late for work tomorrow,' Mammy admonished, her forehead creased.

'Ah, Mrs O'Reilly has four children already, so I reckon this will be quick,' Kathleen replied. 'And she told me and Mrs Clarke that she has the money set aside to pay us.'

'Hmm. You make sure she does, then. I'm sick, sore, and tired of women not payin' you. They're takin the mickey, so they are.'

Kathleen knew better than to respond to this, silently picking up her handywoman bag and her shawl. Ten minutes later she was in the O'Reilly house up on Hawthorn Street, where things seemed to be progressing nicely. Within the hour Mrs O'Reilly ('Call me Eithne') was having pains that were almost on top of one another, and any minute Kathleen expected to hear the distinctive pushing sounds that were now so familiar to her.

Any minute now . . .

An hour passed. Eithne was now struggling with the relentless pains, and Kathleen was beginning to worry about the absence of the urge to push. Eithne had been in labour since about midnight, and exhaustion was a real possibility.

Although she hated to leave the woman's side, all her handywoman instincts were screaming at her. 'I'll be back as soon as I can, love,' she murmured, and Eithne nodded.

Racing downstairs and out, she ran to the next house, knocking the door in a frenzied manner.

'What in God's name—' Recognition dawned on the woman's face. 'Oh, Kathleen, how are you?'

'Mrs Arthurs, I need the doctor for Eithne! Can you get him?'

Mrs Arthurs was already removing her apron. 'Course I will, love. God, I hope everything is all right.'

'Tell him no progress. She's bucked.'

'Ach, God love her.'

With a nod and a wave, Kathleen was gone, on her way back to Eithne, and restoring her own calmness. The last thing she wanted was for the woman to realise how worried she was.

Just ten minutes later, she heard the front door open. *That was quick.* But it wasn't the doctor. Instead a familiar voice sounded. 'Midwife calling!'

'Come on up, Peggy!' She turned to Eithne, who was deep inside herself. 'Peggy's here, Eithne. You know Peggy Sheridan, the midwife?'

Eithne shook her head. Many local women avoided the hospital and its staff, while others were content to stick only with the handywomen. Which was why it was so important for a handywoman to spot when things weren't right, and get help.

Thankfully, Mrs Arthurs had run into Peggy on her way to the doctor's, and Peggy had immediately offered to come instead. Eithne was happy for the midwife to check on her, and so Peggy listened to the baby's heartbeat using her Pinard stethoscope, confirming that baby was doing well, then sat quietly for a few minutes, simply watching, waiting, and listening. Eithne's eyes were closed again, so Peggy and Kathleen exchanged a worried look. Peggy nodded, and in the brief gap between pains told Eithne that she thought it might be best for her to go to the hospital.

'Oh, God, no! What's wrong? What's wrong?'

'Baby is fine, remember? But your labour is very slow, and you seem exhausted.'

'Aye. Bucked, I am. Was never like this with any of the others – not even me first one.' She moaned then as another pain took her over, but once it was done she nodded. 'Right. Get me to the Royal. I can't be doing with this no more.'

★ ★ ★

It was teatime, and celebrations were under way in the Flynn household. The list for shifts at the Blackstaff Mill had included both Therese and Christine, who were both to start tomorrow. The relief flooding through Liam was immense. Even if his sisters only got two or three shifts a week each it would make the difference between the Flynns just about surviving, and actually having a few shillings in the savings box he and Ma kept for the (many) rainy days. The news was enough of a relief for Ma to have bought flour, butter, sugar, and apples last night – using some of her precious rations – and they were all now tucking into delicious apple tart.

Sadie's name was apparently on the list too, with her first shift being a day later, this Thursday. He had heard through his own contacts that the mill was offering shifts to every girl who applied, with the intention of dropping some in the coming weeks, and creaming off the best – who would eventually get even more work. He frowned. Christine and Therese were both good workers, but Sadie . . . he wasn't so sure. A pang of guilt went through him. He really shouldn't be thinking such things of his own girlfriend, who had held down a job in a mill for years until the mass layoffs. No, Sadie would be fine.

Unhelpfully, his mind immediately provided him with an image of her sitting like a queen throughout the wake, while the other women did the work. No, he was being too harsh. It simply meant that she didn't see herself as part of the family yet. *Yet.* Would she ever do so?

And did he really want her to?

★ ★ ★

Eithne had begged Kathleen to stay with her, so when the ambulance came both the midwife and the handywoman accompanied her to the Royal Maternity Hospital. Kathleen had seen it getting built of course – it was on the Falls Road opposite the girls' secondary school – but she had never been inside.

God, it was the last word! Inside it was all new and fresh and fancy, with a smell of chemicals and carbolic soap. This was where Peggy worked, and her friend's calm confidence had a soothing effect on Kathleen. *It will be all right.*

Eithne must surely be uncomfortable, lying on her back on the stretcher. Kathleen, skipping to keep up, still had her hand in Eithne's, and from time to time she was uttering soothing words as they moved speedily along the main corridor. *Labour Ward* pronounced the sign above the wide door to their left, and in they went.

A doctor in a white coat spotted them straight away. 'Report!' he snapped, and Peggy, her face expressionless, talked about a lack of progress, exhaustion, and the fact the baby's heartbeat was normal.

'Very well. Sheridan will see to her.' He glanced at Kathleen. 'No visitors allowed in delivery suite.' And with that he turned on his heel, disappearing into a side room.

Kathleen's jaw was near on the floor. *What a rude man!* She made a face at Peggy, who murmured, 'Dr Fenton. He's the consultant on today. But my Dan will look after Eithne, never you worry. In here, please.' This last was addressed to the stretcher bearers, who took Eithne into the room Peggy had indicated. The door was ajar, and Kathleen saw a high hospital bed, a locker, and a plain stone floor. It was austere, and spotlessly clean, and rather frightening.

As soon as the ambulance men had left, Peggy and Kathleen got Eithne into a sitting position. 'Is that better?' She nodded, her attention being taken up by yet another pain. How the poor woman was sticking it, Kathleen had no idea.

Peggy had gone to fetch her tall, handsome husband, Dr Dan Sheridan. Kathleen, naturally, knew him well, having spent many an evening visiting Peggy at their fancy house.

'Ach well, Kathleen,' he said quietly, respecting the woman on the bed who was clearly in the throes of a contraction. As it ended, he introduced himself, then asked if he could examine Eithne. She agreed, and after feeling her tummy and listening in to the baby's heartbeat, he asked if he could feel inside to try and work out what was happening. Again, Eithne agreed – she was just desperate for some relief, Kathleen saw. Peggy helped Eithne into the position needed for him to feel inside for what was happening. 'Kathleen!' Eithne gasped, and Kathleen approached from the side. The woman grabbed her hand, gripping it so tight it was white, but she

## The Irish Midwife at War

didn't care. Until they kicked her out, she was staying by her woman's side.

'Now, do you want ether, Mrs O'Reilly? It'll make you woozy so you won't be able to feel what I'm doing as much?'

She shook her head. 'I'll never be able to push the baby out if I'm woozy, Doctor.'

'Oh, I'd say you'd manage it, but no worries. This will be a bit uncomfortable, but I'll be as quick as I can.' After donning new gloves he put his left hand on her tummy, while his right went into her birth canal.

'Hmm,' he said, 'presenting part is high. I have the orbital ridge . . . nose . . . Can't get the mouth or chin. Anterior fontanelle . . . slight caput . . . Right! Let's see if I can flex the head.' There was a pause, while Eithne squeezed Kathleen's hand ever tighter. 'Done it!' he declared, sounding pleased. A moment later he had withdrawn his hand and as he removed his gloves, Peggy and Kathleen helped Eithne to sit up again.

'Baby's head was deflexed,' he explained, lifting his chin in the air to demonstrate. 'That means it was trying to come face-first' – he indicated his forehead and nose – 'instead of head first.'

'And what did you do, Doctor?' Eithne, despite her exhaustion, seemed interested.

'Very little,' said Dan with a smile. 'I gently moved the head so that the chin is now tucked in.' He bent his head to demonstrate, his chin pointing down to his chest. 'Hopefully, baby can come now.'

'Thanks so much, Doctor.' Eithne had now abandoned Kathleen and Peggy to grab Dan's hand with both of her own. 'God bless you!'

'Ach, no bother!' With a wink to his wife, he left, carefully closing the door behind him.

'Should I go?' Kathleen could not forget the orders from the rude doctor.

'No, don't leave me, Kathleen!' Eithne sounded distraught. Funny how women formed such a close bond with whoever was looking after them. If it had been Peggy from the start, Eithne would have been attached to her, not Kathleen. And the bond went both ways. Kathleen had occasionally supported women who had had to transfer to hospital, and the wrench as they were separated was almost unbearable.

Peggy was shaking her head. 'Nobody even knows you're here. Fenton will assume you left immediately, and Dan clearly doesn't mind.' She grinned. 'I remember, Kathleen, what it was like. I was a handywoman first, you know.'

Kathleen did know. She nodded, tears misting her eyes. 'Thank you.'

'We're both gonna stay with you, Mrs O'Reilly,' Peggy assured her.

Another pain was coming. Kathleen could see Eithne's breathing change, her face screwing up as it had been since they had left the sanctuary of her home. *I need to help her be calm again.*

'Peggy!' the woman managed.

'Yes?'

'C-call me Eithne!'

# 15

*Wednesday, 4 December 1940*

> *Defence Regulation Order 1305 outlawed lockouts and strikes by workers, and some employers took the opportunity to reduce wages and job security for their employees.*

It was strange to be back at work. As she had done for many years – apart from the past ten months – Kathleen was up at five, and passing through the gates of a mill at ten to six in the morning. This time it was the Blackstaff Mill at the start of the Springfield Road, but a mill was simply another mill.

Eithne had given birth to a healthy baby boy at around half-ten last night. 'Just look at the big Irish head on him!' she had declared on cuddling her son for the first time, her relief and delight clear. 'It's no wonder he near got stuck!'

The baby had been a ten-pounder – even heavier than Eithne's previous babies. Between them, Peggy and Kathleen had managed to create enough of a haven in the hospital room for her to get back into a decent birth trance, and labour had progressed quickly after Dr Sheridan's intervention.

On her way home Kathleen had shared the good news with Eithne's family, who had returned home once the neighbour had informed them that their ma was away to the Royal. Everybody knew that if you had your baby in the hospital you wouldn't be allowed home for days. Eithne's husband and mammy were still up, and delighted to hear that all was well and that there was a new boy in the family. Mr O'Reilly paid her the full fee, which Kathleen tried to protest about, but he was insistent.

'The Royal'll not charge us nahin'!' he reminded her. 'Besides, you were there to the very end.'

And so she took it, conscious of a feeling of optimism within. Eithne and her baby were safe and well, she had a full fee, and she had work in the mill again.

Despite having less than five hours of sleep, Kathleen was feeling reasonably awake by the time she and Bronagh reached the mill. As instructed, they reported to the foreman, who looked them up and down before assigning them to their roles. Bronagh was sent to the weaving shed to work the looms, while Kathleen was told to be a doffer for the day, as they were short. In between, she was to sweep up and help those who needed it.

*Not bad.* The doffers were usually younger girls, and the hardest part was carrying the full bobbins, which were heavy. But Kathleen was nimble, and alert, and would hopefully be quick enough at tying up the ends, removing the full bobbins and replacing them with empties. As she made her way to the weaving factory, a few lines of old songs were going round her mind.

'Oh, do you know her or do you not,' she sang to herself in a low voice. 'This new doffing mistress we have got? Fol de ri fol ra, fol de ri fol ray.' Then the other one. 'You might easy know a doffer, for she'll always get a man.'

This brought her up short. She had no man, and had no wish to *get* one, but something about the conversation with

Bronagh yesterday had unsettled her. What must it be like, to feel as though your chances had passed you by, and that your life would never get better? That everything would just continue, day after day after day, until you were carried off by a heart attack or a stroke or tuberculosis? She shuddered. If the Nazis did decide to bomb Belfast, many would never get to enjoy the privilege of reaching old age. She should be grateful for what she had, and stop thinking about all of the extra things her heart yearned for.

As she and Bronagh crossed the yard a couple of firewatchers were just leaving. This was a new role, required by law in all mills and factories. The firewatchers were guards who patrolled at night, ready to report to the ARP if a bomb or incendiary was dropped. The role was unpaid, with only a meal allowance of three shillings. Kathleen frequently worked overnight sitting with women – and occasionally with the dying – but she did it because she *chose* to. It seemed unfair that this extra rota had been imposed on mill workers without pay. People were so grateful to have a job that owners and bosses were able to push their employees to do more and more.

She stifled a sigh. There was so much wrong with the world, and she could do nothing about any of it. As she began her work, deftly removing the first heavy bobbin of the day, she decided instead to count her blessings. She was well, her family were well, they had a good house, and the extra work meant they would now always have enough to eat. Many's a one around here didn't have those things.

And what of love, and friendship, and companionship? Here too, she was blessed. Her parents were good to her, even if Mammy was a bit stubborn and demanding at times.

Bronagh was the best sister a girl could ever wish for. And she saw her wider family regularly, including her many nieces and nephews.

She had friends too. Good friends. Visiting Peggy was part of her routine – depending on when Peggy was on duty, or if Kathleen was sitting with a woman in labour or someone who had had the Last Rites. She also saw Therese every day, but mainly in the morning or afternoon, since her friend now spent many of her evenings and her Sundays with Jimmy, which was hardly surprising given that they were to marry next Easter.

Jimmy was seen as a great 'catch' because he had escaped the mills and now was a journeyman bricklayer, making decent money. With luck, Therese would have a better life than most women around here. A few shillings extra a week soon added up. Kathleen had kept up her habit of visiting the Flynns' house almost every day, and one small benefit of being out of work was that she and Therese had had more time together this year than they'd had since their school days.

Thoughts of Therese led inevitably to Liam. Liam of the handsome face, the deep blue eyes, the strong frame, and the generous heart. Liam who had never looked at her again the way he had one snowy night, almost four long years ago. Liam who had a girlfriend.

Kathleen knew herself to be a fairly smart woman. She could manage book-learning, and had been gifted with common sense. So why was it that when it came to Liam Flynn, she could be so stupid? At nearly twenty years of age, she should know better. Not all young men were as imperfect as Mugsy Mulligan, nor as perfect as Liam Flynn. She should be open to getting to know some of them, or else risk a life like Bronagh's, where sadness must be contained and hopes abandoned.

Bronagh deserved better, and so did Kathleen. They were respectable, well-behaved women from a good family, with quick minds and kind hearts. Why shouldn't they fall in love and marry? Why shouldn't they have children, if God allowed? Having supported countless women through childbirth, Kathleen was more than ready to have a baby herself. But a baby required a husband, and she knew herself to be altogether too picky. So much for accepting her lot and counting her blessings! She wanted more.

At dinner break, as she and Bronagh walked home, she decided to ask her sister about it. 'I was thinking, Bronagh . . .'

'Oh?' There was a glint in her eye. 'A dangerous occupation!'

Kathleen gave a short laugh. 'True.' She took a breath. 'I think I'm too fussy about lads, but I do want to marry and be a mother. How do I do that, when there aren't any lads I like enough to walk out with them?'

Bronagh slipped an arm through hers. 'We're so alike, you and me. I realise now that I was too fussy when I was your age. I should have walked out with lads and at least tried to find one I liked.' She made a face. 'My other problem was I couldn't forget about Michael. Took me *years* to get over him, and by the time I finally accepted he wasn't coming back, all the good ones were gone. Married, with a rake of children.'

'That bloody boyfriend of yours has a lot to answer for!' Kathleen said hotly, outraged on her sister's behalf. *I'm twenty,* she reminded herself, *not heading for forty.*

'He certainly does,' Bronagh murmured. 'So what's your excuse, Kathleen? Why don't you go out with lads? You must get dances at the céilís?'

'I do.' She sighed. 'But when they ask me to stay on or offer to walk me home, I just say no.'

Bronagh was frowning. 'We might be even more alike than I realised.' She paused, then lifted her chin. 'Right, I'm gonna come out and say it.' She took a breath. 'Liam Flynn.'

Heat rose in Kathleen's face and neck. *Feck!*

'Am I that obvious?' she asked, not without a trace of bitterness.

'Only to me, love.'

Kathleen exhaled. 'I *can't*. None of them are as . . .' Her voice tailed off. 'It's hard to explain.'

'None of them are *him*. Is that it?'

Kathleen nodded. 'He's my best friend's brother. He has a girlfriend. He's never shown any interest in me – well, almost never.'

'Almost?' There was a smile in Bronagh's voice.

'Aye. He kissed me once. New Year's Eve when I was sixteen.'

'The perfect age to make an impression on you.'

'You sound cynical.'

'I don't mean to. But I was sixteen when Michael swore he loved me and he would be back from Dublin as soon as he could. He said he'd write to me as well, but . . .' She shook her head. 'Bloody lads.'

'So he was actually from Dublin, then?' Kathleen was trying to remember what Bronagh had told her.

'Aye. He has cousins up here and lived with them for a few months – 1920 it was, and the War of Independence was in full swing. He said his ma sent him up here to keep him from joining the rebellion. The Black and Tans were starting to appear, and all the young men in Dublin were fired up about fighting. There was less trouble here at the time – now there's something that's changed.' She shrugged. 'I wondered if he was killed in the war after he went back, but I asked his cousin about him one time, years later.'

'What did the cousin say?' Kathleen was fascinated.

'That Micheal was now living in Fairview.'

'Dublin?'

'Yeah. It's the bit up from the North Strand. Only a train ride away.'

'But he never came back here?'

'Nope.'

Kathleen thought about this. Bronagh had wasted the crucial years – years when everyone was pairing up – pining for a boy who had no care for her. 'Liam has a girlfriend.' She needed to say it out loud again, to remind herself of it.

'Exactly.' Bronagh's eyes were full of sympathy. 'Kathleen, you have a chance. Don't mess it up, like I did.'

*Don't mess it up.* Would it really be so hard to try to get to know a couple of young men better? Many of her age group were now going steady, the numbers of single men decreasing with each year that went by. Maybe she should try harder. The dances would start again on New Year's Eve. Maybe, just maybe it could be a fresh start for her, and end the cycle that had begun on that other New Year's Eve, four long years ago.

★ ★ ★

Air raid warden training was fascinating. Seven men were present, along with Mr Seymour. A few of the men were from the Shankill – a Protestant area – and it was strange to be sitting alongside them, everyone's attention directed outwards towards a common threat.

Liam's brain, starved of learning for far too long, eagerly embraced the new knowledge. The ARW role involved much more than Liam had realised. While others took shelter, they would be out and about patrolling, rescuing people, and reporting. Reporting procedures were key, as the main purpose of the role was to be a conduit for communication and coordination. The Warden's Report Form was simple, but as Liam looked over it, he felt a sensation like a punch to the gut. He was to report the location of any areas hit, detailing the type of bomb – with options for both poison gas and incendiary (firestarter) bombs. He was then to record the approximate number of casualties, including how many were 'trapped under wreckage'. He swallowed, hoping to God it would never happen.

'You will, then,' Mr Seymour continued, 'record any damage to utilities including water, electrical cables, or sewers, details of any roads blocked, and the position of any unexploded bombs.'

The very notion brought Liam out in a cold sweat. Being cursed with a good imagination which was currently running away with itself, his mind was full of images of those he loved cowering as bombs fell from the sky, or navigating past unexploded bombs in Beechmount.

He focused again on the training. Mr Seymour was explaining how messages would be swiftly coordinated throughout the city, allowing those in charge to direct the right amount of help from the right service to the right location.

## The Irish Midwife at War

They were then each given a sample form for a test, Mr Seymour barking out a horrifying sequence of imaginary events for them to document. Switching off his emotions as best he could, Liam managed to get most of it down – or at least he hoped so.

'When you are done, write the words *Message Ends* and then bring your completed form to me.'

While Seymour marked their forms the men chatted, mostly about the exercise. They ranged in age from Matt Darcy who was nearly seventy, to Liam who was only twenty-one. How grown-up he'd felt on his birthday last January, and how much a boy he felt standing here among experienced men in their forties, fifties, and sixties.

'Liam Flynn!' Mr Seymour bellowed, and Liam stood.

'Excellent report, young man. You were the only one to include every detail. Come and take your papers back, everyone, and tell me what you each missed.'

After they had done so, Seymour indicated two tea chests in the corner of the room. 'Next, you will be issued with some of your ARW equipment and clothing.' Fishing out a gas mask from one of the boxes, he held it up to them. 'Unlike the standard civilian model,' he explained, 'the air raid warden respirator has separate glass eyepieces and this exhalation valve. Please come forward to be fitted.'

'Right,' Seymour announced, once this had been done. 'Next task. Please find a helmet that fits.' The helmets were brimmed and bowl-shaped, made of steel, with a large white W at the front and a leather chin strap. They looked similar to those Liam had seen in pictures of men in the Great War.

Finally they each took a set of thick cotton overalls. They were dark blue, with the letters ARP embroidered on the left part of the chest in red silk thread. There were three buttoned pockets and smart epaulettes, and Liam felt strange putting them on. It was as though in doing so he was putting on an entire new self. Not Liam, one of the Flynns from Beechmount. Not Liam Flynn, half-timer in the mill. Not even Liam Flynn, who had to be pitied because his da had died young. This was Liam Flynn, air raid warden, and the feeling, strangely, was one of pride.

'You will wear these overalls for every training session and every meeting from now on,' pronounced Mr Seymour, 'and you will wear your helmet and carry your mask at all times while on duty, or making your way to and from training. You are also required to wear an armlet.' He issued them all with a white cotton armband printed with the letters ARP, which they dutifully slid up their right arm. Seymour's own armband was of thick gold wool, with 'Civil Defence NI' embroidered in navy, along with a navy rainbow and a crown. *A good job they didn't make us wear the crown – they'd lose potential wardens in Catholic areas if they tried to force that on us.* The south was still in the Commonwealth – for now, but Liam knew most Irish people wanted to have nothing to do with kings of England.

'Don't forget,' Seymour announced, 'you have first aid training in St John's every Thursday, starting tomorrow, and you are also back here every Tuesday. Next week we shall begin our rescue training, and you will be issued with your haversack. You are dismissed.'

Stepping outside the Falls Road Baths in a warden's uniform was the oddest experience. Liam had bathed here many times as a boy – any time he had had a few pennies to spare he had paid for the privilege of hot water, carbolic soap, and the use of a twill towel in a private cubicle with an enamel bath. That had all ended when his da had died, with every penny needed for rent and food. Nowadays very few could afford such luxuries, and he was used to laboriously boiling water for the tin bath in front of the fire at home.

He had been to the swimming baths in the main part of the building once, but the expanse of water had been daunting, and he had never repeated the experience. Like most people he had never learned to swim, and walking through warm water at chest height had been unnerving. It occurred to him now that he had lived his life so far with a great deal of caution, but the ARW role was stretching him already. His caution – which he dimly knew was to do with having to take on his father's responsibilities at fourteen – would be useful in this role, for there were procedures to be followed, careful notes to be made. Yet the role also required running *towards* danger even as others ran away – a notion that was both preposterous and strangely exciting. People passing were eyeing him as he made his way back towards Beechmount, and not in an unkind way, he realised. It was generally a mix of curiosity and grudging respect.

It didn't even matter that there would be some who would tease him for such an unglamorous role, and one that many believed to be unnecessary. The truth was, everyone hoped that there would be no air raids. But what if there were?

Yes, he had done the right thing. He was certain of it.

# 16

*Thursday, 5 December 1940*

> *By December 1940 the Luftwaffe had around a thousand bomber planes suitable for night flights, with an average of two hundred able to strike on any given night.*

The parish hall was fairly full, for the first aid course was compulsory for all ARP volunteers irrespective of their role. Kathleen and Bronagh had arrived early; Bronagh had brought the paperwork required and sorted it at the desk while Kathleen got them both tea from the lady at the table at the back of the hall. They had barely taken two sips when Liam and Seány Flynn arrived, sliding into seats beside them. Only a day after deciding to put Liam out of her mind and have a look at some of the other lads who weren't yet taken, Kathleen's resolution was being sorely tested by his nearness. How the hell was she supposed to try to fancy other young men when her heart was racing and her mouth dry simply because Liam was sitting beside her?

They had barely spoken after the initial hello, and everyone had listened in fascinated silence to the teacher's words on the immediate assessment of a casualty and the circulation of the blood. Kathleen's head was buzzing with new information, even before the St John Ambulance men announced they would learn the practical skills of bandaging and dressing wounds, starting tonight with instruction on how to use a triangular bandage to make a sling for a broken arm.

Now they were handing out bandages, telling everyone to practise in groups of three or four. It was obvious that they made a four, and so Kathleen was subjected to the exquisite agony of being in close company with Liam, both prompting Bronagh as she attempted to create a sling for Seány, who had gleefully volunteered to be their first 'casualty' and was acting the part with great energy.

It then got immeasurably worse – or better – for one of the teachers came round again with a few spare bandages, handing one to Kathleen with a nod to Liam.

'Here's an extra one,' the man said, seemingly unaware that Kathleen's heart was now ready to jump from her chest. *Not a very observant first-aider*, she thought wryly, trying to distract herself with humour.

Liam looked directly into her eyes. 'Right, let's do this.' His voice changed as he went into his role of patient. 'My left arm hurts, miss, and I'm sure I felt it crack.'

Kathleen nodded. 'Right. So first I assess the arm . . .' She changed her voice to match his. 'Can I take your jacket off, sir?' Her wayward thoughts naturally went to the worst possible place. *And your shirt . . . Stop it!* she admonished herself, but felt her own face blush.

'Any time, miss.' He grinned, and she shot him a quelling look. 'Well, that's what any man would say in the circumstances!'

'Behave!' she said sternly, easing his jacket carefully off his shoulders in the manner demonstrated recently by their teachers. *Any time. If only.* As to whether her instruction to *behave!* was for him or for herself, she wasn't entirely clear. But she couldn't help but notice the firm muscles of his shoulders and upper arms through his thin white shirt.

'Now, where exactly does it hurt?' she asked, in what she hoped was a professional voice.

'I'm not sure exactly. My whole arm.'

'Oh, really?' She raised a sceptical eyebrow, at the same time relishing the notion of what was about to happen. Carefully, using both hands, she gently squeezed his arm, starting from the shoulder and working her way down to the elbow, then along to the wrist. Smooth muscle, smooth skin . . . and this was Liam feckin' Flynn she was touching!

Focused on her task, revelling in the sensations, locking in memories, she was done before she realised that at no point had he signalled mock pain.

'Liam Flynn! You're messing with me! Now where's this flippin' broken bone?'

'Ah, sorry, Kathleen. Go again. I promise I'll do it right this time.' He didn't look sorry, but Kathleen was conscious that Bronagh might be half-listening. And after their conversation earlier, she knew she had to forget about fancying Liam.

'The break is here,' she pronounced firmly, pointing to his upper arm and pushing away the regret at not taking the opportunity to touch him for a second time. 'Now, can I get you to hold your injured arm with your other hand?' She moved his hands into place, noticing they were warm, clean, and slightly calloused.

With crisp efficiency she unfolded the bandage, finding the long edge and placing the top corner to the far shoulder as they had been shown, then gently sliding the soft cloth under the injured arm, bringing the point to Liam's elbow. The bottom corner was hanging down below his arm, so she drew it up to the near shoulder, making sure that Liam's wrist was a little higher than his elbow, then tying it to the first end behind his neck in the reverse knot they had been taught. Finally, she adjusted the sling so that it reached all the way to Liam's little finger, and tucked in the edges at the elbow.

'There. I *think* that's right.' She looked up to find his eyes on her, his expression serious. She caught her breath. *Why is he so feckin' good-lookin'?*

'Let me check that for you.' The St John Ambulance men were going around the room, checking, teaching, and making adjustments. 'Very good. Now swap roles.'

★ ★ ★

*Swap roles.* A simple enough instruction, Liam knew – except when it applied to the girl who haunted your thoughts. *I have a girlfriend.* The reminder was a familiar one, a litany he went to whenever Kathleen was near. Their banter just now hadn't really been flirting, had it? Anyone might have done it when their first-aider was so pretty, as an attempt to defuse any awkwardness.

Yet the awkwardness remained. He had been watching her as she fixed his sling, her face intent, her beautiful eyes focused on her task. And now it would be his turn. His pulse was already racing at her nearness. Had he really kissed her that time, or had it been a dream?

Leaning towards him she undid the knot they had been taught, marvelling at how easy it was to unravel compared to the usual double knot, then folded the bandage, passing it to him.

'Here you go. Now let's see how well you were listening and watching, Liam Flynn!' Her eyes were dancing, and his spirits lifted. She had a gift for making people feel good.

'Not as well as you, I bet!' But his mind was sharp, and in the back of his head he knew he might need these skills some day – some dark day. And so he put on his first aid voice, asking her where it hurt.

'It's my arm,' she said, her brow furrowed in mock pain. She indicated her right upper arm, and he nodded briskly.

'Let me help you with your cardigan.' The cardigan was of dark green wool, probably knitted by Kathleen herself, or perhaps her mother. On this cold December evening, she had buttoned it all the way up over her dress. Her shawl was over the back of her chair.

Careful to keep to her midline, he undid the buttons at the bottom of her cardigan, from her waist up to her ribcage, while she undid some from higher up with her 'good' hand. They met in the middle, just under the swell of her breasts, and he took his hands away as if stung. The last thing he wanted was for her to think he was a creep looking for a cheap feel. She undid the last button and the cardigan fell to the sides, revealing the gentle curves of her figure in her simple linen dress. Carefully he helped her shrug out of the left sleeve, pulling on the ribbed ending and sliding the upper end from her shoulder, then leaning forwards to loosen the garment across her back, his arms either side of her in an almost-embrace. The moment was fleeting, but he felt her breath on his neck, sensed the warmth of her body for the tiniest of instants.

Then he was easing the second sleeve carefully down her 'injured' arm, trying not to think of undressing her in a more intimate setting.

'Right.' His voice was remarkably steady in the circumstances. 'Tell me where it hurts.' Using both hands as they had been shown, he gently squeezed her shoulder, then her bare arm where her short sleeve ended, then—'

'Ow!' Kathleen was very definite when he reached the spot of the supposed break, and he commented before continuing with his examination. Her skin was soft, smooth, and pale, with a few freckles that he longed to kiss, but of course could not.

Creating the sling was straightforward enough, once he had located the long side of the bandage. Initially he had the short side uppermost, and it was only when she bit her lip that he realised he had gone wrong. Well, his mind was in a tangle, so it was hardly surprising that he had erred.

Thankfully, he managed to slide the bandage into place from the top and bottom, without having to so much as brush her dress in the areas he most wanted to touch. Tying the knot behind her neck was also unexpectedly erotic, for he had to move her long hair to the side and lean close enough to see the knot properly. But then, everything seemed erotic when he was with Kathleen.

An image of Sadie came into his mind. She was good craic, he reminded himself, and pretty, and had lots of lads after her, so it had been something of an achievement when she agreed to be his girlfriend. But his attraction to her was like . . . it was like the sparkles on the surface of a millpond on a breezy day. There was no depth to it, no true connection.

With a jolt, he realised he was behaving rather badly right now. Shame flooded through him, and once the St John Ambulance instructor had approved his sling, he undid it briskly, deliberately then turning to Seány and Bronagh. Both had succeeded in their task, and there was a light-hearted air in the hall which was entirely at odds with the reality that they were all only doing this in case the Nazis should bomb their city.

And here was he, obsessing over a beautiful woman when in reality he should be thinking of his family, his community. His girlfriend.

# 17

*Friday, 6 December 1940*

> *'It is useless to expect rational or logical thought or sentiment in Eire. The historical, the religious, the mythical, and the frankly ridiculous continually obtrude themselves. Hopes that a Hitler victory will settle partition are expressed in the same town in which a Spitfire fund is organised; the wife of a German embassy official wins a fur coat in a raffle in aid of another Spitfire fund; and the Local Security Force refuse to patrol a certain beach in Donegal after twelve at night "because they are afraid of the fairies".'*
> British Ministry of Information Secret Intelligence report, December 1940

Kathleen rarely disliked people. She could count on one hand the people she'd known whom she genuinely struggled to like. Unfortunately Sadie O'Kane was one of them, and today they were working alongside one another in the weaving factory. Here a team of women would wind yarn onto spools for the warp and pirns for the weft, the two directions of yarn that would be woven together to make cloth. Some of the girls concentrated on the weft pirns, adding them to the shuttles again and again. This task allowed them to stay in the spacious, airy weaving shed – the only inconvenience the noise, the clack and click of hundreds of looms whirring and whizzing as they worked.

Other girls were on warp duty, taking the spun yarn off the spools and attaching it to the massive warp beams, ensuring the threads rolled without tangling and the lines were stretched perfectly evenly throughout. The women then took the rolled warp to the dressing room where the men would twist four threads into one before passing it back to the weavers for inclusion in the cloth. This meant you got a change of scenery, and a chance to briefly see your menfolk.

Kathleen's parents worked in a different mill, as did Liam and Seány Flynn, so she only vaguely knew the men in the dressing room today. Still, it was nice to vary her task from time to time, even if there was a lot of physical effort in carrying the warp through each time. Two girls would carry the mass of warp between them, and the men would approach to take the burden and sling it up to the harnesses.

It was late afternoon and Kathleen and Bronagh were bringing a heavy pile of warp through to the men. Once Kathleen noticed that Sadie and another girl were already there, she tensed up. Having managed to avoid Liam's girlfriend for most of the day she might now have to speak to her. As she took in the scene though, her jaw dropped. Instead of coming straight back to work, Sadie and her friend had lingered to chat to the men, their attitudes decidedly flirtatious.

Kathleen bit her lip, determined to say nothing. Had she not flirted with Liam just last night at the first aid? Something about her expression must have caught Sadie's eye, for the other girl's lip curled.

'Well, Saint Kathleen of Assisi? Have you something to say?' Both hands were on her hips, her expression disdainful. 'No? I didn't think so. You're so feckin' insipid!'

Bronagh straightened, her dander up, and Sadie's gaze turned to her briefly.

'Aye, and your spinster sister too!' she continued. 'You're no craic at all, either of you. It's no wonder yous can't get boyfriends!'

'Don't say anything,' Bronagh muttered. 'Just ignore her.'

'But—'

'*Ignore* her. Remember what Daddy always says. Getting sucked into an argument with somebody like that is . . .'

'Like trying to debate philosophy with a pig. You'll get nowhere and only end up covered in muck.' Daddy always kept himself to himself. He didn't hold with heavy drinking or fighting, and carefully chose who to discuss and debate with.

'Aye.'

'Are you sayin' I'm a pig?' Sadie looked furious. She stomped forward, her hands closing into fists.

Kathleen rolled her eyes, standing her ground – even as one of the men walked deliberately between them and Sadie, taking the pile of warp with a cheery, 'Thanks, girls!'

Kathleen recognised him: it was Jimmy's friend Mugsy. *Nice one, Mugsy.*

'No bother, Mugsy,' she replied, her tone even. 'You keepin' well?'

'Ah, can't complain. How's your ones?'

'Doing the best. We're all looking forward to the big wedding next Easter.'

'It's all Jimmy talks about.'

'Aye, Therese too. Right, we better get back in before the mistress catches us dawdling. See ya!'

As they made their way back, Kathleen and Bronagh exchanged a glance. 'God, that Sadie one is hard work,' Bronagh muttered. 'What the hell does Liam Flynn see in her?'

'She's good-looking, and popular, and very confident,' Kathleen said.

'Aye, but we all know the rose hides its thorns. You've thought about this, hmm?'

'What do you mean?'

'Liam and Sadie. You've been trying to figure it out.'

Kathleen shrugged. 'I'm not blind, or stupid. I see the way she goes on.'

'A pity *he* doesn't.' She paused, then added in a casual tone. 'Mugsy Mulligan seems like a nice lad.'

Kathleen shuddered. 'Don't. I let him kiss me once – worst experience of my life!'

Bronagh giggled. 'Really? That's a pity.'

'Aye. He's a bit more to say these days. He could hardly say a word to girls when he was sixteen.'

'There's a big difference between sixteen and twenty. Look at you, the change in you.'

'What do you mean?'

'You've grown into yourself, Kathleen. You always had a kind of inner calm, but now . . . you *radiate* serenity. You're comfortable in your own skin, comfortable with who you are.'

'I dunno about that,' Kathleen replied, thinking of how tongue-tied she sometimes felt with Liam. 'Apparently I'm shit craic. We both are.'

Bronagh laughed. 'Never you let somebody as twisted as that bother you. You don't have to be loud and brash to be good craic. In our own quiet way, we're both rebels.'

'Are we, though? We live quietly with Mammy and Daddy, and Sadie is right. We don't have boyfriends.'

Bronagh sniffed. 'We're rightly fussy, that's all. No point in taking a boyfriend just for the sake of it. I'd rather be a spinster than married to an eejit.'

'And back in the day, spinsters were women who made enough money from weaving and spinning that they didn't have to marry. Isn't that right?'

'It is. They were well respected in my granny's day. And they were rebels too. They didn't do what everybody expected. Like me, not marrying. You know the old saying: there'll be white blackbirds before an unwilling woman ties the knot. Well that's me, an unwilling woman!'

'And yet part of you wished for a home of your own, and children,' Kathleen said quietly.

She sighed. 'True. But only if I could find a man I could put up with. And sadly, for me there's no such man. But *not* to marry is rebellion in a way.'

'And me being a handywoman is another type of rebellion. Therese couldn't understand why I'd be bothered, Mammy worries about me not getting paid, but I'll keep doing it anyway. It's *in* me now, you know?'

'Aye. I do know.' She sent Kathleen a curious glance. 'Did you ever wish to be a qualified midwife, like Peggy Sheridan?'

Kathleen thought about the Royal, with its white walls and clinical smell. Doing only births, and not being able to sit with the dying or help the bereaved. She shook her head.

'Nah, I'm better being a handywoman. I wouldn't be one for hospitals. Like, Peggy was great to go away and train and all, but I have everything I need here. I like helping people, you know? Besides, I am sort of a midwife already. Even though I don't have a fancy certificate.'

Bronagh smiled mistily. 'I'm so proud of you, Kathleen.'

Satisfied with their assessment of the world, they split then to pick up their next tasks, avoiding the eye of the mistress, who was frowning.

'Where are the other two?' she demanded, but Kathleen and Bronagh said nothing, then exchanged a grimace as the mistress headed for the dressing room, clearly intent on finding the two missing millies.

Why Sadie and her friend had taken such a risk, Kathleen couldn't understand. With hundreds on the waiting list for casual shifts, the mill was hiring and firing new girls all the time.

Keeping their heads down, they went back to work. Sadie and the other girl appeared a few minutes later, Sadie's expression one of defiance. Kathleen and Bronagh kept away from her until the end of the shift, but as they were leaving Kathleen saw the factory mistress call them aside.

'Uh-oh. Mistress wants them two.' Bronagh's eyes were wide.

'They've brought it on themselves,' said Kathleen, yet her heart was sinking. Nobody liked to hear about millies getting fired, for it was always a blow to their family. It would be a blow to Liam too, no doubt, and Kathleen couldn't bear to think of how it might add to his burdens.

She sighed. There was absolutely nothing she could do about it. Liam was his own man, and had made his own choices. If-onlys had no place in her heart.

# PART III

# 18

*Tuesday, 14 January 1941*

> *The British government has announced new price controls on food to combat profiteering. More than twenty items including rice, jelly, biscuits, and coffee will be subject to price freezes.*

'Tonight, you will learn how to assess the safety of a building, and how to identify structural issues.'

Liam was already fascinated. Mr Seymour was a builder, and was bringing his considerable expertise to tonight's training session, the fifth in the series. They had had three lessons before Christmas, and last week both ARW and first aid training had started up again.

*First aid.* Fleetingly an image of Kathleen flitted through his mind, before he banished it ruthlessly. He and Seány had developed the habit of sitting with the Gallagher sisters every time, and every time he had been impressed by Kathleen's competence and quick mind. Like him at ARW training, she stood out – the instructors frequently praising her for remembering the details of their teaching session, applying yet another perfect bandage, or demonstrating effortlessly how to treat someone who was choking.

He was unsure why he himself was doing so well at Mr Seymour's training. Perhaps his mind had been starved of stimulation since leaving school; they had very few books at home, could barely afford newspapers, and had no radio, so his main source of information was old newspapers he took home from the mill, and anything shared by people he knew.

Shockingly, Nazi bombs had been dropped on Dublin again a week ago, despite the south having declared themselves neutral. By some miracle no one had been killed, yet the incidents had served to sharpen the minds of citizens in Belfast, only a hundred miles away. The Nazis were apparently claiming the bombs were a 'navigation error', but no one quite believed their 'Ministry of Public Enlightenment and Propaganda'.

His stomach churning, Liam had read accounts of the scene in week-old newspapers and seen photographs of a huge crater behind houses in Terenure. Had it landed only a few feet further along, there would likely have been people killed. And as an ARW, he would be among those going to the site of such devastation. Often, Mr Seymour had reported, ARWs were first on the scene when bombs hit in England.

Which was why Liam needed to focus tonight. Mr Seymour was sharing his considerable expertise while employing his usual technique of trying to get them to figure things out for themselves rather than simply giving them the facts. Just now he had asked them to share what they thought might be possible signs of structural damage in a building they were entering. Matt Darcy instantly mentioned cracks in walls or ceilings, which was correct, but Mr Seymour urged them to think of what else they might notice. Liam conjured up a damaged building in his mind, and stuck his hand up.

'Mr Flynn.' Seymour's expression was encouraging; he seemed to like Liam, and Liam's confidence was increasing the longer he spent in the man's company.

'Would you notice things that are like, out of line? Like a wall or a ceiling that's a funny shape?'

'Precisely.' Seymour beamed at him. 'A sagging ceiling or a bulging wall, a chimney stack that is no longer perfectly straight, a floor that slopes, a window that looks out of line . . . you must train your eye to notice these details. The last thing we need is to lose men who rush in without first thinking of safety.'

Walking to the side of the room, he picked up a long metal pole with a pointed end, a sharp hook below the point. 'Now, how might this help you in a damaged building?'

Liam worked it out straight away. 'You could use it to prod or poke a wall or ceiling from a safe distance.'

Seymour beamed at him. 'Once again, Mr Flynn has it. Yes, from the safety of a doorway you can use this ceiling pike to test an area that might be unsafe, while the hook can be used to snag and dislodge debris. You are each to be issued with a similar pike tonight.'

Liam digested this, wondering where he was to store it. His home was tiny, and already Liam's haversack, first aid kit, uniform and helmet were taking up space, along with Seány's fireman's gear. The ceiling pike would have to go into the tiny yard.

'. . . if you found a small fire?' Seymour was asking, and John O'Toole replied by speaking of water or dousing it with a soaked curtain.

'Both good suggestions. We will also have access to this.' Seymour pulled across a metal bucket containing a strange looking object with a rubber tube and a metal stand, topped with a U-shaped bar supporting a wooden handle. There were two others, identical, standing beside it. 'This,' he announced, 'is a stirrup pump, and we are going to practise using it in a bath. Follow me – and bring the other pumps!'

He led the way to the row of bathing rooms, allocating them to a pump in groups of two or three. He himself joined Matt and Liam, directing them to fill the bucket with water then use the pump to produce a fine spray into the bath, thereby minimising the clean-up needed after training. The spray, he explained, could be targeted precisely at a fire, and was a much more efficient way to use limited water supplies. The fine mist produced would also be effective at extinguishing incendiary bombs if used carefully; pouring water directly onto the chemicals might cause the device to explode. He left them, then, to practise, heading for the adjoining bath cubicles where the other ARWs were figuring it out. A few more men had come forward to be trained, which Seymour seemed relieved about. *God, he really thinks we'll be needed!*

'He's a good 'un, isn't he?' Matt said, jerking his head towards the door. 'Seymour, I mean. And him a Protestant.'

Liam smiled. 'It's bad that this place makes us surprised to find a good one. But you're right, he is a good one.'

'And you'd never know it by him, but he's loaded.' Taking the hose, Matt began pumping the stirrup handle until water emerged. 'His building company is one of the biggest in West Belfast, and he has a big fancy house on the Springfield. I arrived early tonight, and had a good chat with him. He was from the Shankill originally, and he's very loyal to the people there. His da was a millworker.'

'Interesting.' It actually increased Liam's admiration of the man, for Seymour had no need to do any of this, having somehow escaped the destiny of most mill-hands. 'Has he family, do you know?'

'Two daughters, both married. The oldest lives in Scotland, and the younger one has apparently moved back home to her parents.' He grimaced. 'Her husband is in the army and has been deployed somewhere, and the daughter's expecting. First grandchild, he was tellin' me.'

'God love them.' Everyone had their problems to bear, Catholic or Protestant, rich or poor. Mr Seymour's riches could not protect his son-in-law, though at least the daughter could retreat to a big house with, no doubt, a decent shelter where her chances would be much better than families on the Falls. Or, indeed, the Shankill. 'Fair play to Seymour for leading this.'

'Aye. A good 'un, like I say.'

Liam reflected on this as he made his way home, carefully carrying his ceiling pike. Seymour was no doubt a member of the local Orange Lodge, would march with the others on the Twelfth of July and be heartily glad that the north hadn't gained independence from Britain as the Free State had. He was perfectly entitled to that view, and Liam suspected Seymour might say the same about Irish nationalists. Unionist yes, but there were no signs of sectarian prejudice in the man. Funny how being on the same side against a common threat – the possibility of Nazi bombs – made such things seem less important, for now anyway.

He frowned. No, not less important. As an Irishman he passionately hoped that this partition experiment would be very temporary. It made no sense to split such a small island into two jurisdictions, with this northern statelet comprising only six small counties. There were apparently twice as many people in London city as there were in the whole of Ireland, and yet London hadn't been partitioned . . . but then again, the people of England knew they were English, whereas here, people's very sense of nationhood was contested.

He was home. Heading straight through the house to the backyard, and ignoring the exclamations from Mammy and the others, he leaned the pike carefully against the wall of the outhouse, then glanced at the cloudy sky. One night, sometime soon, would those clouds be pierced by aircraft laden with destruction? It didn't bear thinking about.

# 19

*Thursday, 23 January 1941*

> *January saw heavy snow in Belfast, with a major snow storm on January 18. Delivery men used horses and slipes – a type of sled – to deliver their goods, and some rural communities were cut off for days.*

Finally, the first aid course was coming to an end. This last night was an examination, a test of learning, and the St John Ambulance tutors had brought a team of extra colleagues to do the testing. Mr Seymour was there again, organising proceedings and thanking the St John Ambulance personnel, who were all, he reminded them, volunteers. Despite feeling a little nervous, Kathleen was able to provide reasonable answers to all of the examiner's questions, and her bandaging went fairly well, she thought. They all had tea, then, while the examiners were totalling scores and filling in forms.

'What's this I hear about you and Jamesy Mackin, Kathleen?' asked Seány with a teasing look, and she almost spat out her tea, conscious that Liam was *right there*.

'What do you mean?'

'Apparently he's delighted you let him walk you home from the dance last week.'

She sniffed. 'Oh, is he?'

'Aye. Everybody knows how fussy you are, so he thinks he's class now.'

'All girls should be fussy,' Bronagh said firmly, a twinkle in her eye. 'Lads too. Nobody should just settle for whoever comes across their path.'

Liam's eyes widened, Kathleen saw, then he dropped his gaze to his cup.

'Aye, fair enough,' said Seány breezily. 'I've no notion of a girlfriend meself. Far too young for that carry-on.'

They all laughed, since Seány was twenty – the same age as Kathleen – and was more than old enough for a girlfriend, if that's what he wanted. Vaguely, Kathleen was aware that boys were much less likely to be criticised than girls for being single, but before she could focus on this, Mr Seymour was calling for their attention.

'Congratulations!' he announced. 'Everyone has passed the examination, which means you are all now qualified first-aiders. Well done!' There was a murmur of delight around the hall, as most people present would never have qualified as *anything* before. It sounded very grand.

'As you know,' he continued, 'we have been carefully considering all of you, your skills and abilities, and we have allocated you to different roles according to your training, your registration, and your abilities. Firstly, I would like to call upon our air raid wardens to make themselves known.' He read out a list of names including Liam's, and Liam stood with the others, looking uncomfortable.

'These men,' said Mr Seymour, 'will lead us should the worst happen. They will be responsible for communication and coordination, and will have the power to give orders to the rest of us.'

*It's a leader role*, Kathleen realised abruptly. Most people hadn't really taken the ARWs seriously until the bombs in Dublin, and Kathleen noticed how some of the men now looked a little regretful at their choice of fire or rescue. Liam and the other ARWs would be in the thick of the action too, but as leaders. She was delighted for him.

'Next,' Mr Seymour was saying, 'we have selected five of you to be trained as ambulance drivers. This is based on your tutors' assessment of you, as well as your scores in the first aid examination. Each of you selected to be drivers will receive full driving instruction, as well as extra training in stretcher drills.' He referred to his list. 'The five selected are . . .' He read out a list, while everyone waited with breath held, '. . . and Bronagh Gallagher!' he concluded with a flourish.

*Bronagh!* Kathleen clapped with the rest, then hugged her sister, who looked astounded. 'Me?' she kept saying. 'Did he say me?'

'He did, and I'm delighted for you!' *A woman, driving!* Very few in these parts knew how to drive at all, and Kathleen was sure she didn't know any woman who had learned to drive. For Bronagh to be selected was wonderful.

'Finally . . .' Once the clamour had died down Mr Seymour brought their attention back to himself, 'we have four first-aiders who achieved perfect scores on their examination, as well as being highlighted by the tutors as having a gift for the role. These four will be given additional training in March, with the opportunity to become a corporal in the commandery. Congratulations to the following . . .' He took a moment to check his various lists, then lifted his head again.

Kathleen was frozen in anticipation. Of all the roles and accolades, this was the one she had secretly been praying for. As a handywoman she had learned to be calm, to deal with distressed people – both pregnant women and families where a loved one was dying – without increasing their distress. She had studied Peggy's text book from cover to cover, and had been fascinated by the first aid lessons covering the heart, the circulation, bleeding, choking, and shock.

The first aid course had come easily to her, as it built on her existing knowledge and what she believed to be her talents. And so when Mr Seymour called out her name she was both astonished and yet *not*, for she had known deep inside that this was her calling. To support people who needed her skills, whether as a handywoman, or as a first-aider.

Bronagh hugged her, and Seány too, and then – then Liam's arms were around her briefly, his body warm and his breath sweet. 'Well done, Kathleen,' he said, pulling back to look at her. 'You're a wonder.'

*A wonder.* She kept the words within her heart – not the physical one that pulsed and beat, but the heart of her soul where Liam remained king, no matter how hard she tried to oust him.

The walk home was filled with excitement; she and Bronagh both delighted with themselves. Even Mammy was impressed, telling Bronagh that being able to drive would open the door to all kinds of work, while maybe Kathleen would get selected to become a nurse or something – which, she asserted, had happened before, or so she had heard. Somewhere. *Aye, right.* The fact Kathleen had no interest in becoming a nurse was not, apparently, relevant.

*The Irish Midwife at War*

And so there was an air of celebration in the Gallagher household that evening. Mammy even agreed the girls could use a couple of extra coupons to get eggs and flour the next day, for pancakes. As they sat in their cosy home – the radio on, the fire lit, and notions of Nazi bombs far, far away – Kathleen was conscious of a feeling of gratitude, of everything being right with the world. Well, why wouldn't it be? He had told her she was a wonder.

# 20

*Sunday, 23 February 1941*

> *After three days of bombardment the Swansea Blitz ended on 21 February with the town centre devastated, fires still alight, and over two hundred people dead. Over seven thousand people have been made homeless. The town had been targeted by the Nazis due to its strategically important port, docks, and industry. After similar bombing raids on Bristol, Portsmouth, and Plymouth, people begin speaking of a 'Luftwaffe Tour of the Ports'.*

It was a dreary Sunday afternoon, the first Sunday of Lent, and Sadie had called. She usually did call on a Sunday, but Liam was feeling increasingly unsettled in her company. Everybody knew that once a lad chose a girlfriend and stayed with her for more than a few months, that was that. Couples rarely broke up, and there was generally talk of marriage after a year or so. He and Sadie had started walking out last August, and so there would soon be pressure building within him to think of proposing to her.

But how could he marry, with barely a few ha'pennies left at the end of some weeks, and his family relying on his meagre earnings? Therese and Christine had the temporary shifts, which helped, but that could go at any time. Sadie and her friend had had the misfortune to be laid off again after only a couple of days. The work simply wasn't in any way secure.

No, it was impossible to think of marriage. He wouldn't dream of walking away and leaving his mother and younger sisters destitute. He could see it all around him. One more lay-off, one wage-earner lost to a household, and they went from just about managing to full-on poverty. *Is this it? Is this my life?*

What was it Bronagh Gallagher had said at the first aid that night? *Nobody should just settle for whoever comes across their path.* The words had been haunting him for weeks.

He wasn't at all sure he wanted to spend his life with Sadie O'Kane.

Oh, on the surface she was a good choice. She was pretty, and vivacious, and her family was sound. He had thought that her outgoing nature would bring him out of himself, but instead he had become even more subdued in company, allowing her to do the talking for both of them. The longer they were together, the more uncertain he was becoming.

There was also Kathleen. Surely, if a man was committed to his girlfriend, he wouldn't be thinking of another girl? And Liam thought about Kathleen. A lot. *I should have asked her out once she was eighteen.* Two years ago he had thought of it but had hesitated, afraid to spoil the friendship she had with him and Therese and all the Flynns. The opportunity had passed, and Kathleen seemed perfectly content letting boys walk her home occasionally. So why, then, did she haunt him?

There was a sort of hierarchy among lads and girls. Rich ones dated rich ones, and poor the poor. Good-looking dated good-looking, and people generally matched in terms of intelligence too.

He had been told he was handsome, and did seem to attract the right sort of attention from the good-looking girls. He knew himself to be smart – frustratingly so, given his destiny to live and die as a mill-hand. But he was poor. His family were poor. They had so far managed to keep their heads above water, but all it would take would be one moment of misfortune – Seány or Liam losing more work, somebody needing the doctor regularly – to make them sink, and then they would join the ranks of those without enough food, or money for rent.

Kathleen's family were mill-hands too, but so much better off, with four adults all bringing in money. For Kathleen to end up with someone like him would be a step down. Yet she haunted his thoughts.

The pressure of it all was relentless. And Sadie, without meaning to, was adding to that pressure. As they walked out into the cold February air, the light dimming, she talked about Therese's upcoming wedding, sighing at how romantic it all was.

'Romantic?' he replied, probably with more vehemence than was needed. 'With no savings, and planning how to use coupons to put on some sort of wedding breakfast?'

Sadie tossed her head. 'Well *I* think it's romantic, and I can't wait until it's our turn!'

He said nothing, which made her mouth set into a hard line. *God, I'm such an awful person!* It was perfectly reasonable for her to be hinting at marriage. It was him who was the blocker. Him who was hurting her. But what could he do?

★ ★ ★

## Seána Tinley

The McGowans' house was exactly as Kathleen had remembered it. It was bare, and plain, and there were no comforts or luxuries on display. But this time it was clean, and the fire was already lit. Mrs McGowan had posted a note through the Gallaghers' door earlier, asking Kathleen to call round after work, and Kathleen was unsure why.

The family were clearing up after tea, the place a hive of chaotic activity. Families with smaller children always had the tea very early, so they could get the wee ones to bed. In the Gallagher house – and the Flynns' – they would not be thinking of their tea for another couple of hours yet.

One of the girls was holding the new baby – wee Mary, Kathleen recalled. At three months old, she looked healthy and well. The children were all clean too. Mrs McGowan had clearly got on top of things again. Wee Alice came running to hug Kathleen, her little face shining with happiness.

'What's *she* doing here?' Mr McGowan's comment was in the running for the least welcoming greeting Kathleen had ever received on a house call. 'You're not in the family way again already, are you?' His tone was accusatory, and Kathleen's hackles abruptly awoke on behalf of Mrs McGowan.

'Not that I know of,' Mrs McGowan declared calmly. 'Now, yous keep tidying up. We're going upstairs.' She led Kathleen out of the living room and up the stairs, where the air was cold. 'In here.' They went into the back bedroom and she closed the door. 'It's our Cora.'

Kathleen's heart sank. 'What's the craic with Cora?'

Mrs McGowan shook her head. 'She hasn't been right for a while, but it's only today that I started to wonder if maybe . . . She seems to be in pain, but doesn't want a doctor. Not that we could afford a doctor anyway.'

Kathleen nodded grimly. 'Where is she?'

'In the front bedroom. Says she doesn't want to talk to anybody. But she liked you. And besides . . .' She didn't finish the sentence. Kathleen nodded, then squared her shoulders, crossing the landing to the other door.

Knocking the door softly, she said, 'Hello, Cora. It's Kathleen, Kathleen Gallagher. Can I come in?'

'No!' There was a pause. 'Yes, all right.'

The room was in darkness, so Kathleen paused with the landing light behind her, as Mrs McGowan made her way downstairs.

'Is she gone?'

'Your mammy? Yes.'

'Right. Close the door. You can turn the light on.' Cora's voice was shaking, and Kathleen's heart was thundering, unsure what she was about to see.

Cora was sitting on the large bed where all the girls slept, her eyes red, her expression one of wariness. Kathleen sat on the edge of the bed, giving what she hoped was a reassuring smile. 'What's happening, Cora?' she asked gently.

'I dunno. I'm scared, and I dunno. It might be . . . but it can't be! It can't!'

'All right. Shhh. It's all fine, Cora. Can I give you a hug?'

She nodded, and the hug allowed the girl to cry properly. As well as being compassionate towards the terrified girl, Kathleen's handywoman brain was noticing important details; despite generally being on the thin side, Cora's abdomen was definitely enlarged.

'Now, tell me what's happening in your body. Have you a sore head?' The girl nodded. *Unsurprising*. Kathleen continued with other parts of the body unrelated to pregnancy. 'Any earache? Toothache? How's your neck? Sore at all?' In the same tone, she eventually got to the stomach, and Cora confirmed that yes, her stomach was sore. 'Only on and off, Kathleen,' she said earnestly. 'It's not sore all the time.' She clearly had no idea that this was the opposite of reassuring.

'Right. Can I feel it?'

When Cora nodded, Kathleen put a hand on the top of her neat bump, feeling no tightening. 'Would you lie down for me, and let me feel your tummy with two hands?'

Cora did so, and Kathleen took a thin blanket from the bottom of the bed, draping it over Cora's hips and thighs. 'Now, lift your dress up a wee bit, so I can feel your tummy. Is that all right?'

The girl's bump might be neat, but it followed the typical contours of pregnancy. Kathleen's heart was sinking as she placed her hands either side to ascertain if the bump was in fact a pregnancy.

It certainly felt like one. Yes. There was the baby, and here was its spine, space at each side . . . she checked again. The head was likely at the top, under Cora's ribs. *Lord, that's all we need.* A young girl of only sixteen. A concealed pregnancy. A breech baby.

She had only just helped Cora back up into a sitting position when the girl's face screwed up, 'Ow, ow, ow! This is like the worst monthly I ever had!'

Immediately Kathleen's hand was on Cora's abdomen again, her voice soothing as she encouraged the girl to breathe calmly. A good strong contraction. Once it ended she asked, 'Are you bleeding?'

'No. It's like it's been trying to come all day but it won't actually come. And I haven't had a monthly for a while so it's probably gonna be a massive one.'

Kathleen took a breath. 'Cora. Cora, look at me. Do you know the most common reason for monthlies not happening?' She was going to have to go carefully here. Cora's furtiveness suggested she knew deep down what was happening, but the poor girl also would be wanting to deny it. The last thing Kathleen wanted was to push too hard and send a vulnerable sixteen-year-old round the bend.

'No?' Her gaze slid away.

*She knows.* 'Cora.'

'It can't be!' The words erupted from her. 'It was only the once, and it was so long ago!'

'How long ago?'

'June.' Her voice was small. 'It was that day when the Italians declared war on Britain and France. I'll never forget it. He said we might as well do it cos we're all gonna die soon anyway.'

Kathleen managed to not roll her eyes. *Feckin' lads.*

'Do you remember the date?' Kathleen's tone was gentle as she questioned Cora. 'When you – you know . . .?'

She nodded. 'It was the tenth.' Her voice was small.

*Almost full term, then.* 'Right. Cora, I'm gonna say it. Are you ready?'

The girl lifted her chin. 'Yes.'

'You're expecting a baby, and it's due to be born.'

'Oh, God. Oh, God.' She began rocking like a child. Hearing it out loud meant she couldn't pretend any more. 'My ma and da are gonna kill me.'

Kathleen wrapped her in another hug. 'It's all right, Cora. It's all right.'

But it wasn't all right. Cora's life would never be the same again.

'Shit! Is that my ma coming?' Cora sounded panicked at the sound of someone coming up the stairs. 'Don't tell her!'

'Cora, she has to know.'

The girl started crying again, and Kathleen put an arm around her. Mrs McGowan came in then, closing the door behind her. Her gaze sought out Kathleen's, and Kathleen grimaced.

'Well? Is she . . .?'

They were all waiting for her to be the one to say it. And she couldn't. It wouldn't be right. Not without Cora's agreement.

'Cora. Cora, listen to me. I have to tell your mammy what's happening. All right?'

Cora buried her face in Kathleen's neck, sobbing. Crucially, though, she nodded.

Kathleen took a breath. 'Cora is having a baby.'

Mrs McGowan paled, a hand flying to her mouth. 'I knew it! Well, I suspected it anyway. All day I've been driving myself mad going maybe it is, maybe it isn't. Pains in her stomach, on and off, so I felt her stomach. When you've had fifteen babies yourself you know the craic.' She shook her head sadly. 'Fer fuck's sake, Cora!'

Kathleen eyed her evenly, and she sighed. 'Come on now, Cora. We'll manage some way or another. Come here.' Cora transferred to her mother's arms, still sobbing, and Kathleen was relieved to see Mrs McGowan's arms tightening around her daughter.

*Thank God for that!*

★ ★ ★

*I am hurting Sadie.*

As Liam and Sadie made their way back to the Flynn house after their walk, Liam's mind was reeling. The revelation about him and Sadie had hit him like a punch to the gut. Why had he not seen it before? He was *hurting* Sadie by being her boyfriend when he couldn't commit to marrying her. Worse, he had suspected they weren't suited for some time now. But with everything else that was going on, he hadn't been brave enough to look at it.

Strangely, the ARW training was part of this. He lived for the weekly sessions, and had slowly felt some part of him re-emerge that had been long buried. He was discovering a new self within him. Liam Flynn, air raid warden. He had even been given a card now that Seymour had deemed they were ready. Issued by the City and County Borough of Belfast, it looked impressively official, and certified that Liam Flynn of Clowney Street, Belfast, had been duly appointed as an air raid warden. The card stated, *This is his authority to carry out the duties laid upon Wardens by the County Borough of Belfast.* He would have certain powers in the event of a raid, like enforcing the blackout, evacuating people, and coordinating emergency responses in his area.

He and Seymour had added their signatures in the appropriate places, and Liam now carried the card everywhere he went, for who knew when he might have to transform from Liam Flynn, nobody, into Liam Flynn, air raid warden.

At school he used to believe he could one day be something, be *somebody*. Mr Seymour and the warden training was helping him to believe it again. Tomorrow he was going to Mr Seymour's office in the Shankill, for the man had invited him and Matt for extra training on the basics of what he called structural engineering. Unpaid, of course, yet Liam would be grateful for the learning.

As he took off his cap and donkey jacket – the uniform of his life as a poor mill-hand – he laughed inwardly at his own foolishness. Hanging them on the hook by the front door, he followed Sadie into the living room, where Therese was sitting with Mammy, writing lists. More wedding preparations, no doubt. While he understood their enthusiasm, he couldn't share it. Therese leaving meant less income, and less help around the house. Yet, looking at her shining eyes right now, he could begrudge her nothing. His sister deserved every bit of happiness.

Sadie, however, was less generous – hardly surprising, given their squabble just now. 'Ach, not wedding stuff again,' she declared sullenly. 'Do yous never get tired of it?'

'No, never!' There was defiance in Therese's eyes, and Liam made haste to intervene, fearing a row.

'I'm putting the kettle on,' he said evenly. 'Cuppa tea, anybody?'

While this served to prevent any further cross words immediately, it unfortunately meant Liam left them all to go to the kitchen. Once the kettle was on he returned, unsurprised to find the air thick with tension, and Mammy sending him a warning look. He stifled a sigh. This was all he needed.

★ ★ ★

After the hugging had ended and Cora had got through another pain, Kathleen spoke about the plans she had been making in her head. 'We'll need to get the wee ones to bed. All the girls normally sleep in here, don't they?'

'Aye.' Mrs McGowan nodded. 'All but the baby. She sleeps with me downstairs.'

'And you've three boys?'

'Aye. They sleep in the back room.'

'Right, I remember. I suggest the three boys sleep downstairs and we use this front room for Cora tonight. The girls can have the back bedroom, since there's four of them. We'll need the fire lit in here.'

Mrs McGowan nodded. 'My man will have to sleep on the settee. He'll not be impressed.' She shook her head again. 'I'll have to tell him.'

'He'll go mad, Ma!' Cora's voice was trembling.

'Aye, he might.' Mrs McGowan made an exasperated sound. 'What were you *thinking*, Cora?'

Cora's face flamed. 'Don't.'

Mrs McGowan rose. 'Right. I'll go and get him.'

Cora was shaking all over, and Kathleen sat in the place the girl's mother had just left, taking Cora's hand in her own. 'This is the worst bit. Once he knows, he knows.'

A few minutes later Mrs McGowan returned, accompanied by her husband, who was wearing a perplexed expression. As they entered the room, Cora's grip on Kathleen's hand tightened in a clear message signalling, *Don't leave me!*

Kathleen had no notion of abandoning her woman, and sat with a calm expression. It was hard on Cora's parents, she knew. This was not what they would have wanted for their eldest daughter.

'What's going on?' he said, his brow furrowed.

'Our Cora is expecting,' said his wife baldly. 'She's in labour.'

'She WHAT?' he roared. 'She WHAT?' He leaned over his daughter. 'What the FUCK have you been up to, Cora?'

Cora shrank back in fear, and Kathleen slid her right arm around her, taking Cora's left hand with her left. Her own heart was pounding with fear. An angry man was an angry man.

'Answer me!' His face was filled with rage. He lifted a hand, hovering it threateningly over his daughter. 'Answer me, fer fuck's sake!'

'That's enough.' Kathleen stood, inwardly quaking, but filled with outrage on Cora's behalf. 'That won't change anything, and it certainly doesn't help.'

'Who the fuck are *you*,' he sneered, 'to come into *my* house and give me orders?'

He was a hair's breadth away from violence. Kathleen knew it. Protection of the young mother and her baby had been her first priority, but her actions had drawn his eye to her. *Exactly as I hoped.*

She lifted her chin. 'I'm the handywoman, and this young woman and her baby are my responsibility until the baby is safely born.'

There was a silence, the tension growing. Kathleen could barely breathe. Fear was pooling in her stomach, moistening her palms, and making her heart race. *What is he going to do?*

★ ★ ★

'What days are you working this week, Therese?' Mammy asked mildly, clearly trying to find innocuous topics of conversation.

'Tuesday, Thursday, and Friday,' said Therese, adding pointedly, 'It's so great to have the guaranteed three days. Long may it last!'

*Therese!* Liam sent her a look, but it was too late. Sadie, already angry, took the bait.

'Yeah well, I still woulda had a job too, if *certain people* hadn't informed on me to the mistress!'

'Certain people?' Therese's tone was innocent. 'Who do you mean, Sadie?'

They were like two cats in a stand-off on the street, Liam thought, looking from one to the other. Entirely focused on one another, oblivious to anyone or anything else – including common sense. Fire in the eyes, polite expressions, and a sweet tone to their voices. Danger was in the air, for he knew these two young women well, and suspected neither would back down.

'Kathleen and Bronagh Gallagher, if you must know!' Sadie practically spat the words out. 'They told on me, and got me fired!'

Liam felt shock ripple through him. Sadie had been cagey about the reasons why she had been let go, but he had never thought to delve deeper. What she was saying now though . . . it didn't seem right. Kathleen and Bronagh would never do something so awful. Work was *everything*. Without money, people could starve.

'That's so *interesting* you would say that, for I heard a totally different story.' Therese's tone was sugar-sweet, but Liam's senses were now on full alert. *This is not going to end well.*

'The mistress said to my friend Annie,' Therese continued, 'that you and your chum had been caught dawdling and flirting with the men in the warp room. Nobody told on you – the mistress was already looking for you.'

'That's not true!' Sadie spluttered. 'I wasn't flirting with nobody! And—'

'And *nothing*!' Therese was standing now, her face flushed. 'You got yourself fired, Sadie O'Kane. You wouldn't know what work was if it came up and slapped you in the mouth!'

'I'll slap *you* in the mouth, you dirty hallion!' Sadie's face was twisted with rage.

As they reached for one another, Liam started forward, placing himself between them and saying loudly, 'That's enough! Both of you!'

'She started it, telling lies about Kathleen!'

'Ah, Saint Kathleen of Assisi! The girl who can do no fucking wrong!' Sadie's tone dripped with contempt.

'Well, she's worth a hundred of you, Sadie!' Therese wasn't giving an inch.

'Therese Flynn!' Mammy had joined the fray. 'Not another word from you!'

'But—'

'Not one word!' Mammy repeated, her finger raised in front of Therese's face. 'Liam, take Sadie home.'

Turning, Liam reached for his jacket and cap. His heart was racing and he felt queasy. They had been in the house for less than fifteen minutes.

'Let's go.'

# 21

Kathleen stood firm, hoping that her fear would not be obvious to Cora's angry father. She needed to divert the focus away from him. 'I think the baby is breech,' she said, directing her words to Mrs McGowan.

'Ah, no.' Mrs McGowan rolled her eyes. 'That's all we need.'

'What does that mean?' Mr McGowan was looking from one to the other, while Cora sat stock-still on the bed, safely beneath their line of vision.

'It means the baby is the wrong way round, so instead of the head coming first we'll get the feet or the backside.'

He was pale, Kathleen saw. *Shock. And anger.* 'What does that mean? Is it bad for Cora?'

*He cares.* 'It means we'll have to handle the birth differently.' Kathleen's voice was remarkably steady, considering.

'Cora.' He turned back to his daughter, his tone a bit quieter. 'I am so disappointed in you. We didn't rear you to get up the stick at feckin' sixteen.' The milder expletive was significant. The man was calming down.

'Now that I can agree with,' said the girl's mother, and Cora hung her head, avoiding their gaze.

'Who's the father?' Mr McGowan demanded suddenly, his voice cracking.

Cora's head whipped up, her eyes ablaze. 'What do you mean, who's the father? Tony is the only boyfriend I ever had. What sort of girl do you think I am?'

'Well, at least that.' His tone was begrudging.

'Mark, them that is without sin . . .' Mrs McGowan's tone was firm, and Kathleen's eyes widened at the implication.

'Aye, but we got married before the chile was born. She should have told us sooner.'

'She should, but we can get it sorted. I'll go and see the priest the morra, with Tony's mammy. We'll get it all organised.'

'Get what organised?' Cora was looking from one parent to another, her brow furrowed.

'Your wedding.' Her mother's tone was clipped.

'My wha—' Her jaw dropped.

'Well, you don't think you're gonna *not* get married, do ya?'

'I suppose.' Her eyes took on a wistful look. 'Only, it would have been nice to have him propose and to plan it and all.'

'Well, you should have thought of that before you—' A quelling look from his wife prevented Mr McGowan from completing the sentence.

'Anyway,' Kathleen intervened, 'I've suggested the boys sleep downstairs, and we get the fire lit in this bedroom.'

'I'll do that.' Mr McGowan's tone had changed. Having something to do would help him. 'I'll go and get the stuff.'

'Thank you. Also, hot sweet tea all round, I think.'

'Aye, a good notion.' Mrs McGowan nodded. 'I'll go and put the kettle on. This sort of thing is bad for the nerves.'

★ ★ ★

Liam and Sadie were walking a foot apart, but it might as well have been a mile. Liam felt sick inside. Initially, Sadie ranted loudly, venting her anger about Therese, about Mammy, about Liam.

'And you!' Her face was twisted, her skin flushed with anger. 'You just stood there and let them abuse me!'

'Sadie, stop.' His voice was low. There was no coming back from this. He knew it as well as he knew his own name.

'No! You're supposed to stick up for me!'

'Why?'

'That you would even ask that! You're my boyfriend, for fuck's sake!'

'And Therese is my sister. Yous were both in the wrong for fighting like that.'

'But she's telling lies! I—'

'I don't want to hear it, Sadie.' His voice held a tinge of sadness, as he confirmed what Sadie surely suspected – that it was Therese he believed.

'Well, you can fuck off, then! I'm sick of your moaning and moping anyway. Boyfriends are supposed to be fun!'

He stopped, right there in the street. *Fun.* He had never in his life been *fun*. 'Sadie, I'm sorry. I can only be who I am. I—'

'Well, who you are is *boring*, and *judgy*, and – and no craic!' She took a breath. 'I think we should break up.'

He caught his breath, his heart thumping like a piston. 'You do? Are you sure?'

'Yes, I feckin' am! I've had enough of you, and your stupid family! I'm going to find somebody better – just you wait and see!' She spun on her heel, and he followed, his head reeling.

'Sadie, wait! I—'

## Seána Tinley

'I can walk myself home, thank you very much!' she declared primly, then marched off, her head held high. Liam simply stood there, a whirlwind of emotions within him. Already troubled from the row between the two women, the events of the past few moments had added to his agitation. His heart was pounding, his mouth dry, and his stomach sick. Sadie had been a big part of his life for months, and now she was gone.

As he retraced his steps towards home, he recognised that amid regret, distress, and quite a significant dose of guilt, the main emotion he was feeling was obvious. He felt relieved.

★ ★ ★

Once Cora's parents had gone, Kathleen's attention returned fully to Cora. The girl's brow was furrowed, her shoulders raised, and her hands were in fists. She hadn't had a pain since the row kicked off. *That'll be the stress of it.* Kathleen's challenge now was to get the mother-to-be into the right frame of mind for birth.

'Now. That's all done, and it's over. You'll never have to go through it again.'

'God that was kyet! I've been dreading it, cos I was afraid I was expecting.'

'How long have you been thinking you might be pregnant?'

She shrugged. 'Months, probably. I dunno. It was easier not to think about it. Just do my work and help Mammy and not even look at it, you know?'

'Aye. It must have been hard.'

'But then I kept getting them pains in my stomach. Like monthly pains only worse.'

'When did the pains start?'

'Thursday morning, early. Scared the life out of me, but thank God they stopped after a few hours. Same thing happened on Friday night when everybody was sleeping. I was so scared!'

'I'm sure. And they stopped again?'

'Aye. But then they came back this morning.' She rubbed her abdomen. 'But this time they didn't go away. They just keep coming, and there's more of them.'

'Aye, that's normal.'

'Is it?' Her eyes were big and round. 'I don't really understand it all. What's gonna happen?'

'Well, the first bit is that the pains will get longer, with less time in between them. That's your womb opening.'

'My womb? Like in the Hail Mary? The fruit of thy womb?'

'Exactly. Your womb is the place inside your tummy where the baby has been growing.'

'And like, when I eat, does my dinner go all over the baby?'

'God, no. They're like . . . separate rooms inside you.'

'Right.' She thought about this. 'And how does the baby, you know, get out? I've heard sometimes women have to go under the knife. Like, they cut your stomach open.'

'That does happen sometimes. But most babies come out the natural way. Between your legs.'

Her jaw dropped. 'From my bum?'

'No. From your . . . doctors call it the vagina. It's where your period blood comes out.'

She gaped. 'But how can a whole baby come out of such a small place?'

*I remember asking the exact same thing.* She gave Cora a reassuring smile. 'Because women's bodies are amazing, Cora. Your body is amazing. You will do this. Everything will be good.'

'Will it?' Her voice was small. 'I'm scared, Kathleen.'

'It's all right to be scared. Look at the day you've had. But things are better now. You're over the worst of it.'

'Maybe. What about Tony, though?'

'Does he know?'

'No. He has no idea. See, if I said it out loud that would have meant it was real.'

Kathleen smiled. 'He's gonna get a shock when your mammy calls round in the morning.'

'He is!' Her gaze went distant. 'We really love each other, Kathleen.'

'That's good. Yous will be all right, then.'

'Will we? Where will we live? What will we do for furniture? And baby things? We have nahin'! Literally nahin'!'

'Has Tony a job?'

Aye, he's still a full-timer.'

'Well, then. That's something.'

'I suppose.'

'I'm gonna give you some advice now, Cora.'

'What is it?'

'Today you have one job, one thing to do, and that's to get this baby out safe and well. The best way to do that is to focus on that and only that. All the problems of tomorrow can wait for tomorrow.'

'Like the song!'

'What song?'

The girl sang softly, her voice sweet and true. 'And the cares of tomorrow must wait till this day is done.'

'Beautiful. You've a lovely voice.'

She blushed. 'Thank you. I used to sing at Mass.' She grimaced. 'They won't want me any more, now I'm a bad woman.'

Kathleen hugged her. 'You're not a bad woman, no matter what some might say. Did Jesus not make friends with Mary Magdalene, even though she's supposed to be a . . . you know?'

'That's true.'

'So don't be worryin' about it. If Mary Magdalene was good enough for Jesus himself, then you're good enough for me!'

'Thanks, Kathleen.'

'Don't mention it.' Inwardly though, Kathleen knew it wasn't quite so simple. Cora would be talked about once the word went round that she'd had a baby. Oh, maybe in a few years, married to Tony and with a brood of children, the fact that their first child had been born before the wedding would be forgotten by some. But there would be others who would never forget. Would make a point of not forgetting. And it was always the girl who got the blame. She stifled a sigh. Why did things have to be so hard, especially for girls and women?

★ ★ ★

All the way home, Liam kept going over it in his mind. Again and again. The row between Sadie and Therese. The lies about Kathleen and Bronagh. The fact Sadie was no longer his girlfriend.

Couples rarely broke up, and if a lad broke up with a girl he was always looked upon with suspicion. His stomach churning, Liam tried to take in what had just happened. *But she finished with me*, he reminded himself, as he let himself into the house.

'You're back quick,' said Mammy, her eyes narrowed.

'Sadie's walking herself home.'

'Are yous finished?' Therese, always astute, was straight to the point.

He nodded, then turned to hang up his cap. So much had changed in the past hour.

'Hallelujah! Finally!' Therese's delight was clear.

'Therese!' Mammy intervened. 'Liam's probably disappointed!'

'He'll get over it. She's a witch that one. You're well rid of her, Liam!'

While he couldn't agree with Therese's words, he was guiltily aware of the relief within him, so said only, 'I don't want to talk about it.'

'Right so!' said Mammy briskly. 'Time for us to get the tea ready anyway. Therese, go and call the girls down from upstairs. About time they started taking a lead on some of the cooking, for you'll be married and gone soon enough.'

'Good idea! I'll teach them the way you and Granny taught me. I'll have them baking and making stew in no time!'

Therese squeezed his shoulder as she passed, and he allowed it. Following Mammy into the kitchen, he watched as she put the kettle back on – the same kettle that he'd set to boil a wee while ago. The whole thing was just surreal.

★ ★ ★

Mr McGowan lit the fire, then Mrs McGowan returned with sugared tea and a soda farl for Cora, as well as tea for herself and Kathleen. The three women sat there on the big bed, drinking tea and talking about nothing important, while half-listening to the children playing downstairs and the occasional sound of passers-by in the street outside. Cora had two more contractions, and her shoulders were no longer up by her ears.

A little later Mrs McGowan disappeared for a while to put the other children to bed. The quietness was beginning to come over Cora, as she let go of some of the worries she had been hiding for months. *Birth works best when the women forget about the past and the future.* Cora had had plenty to be chewing over, and new challenges would await once the baby was born. But for now the girl's only business was birthing her baby.

★ ★ ★

Tea had been strange. Therese was clearly delighted by recent events, the younger girls agog at the notion of drama, while Seány was maintaining a carefully neutral expression.

Mammy had also been hard to read, saying only, 'A questioning man is halfway to being wise.'

This was one of many *Seanfhocail* she liked to spout. The old sayings were sometimes cryptic, and it was hard to understand what Mammy was trying to convey here. Was she saying he had been right to question his relationship with Sadie, or that he should question recent events and try to win her back?

The problem was, he didn't *want* to win Sadie back. As his distress settled, the relief remained; if anything, a conviction was growing that they would both be better off without one another. Still, he hated being the centre of attention, so after tea he donned his cap and jacket, making for the dusky streets.

He was single once more, and despite a brief pang at the loss of a possible future that included Sadie and her family – who were all perfectly nice people – he was content. He would walk for a while, then head back home. Tomorrow was a new day, and he would soon get used to life without Sadie.

\* \* \*

By the time Mrs McGowan returned and the house had quietened, Cora was progressing nicely. The baby was still breech – at this stage there was so little room for babies, they rarely turned – so Kathleen was going over in her mind all she had seen and learned from Mrs Clarke and Peggy at various breech births. The child was moving nicely inside the womb, and Kathleen found it hard to comprehend how desperate Cora must have been to hide her pregnancy from everyone – including herself. The girl had been through a difficult few months, yet watching her follow instructions and breathe calmly through the latest tightening, Kathleen's heart swelled with admiration.

Around five in the morning, as they reached the intense end of the pre-pushing stage, Cora got herself into something of a state. The pains by this stage were on top of one another with only a few seconds' rest in between, and some of them even had double peaks, it seemed. This was a part of the process that many women found tough.

Cora, who had been fairly calm for hours, was gradually getting worked up, and kept telling them how awful it was. 'Here's another one! Oh, God, Ma, I can't do this!'

'Course you can!' Mrs McGowan's tone was brisk. 'Sure, haven't I had fifteen babbies? All women go through this. It's nothin' to be afraid of.'

This was exactly what Cora needed, it seemed. Her mother's matter-of-fact tone signalled to the girl that what she was experiencing was normal, which seemed to lessen her fear.

'Now, do your breathing again, Cora. Yes, that's it. Good.' Kathleen's tone was slow and soothing, and it seemed to help Cora get back into a more relaxed frame of mind. She exchanged a satisfied glance with Mrs McGowan. Between the two of them, they had hopefully staved off any panic.

A little later Cora began making classic pushing sounds, and Kathleen suggested she get on all fours.

'Can she not do it sitting?' asked Mrs McGowan. 'I always like to be sitting for the pushing.'

'Not for a breech baby,' said Kathleen. 'It's always better to be kneeling.'

Kathleen felt a flutter of nerves inside. While doctors, midwives, and handywomen all agreed that breech was simply a different version of normal, Kathleen hadn't assisted many breech births by herself. *Please don't let it be a footling breech!* she prayed. The less complicated, the better.

Thankfully the child's bottom was coming first, with no sign of a little foot alongside it. As Cora strained and pushed, Kathleen gave words of encouragement, while Mrs McGowan wiped her daughter's face with a damp cloth. Three women, working together in perfect harmony. Two supporting, one doing. Cora at sixteen, Kathleen feeling old at twenty, and Mrs McGowan who was probably in her mid-thirties. Steps and stairs. Wisdom being passed on from woman to woman, generation to generation. There was something about it that was just . . . *right*, somehow. As it should be.

Gradually, gradually the child emerged. First the bottom, then both legs fell down at once. The baby's hips and abdomen began to emerge immediately afterwards – breech births tended to be quick once they got going, thank God. The little body was sideways on, the tummy facing Cora's left leg.

'It's a girl!' Kathleen announced. 'You're doing great, Cora! Now keep pushing whenever you feel the urge.'

Kathleen bent to reposition the old clean towels under Cora, satisfied with how the birth was going so far. She and Mrs McGowan had earlier dressed the bed with a rubber sheet to protect the mattress, and the towels were clean, well used, and soft. A loop of purplish pulsing cord was now hanging down by the baby's tummy, and the baby's colour was reasonably good too. Kathleen's hands were itching to touch the baby, but the other handywomen had drummed into her never to touch a breech, as it could apparently disrupt the birth.

*Rotation next*, Kathleen said inwardly, running through what she had been taught. Sure enough, the baby was turning slightly so that her front was now fully aligned with Cora's back. It was miraculous for Kathleen to expect this, then see it happen. Women's bodies were truly amazing.

The baby was continuing to steadily emerge. Peering closely, Kathleen was reassured to see a cleavage on the baby's chest – a skin crease right down the middle which suggested that the baby's arms had been tucked to the front, and should emerge next. The baby was now moving, bringing her legs sharply up into the position they had been in for months. At the same time, Cora spontaneously dipped her bottom towards the bed and the arms appeared together, flopping down to the baby's sides, almost immediately followed by the head, Cora's groans changing to a brief squeal as it emerged. Fresh blood indicated a tear, but an initial glance suggested it was fairly small.

The baby meanwhile had landed square on the towels on her back, her arms and fingers opening wide before closing again, and her mouth opening as she took her first breath. A lusty cry followed, and Kathleen swiftly directed Cora into a sitting position. While Mrs McGowan arranged pillows behind her, Kathleen handed the baby up to Cora.

'Congratulations, Mammy,' she said, feeling it was important to give Cora her new title.

'Oh, my God. I can't believe it! It's an actual baby, look!' Cora looked and sounded every inch a sixteen-year-old, and Kathleen felt a momentary pang of concern. Would the girl manage?

*Of course she will.* She would stay with her own mother for the first few weeks, wedding or no wedding. Plus the girl had years of experience of looking after babies. As the eldest daughter she'd have helped her mother every single day. *Like our Bronagh. Like Therese.* Girls and women were strong. They had to be.

# 22

*Monday, 24 February 1941*

> *In early 1941 British planes began using the 'Donegal Corridor', a narrow strip of Irish airspace between Lough Erne and the Atlantic, with Dublin's tacit agreement. This constituted an unpublicised contravention of Ireland's neutrality.*

Liam was conscious of nerves fluttering in his gut as he made his way up the Falls, heading for Mr Seymour's yard which was apparently between Dover Street and Percy Street, off the Shankill Road. This was a Protestant area, and one where Catholics normally didn't go, but hopefully Liam would be safe on a damp Monday morning in late February. His working man's uniform of donkey jacket and cap was no different to that worn by men in the Shankill, so there was no reason why he should stand out.

Still, his back was itching as though any minute a bullet would fly from one of the surrounding buildings. *Why in God's name did Seymour want us to come to him? Why couldn't we have met in the Baths as usual?* There was something fishy about the whole thing, yet he had said he would come, and so he would. Extra learning was welcome; going to the Shankill was not.

There was a large air raid shelter on Percy Street, its sturdy concrete roof reminding Liam that there was work to do to get similar shelters built in his own area. He and the other wardens had begun a programme of assistance with shelter building; both the small ones that some men were constructing in their tiny back yards, and the large community shelters like the one on the Springfield and this one.

*Seymour and Son.* The painted sign on a red-brick wall told Liam he was in the right place. But Mr Seymour had no sons. *Ah, it'll be his da and him.* The yard was filled with building supplies, and surrounded by a high wall. Theft must be a nightmare for Seymour. Still, it was a good problem to have – those supplies were worth many hundreds of pounds. Glancing around, he spotted the tiny office building at the far end, and made his way across. Matt was already ahead of him, and turned on Liam's shout, looking relieved when he saw Liam.

'Well, Matt. What about ye?'

'Well, L— Ach, I'm grand. You?'

'Can't complain.'

They exchanged a knowing look. Matt's name was common in both communities, but the Irish name Liam would mark him out as a Catholic, hence Matt's last-minute veering away from saying it.

Entering, they found themselves in a small reception area. It had a desk containing a telephone, a notebook, and a potted plant. The middle-aged woman behind the desk was looking enquiringly at them, so Liam said, 'I'm here to see Mr Seymour, along with Matt here. We're air raid wardens. He's expecting us.'

'I'll let him know you're here.' She disappeared through the door at the back of the room, returning seconds later.

'Go ahead there. I'll bring the tea. Milk, no sugar?'

They both confirmed it and went through to the inner office, a small room with cabinets, noticeboards with various papers pinned to them, and a desk overflowing with papers. Behind it was Mr Seymour, and he rose as they entered.

'Darcy! Flynn!' He shook their hands with great enthusiasm. 'Thank you for coming. Sadie will bring tea in a minute. Here, have a seat!'

Bustling about, he lifted a pile of papers off one chair, and a box of what looked like door latches off another. Vaguely, Liam noted that Seymour's colleague was called Sadie, which gave him a pang until his mind reminded him that Sadie was, in fact, a Protestant name. He suppressed a smile as he recalled Granny's outrageous teasing of his girlfriend. *My former girlfriend, as of yesterday.* He had not slept well, but remained convinced that the break-up was the right thing to do.

'Right.' They were all seated, and Seymour was back behind his desk. 'I asked you to come here today as you two are the best and brightest of the air raid wardens in my district, and should a raid ever happen, I will rely on you two as my key assistants.'

'Thank you, sir,' said Matt. Liam said nothing. *Where is he going with this?*

'As you know, there are ARWs from the Shankill as part of our team, but I am no bigot, and believe in choosing the best man for any job.'

Liam wanted to believe it, but scepticism held him back. Was this really Seymour's motivation, or was he basically planning to send Matt and Liam into danger? *My key assistants.* One a grandfather, the other a young unmarried man.

Both Catholics. *Are we expendable?* Despite the previous conversation he and Matt had had about Seymour being a 'good 'un', there was always the possibility that the man was simply good at hiding his sectarianism.

'With that in mind,' Seymour continued, 'I want to offer you two additional training – training which I believe will help more people stay safe. The last thing we need is for rescue teams to go flying fearlessly into damaged buildings and get themselves killed.' He took a breath. 'Part of my work is demolition; we often have to pull down old buildings to clear a site. Doing that safely is important – I've yet to lose a man from my company.' He sounded proud, and despite himself Liam began to warm to the man again. That safety record was something to be proud of, if true.

'This week we've a couple of houses to pull down in Boundary Street round the corner. I thought you might like to see them.'

'Sounds good,' Matt offered.

'Mr Flynn?'

Liam nodded. 'Aye. We can take a look.'

'Good, good. Ah, Sadie! Just in time!'

There was a pause while they each took a cup from Sadie's tray, sipping in unison. 'Thanks, Sadie. I'll need you to sort out some of these invoices later.'

Sadie looked dubious, but said only, 'Yes, Mr Seymour.'

There was a knock on the door. 'Come in!'

A solemn-eyed man in his sixties appeared. 'Morning, Mr Seymour. I wondered if you'd been able to get that extra wood ordered?'

Seymour clapped a hand to his head. 'I'll do it today, Stanley, I promise.'

*The Irish Midwife at War*

'If we don't get it by Thursday there'll be ructions, so there will,' Stanley replied firmly. 'Ructions and shenanigans, if I'm not forsaken.'

'No, you're right. I haven't had the time . . .' Seymour glanced vaguely at the piles of papers around him. 'I'll do it today though. I will.'

This appeared to satisfy the blank-faced Stanley, for he nodded, turned on his heel and left.

'He worked for my father,' Seymour said, adding ruefully, 'The problem is, I love the business, but hate the *detail* of the business, you know?'

Liam nodded, though truthfully he had no idea what it must be like to have to manage something like this. Thinking about it, Seymour clearly got excited by leading, by bringing through new ideas, by thinking about the broader view. It was interesting to discover that Seymour's ability to strategise came at a cost: a dislike of the smaller aspects of the work.

Seymour went on to describe the steps his team took when entering a derelict building; the signs they looked for, the tests they did. This was old ground, already covered in the ARW training, so Liam's mind wandered a little. Seymour had clearly inherited the company from his father; all Liam had inherited was the responsibility of being a man at fourteen. Yet Seymour's da had started out as a mill-hand; clearly he had instilled in his son some feelings of solidarity for working men, for Seymour's speech was peppered with hints that he cared deeply for the welfare of his workers. A good man, then.

*Still doesn't mean he cares about me and Matt. We could be lesser people in his eyes, and undeserving of the same protection he'd offer to his own people.*

Another knock at the door. Stanley had returned, his demeanour unchanged. 'Mr Seymour,' he declared, 'there's a man here from Boyd's lookin' for his list. He's fairly agimatated, so he is. Says he should have had it a week ago if you want the stuff on time.'

'Lord, I forgot!' Jumping up, Seymour began looking through the papers on his desk. 'Sadie! Sadie!'

Sadie appeared, looking displeased.

'Where's the Boyd's order?'

'I have no idea, Mr Seymour.' She picked up the paper closest to her, peered at it, then set it down again. 'What does it look like?'

'It's a list,' said Seymour, his tone one of careful restraint. 'Different sizes of nuts, bolts, nails, and screws, and the quantities we need.'

'Oh.' She picked up another paper, holding it out at arm's length, her eyes almost closed. Stanley, meanwhile, was still standing in the doorway, one arm as long as the other.

Suppressing a sigh, Liam stood. 'Happy to help. Is the list handwritten or typed?'

'Ah, good lad. It's handwritten. Sadie can't—' He broke off, clearly not wishing to highlight his assistant's inadequacies. *I bet she worked for his da too.*

Reaching for the nearest pile, Liam began searching through it with brisk efficiency, automatically separating out the papers into different groups: invoices, orders, bills, general correspondence, and informal notes that Mr Seymour clearly intended to help his memory of tasks to be done. Setting each new pile on the large table at the side of the room, he returned to the desk where Seymour was rummaging. Sadie was on only her fourth or fifth document by this stage, while Matt had remained seated, explaining that he had left his glasses at home, his eyes sliding away from Seymour's gaze.

A pang went through Liam. He knew Matt had learned to read, for he had managed the paperwork at the first session of the ARW training, but since then Liam couldn't recall seeing Matt with glasses on more recently. The most likely explanation was that they had broken and he couldn't afford a new pair.

Taking another pile from the desk, Liam continued with his sorting, absently noticing red reminders on some of the outstanding bills. Was Seymour's firm in financial difficulty? Or was it simply another symptom of the chaos in the office?

*Anyway*. It was none of his business. It took almost fifteen minutes, but eventually the order list was unearthed and passed to the laconic Stanley. Once he and Sadie had left, Seymour collapsed into his seat, mopping his brow with a cotton handkerchief. 'Thank the good Lord we found that! Now, on to more interesting things. Shall we walk to the site? We can take a ceiling pike with us.'

As they walked through the yard, Liam noted that Seymour still seemed a little tense. It was only when they got out onto the street that his affability returned and with it, his talkativeness. 'Did you know,' he said, 'that Boundary Street marked the old edge of Belfast? Townsend Street too, the next street over.'

Matt and Liam confirmed they had not in fact known this, and to be fair it was an interesting piece of information.

'Here we are.' Seymour paused, pointing at two derelict houses opposite. 'Those two are coming down tomorrow, and they're in bad shape, as you see. Now, what can you notice from here?'

It was astonishing, Liam thought later, just how much one could learn from real life experience rather than theory. They assessed both houses, venturing well into the first one safely, but immediately realising that the second one was dangerously unstable. The ceiling pike proved invaluable. One single poke at the bulging living-room ceiling from the safety of the doorway brought the entire ceiling and half of the upstairs down in a shower of bricks, wood, and dust. Coughing, they all stepped backwards into the road, Liam's heart pounding at the potential danger they had just avoided. Matt had managed to hold on to the end of the ceiling pike, but the sharp end was now stuck in piles of rubble. By dint of twisting and jerking it, they succeeded in working it free, and as they returned to Seymour's yard Liam was conscious of a feeling of satisfaction. Today's lesson would be so useful if they ever had to deal with a real-life situation.

A smart red-and-black motor-car was parked outside the yard – a Morris Eight, if Liam wasn't mistaken. *Those cars cost nearly a hundred and fifty pounds!* Seeing the motor-car, Seymour rubbed his hands together. 'Ah good!' Stepping inside the building, he sent a jovial greeting in Sadie's direction.

'Oh, Mr Seymour, your wife and daughter are here.'

'Yes, I know,' he said bluntly, heading straight into the inner office. 'Come with me.'

They obeyed, Liam decidedly curious about Seymour's family. If the expensive car was theirs, that meant Seymour's business was in fact thriving. No doubt about it.

'Oh, there you are, George!' The speaker was a middle-aged lady in a pale blue dress with a matching coat, hat, and gloves. 'We've ordered the most darling little crib for the baby! They're delivering it in three weeks. I—' She broke off, sending a curious glance towards the two men.

'It's the most gorgeous thing – hand-crafted, of course,' the younger woman added. She too was dressed in finery, including gloves and hat, her coat open to reveal a maternity dress and a swollen belly. Idly wondering when the baby was due, the thought came instantly; *Kathleen would know.* Damn it, he had to stop thinking about Kathleen Gallagher!

Mr Seymour was performing introductions. 'This is Mr Darcy and Mr Flynn, two of my air raid wardens. My wife, and my daughter, Mrs Newsome.'

'How d'ye do?' the ladies murmured politely. Neither offered their hand. Well, why should they? Two men in donkey jackets and flat caps were clearly not their social equals.

Resisting the urge to rub the back of his neck, Liam stood impassively as the Seymours continued their conversation. God, he couldn't wait to get home! Despite Mr Seymour's affability, these people were alien to him. Standing in the small office, surrounded by middle-class Protestants and piles of papers, Liam's mind went a-wandering, imagining himself asking Kathleen how she would know just by looking how far on a woman was with her pregnancy. She would smile with that gorgeous mouth of hers and then tell him some intriguing fact, yet his eyes would be drawn to the fascination of her face, her eyes, her lips . . . *I'm doing it again!*

The ladies were leaving. Liam took his part in the polite farewells, wondering if they knew he was Catholic – that he and Matt were both Catholics. Just because Mr Seymour seemed tolerant it didn't mean his wife and daughter were.

Mrs Newsome's husband, Seymour was explaining, was on active duty somewhere in Europe.

'That must be hard on your daughter,' Liam offered. 'Especially with the baby coming.'

'Aye, hard indeed. He'll not be back till well after Easter, so he'll definitely not be here when the chile is born. But our Lily's a good girl. She'll manage.' He eyed Liam curiously. 'Are you married yourself, Liam?'

'No.' Liam shrugged. 'And not likely to be, any time soon.'

Matt sent him a puzzled frown. 'Are you not walking out with the O'Kane girl?'

Liam shook his head. 'Not any more. Besides, what have I to offer a girl?' His lip curled as he thought about his poor prospects.

Seymour's eyebrows shot up. 'What have you to offer? A good lad like you would make a great husband. You're smart, and hard-working, and well-mannered . . . any man would be proud to have you for a son-in-law. Not that I'm suggesting anything,' he added, chortling, 'for both my girls are settled. But is there not a girl you'd like to have for your sweetheart?'

Liam could feel his face flaming. 'That's not the point.' Mr Seymour was looking at him with great interest, so he hurried on. 'The point is I *shouldn't* be asking a girl to walk out with me when I have nothing for her.'

Mr Seymour was still eyeing him intently. 'Nonsense!' he declared. 'You work in one of the mills, yes?'

'Aye, as a half-timer. They've cut back on most millhands' hours. And I've my family to look after. Me da died when I was fourteen, and I'm the eldest.' He shrugged. 'I'm not complaining. But it is what it is.'

'I see.' He turned to Matt. 'And have you work enough, Matt?'

'I do, aye. My ones is all up and away, so I've only meself and the wife to feed. Half-time suits me lovely, so it does.'

Seymour nodded thoughtfully, his gaze returning to Liam. 'I don't suppose . . . but no, you'd probably not want to be up here all the time.'

'What do you mean?' Liam's heart was pounding as he realised what Seymour might be trying to say.

Seymour indicated the piles of sorted papers. 'I could do with getting on top of all of that. What with being in charge of civil defence in the district, I've let things slide a bit with all the office work this last while. And Sadie means well, but she's a receptionist, not a . . . Anyway, would you be interested in a few hours' work this week and next, Liam? Just till I get these orders and bills sorted?'

'I—' Thoughts were racing through Liam's mind. Not everyone was as tolerant as Mr Seymour, and there were very real dangers in him coming to the Shankill on a regular basis. But could he really turn down paid work? Of course he couldn't. And it was only for a few days.

'Thank you, I'd be happy to do that.'

Mr Seymour shook his hand, and then clarified which days Liam would be in the mill that week, immediately booking him for the other days – even Saturday. Six days' wages instead of three would be such a boon, even if it was only for two weeks.

'Maybe,' Liam added, thinking it through, 'you should call me William while I'm here.' The two names were similar, and Liam knew lots of lads who'd changed their names to sound more Protestant when working outside their own community. Lads called Sean became John, Seamus was James, and Liam was usually William.

'No problem, William!' There was a twinkle in Seymour's eye. 'D'ye want to stay now and get started?'

'Ah, I can't today. I need to head home.' It was nearly dinner time, and his ones would worry if he didn't show – they all knew he was in the Shankill this morning. 'I'll come back tomorrow, if that's all right?'

'Aye, no bother.'

Liam's head was reeling as he and Matt walked back down the Falls. Had he done the right thing? Was he going to get himself killed? There were headers in both communities who occasionally took to violence, and the wounds of the Irish War of Independence had not yet healed.

He shrugged. He had no choice, not really. Work was work, and money was money. And he'd had little of both recently, so even two weeks of extra hours was welcome. He'd take the work, and hope for the best.

★ ★ ★

'Well, Kathleen.' It was Jamesy Mackin, the lad who had walked her home after the dance a few weeks ago, before Lent. Dances weren't allowed during Lent. Sticking to her plan, Kathleen had allowed various lads to converse with her at the dances, going so far as to let two of them walk her home and kiss her. Both had been a disappointment. Oh, the kisses hadn't been horrible like her experience with poor Mugsy when she was younger. But they had been . . . forgettable, and she had no intention of going steady with either lad.

She squirmed at the bad luck that had made her and Jamesy both be walking along the Falls at the exact same

## The Irish Midwife at War

time, but really, in such a small community it was inevitable Kathleen would bump into him again.

'Och well, Jamesy, 'bout ye?' She paused as he had stopped at the corner of Islandbawn Street, clearly wishing to talk to her.

'Aye all good, all good.' His eyes fixed hers. 'Working away, like.'

'Aye, me too, and glad of it.' She pretended to be fixing her shawl, glancing down so as to break his gaze.

'Too right. Are you in the Damask?'

'No. Blackstaff.'

'Oh aye, that's right. You told me.'

She had, the night he walked her home. *God, this is so awkward!*

'I was hopin' to run into you, so I was.' Was he? Why? *God, is he gonna ask me out?*

Inside she was filled with sudden anxiety, but politeness demanded she respond. 'Oh, why's that, Jamesy?'

'You see . . .' He ran a hand over the back of his neck. 'Eh, I was wondering, eh, if mebbe me and you could – I dunno, take a walk sometime?'

*Here it is.* She was at a crossroads. This was her chance to truly forget about Liam Flynn. To move on from him. To have a chance at a different life. She froze, feeling the weight of the decision. *Say yes!*

'No.' The word was already out. 'I mean – I'm sorry, but . . . but no.' He looked crestfallen. 'You're really nice and all, Jamesy. I . . .' She shrugged. 'It's me, Jamesy. It's me.'

He nodded. 'Aye, I thought it was a long shot. Good luck to ya, Kathleen.'

He walked on, crossing the road towards Fallswater Street, leaving her agitated and slightly sick inside. *What the hell is wrong with me? Why can I not just*—With a muffled expletive she walked on. *I am a feckin' disaster, so I am.*

★ ★ ★

Liam saw her as she made her way up the Falls from the Whiterock Road direction. *Kathleen Gallagher.* He knew her face and form as well as he knew his own family, for she had been part of their clan ever since she and Therese had bonded at school. And yet . . . she had never been his sister, nor anything like it.

She had been talking to Jamesy Mackin, though Jamesy had now disappeared over the road. *Are they a couple?* Was that why they had been talking? God, he was altogether too interested in Kathleen Gallagher.

Once more he allowed himself to recall their kiss, amid the magic and snowflakes of a New Year full of hope. There had been no war then, no threat of Nazi bombs, no need to wear a steel helmet and practise using a stirrup pump.

Guilt raced through him as he finally acknowledged that he had never truly committed to Sadie because of Kathleen. Well, not only Kathleen. He had also wondered if he and Sadie had been a good match for one another. But it had been Kathleen who haunted his dreams, Kathleen who had been his near-obsession at times, Kathleen who had fitted so well into his family . . .

They had been too young back then, and the gap in their ages too wide. Now, he was twenty-two and she was twenty – both adults. Was there any chance for him?

She'd had no serious boyfriend, he knew, although recently she had been staying on with lads at the céilís, and had allowed

Jamesy to walk her home after the last dance before Lent. He had noticed it. Jamesy had probably kissed her.

*Stop it!* he told himself, Sadie had only just broken up with him. It would be totally disrespectful to her to start planning to ask another girl out, only a day later. *God, I am such a buck eejit!*

And besides, what did he have to offer a girl like Kathleen? A pang went through him. This was the other thing that had been stopping him, all these years. He didn't want to pull her down to the Flynn level of poverty. The Gallaghers had a comfortable life: a bed for everyone, a radio, a few extra shillings each week . . . What had he to offer someone like Kathleen?

She hadn't yet seen him. Filled with shame and guilt, he ducked into Rockville Street, unable to face speaking to her.

★ ★ ★

*Liam!* Kathleen had spotted him straight away, but was studiously avoiding looking at him. Her head and heart was already in turmoil after her cowardice in rejecting Jamesy, who was a perfectly nice lad and deserving of more from her than a flat *No.*

Yet any day she saw Liam Flynn was a good day, and right now he was walking towards her! She turned her head slightly to the left, pretending to be eyeing the notices in the shop windows, but in reality she was keeping an eye on Liam, her heart pounding in anticipation.

He had reached the junction of Rockville Street, and was walking with determination – until he abruptly and shockingly veered to his right, up the street.

*He's avoiding me!*

Shock rippled through her, swiftly followed by confusion. *But why? What did I do on him?* She racked her brain, but the only possibility she could think of was too awful to contemplate.

She fancied him. More than that. She wanted him. Had always wanted him. And Bronagh had known it. Her face flamed anew as she realised her yearnings had been perfectly obvious to her sister.

*Do they all know? Does Therese know? And Mrs Flynn?* Granny Flynn had certainly hinted that she suspected. God, it didn't bear thinking about – but it did provide a logical reason as to why Liam was avoiding her. *He knows, and he's scundered.*

She put both hands to her face, which was hot with shame and mortification. What must it be like for him, to know that your sister's best friend was obsessed with you, not wanting her, yet being unable to avoid her?

'Jesus Christ, Kathleen, you are the biggest eejit God ever put on two feet!' God, now she was talking to herself, and somebody was approaching on the footpath. 'Hello, Mrs Thompson. How are you?'

'Ach, well, Kathleen-love. How's you?' Mrs Thompson paused, clearly ready for a big conversation, even though Kathleen was dying inside.

'Ah, can't complain. Is this Francis?' She bent to speak to the little boy clutching Mrs Thompson's hand. 'Hello, Francis.'

'Aye he's quare and big now.'

'God, he is. He must be what, three now?'

'He'll be four next month!'

'Which means I've been a handywoman for nearly four years!'

'That's right! Our Francis was your first ever birth, was he not? God, I dunno where the time goes!'

'Too right!' As she walked on a few moments later, Mrs Thompson's words were echoing in Kathleen's brain. The time really had flown since she had begun her apprenticeship. She was twenty now – an age when many young women were getting engaged or simply going steady with a lad. If she wasn't careful, the chance to marry and have babies would pass her by. Liam didn't want her, clearly. Maybe if Jamesy were to ask her now, she would give a different answer.

*Right.* It was well past time for her to wise up. She would avoid the Flynn house, stop thinking about Liam, and say yes to the next lad who asked her out.

★ ★ ★

Christine had the dinner ready when Liam arrived. Seány was there, and Mammy, and Therese arrived just as he was hanging up his coat.

'Well? How did it go?'

His head full of Kathleen, he had to think for a minute what they meant. *Seymour!* He nodded. 'Better than I thought. Checking the derelict houses was really useful.' They were all looking at him, except Christine, who was busy in the kitchen. 'He's given me some paid work.'

'Paid work! Hallelujah!' Mammy clapped a hand to her chest. 'Wait. In the Shankill?'

'Aye. It's temporary. Three days this week, and the same next week.'

Mammy was frowning. 'I dunno, Liam. Things could get bad very quick.'

'I promise you, at the first sign of trouble I'll be out of there like a hare that's seen a fox.'

'Aye, you make sure you do. How much is he payin' you?'

Liam shrugged sheepishly. 'I didn't actually ask him. Not very much, I'd guess, but sure it all helps.'

'And of course now you don't have a girlfriend making you buy her pokes and sweets!' Therese added tartly.

'Therese!' Mammy looked outraged. 'Leave him alone. He might be gutted at them splitting up.'

Therese sniffed. 'Thon one was busy gossiping in a corner when God was giving out good sense. She mightn't be much good at boiling a pot of spuds, but she'd look *lovely* carrying them to the table. No bloody work in her.'

'That's enough, Therese. Our Liam liked her, and that was what matters.'

'Our Liam can do ten times better, and we all know it. Thank God she won't be back, with all her dramas.'

'The house'll be a lot more peaceful, that's for sure and certain,' said Mammy.

'Wait – did none of yous like her?' Liam was astounded. 'Therese, I knew you weren't a fan, but—'

'No more speaking ill of the girl,' said Mammy primly. 'She's gone, and that's that. Now, let's get this table set.'

As he ate his spuds, Liam was taking in the fact that it seemed his family had not been keen on Sadie. Her dramas, her abrasiveness, her self-centredness . . . He shouldn't be thinking ill of her, and yet it was important to understand that their break-up had been for the best. Sadie had flared into his life like a bright match, only for the light to fade almost instantly. *Our Liam can do ten times better.* Could he, though? Could he really?

# 23

*Sunday, 2 March 1941*

> *A convoy en route from Britain to Gibraltar was attacked off the north-western coast of Ireland by German U-boats, resulting in the sinking of eight merchant ships and two naval escorts. Over four hundred lives were lost.*

The advanced first aid course was due to start this afternoon, and Kathleen was late. Mrs Murphy from Lincoln Street was only after giving birth to her first child, and Kathleen knew not to leave the house until everything was well with the new mother and her baby. Mrs Murphy's own mother was there, but the baby had been fussy at the breast, and they had both sat with Mrs Murphy until she was calm enough to let the baby find her own way.

Which was why Kathleen was now hurrying down the Falls to the parish hall. She hated being late – years of the fear of missing the factory whistle ingrained in her bones. Ideally she would have been there twenty minutes early, but as it was, she would likely only be five minutes ahead of the two o'clock start.

Kathleen had had the busiest week she could ever remember. As well as doing three full days in the mill, she'd sat with three women in labour and a dying man, and her evenings had been spent doing follow-up visits to the families. She had seen neither Peggy nor Therese, and hadn't so much as darkened the door of the Flynns' since Saturday a week ago. Since before Liam had avoided her. It was good to be busy, since it kept her mind active and herself far, far away from him.

Hopefully now that Mrs Murphy's baby was here, things would settle down a wee bit. The extra money was great, but the breathlessness of it all was exhausting. And she needed to be mentally ready for the advanced first aid course; this opportunity was important. As a cadet corporal, she had the chance to become an *actual* corporal with a fancy uniform and all the authority of being a properly qualified senior.

A pang went through her. She was missing a visit to Jane's for this – her other sister was thirty today, and so Mammy, Daddy, and Bronagh were calling round with little gifts for her. Jane was the nearest to Kathleen in age, but with ten years between them they had never been particularly close. Fifteen-year-olds don't typically befriend five-year-olds, and so it had fallen to Bronagh, who would have been twenty-two when Kathleen was five, to look after her.

The first aid people were using the wee room in the parish centre, rather than the big hall, and when Kathleen went inside she saw a woman and a man in St John Ambulance uniforms, along with Mary, the other girl selected for advanced training. There was no sign of the two lads whose names had been called out.

'Well,' said the woman, 'you must be Kathleen!' She made her way to a small table near the door, where Kathleen saw various forms and a pen. 'Fill this in, please, and let me check your birth or baptism certificate.'

'Certificate?' Kathleen vaguely remembered them mentioning that last night, but it hadn't really sunk in. 'But me and my sister brought them at the start of the other course.'

'Aye, well, you need it again for this one. You can't start without it.' The woman's expression was kind. 'Is your house far from here?'

'No, I'm from Beechmount.'

'Well, why don't you run and get it, then? Two of the students aren't even here yet, and we'll be starting with a wee cuppa tea anyway, so you'll be grand.'

'Right, no bother.' Kathleen moved swiftly, heading out the door, through the main hall and out into the yard. A young man she vaguely recognised was walking towards her, frowning as he noticed her.

'Is it not on? The first aid, I mean.'

'Oh no, it is. In the wee room. But I haven't brought my baptism certificate and I can't start without it.'

'Ah, shite.' He turned. 'I'll have to go home for mine too.' He stuck out a hand. 'Johnny. Johnny McQuillan.'

'Kathleen Gallagher.' They walked together, both turning right onto the Falls Road.

'Have you far to go?'

She shook her head. 'Beechmount. You?'

'St James's.' He grinned. 'Not a great start, eh? They'll think we're disorganised.'

'I know! And I hate being late. All those years of working in the mill.'

'Aye, the terror of missing the gates. I'm grateful to still have a job, though. I'm full-time in the Damask. You?' She shot him a sideways glance, liking what she saw. He was around her own age or maybe a little older, and was good-looking, clean, and well-presented, with dark hair and dark eyes. His conversation to this point was good too; he seemed smart, and not the sort of lad to leer at a girl. Well, not so far, anyway.

He was waiting for an answer. 'My mammy and daddy are in the Damask. I'm in the Blackstaff Mill as a half-timer.' Both she and Bronagh had been told they were being kept on three days a week for the foreseeable future, which had come as a great relief to Mammy. It could end at any time, like, but the longer it went on, the better.

Sadie O'Kane, on the other hand, had been let go that day along with her friend, which had surprised nobody in the weaving factory. It hadn't even seemed to worry her that much. Why Sadie and her friend had risked the wrath of the mistress, Kathleen would never understand. As she and Johnny walked along the Falls, chatting lightly, half of Kathleen's mind was on Sadie O'Kane.

What had Liam thought about his girlfriend getting fired? He was very loyal, and it was likely that he would stick with Sadie through thick and thin. Which was exactly why Kathleen should be forgetting about him, and focusing on other possibilities. And chatting with a nice lad like Johnny was a good start.

'Right, I'm crossing here.' She gave Johnny a bright smile, and he blinked.

'Hang on.' His look was intent. 'Would you like to go for a wee walk with me sometime?' *He's asking me out.* This time, there could be no hesitation. *Say yes!* 'Aye, why not?'

He was beaming. 'I'll be in the mill all week, but Saturday afternoon, maybe?'

'I'd like that.' The look he was sending her was nice. *I can do this!*

'See you back there shortly.'

'Looking forward to it!' he declared, his eyes warm, and she crossed the road with a spring in her step. Maybe, just maybe, she could get over Liam after all.

She vaguely remembered Johnny from the basic first aid course, but naturally she had been so focused on Liam that she hadn't really talked to any other lads there. And the advanced course would be the perfect opportunity to get to know Johnny McQuillan a little better. They would walk out (and maybe even kiss) next Saturday, and maybe he could be her boyfriend. Her first ever proper boyfriend.

With a definite sense of satisfaction at having made a plan, she went straight into the house, making for the locked box in the living-room cupboard. She knew exactly where the key was kept – Mammy was always a bit furtive about it, but Kathleen wasn't in any way slow. Rummaging in the third drawer, she found it, fitted it to the tiny lock, and opened the box.

Inside, at the top, was an envelope containing notes and coins: Mammy's meagre savings. The rest was piles of papers, and as Kathleen started rooting through them she had to remind herself that she was in a hurry and couldn't linger, no matter how fascinating the papers were. Here was Mammy and Daddy's wedding certificate: 1902 they were married, apparently. And here was a school report on Kathleen dated 1926. She picked it up, unable to resist taking a few seconds to run her eye over it. Apparently she had been 'A good student, well-behaved and well-mannered . . . Picks up new learning very well.'

There were other school reports too, for all of Kathleen's siblings. God, Mammy had kept everything! Then the birth and baptism certificates started appearing – Mammy had clearly organised the box to more or less keep things together. Kathleen sifted through the certificates, frowning as the time went on. Everyone's was here, except hers.

Had they been lost when Bronagh brought them to the registration before Christmas? But no, for here were Bronagh's, and they surely should have been together?

Taking the box to the table, Kathleen began going through it again, this time methodically. Trying not to rush, and banishing from her mind thoughts of the St John people tutting at her tardiness, she laid them out into piles: money, Mammy and Daddy's papers, school reports, certificates. No, she hadn't missed it. Hers simply wasn't there.

An envelope caught her eye then, at the very bottom of the box. It was sealed and unmarked, and she hesitated for a moment. But desperate measures were needed, and so she opened it carefully, withdrawing two pieces of paper and running her eye over the first.

Certificate of Baptism, she read. Diocese of Dublin. Name of child: Kathleen Mary Gallagher. *Dublin? I was baptised in Dublin? But how?* Vaguely, she recalled that Mammy and Bronagh had lived in Dublin for a while, and the hairs at the back of her neck stood to attention as she realised she must have been born during their time away from home.

And why were her certificates hidden away in a sealed envelope? She looked at the certificate again. Mammy's name was there, and Bronagh's. Bronagh was her godmother, so that made sense. Stupidly, though, the priest had put the wrong name in the wrong box.

There was a swirling feeling inside her as she flicked to the other paper. It was just a mistake. *Just a mistake.* And here was her birth certificate, again specifying Dublin. Date of birth: 27 December 1920. Place of birth: Gloucester Street, Dublin. Name of mother . . .

She stared, scarcely able to believe what she was seeing.

Name of mother: Bronagh Anne Gallagher.

# 24

Kathleen stood there for what felt like a year, not moving, as her heart thundered and the words on the paper in front of her danced and blurred. Then Mammy's good clock struck the quarter-hour, and her mind returned, a little. *No time. I have no time.*

Carefully placing her birth certificate and all the other papers back in the box, she kept the baptism certificate, shoving it into the pocket of her dress. Then, her mind blank and her pulse tumultuous, she made her way back to the parish hall.

The woman glanced over the certificate, barely seeming to read it at all, then ticked a line on Kathleen's form and handed the certificate back to her.

'That's us now!' *Ats us nai.* 'Have a seat and I'll bring you your tea; they're just about to start.'

Kathleen sat between Mary and Johnny, managing to give each of them a light smile. It all felt as though nothing was quite real, but a moment later the woman brought her tea, as promised. 'Thank you.'

'I didn't know if you take sugar, so . . .'

'Oh!' Sugar was a good idea. *Shock.* She had learned that in the basic first aid course. 'I do, thanks. I'll get it.' She didn't normally, but today . . .

Rising, she went to the tea table, checking that no one was watching before adding three heaped teaspoons of the precious commodity. The woman had gone to the front of the room to join her male colleague, and they then began the session.

Somehow Kathleen was maintaining a semblance of calm – years of handywoman work standing her in good stead. Her mind was blank, her attention focused only on doing what she had to do in order not to look like an eejit. And so she introduced herself when prompted, listened as best she could to the others: Mary, a middle-aged man called Pat, and of course Johnny McQuillan. Strange to think that only half an hour ago she had agreed to walk out with Johnny. Now her world had been entirely shaken and she had no idea who she even was.

The tutors, Mr and Mrs Anderson, a married couple, then outlined the training they would provide, leading to the advanced qualification. As the hot, sweet tea did its work Kathleen focused on the lesson, reminding herself that she might save someone's life one day.

As for her own life, she had none. She had no heart, no mind, no sense of self. The only reality was the hard chair beneath her, the hot tea in her throat, and the voice of Mr Anderson. The cadets would learn how to give heart massage – CPR, they called it – as well as dealing with choking incidents where a tracheostomy was needed. This, he explained, was where the advanced first-aider made a cut in the front of the neck to allow the person to breathe. The very thought of it was daunting, but then, life was suddenly daunting in all manner of ways.

Shying away from the darkness, Kathleen gripped her cup tightly and focused on the present. She wasn't being asked to perform a tracheostomy today; right now she only had to learn about it. *I can do this*. Minute to minute, breath to breath.

★ ★ ★

'Did you see who came to eleven Mass this morning?' Therese was big with news – and outrage, if the look in her eye was anything to go by.

'Who?' Ma was determinedly calm as she stood ironing shirts with their old cast-iron plate. Liam looked up from reading yesterday's paper, which was filled, as it always was these days, with news of death and destruction right across Europe.

'Sadie O'Kane! She's not even from our parish!'

Liam felt his shoulders tighten. He didn't want to think about Sadie O'Kane.

'And wha'?' Ma remained impassive. 'There's no law against goin' to Mass in a different chapel.'

Therese tossed her head. 'I reckon she was there to try and see our Liam!'

*God, I hope not!* But Therese's words were not particularly surprising. He had wondered a few times this week if Sadie would regret her impulsive decision to break up with him.

Ma snorted. 'Well, she doesn't know him very well if she thinks he goes to eleven Mass. Always out for nine Mass, our Liam.' She sent him a wink. 'Not like you and Christine. Yous love your sleep on a Sunday, so yous do!'

'I doubt Sadie even knows what Mass he goes to!' Therese retorted. 'Interested in nobody but herself, that one!'

'Now,' said Ma in her be-nice tone, 'don't you be speaking ill of the girl!'

'She's not *dead*, Ma!'

'Even so. We don't do that. She's gone, and that's that.' Ma headed into the kitchen to re-heat the iron over the stove.

'Don't you even *think* about getting back with her, not even if she comes crawling on her knees, Liam!'

Liam eyed his sister, but said nothing. The chances of him getting back with Sadie were, he believed, close to zero.

★ ★ ★

Kathleen had made it to the break, and there was more tea. Excusing herself, she made for the toilet at the back of the building – like the mills and factories, the parish hall had an inside toilet, the height of luxury. Leaning against the door she took three ragged breaths, yet still resisted thinking about . . . about anything. Afterwards she went back to the wee room, and was even able to smile and make small talk.

'It's a real honour to be picked for this,' said Mary. 'I could hardly believe it when they called out my name.'

Kathleen joined in with general agreement, but it was all only on the surface. She couldn't remember that feeling of achievement, of delight, because her insides were locked down in rigid control. She must not think, must not feel. She needed *time*. And being alone. And right now she had neither.

Finally, it was over. Being in such a formal environment where she had to be polite, and listen, and be ready to answer questions, had turned out to be a good thing, for Kathleen's nerves had settled a little. As she said goodbye to the others, noting Johnny's smile, the tutors cheerily called, 'See you next week!' and a shudder ran through her.

*Next week.* How could she think about next week, when everything had changed? Everything she had believed. Everything she had thought she knew – about herself, her parents, her sister . . . Her entire life was a lie.

Did everyone know? Was the truth of her origins known by all the adults? By Therese's mammy, and Mrs Clarke, and her teachers?

Maybe not. Surely the whole idea of going to Dublin was to hide the fact the baby was Bronagh's? Or at least have the ability to deny it was Bronagh's. Although people must surely have suspected . . . Unlike poor Cora, whose baby was undeniably her own.

As well as Cora, Kathleen had supported two other unmarried mothers living with relatives in Belfast, and Mrs Clarke and Peggy sometimes attended mothers in St Mary's Home on the Ormeau Road, taking turns with Catholic handywomen from all over the city. The Home doubled as a laundry, and the girls there worked for their keep. From Mrs Clarke's expression when she talked of the institution, Kathleen had gathered it was not a nice place, and her insides twisted as she tried to imagine being sent there.

The date of birth on the form was accurate, so that part was safe, factual, real. But it meant that Bronagh had been seventeen when the baby had been born, which meant in turn she had been just sixteen when it had been conceived.

*It? Me. That baby was me.* As she walked slowly along the Falls, Kathleen's head was spinning. In a few minutes she would be home, and she had no idea what to say or how to be. How did you casually announce that you had discovered that your entire existence was a lie, and that the secrets everyone had held from you were now exposed?

*I can't.* Yet the thought of colluding with the secrets and lies was impossible.

Turning, she headed in the opposite direction. It wasn't dark yet, though the light was dimming. *I have time.* Briskly she headed for the nearby Milltown Cemetery, making for her grandparents' graves.

*Not grandparents: great-grandparents.* Even that had been taken from her. She had not known either of her grandfathers, for they had died before she was born, and Mammy's mammy had only lived until she was three. But she had clear memories of her Granny Gallagher – a formidable woman who had adored her youngest, last grandchild.

*But I was never her grandchild.* Instead Kathleen, as it turned out, had been the first baby of the next generation. A baby born to an unmarried girl. It meant that Jane was not her sister but her aunt, and John and Dominic were not her brothers, they were her uncles. She had no brothers or sisters. Not one. And the children? Her nieces and nephews? *No.* They were . . . her brain struggled with it . . . were they cousins?

Whatever. Her entire family had taken a step back from her. She was once-removed from everyone, except Bronagh. Bronagh, her supposed sister. Anger surged through her – the first clear emotion she could recognise amid the fog of bewilderment inside.

Having pulled out a few weeds from the Gallagher grave, she rose, brushing dirt from her hands, and noticing the sound of paper crackling in her pocket. No, she wouldn't look at it again, for the information written on the certificate was seared into her brain. As she made her way out of the gate and turned towards home, she was conscious of walking very, very slowly. It was odd to see familiar buildings, to understand that she knew every house and shop in this part of the Falls. Odd because none of it seemed real, for she was not who she had believed herself to be, and the world would never again be the same.

'Well, Kathleen!' A cheery voice hailed her.

She started. 'Seány! Well, I didn't see you there!'

'Aye, you looked like you were sorting out the troubles of the world in your head!'

She managed a light laugh, diverting him by talking of today's first aid session. Like her, he had been at training, and regaled her with a tale of a fire hose that had briefly escaped from the hands of a trainee, and it writhing like a massive snake while they all jumped out of the way of its spray.

He walked on a few minutes later, and Kathleen continued towards home, her thoughts tumultuous. *Could Seány possibly know about what I discovered?* Shame rippled through her as she realised that her entire status had changed. Instead of being the youngest daughter of respectable parents, she was the illegitimate child of an unmarried mother. The piece of paper in her pocket had changed her entire life.

How could she continue to be friends with respectable people like the Flynns, when she was herself anything but respectable? And how could she lead any lad on to be her boyfriend, when she knew what she was? Now she understood why Bronagh was single. No good-living family would want her, and Bronagh could hardly lie about something so important to a potential boyfriend or husband. No. Atonement had to be made, and Bronagh being unmarried was part of that atonement.

Kathleen had never been one of those who hugged the altar rails or signed up for bible classes, yet her religion was an important part of who she was. Well, she knew the disdain with which fallen women were treated. In school, pregnancy outside marriage had never been discussed, yet they had all known of those older sisters who were rumoured to have been sent away to work in the mother and baby home – also known as the Magdalene laundry, after the biblical fallen woman.

Kathleen had always prided herself on thinking compassionately about such women, avoiding judging them as some did, and focusing only on how hard their lives must be. They either stayed in the laundry with their child or they gave their baby up for adoption to married couples who couldn't have children of their own.

God, how sanctimonious she had been, secure in her little bubble of ignorance, and bestowing compassion on those she had seen as beneath her in some way! *She* would never be like that. *She* would never allow herself to fall pregnant outside marriage. And yet, here she was, bastard child of an unmarried mother.

She too would atone. Through silence, through the burden of knowledge that could never now be unknown. She could never marry, never again allow a lad to kiss her. Wistfully she thought one last time of Liam Flynn, of Johnny McQuillan – even of Mugsy Mulligan, whom she had rejected in her mind, and yet who was now as far above her as the Pope was above a parish priest.

Whatever Liam's reasons for avoiding her – and her anxious mind was unhelpfully reminding her that he had clearly realised she still liked him – he was smart to have done so.

She was bad news. Unworthy of the attention of any respectable young man.

Her life, her dreams of marriage and motherhood, was destroyed, through no fault of her own, but those dreams could now never be. Her rational mind tried to muscle in. Was she being over dramatic? Was her thinking being led by emotion? Was there any counterargument to her sense of hopelessness? As she turned into Beechmount Avenue, she searched her brain for any examples of illegitimate children who had grown up to marry well. She could think of a couple of lads who had done it, but they were lads lucky enough to have made something of themselves, like having a trade. She could think of no examples involving young women. But, then, women were always judged more harshly than their male counterparts, so they were.

★ ★ ★

Seány was home from fireman training, and was regaling them all with the details. As he listened, Liam felt a slight sick feeling in his belly. The notion of his younger brother putting himself in danger – running towards fires and bombs when everyone else was running away – did not sit well with him.

*This feckin' war!* The arrogance of countries thinking they could simply walk in and take over their neighbours! Ireland had suffered under British rule for centuries, those who led the Empire treating anything outside England as simply a property to be exploited. Oh, they were not the only ones, he knew. Africa and South America and parts of Asia had been exploited in similar ways by the so-called European

Powers – and worse. But Ireland being so close to Britain had allowed a particular form of abuse to thrive.

And now the Germans and Italians were at it. He could try his best not to care, for there was nothing he could do about it, but Seány's humorous tales of mishaps with hoses this afternoon concealed a grim truth: that even Ireland, on the edge of the Old World and surrounded by water, was susceptible to Nazi bombardment.

'. . . Kathleen . . .' Liam's ears pricked up, and he focused on Seány once more. His brother had met her there now, it seemed, and she had been attending her advanced first aid training. Abruptly Liam's heart was pounding, and he knew exactly why. He was single again, which meant the whole question of asking her out was a possibility. To reassure himself, he deliberately recalled those moments when Granny had been dying – moments when it had seemed as though the world held only himself and Kathleen. Was it real? Would it mess everything up to ask her out?

He couldn't do anything about it yet anyway. He had to wait until a decent amount of time had passed after breaking up with Sadie. To do otherwise would look bad on the girl. Which meant he would end up torturing himself mentally for weeks. And even then he might not do it, no matter how much he wanted to. God, how was he supposed to know what to do for the best?

★ ★ ★

It was nearly dark as Kathleen finally approached her own front door. When the sun had risen this morning, all had been well in her world. She had been safe and secure, sure of who she was and her station in life. Her biggest worry had been about not letting herself down in the advanced first aid class. How strange that seemed now. Everything had changed, and she was expected to change along with it.

Anger, hurt, and a strong sense of injustice raged through her, and she took a breath as she entered the house. She had no idea what to say, nor where to start, but before she could even get a word out, Mammy was there, her expression cross.

'Where the hell have you been, Kathleen? Mrs Clarke has been looking for you for nearly an hour. No, keep your coat on. You may get over there as quick as you can.'

They were all looking at her. Mammy, who was not really her mother. Daddy, who was not her father. And Bronagh, who—

Picking up her handywoman bag, she turned on her heel and left again without a word.

# 25

*Monday, 3 March 1941*

> *At least eight men from Belfast, Glenarm, and Killyleagh died when the merchant navy cargo ship SS* Castlehill *sank in the Bristol Channel after a U-boat torpedo attack.*

Kathleen arrived home late in the morning to an empty house. Mrs Clarke had needed her for a birth in St James's. The mother had been in labour for nearly two days, and Mrs Clarke had been with her the whole time. The handywoman was so tired she had needed a second, fresher pair of eyes on the situation. In the end the birth had gone well, the mother persevering through her fatigue.

Although exhausted from being up all night and the mental weariness following the stress of yesterday's discovery, Kathleen knew she couldn't go to bed yet. Bronagh was at work, as were Mammy and Daddy, so it was up to her to get the dinner on. Thankfully the spuds were already peeled, so she turned on the cooker and had a look in the larder.

Once the dinner was on she took the certificate from her pocket, looking at it one last time. *Who's the father?* Mr McGowan's words had come back to her, as Cora's situation had been echoing in her head all night long. She and her Tony were to get married tomorrow. Carefully she withdrew the birth certificate for another look. The space for *Name of Father* was blank. Of course it was. Carefully, she replaced it in the envelope alongside her birth certificate, putting the locked box back in the cupboard exactly where she had found it.

So who *was* her father? Was it that boyfriend who had told Bronagh he loved her, then abandoned her? It seemed likely. Or had there been another man in Bronagh's life?

The sense of betrayal was still strong. Her entire life was a lie, her future in jeopardy. Far from being respectable, from a respectable family, she was no better than the unmarried mothers she had been judging for years. *Judging? Yes.* It was only now, on learning she too was among them, that she realised she had been judging others. Now every unmarried mother was Bronagh, and every illegitimate child, her own self.

A priest had once spoken of a missionary colleague who had lived among a leper colony, and who began his homily every day with 'You lepers', acknowledging their disease, acknowledging his own decision to be among them. One day, he had instead begun with 'We lepers', and the condition had eventually killed him.

Unmarried mothers and their children did not have leprosy, but in Ireland right now, in 1941, they were seen as *lesser*, as flawed, as damaged goods. The only difference between Cora and Bronagh was that Bronagh's pregnancy had been successfully concealed, and Kathleen accepted as the girl's younger sister.

Now that she knew the truth, Kathleen could not un-know it. In an instant the knowledge had changed how she viewed herself, and Bronagh, and her parents.

*No.* They were her grandparents.

Anger boiled within her, making her hands shake and her insides tighten. She slammed a hand on the table, welcoming the pain that jarred up her arm.

Exhaling carefully, she went upstairs and opened the tiny wardrobe in the room she shared with Bronagh.

There it was – her blue dress. The one she had worn to her first ever dance, and had worn multiple times since, her figure having not changed much in the past few years. It was a thing of beauty, the tiny embroidered flowers, tucked bodice and full skirt never failing to make her feel pretty when she wore it. Removing it, she went to the mirror in the front bedroom and held it up in front of her, one last time.

Tears started from her eyes – the first tears she'd shed since discovering the awful truth. With resolution she bit them back, carefully folding the dress and putting it into a cloth bag beneath her bed.

★ ★ ★

Returning downstairs, Kathleen was mashing the spuds when Mammy and Daddy arrived, right on time. Bronagh joined them soon afterwards, and in the bustle of dinner and talk of the dreadful bombing raid on Swansea last week, no one seemed to notice anything wrong with Kathleen. *Nobody ever sees me. Not really.*

Always preferring to be quiet, never seeking to be the centre of attention. A grey mouse in the corner. Funny, she had never minded before. Mammy usually spoke for her in social situations, Therese at dances. Becoming a handywoman had helped her find out who she was, had helped her recognise her inner strength and find her voice.

She had even stood up to Mr McGowan that time when he had been in danger of losing the run of himself. Mrs Clarke and Peggy were her idols – calm women who managed to keep control in situations that might frighten the life out of most people.

But both Peggy and Mrs Clarke were respectable. Mrs Clarke had married a lawyer, Peggy a doctor. Kathleen herself would now be lucky to marry at all. An image of Liam came to her mind and pain stabbed through her. Dropping her eyes to her plate she chewed carefully, hoping no one would notice her distress. They knew she'd been up all night and was exhausted. That would surely be enough.

Daddy was still talking about the carnage in Swansea. Details continued to emerge about the ongoing rescue efforts following three nights of Nazi air raids which had ended on Friday just over a week ago. The Swansea Blitz, they were calling it. Hundreds were apparently dead, though as usual, the news was frustratingly vague – not wanting to give Hitler too much information about the impact of his raids.

'Swansea isn't that far away from us,' Daddy was saying, his expression grim. 'Less than 250 miles for a plane. Their range is getting longer now they have France and Holland. They bombed Wexford and Kildare, and even Meath, though they're saying it was accidental. And look at how they're hitting the port towns in Britain!'

Mammy glanced towards Bronagh, who was wearing a frown, and Kathleen, who was probably not looking her best, then looked back at her husband. 'Yes, well, nothing we can do about it, so there's no point in worrying over it, is there?'

He commented the whole way through dinner, and Kathleen came out of her own worries long enough to realise that yes, the likelihood of Nazi bombing raids here seemed to be increasing. Which was why she was training as an advanced first-aider, she reminded herself.

Going through to the kitchen, she started the dishes. 'What's that you're humming?' Bronagh's tone was sharp.

Kathleen started in surprise, then lifted her chin. '"My Aunt Jane". Why?'

'No reason. I thought that was it.'

Deliberately, Kathleen sang the song, a favourite among the girls playing in the street every day after school.

> *My Aunt Jane, she called me in*
> *Gave me tea outta her wee tin*
> *Half a bap with sugar on the top*
> *And three black balls outta her wee shop.*

She had been singing it for years in innocence, unaware that her 'sister' Jane was really her aunt. Now she sang it deliberately, wanting to cause Bronagh a moment's discomfort.

After they had gone again Kathleen finished cleaning the kitchen, then set off to visit Cora. She was a handywoman, and had responsibilities. That, thank God, was the one thing that hadn't changed.

★ ★ ★

Liam had spent the morning working on a back-yard shelter for one of the pensioners in Beechmount Street. It wasn't much, but it looked increasingly likely that Belfast would be targeted at some stage, so it was important to have as many shelters as possible. Mrs Kelly was grateful, and a little weepy, and Liam sat for a cup of tea with her before heading home.

It was early afternoon, and as he was passing Kathleen's house he couldn't help but glance towards it. Was she in there? God, he'd love to catch a glimpse of her.

There must have been some sort of magic in the air, for as he drew level the front door opened and she stepped out. As if conjured up out of his head, there she was, her shawl wrapped around her and a cloth bag in one hand, an unlit lamp in the other. Wherever she was heading, she mightn't be home before dark.

'Och, well, Kathleen!' he declared, hoping he wasn't sounding too enthusiastic.

Her head whipped round, eyes wide, then her expression closed. 'Well, Liam.'

This was the opposite of encouraging. Politeness alone meant they walked together to the end of the street. 'You going to somebody's house?'

'Aye. A baby born a week ago.'

'We haven't seen you for a while.'

'Aye. Been flat out.'

She was definitely cool with him. He tried a different tack. 'I was in with Mrs Kelly.'

'Very good. She likes a bit of company.' They had reached the corner. 'Right. See you.'

'See you, Kathleen.'

He walked on, feeling deflated. Now he had no girlfriend, no prospects, and even Kathleen Gallagher had gone off him. They had always got on well, and there had been a wee spark between them for years – or so he had believed. Well, whatever it had been, it wasn't apparent there now. Kathleen had been curt, and closed, and . . . distracted.

The girl was entitled to her own troubles. Maybe she was preoccupied with something else; maybe the baby she was going to visit was unwell. Maybe – a sudden notion struck him. Had she heard about Sadie slagging her off? Telling lies about her and Bronagh? Or had she realised he had deliberately avoided her that time?

God, he hoped not. Impulsively, he turned. She was only a few yards away. 'Kathleen!'

★ ★ ★

*Liam Flynn.* That was all she needed. Her naive former self had dreamed of him for years, not knowing she wasn't fit to be associated with a respectable family like the Flynns. The last time she had seen him he had avoided her – last Monday. A full week ago. God, she wasn't sure she'd ever gone a week in her life without seeing him.

He had avoided her. Almost as if he had *known*.

Who knew? Did everyone know? Was she the only person in West Belfast who had stupidly assumed that Bronagh and Kathleen Gallagher were sisters? Was everybody secretly laughing at her for being an eejit? Was she an object of pity? Her head was in turmoil, her stomach matching it.

*I am such a coward.* She had hidden away the evidence, and said nothing, complicit in the conspiracy of silence that had surrounded her since birth. But she was only one girl, and it all felt too much to take in. A full twenty-four hours had passed since her shocking discovery. It felt like forever, and at the same time she understood she was still stuck in the first moment of realisation. *Shock.* She should be on round-the-clock sweet tea. Like the McGowans. They, too, had experienced a shock a week ago. They needed her.

Squaring her shoulders, she decided to focus on her next task – checking on Cora and the baby, checking on the whole family. A shout came from behind her. 'Kathleen!'

She turned, confused. Liam was hurrying towards her and *oh!* It was impossible not to notice again how handsome he was.

'Kathleen.' He had reached her. 'I have to say sorry for something.'

She frowned, entirely bewildered.

'Last Monday. I was walking up the Falls. I was . . . annoyed about something. I saw you, and I couldn't cope with speaking to anyone at the time, so I went up Rockville Street so's I could be on my own. I didn't mean to be rude. Especially to you.'

His words came out in a rush. He was on edge, she sensed. But why?

'Anything I can help with?' Oh, why did she have to be such a damned handywoman all the feckin' time? The last thing she needed was to take on yet another person's troubles. Not today.

His gaze softened, and her stupid heart melted. *Liam. Feckin' Liam.*

'Me and Sadie broke up.'

Somehow, her hand was on his arm. 'I'm so sorry, Liam.' Sorry because he was sad. Not sorry because he was away from Sadie bloody O'Kane.

He shrugged, moving his arm so that his hand slid towards hers. 'It's for the best.'

'Was it – a mutual decision?' *Stop prying, for God's sake!* But she couldn't help herself. Not when his eyes were on hers and his hand had now enfolded hers in a warm grip.

'Not really.' He grimaced. 'There was a bit of a row at our house then she finished with me on the way home to hers.'

'A row?' She couldn't imagine Liam rowing with anybody. Like her, he was a quiet person. It was one of the things she liked about him.

His mouth twisted. 'Not me. Sadie and our Therese.'

Her eyes widened. 'Jesus! Now that I'd like to have seen!'

'So you didn't know about it?'

'No. I haven't seen Therese in over a week.'

He was grinning. 'Our Therese is quite the hallion when she gets going.'

'Aye, she sure is. So what was the row about?'

'Ach something and nothing . . .' His voice tailed off, then he shook his head. 'No. I can't lie to you.' He took a breath. 'Sadie said you and your Bronagh got her fired.'

Her jaw dropped. 'What? No way! I wouldn't *dream* of getting anybody fired!'

He squeezed her hand. 'D'ye think I don't know that? No, our Therese put her right – the mistress apparently said she was idling.' He sighed. 'Which is actually believable. Sadie is great and all, but . . .'

*There's no work in her.* The words hovered unsaid between them.

'Anyway. I wanted to make sure you're not annoyed with me.'

'I'm not annoyed with you.'

He grinned. 'Good!' He squeezed her hand once more, then stepped away. 'See you.'

'Bye, Liam.'

She walked on, her heart pounding and a strange sensation running through her, almost as if she was floating a foot above the footpath. Liam liked her. She knew he did. But did he also *like* her, in a particular way?

*God, don't you be reading anything into it!* Just because he and Sadie were finished (thank God) it didn't mean that he was even looking for a new girlfriend, never mind considering her as an option. And besides . . .

Her heart lurched as she remembered her secret. A secret so big it defined who she was. A secret that would change how people saw her, for it was changing how she saw herself.

The cloth bag was hanging from her arm, and briefly she lifted it, pressing it to her cheek as memories ran through her – of a snowy night, and a world full of possibilities. But that world was gone. She was now Kathleen not-Gallagher, a girl who didn't even know her father's name.

★ ★ ★

Cora's wedding took place the next day, with both the bride and the groom looking slightly bewildered throughout. Tony wore a suit that did not quite fit, while the bride wore a beautiful blue dress with tiny flowers embroidered on the bodice. The two babies – Cora's and Mrs McGowan's – were thankfully quiet during the administering of the sacrament, for the priest seemed not to be in a mood for joviality. The two baby girls were not twins nor even sisters, but aunt and niece. Such an odd thing, and with shades of the Gallaghers' fecked-up arrangements.

Kathleen had taken it upon herself to keep little Alice entertained, for it was hard to sit through a ceremony when you were three. Eventually the child settled on her lap, relaxing into Kathleen. Her blonde curls tickled Kathleen's chin, and she couldn't help but stare at the child's perfect little hands, with dimples at the base of each finger.

*Will I ever be a mother?* It was only two days since she had discovered the truth, and the questions were still piling up in her head. Question upon question, emotion upon emotion. The shock was still there, though not as acute. It was layered under anger, hurt, confusion, and worry. Worry about the future, about what would happen if the truth came out, about how her options had now changed.

Liam was free, but that didn't mean anything. And she had decided to stop hankering after him even before she had found the certificates. Their warm conversation last night hadn't changed anything, except for her now knowing that he hadn't avoided her because she was chasing him, or because he secretly knew she was illegitimate. No, he didn't need any particular reason not to have asked her out all these years, apart from not liking her the way she liked him.

And yet . . . her heart warmed as she recalled his hand in hers, the sincerity in his eyes as he'd told her about his break-up with Sadie, and his reasons for avoiding her that day. *I wanted to make sure you're not annoyed with me.* He was kind, she knew. And sensitive. He wouldn't want anybody to be annoyed with him. She stifled a sigh. Yes, perfectly understandable – and once again, nothing to suggest he *liked* her.

She was supposed to meet Johnny McQuillan on Saturday too. Maybe she should go ahead. Bronagh's life had been wrecked – no reason why Kathleen should quietly take her punishment too. The priest's homily had contained some pointed references to the forgiveness of sins. *They are not my sins*, Kathleen reminded herself. Why should she bear the consequences?

No one had even noticed. Here she was, going through inner turmoil, and not a single person in the world knew about it. Bronagh had maybe picked up on something, for last night she had commented on the fact she and Kathleen hadn't had a good conversation in a while. Kathleen had brushed it off as tiredness on her part, but it was astonishing to her that people couldn't see any hints of the feelings raging within her.

This was how it had to be. *Say nothin', and it isn't real.* Bronagh and the people she believed to be her parents had kept this secret for over twenty years. Maybe she would have to do the same.

# PART IV

# 26

*Monday, 7 April 1941*

> *Most ministers in the government of Northern Ireland believed it unlikely that Luftwaffe planes could reach Belfast from their bases in northern France. Only four public air raid shelters had been built in Belfast city centre, and the majority of the searchlights allocated to Belfast had been sent back to England. More than a thousand evacuees from England had arrived as the city was believed to be safe.*
>
> *In early April the head of the NI civil service recorded his 'relief' that the Westminster government was planning to allocate building materials for the construction of more shelters in NI.*

It seemed like any other Monday. Kathleen had spent the day in the Blackstaff Mill, walking home with Bronagh as if they were sisters. Therese's wedding was just over a week away – booked for Easter Tuesday when the mills would be closed for the holiday. Kathleen's friend had gone from being calm and prepared to being on edge and saying she was disorganised. Kathleen had reassured her as much as she could, reminding her that making her vows was the only thing that mattered.

*She has little to be worrying about.* Kathleen's discovery about her own past had made everyday worries shrink into insignificance.

In the evening she had joined Bronagh in the parish hall, which they and others from the new Women's Voluntary Service were setting up as a so-called 'rest centre'. The authorities had already commandeered local schools as rest centres to be used in the event of a raid damaging local houses, and now they were equipping buildings such as the parish hall to serve as reserve rest centres. Food, blankets, and even makeshift beds had arrived during the day, and another delivery of canned goods then landed in, meaning they had to reorganise the space once again.

'I dunno who they think is gonna eat all this!' Mrs McKenna, a widow from the Whiterock, tutted in irritation as she stacked cans of Heinz Oven Baked Beans with Tomato Sauce three high on the meagre shelves at the back of the hall. The top shelf was a little too high for her, and she stretched with effort to slide each can onto it. 'And it looks a sight! Our lovely parish hall . . . it's like a bloody jumble sale!'

To be fair, the hall bore little resemblance to the normally pristine venue for dances, meetings, and Christmas parties. Boxes and tea chests were piled everywhere, the twenty or so women busying around it all like ants.

'Let me help you.' Kathleen was a little taller, so could reach all the way to the back. 'Right, pass me them up and I'll arrange them.'

'Ah, thanks, Kathleen. We'll soon have it sorted between us.'

Out of the corner of her eye, Kathleen saw Bronagh give up and walk away. Back in the day, before everything changed, they'd have chosen to do a task together, working side by side. These days, Kathleen could barely look at her sister. The sister who was really her mother.

Carrying the knowledge was a burden that grew heavier by the day. Kathleen had known the truth for five weeks now, and it felt almost impossible to bear. How Bronagh and Mammy and whoever else had managed to keep the secret for more than twenty years was incomprehensible.

The war too, was affecting everything. Kathleen and Bronagh had both finished their training; Bronagh had qualified as an ambulance driver, while Kathleen was now a corporal in St John Ambulance.

Today's papers had carried news that they wanted to recruit another 450 auxiliary fire officers, which was hardly surprising given that the raids over in Britain had involved many incendiary bombs, or firestarters as they were known. For the auxiliaries to be going from only 150 to 600 full-time firemen was significant. Seány Flynn would likely join up; instead of risking life and limb among the same machinery that had killed his daddy, Seány would soon be running towards fires, trying to rescue people. But at least the work was better paid than the mills.

There had been some criticism of the slow growth in the numbers of firemen. Apparently the city of Glasgow fire brigade had seen a twenty-fold increase since the outbreak of war, whereas Belfast's fire service had only tripled in size. Seány and his colleagues could find themselves mightily overstretched if a raid ever happened, Kathleen knew. God, the very thought of it sent shivers through her!

An hour later they were done. Walking home with Bronagh, Kathleen could not help but notice that the moon was more than three quarters full, and anxiety pooled in her belly. Everyone knew the Luftwaffe attacked when the skies were bright, and unfortunately the cloud cover tonight looked to be breaking up. The full moon wasn't until Saturday, and all the nights before and after would be bright with the pale silvery light that now signalled danger, not romance.

'Kathleen, what's wrong?'

She stiffened. 'Nothing, why?'

'For the past few weeks something's been different about you. You're not happy.'

'In case you hadn't noticed, we're in the middle of a bloody war.'

'Aye. That's not it, though. There's something else. Is it – is it Johnny?'

Kathleen closed her eyes briefly at the mortifying reminder. She had walked out with Johnny for the entire month of March, had chatted with him and kissed him and held his hand. But it was no good. She was too messed up inside, too ashamed by her own past, too hung up on Liam . . . In the end, she had gently told Johnny that it wasn't working, and he had agreed, sadness in his eyes. A perfectly nice lad, and she couldn't even allow herself to *see* him properly.

'No. Me and Johnny broke up.' Nobody knew about the break-up yet. Neither she nor Johnny seemed to have got round to telling people. It didn't matter. Nothing mattered, really.

'But why? I thought he was lovely.'

Inside, Kathleen's self-control was thin, overstretched, fracturing. 'If he's so lovely, you go out with him, then!' she snapped.

Bronagh was frowning. 'I know we talked about Liam Flynn one time. Are you still—'

'No, it's not bloody Liam! Or Johnny!' The words erupted from her. 'Unlike you, I have the ability to live without a man!'

'What the hell does that mean? I haven't had a boyfriend since I was sixteen, and well you know it!'

The rage and hurt Kathleen had been containing for weeks had been unleashed, and she was lost to it. 'Bloody sures I know it!' The words erupted from her. 'It's the only reason I'm here, isn't it?'

They had both stopped, and in the moonlight Kathleen could see how pale Bronagh was. 'Wha-what do you mean?'

'I know, Bronagh. I *know*.'

'Kn-know what?'

'Jesus Christ, do I have to say it out loud?' She took a breath. 'I've seen my birth certificate.' Her tone was flat. 'And my baptism certificate.'

There was a silence. Bronagh looked like she was attempting to speak, but nothing was coming out.

'I know the truth, Bronagh. I know who you really are. You're not my sister.' *Not my sister. But by God, not my mammy either.* Oh, Bronagh had given birth to her, but even though her brain understood the facts, Kathleen could no more say 'Mammy' for Bronagh than she could fly.

'Well, thank God for that!' Bronagh had found her voice, though there was a clear tremble in it. 'I've been arguing with Mammy for months about telling you.'

'You have?' Vaguely Kathleen recalled sudden silences when she entered the house on more than one occasion. But she had passed no remarks, for all of them occasionally got annoyed with each other.

'Yeah. You have the right to know.'

'And?' *Too little, too late.*

'Mammy said she wouldn't even discuss it until you're twenty-one.'

'Mammy? *Mammy?* She's not my feckin' mammy!' Kathleen was almost shouting, her words hard as bullets in the night air.

Bronagh simply looked at her.

'And you were only sixteen when you got pregnant. She forced you to lie to me, didn't she? Didn't she?'

'I—' Bronagh's brow was furrowed. 'It wasn't that simple, Kathleen.'

'What's *simple* is that my entire life is a lie. Yours too!' She stabbed an accusing finger in Bronagh's direction, and Bronagh's face crumpled.

'I know! D'ye think I don't know? But what the fuck was I supposed to do?'

'I don't care!' It was almost a wail. 'I don't care! I just want to be normal again, and that's gone! *Forever!* Do you not get that?'

'I . . . Yes. Yes, I suppose I do.' She reached out a hand. 'I'm so sorry, Kathleen. Truly.'

Kathleen slapped her hand away. 'Aye, right. Sure you are.' Her tone was venomous, as pain raged through her. She *wanted* to be unkind, to hurt Bronagh and Mammy and God and the world. 'A pity you didn't think of that when you were letting some fecker have his way with you.'

Bronagh flinched.

'What was the point of me being such a feckin' good girl and keeping myself for marriage?' Her tone dripped with contempt. 'I'm illegitimate, Bronagh! An actual bastard. I have no *reputation*' – she almost spat the word– 'to protect! All my life I tried to be good. To do what I was told. To help others. And all my life I've felt I was never good enough for Mammy. Well, now I know why. I'm not even her child. I'm the reminder that her *actual* child got pregnant at sixteen!'

'No, Kathleen. She loves you! She loves the both of us!'

'Sure she does! That's why she never lets you out to dances, or anywhere you could meet a man. She's been controlling you – yes, and *punishing* you – for twenty years, and still you're sticking up for her! Sad, Bronagh. You just let her walk all over you. So did I. But that's gonna change. I don't owe either of yous anything.'

Turning on her heel, she marched off towards home. Where her heart should be was a cold hard stone. She was done with the whole feckin' lot of them. Bronagh. Mammy. Daddy. Liam. From now on there was only herself to worry about.

'Where's Bronagh?' Mammy's tone was sharp. Avoiding looking at her or Daddy, Kathleen went straight through to the kitchen, making for the outhouse. 'She's coming.'

Let them think she was in a hurry to use the toilet. She didn't care. After her ablutions she went straight up to bed, and was already pretending to be asleep by the time Bronagh came upstairs. *Feck you, Bronagh. And feck you, Mammy. Feck yous both.*

*11.55 p.m.*

Liam was lying wide awake, unable to sleep worrying about Kathleen Gallagher and why they so rarely saw her these days. He simply couldn't figure out why she had so abruptly changed. For she had changed.

Oh, she had accepted his reasoning for the day he had avoided her. Had been kind about Sadie. But there had been an aloofness in her that he had never sensed before. She still called at the house sometimes, but had been even less talkative recently – maybe because Therese's wedding chatter dominated every conversation at home. She was apparently walking out with Johnny McQuillan, a fella he knew from the football. Johnny was a good lad, and was said to be good-looking, so he might actually have a chance to keep a girl like Kathleen.

*What is that noise?* His breath caught as he heard the sounds they had all been dreading for months. First the unmistakable drone of aeroplanes, then the sirens. By that stage he was already up and donning his ARW uniform, Seány getting dressed beside him.

He had the whole Flynn family well-drilled, and so took comfort in the fact they had jumped out of bed so quickly. Mammy and the girls were even now heading through the house, clothes and blankets in hand, making for the tiny yard at the back where he and Seány had built the half-submerged shelter. Belfast was built on boggy land, the runoff from the hills, the frequent rainfall, and the nature of the rocks beneath leading to a plentiful supply of groundwater for wells and, more recently, pumps. The disadvantage was that when you started digging – as many men had discovered while building their Anderson shelters – the subsoil was hard to manage, and in many places was waterlogged. The Flynn shelter basically had a mud floor. *I wonder if I could get some gravel or flags from Seymour?* The truth was Liam had never imagined his family *actually* having to use it. Not really. Despite the fear, despite the news, despite all his training and preparation, it had been hard to picture a time when the Nazi planes would actually arrive.

Securing his helmet strap as he walked, and ignoring the occasional sounds of explosions and gunfire, Liam tried not to look at the sky. Instead he slid his ARW armband up his sleeve and set to work.

*Midnight*

There was a strange sound in Kathleen's dream. It started low, the pitch rapidly increasing along with the volume, piercing through to her brain with painful intensity. *Air raid siren!* Before she was even fully awake she was moving, rising, reaching for her clothes and shoes.

'Don't forget your gas mask,' Bronagh muttered, as the siren reached its height. Reaching under the bed she pulled out the two small boxes made of stiff cardboard, checking the luggage labels attached for the names. 'This one's yours.'

Within seconds they were heading downstairs, grabbing their ambulance bags as they went. Every night, Kathleen put her handywoman bag inside her large St John Ambulance bag, just in case. But she had never anticipated an air raid actually happening.

In the yard they joined Mammy and Daddy in the Anderson shelter that Daddy had painstakingly built six months ago, with the help of a couple of the neighbours. They had all helped each other – those who had bothered to build them. Others had laughed, saying the Nazi planes could never come this far.

As she crossed the few steps to the shelter entrance Kathleen had glanced anxiously at the dark sky, but could see nothing. *Where are they?* Was a gas bomb or an incendiary about to fall from the heavens, wiping out Kathleen and her entire family in an act of revenge for their sins? But no. There had been nearly twenty false alarms so far. No reason why tonight should be different.

She was wrong. 'Did you hear it?' Daddy asked. 'Bombs. And gunfire! I bloody knew it would happen eventually. Didn't I tell yous it would?'

'No, really? All I heard was the siren.'

'We better report for duty, then!' She and Bronagh quickly donned their St John uniforms, Daddy respectfully turning his back. It was safer to dress here rather than linger in the house. Tightening the slim belt of the dress around her waist, Kathleen wrapped her shawl around her and said, 'I'm ready.'

*Boom!* The sound of a distant explosion stopped them all in their tracks. The muffled thud of anti-aircraft gunfire followed.

'Do yous have to go, girls?' Daddy's face was in shadow, but Kathleen could hear the tightness in his voice.

'This is what we signed up for,' Bronagh replied crisply. 'Let's go, Kathleen.'

Daddy then Mammy held them each in a rough hug for a moment, then the girls stepped out into the night.

# 27

*12.20 a.m.*

People were everywhere, hurrying from their houses in various states of undress. Some were scurrying, even in the darkness, and Liam reminded them to walk rather than run. One man had his lamp open – a beacon in the darkness for any planes overhead. Sternly, Liam ordered him to hood the light, directing him to the large shelter on the main road. His mind was everywhere, his eyes darting left and right, looking for lights to be dimmed or people to be assisted. Families with elderly relatives or neighbours were helping them slowly along the footpaths, those lucky enough – or sensible enough – to have Andersons in their backyard or Morrison shelters in their homes would even now be cowering there, most likely praying for the all-clear.

As Liam had been appointed senior warden for this part of the Falls, he went round all the posts ensuring that the wardens were in place and patrolling their areas, then made his way towards the ARW meeting point, a disused shop on the northern end of the Falls Road that had been set up as Seymour's control centre. Slipping inside, Liam made his way through the darkened hallway and into the duty room, blinking at the light. Seymour was on the telephone, three other senior wardens already there pointing to the map.

'Well.'

'Well, Liam. Bombs at the docks.' *Four words. Only four words.* A shiver went through him. This was actually happening. Everything they had trained for, yet hoped would never be needed. The question as to whether the Luftwaffe could range this far had been answered in the worst possible way.

He stayed until Seymour had finished his call, clarifying that the activity so far was indeed limited to East Belfast and the docks. Everyone was on edge, the tension in the room palpable.

Once updated, Liam went back out into the silent darkness of the night. There was no light anywhere, and he felt as though he was looking out over a vast, empty plain. Never had he seen his city so quiet, so desolate.

Briefly, he allowed himself to think of his loved ones. His family, hopefully sheltering safely in the Anderson. Seány, waiting at the fire station to be called to who-knows-what. Kathleen, at the ambulance point, unless she was attending a woman in labour. He frowned. How could they best protect a woman about to give birth? The notion hadn't occurred to him before, and he resolved to ask Kathleen about it when next he saw her. *Kathleen.* Who was seeing Johnny McQuillan. Sighing, he put all of it out of his head and began making his way to his allocated zone.

*12.30 a.m.*

The ambulance station was an old single-decker bus that had been converted into a first aid centre in the large yard between the church and the parish hall. As soon as they arrived Kathleen and Bronagh were directed to help prepare station number three, where they would receive casualties assigned to them.

'I'm also a driver,' Bronagh reminded the coordinator.

'Good stuff. Bronagh Gallagher, right? We might need you to take casualties to the hospital as the night goes on. Depends.'

*Depends on how bad things get. Depends how badly people are injured.* Kathleen felt sick inside. This was nothing like her work as a handywoman. Being with women giving birth was hard work, but joyful. Being with someone at the end of their lives was a privilege. Tonight was different. Tonight, people's bodies might be ripped, broken, or burned, and she would have to tend them. Squaring her shoulders, she began setting out bandages and antiseptic. She was a corporal in the St John Ambulance now, and she could only do her best.

*1 a.m.*

Making his way carefully back to his assigned area, Liam made a tour of each warden's post, relaying information and checking that all was well. Many of the men had only signed up in the past few weeks, but they all knew this area like the back of their hands; every entry, back lane, and alleyway, every house on every narrow street. They knew who lived where, and had personally checked houses where they knew there were elderly people living alone, ensuring they had been brought to shelter.

Standing at the corner of the Falls and the Whiterock, Liam stiffened as he heard a distant bang. Somewhere to the east a bomb had just exploded – a bomb large enough to be audible all the way over here in the west of the city.

Muttering a prayer for whoever had been affected, Liam looked to the skies but could see little among the clouds. Exhaling, he resumed his patrol. It was all he could do.

*2 a.m.*

The ambulance station was eerily quiet. Sitting in the light and the warmth – for the converted bus even had heating – Kathleen felt guilty thinking of all of the people cowering in damp shelters, many of them standing holding babies and children. In the morning she suspected a lot of families would be putting chairs inside, or building shallow platforms for people to rest on.

No one was talking. They had all set out their stations with equipment and supplies, and the sense of waiting was everywhere, until a distant bang made them all exclaim in shock.

'Jesus, Mary, and Joseph!' One of the women at station two blessed herself, and then someone started a decade of the rosary followed by one of the litanies. The familiar words and the back and forth sequence was soothing, and would hopefully help someone affected by the terrible, terrible events now unfolding.

Mirror of justice . . . pray for us. Seat of wisdom . . . pray for us. Mystical rose . . . pray for us. Morning star . . . pray for us.

Oh, to see the morning star again! To have the sun come up and the planes go away. To go to work and cook dinner and have all her family safe!

She pictured Mammy and Daddy, cowering in the shelter, sitting all this time on the hard little bench that was the only furniture. A wave of love went through her. They were her family. As Bronagh was.

Suddenly the lies seemed to matter less, as Luftwaffe planes circled above, deciding where and when to release their deathly cargo. Family mattered. Like Bronagh, Kathleen was now probably destined to remain unmarried, to look after Mammy and Daddy as they aged. To accept her fate. Tonight, she prayed only that they would all be alive come morning. That would be enough.

*4 a.m.*

Liam was on his third tour of the area when the all-clear sounded. He had been hoping for it, as he had heard no explosions in the last half hour. Instantly a wave of relief rushed through him: his community was safe – for now. He put a hand on the wall beside him, breathing deeply. *I am alive. They are all alive.* Within minutes people began emerging from the main shelters, chattering and exclaiming. Some were weeping, but the majority seemed almost euphoric, so great was their relief. A few were injured, mostly twisted ankles or fall injuries from rushing to the shelters in the darkness. One woman was struggling to support her large husband as he limped along, and so Liam went to the man's other side. 'Let's get you to the first aid station,' he said. He knew he should be reporting back to Seymour as soon as he could, but he just had to do this one thing first.

*4.15 a.m.*

Ironically, the all-clear had signalled an inrush of casualties to the ambulance station. Kathleen and Bronagh strapped up ankles and made slings for broken arms, as well as tending to cuts some people had received from falling in the darkness. The radio announcements about what to do in an air raid always emphasised the need to walk rather than run, and this was why.

Amid the cuts, bruises, and strains, there were a few more concerning casualties. An elderly lady from nearby Clondara Street looked very unwell – her breathing rapid and shallow, her skin clammy, and her face pale. Medical shock, perhaps, or heart problems. Quickly they determined she would need hospital treatment, and Bronagh walked briskly outside to start up the ambulance as the others followed with the lady. The woman's daughter went with her, talking calmly to her the whole time. Once they had gone – Kathleen pausing for a second to wonder at the spectacle of Bronagh driving – she turned to go back inside, then paused as another small group of people were approaching, lamps well hooded. In the dim light she could make out three figures, the middle one limping and being supported by the others.

'Well,' she said softly, walking towards them, 'is there somebody who needs first aid?'

'Kathleen!' Her heart immediately began racing as she recognised the voice. 'This is Mr O'Donnell. He's hurt his ankle.'

'Well, Liam. Hello, Mr O'Donnell. Let's get you inside and I'll take a look at the ankle.'

'It's grand,' the man protested. 'Be fine in an hour or two. I didn't want to come but the wife insisted.'

'But nothing!' said the woman accompanying him, presumably 'the wife'. 'You'll get seen to, and that's that!'

'And sure why wouldn't you?' Kathleen allowed a little humour into her tone. 'It's free!'

'Well, there is that!' the man chuckled. 'Fair enough.'

Leading the way, she opened the door, noticing they were all blinking at the sudden light. 'Over here.' Indicating station three, she went ahead and pulled out a chair for the casualty. As 'the wife' was helping him into it, Liam straightened, catching Kathleen's eye, and she couldn't help smiling. Despite dealing with injured and upset people, the feeling of relief within was akin to joy. And now Liam was here.

'You all right?' he asked softly, and she nodded, a pang going through her at the warmth and sincerity in his eyes. Those gorgeous eyes.

'You?'

'Aye. Glad it's over.' His tone changed. 'Right! I better report to the duty room. All the best, Mr O'Donnell.'

'Thanks, lad,' the man said, and Liam left.

God, it was all so confusing! She had tried so hard to simply treat him the same way she treated Seány, but the truth was she had had a notion for Liam Flynn since she was no age, and it wasn't going anywhere. And him and Sadie hadn't got back together, despite Kathleen worrying they might. *Worrying?* Well, yes. She wanted him to be happy, and Sadie was far too self-centred. She'd have made his life a misery with her demands.

*I would never do that.* But there was no sense in even thinking about such things, not when she now knew the sordid truth about herself and her background. Fixing a bright smile to her face, she turned her attention to Mr O'Donnell.

*5 a.m.*

'Five confirmed dead so far,' Seymour announced crisply. 'Four firewatchers and a fireman. The papers have been instructed to play it down, though. Can't give the enemy any cause for celebration.'

*Celebration?* That ordinary working-class men had been forced to work as firewatchers was bad enough. The fact that it had exposed them to this level of danger was disgusting. And Seány was intending to apply for a full-time fireman role. He swallowed. No doubt people would say Liam was mad too, for becoming an ARW. While everyone else had been huddled in shelters, he and the other wardens had been assisting and patrolling.

One thing was certain; last night had proved the need, for Liam had had to remind dozens of eejits about blackout rules. One stupid fecker leaving a light on could have exposed their whole community to a higher risk of bombs being dropped on them.

After receiving all their updates Seymour sent a 'No Damage' report to the Belfast Civil Defence Headquarters. 'We were lucky last night, lads. Very lucky.'

As he had during their exercises – pretend emergencies – Seymour took them through the aftermath, leading a discussion aimed at working out what they could do better. Things that had worked well, things that had gone badly, new learning for the wardens. They discussed it all at length until the Stand Down orders came through. At that point Seymour thanked them once more, then dismissed them to go home to their beds.

As Liam walked towards Beechmount, dawn was breaking. The sky to the east was orange-pink and beautiful, belying the horrors that had unfolded in the city only hours before. Quietly entering the house, he saw that Seány was already back and asleep in the living room, and as he took to his own mattress he was filled with gratitude that his family was safe. But as he drifted off to sleep his thoughts, as always, turned to Kathleen.

# 28

*Tuesday, 8 April 1941*

> *On returning to their base in northern France, the Luftwaffe crews reported that Belfast's defences were 'inferior in quality, scanty and insufficient'.*

Kathleen had work in the mill the morning after the air raid, and the place was agog with stories of how people had felt on hearing the siren, how they had managed in the shelters, and what they would add to their air raid bag or shelter for the next time. Despite the lack of sleep, everyone worked their full shift in the mill, grateful for the wages. Afterwards, she and Bronagh walked together down the Falls Road in the late afternoon sunshine, the silence between them taut as a fiddler's bow.

'I'm going to say something to Mammy.' Kathleen's words were terse. When she thought about her family, her innards were a confusing mix of love, fear, and yes, anger. Last night she had felt love, anxiety, and relief that they were all safe. Today she was discovering it was possible to feel conflicting things at once. She could acknowledge she loved them all, yet still be raging at the lie that was her life.

'Do you think that's a good idea?'

She sent Bronagh an angry glance. 'You're not seriously suggesting I keep quiet after twenty years of yous holding secrets from me?'

'I suppose.' She exhaled. 'It's a nightmare. I'm so sorry, Kathleen. Nobody was trying to hurt you.'

*They may not have been trying to, but—*

Her thoughts were interrupted by a cheery greeting. 'Kathleen! Bronagh! Well, how are yous?'

'Cora!' Kathleen managed a smile. 'Well, what about you?' The young woman had her baby tied to her chest with her shawl, and had wee Alice by the hand. 'And hello, Alice!' Alice was Cora's little sister, the baby on her chest her own birth child, yet it wouldn't be obvious to a passing stranger if Cora was Alice's sister or her mother . . . This was how Mammy and Bronagh had managed it.

'I'm good thanks, Kathleen. Married life suits me!'

'Did you and Tony manage to find a house?'

'We did, aye. A wee kitchen house at the top of Dunlewey Street. Two bedrooms and all. We're just about managing the rent, but it's lovely to have our own place. Our Alice comes to stay with us half the time. Don't ya, Alice?'

Alice had slipped a little hand into Kathleen's and was looking up at her adoringly. 'Kathleen, Kathleen!'

She hunkered down so she was at the same level as the child. 'Yes, what is it, pet?'

'I got a sore finger.' She held up her other hand and Kathleen studied the tiny cut on her index finger.

'Aww, poor you. Did your mammy kiss it better?'

The little girl nodded solemnly. 'Kathleen.'

'Yes, Alice?'

'Will you come to my house again?'

'I will of course.' Her heart was hurting, knowing that brief connections with wee ones like Alice may be as close as she would ever get to motherhood.

'You've a great way with her,' Cora commented, as Kathleen straightened. 'She always bees talking about you.'

'Aww that's so nice. We're friends, aren't we, Alice?'

'Aye,' the child pronounced with great seriousness, and Kathleen ruffled her blonde curls.

Bronagh joined in. 'Wasn't that desprit last night, Cora?'

They stood on, chatting for a few minutes about the air raid. Neither Cora nor her parents had a shelter, apparently. 'Me and Tony took the baby and went to the big shelter up there on the Springfield Road.'

'And what about your ones?'

'Me da took the older ones up the road to the shelter, but Mammy and Alice and wee Mary went under the stairs. We have a wee cubbyhole there.'

Bronagh frowned. 'They don't recommend that, you know.'

Cora rolled her eyes. 'Here, you may have a go at trying to tell my ma, for she knows her own mind! Besides, there's literally not enough shelters for us all!' She readjusted the baby in her shawl slightly. 'Right, I better go. My fella will be wantin' his tea!'

They walked on, Kathleen pleased at Cora's confidence. 'She's enjoying being a married woman.'

'She is. Her own house, her man, her babby . . .'

'The independence.'

'Aye.'

'We'll never have that.'

'What do you mean?'

'Mammy is the boss of our house. I understand now why you never married, but so long as we live under Mammy's roof she'll be telling us what to do.'

'There's no reason why you can't marry, Kathleen.' Bronagh's brow was furrowed.

'Yeah, right. As if anybody I'd want to marry would want a bastard.' Her tone was harsh, and Bronagh flinched.

'Don't say that!'

'Why not? It's the truth! No point dressing it up with fine words.'

'I'm serious. You're smart, and good-looking, and kind. Any man would—'

'Even if they knew the truth?'

'Do you have to tell them?' She shook her head. 'Sorry. Of course you wouldn't want that between you. But a good man won't care.'

*I wouldn't ask someone like Liam to make that choice. Or Johnny either.*

'If that's true, then why are you still a spinster?'

'Because. . .' She exhaled. 'I told you before. I was hung up on Michael for too long. Like, years.' She grimaced. 'The romantic eejit that I was. And by the time I finally put him out of my head, all the good lads were married.'

'That fecker ruined your life.' *And mine. He has to be my father.* She wanted to ask, but the question stuck in her throat.

Bronagh sighed. 'Maybe. But I'm all right really. I have my work and my family. And I drove an ambulance last night!'

'You did.' She eyed her curiously. 'How was it?'

'Strange. Scary and exhilarating at the same time. That wee woman is doing all right, thank God.'

'Good.'

They were nearly home. 'Aren't you going round to Therese's tonight?'

'Aye. She's picking up her outfit the day.'

'Good. Think about what I said.'

*She means Liam. Impossible.* But there was no point in arguing. 'All right.'

★ ★ ★

'Well.' Liam sent Kathleen a crooked smile, making her heart seem to swell in her chest. 'Haven't had the chance to have the craic with you yet among all this excitement.'

'It's great news, though.' Therese had managed to get enough donated and swapped ration vouchers to get all the ingredients for a fruit cake. 'We'll have wedding cake after all.' She thought for a minute. 'Such a small thing, I suppose, but it'll make the day seem special.'

He nodded. 'Are you looking forward to it?'

'I am. God knows we need something to cheer us all up!'

'We do!'

'Kathleen!' Therese was calling from upstairs. 'I'm ready.'

Kathleen rose. Therese was trying on her wedding outfit and wanted Kathleen to get the full effect. Unusually, there were only the three of them in the house: Therese, Liam, and Kathleen. And Kathleen had just spent a butterflies-filled five minutes alone with Liam. 'I better go and see this dress!'

'Kathleen!' He caught her hand as she went to pass him, and all the breath left her body. 'I. . .' He seemed to falter. 'I need to talk to you properly about what we should do with a woman in labour during an air raid.'

He had let go of her hand, but it still tingled. 'Of course! When would suit you?'

'Tomorrow afternoon, maybe? Therese said yous aren't at the mill again until Thursday. I'm up at Seymour's in the morning.'

'Are you still helping with that paperwork?'

'Aye. I'm enjoying it, so I am.'

'Well, good for you! I'll meet you outside the parish centre at one, if that works?' *That's the end of Mammy and Daddy's dinner break, so I can hopefully avoid any awkward questions about where I'm goin' and who I'm meetin'.*

'Perfect!'

'Kathleen!' Therese was sounding impatient, so Kathleen gave Liam a farewell smile and headed up the narrow stairs. God, the way he'd looked at her there now! Almost as if . . .

# 29

*Wednesday, 9 April 1941*

> *The first raid of the Belfast Blitz, 7 April 1941, was later understood to be a test run to assess the city's defences. Given the events that followed, it subsequently became known as the 'Wee Raid'.*

'Lia—, er, William!' Seymour was calling, so Liam went back into the inner office. He had been working for Seymour for over six weeks now, part-time, and loving every minute of it. Seymour had seriously underestimated the amount of paperwork to be sorted, and kept extending Liam's involvement. The work was interesting, the wages excellent, and the effect on his self-confidence profound. Such a pity it couldn't last forever.

Stanley had arrived, and that did not bode well. Stanley was eccentric, entirely dedicated to his work, and strangely intimidating.

'Yes?'

Seymour nodded to Stanley, who declared, 'Not enough cement. Only four bags left. The boys'll be lookin' it for that job up at Dunmore, so they will.' One of Seymour's teams were repairing a wall and path outside the Jewish Club. Fleetingly, Liam wondered how many of the club members had family in Germany.

'Right. I'll get some ordered, if I can. How many bags?'
'Ten.'

'Look, why don't you go directly to William from now on, Stanley?' Mr Seymour was mopping his brow, seemingly more unsure of himself with Stanley than he was as group warden for the entire district. 'He'll sort you out.'

Stanley eyed Liam impassively. 'Aye. He gets things done, so he does. But he's not here every day.' He continued to stare at Liam, unblinking. 'When he's here there bees no ructions. Even if he is a taig.'

Liam gasped. 'Taig' was the derogatory word loyalists used to describe Catholics.

Well, he might have realised the boys here would work out he wasn't one of them. The hairs on his arms stood up as he realised he had developed a false sense of security these past weeks. He could be in real danger working here.

Seymour knew it too. Once Stanley had gone, he muttered, 'Sorry about that. He means no harm.'

'Aye.' Liam sensed no danger from Stanley. But if Stanley knew, then they all knew. And if things kicked off again it would take only one hothead with a gun to remember there was a 'taig' working in Seymour's office, slap bang in the middle of what they would see as *their* territory . . .

He shook his head, imagining the conversations. *Why did a taig get a good job like that? That job should have gone to somebody from our side, somebody local.* The thinking was the same on both 'sides', and was strongly influenced by what people perceived as a Catholic/Protestant 'area'.

He looked back at Seymour, deciding to be honest. 'But I need to think about whether it's safe for me to keep working here.' He hated saying it, for he loved the work.

He was using his brain, learning more and more each day, and he knew – without false modesty – that he was improving the efficiency of Seymour's entire operation. And Seymour knew it too. What had begun as a couple of days' work had become two or three days a week, every week.

Seymour sighed. 'I'm sorry, Liam. So sick of it.' His eyes narrowed. 'There's a thing I've been thinking of doing . . . maybe now's the time.' His gaze became intent. 'Give me a week or two, all right? I'll see what I can do.'

This was a bit cryptic, but Liam nodded. 'A week or two is all right. But the longer I stay . . .' He left the sentence unfinished, for they both knew the craic.

An hour later he was done for the day, and heading back to his own area. It was a good thing he hadn't quit his mill work during his recent employment with Seymour. To do so would have been foolish, for the work with Seymour had always been intended to be temporary.

This lucrative, enjoyable job would have to end, and Liam would have to go back to near-poverty and his only work being the grinding, exhausting, soul-destroying labour of the mills. But there was many's a one with worse troubles to bear . . . He thought of the firewatchers and the fireman who had died on Monday night. They would have had families. Loved ones who were grieving today. He was alive, and he intended to stay alive. If that meant leaving the best job he had ever had, then so be it.

His heart lifted as he thought about his next assignment: meeting Kathleen. Kathleen wasn't a lit match, like Sadie. Instead her light was like the steady warm glow of a candle; just being in her company was enough to brighten his day.

He might be losing his job, but at least today he could enjoy the company of the best-looking girl in West Belfast.

★ ★ ★

Kathleen's excitement was like a fever. Only twenty minutes until she would go and meet Liam. Oh, she shouldn't read too much into it. She knew that. He wanted to talk about supporting women should there be someone in labour during an air raid. Very sensible. But Kathleen was not feeling in the least sensible. And that was not the best frame of mind to be meeting Liam.

Did he like her? God, she wished she knew. She saw signs sometimes: a look in his eyes, the way he spoke to her, the way he took her hand every chance he could . . . She had tried so hard to keep a distance since hearing the truth about herself, but it had been hard, especially since he and Sadie had split up. She had managed to dance with Liam at the last céilí and remain cool, even though her heart had been pounding fit to explode. Sadie had been there with her new fella – a lad called Barney – but Liam had seemed unbothered.

And now, today, she was meeting him. Only the two of them. A wee bit further down from the parish centre was the Falls Park. Could they maybe . . .? The last thing she wanted was anybody seeing them and making something out of nothing.

'Kathleen! Answer me when I'm talking to you!'

Mammy sounded cross. 'Sorry, what did you say?'

Mammy tutted. 'I am sick of you giving me cheek and disrespect.' Bronagh and Daddy had stopped eating; nobody liked it when Mammy delivered one of her occasional rants.

'If you're not lyin' in your bed you're out gallivanting with thon Therese,' she continued, her face *dearg le fearg* – red with anger. 'Well, it's gonna stop, you hear me? Sick of it, I am!'

Kathleen's jaw dropped, then anger raced through her. She was angry a lot these days. The only time she slept late was when she had been out during the night as a handywoman, and Therese was taking up so much of her free time because of the wedding in a few days. *Enough. No more.*

Rage rose within her. 'Aye, well I'm sick of you talking to me like I was ten! I'll be twenty-one in December and you're still at it! Still telling me what to do!'

'Kathleen Gallagher!' Mammy's face was now almost purple with outrage. 'I'll be telling you what to do till the day I die! I'm your mother!'

'No, you're not!' Kathleen pushed back her chair with an audible scrape. 'You're not my mother. She is!' She jabbed her fork in Bronagh's direction. 'And yous have all been lyin' to me my whole feckin' life!'

# 30

'Kathleen!' Bronagh was ashen, her voice little more than a croak.

'And my surname isn't Gallagher! There is literally no father on my birth certificate! I'm a bastard!'

'Jesus, Kathleen!' Daddy was pale too. 'No need for that. Now calm down and we'll explain. You see—'

'No!' Nowhere inside was there a place of calm, and Daddy telling her to 'calm down' had simply fuelled the flames – as if her anger wasn't allowed. Her heart was pounding fit to burst, and she could feel her stomach sick and her palms damp. 'Yous are all liars, every feckin' one of yous!'

Daddy winced, while Mammy's expression hardened. 'Not by choice. If our Bronagh hadn't let some fella have his way with her, none of it would have happened.'

'And I wouldn't exist! Is that what you're sayin'? That yous would all be better off if I'd never been born?'

'Now don't you be putting words in my mouth, miss!' Mammy looked fierce. 'That's not what I'm sayin', and well you know it!'

'Do I? Everything I thought I knew turned out to be wrong, so why the hell should I believe anything yous three say to me ever again?' She glared at them.

'If you would just listen for a minute—' That was Daddy, ever the peacemaker. Oh, Kathleen could see how uncomfortable he was – how they all were. But she didn't give a flying fuck.

'Go on, then!' she challenged. 'Tell me all about it! How exactly did I end up being lied to my whole life – a bastard without a father?'

'Your *father*,' Mammy snapped, her tone contemptuous, 'was apparently a married man that our Bronagh was stupid enough to . . . to . . .'

'That's not true!' Now Bronagh was fired up too. Her face twisted. 'I only told you that so you would stop torturing me.'

Mammy's jaw dropped. 'He wasn't married? So we could have found him and made him marry you!' She rolled her eyes. 'Jesus, how stupid can one girl be?'

Bronagh's voice dropped, her expression closing. 'Not stupid. Realistic. He dumped me and disappeared. Last thing I wanted was to be forced to marry somebody who would hurt me every day of my life.'

'I cannot believe I'm hearing this!' Mammy's face was now somewhere between red and purple. 'To think of the lengths I went to . . . I should have bliddy left you with them nuns in the laundry.'

'Aye, you'd have liked that, wouldn't you?' Bronagh's voice shook with emotion. 'Years of so-called penance for my sins, and the baby taken off me!' She glanced towards Kathleen, her expression ferocious. 'At least this way I got to keep my baby, even if I had to pretend she was my sister.' Her voice softened. 'You were always mine, Kathleen. Always.'

A million memories flooded through Kathleen's mind. Bronagh tending to her as a child. Bronagh taking her for walks, helping with homework, telling her stories. Listening to her. *Loving her.*

'You were never not mine, Kathleen,' Bronagh muttered fiercely. 'No matter what they all said.'

'Aye, well the least you could do was rear her, after getting yourself in trouble like that.' Mammy was unrepentant. She pronounced it 'rare' rather than 'rear' as everyone did around here, but it suddenly struck Kathleen that, although her upbringing had been 'rare' – unusual and different as it turned out, she had not lacked for anything. Food, clothes, schooling, fun . . . love. Abruptly, the anger drained out of her.

'I was well reared,' she said quietly. 'I only wish yous had all told me.'

'I know, and I'm sorry.' Bronagh's voice cracked.

'It wasn't easy for your mammy either.' Daddy's voice was low. Noting fleetingly that no one was calling Bronagh her mammy, Kathleen considered this. She didn't have to seek too far in her memories to find examples of Mammy being loving. Hugs, and treats, and letting her away with things at times. It had been Mammy who had scraped the money together to buy her the beautiful blue dress for her sixteenth birthday. The dress she had recently given away.

She sighed. It was all a feckin' mess.

'So, who *was* the father?' Mammy's question was directed to Bronagh, her tone sharp, and Kathleen held her breath. *Who's the father?* Cora's da had asked the same of her.

'He was a young fella from Dublin. He was my boyfriend that spring.' She grimaced. 'The only boyfriend I ever had.'

There was pain in her eyes. 'He said he'd write to me once he went back to Dublin, but he never did.'

'Right.' Daddy looked angry. 'If I got a houl' of him—'

Bronagh grimaced. 'Water under the bridge. It was over twenty years ago.'

'Was it . . . was it that fella Michael – the one you told me about?' Kathleen's voice sounded small.

'Aye.'

There was a silence. 'Finish your dinner,' said Mammy. 'No point in good food goin' to waste.'

'I'm not hungry.'

'You'll follow the crows for it some day,' said Mammy firmly; a throwback to the Great Hunger that had plagued Ireland less than a century ago. 'Just eat it.' Kathleen hesitated, but Mammy added in a kinder tone, 'That's the girl. You'll be glad of it.'

And so Kathleen sat, forcing herself to eat the remainder of her meal, such as it was. Spuds, turnip, and cabbage. And yes, her ancestors would have been glad of it.

They were still her ancestors, she mused, as the table went silent but for the sounds of dinner and the ticking of the clock. All Mammy's side and Daddy's side too. They were all part of her. She hadn't lost a single one of them.

They left soon afterwards, all three of them, for Bronagh had been given an extra shift in the Blackstaff Mill. She always got more shifts than Kathleen, for Kathleen was often busy with her handywoman work. Luckily, the mistress took it into account, giving Kathleen flexibility that wasn't permitted to any of the other girls. Well, and why wouldn't she, since Mrs Murphy was her sister, and had raved to the mistress about what a good handywoman Kathleen was?

Kathleen washed up, enjoying the stillness. Gradually her agitation was settling, replaced by a sense of relief. *At least we all know that we all know.*

Shaking her head at the convoluted thought, she allowed herself to think about what lay ahead: an uninterrupted conversation with Liam-dreamboat-Flynn. Even if her destiny was to end up unmarried like Bronagh, she could still enjoy a few precious moments here and there, could she not?

# 31

The day was mild so she left her shawl at home, enjoying the sense of anticipation inside as she made her way down through Beechmount, noticing all the babies sleeping in prams outside the front doors. It was a lovely thing, the way people put the babies out like that, then carried on with their housework knowing they'd hear the child's cry if it woke up. Until recently Kathleen had assumed she might one day be a mother too. *Bronagh was never allowed to be a mammy.* What a mess!

*There he is!* 'Well, Liam!' She gave him her brightest smile, a strange recklessness running through her. Dimly she knew it had been formed of many elements: the air raid dangers and subsequent relief, the row with her family, her steely determination to accept her lot like a good girl, yet at the same time rebel against it. *A feckin' good girl. Feck that!*

'Kathleen!' His eyes roved her face. 'You're lookin' well.'

'Thank you.' He had joined her, and they turned and walked together away from the Whiterock, from St James's, from Beechmount. Like her, was Liam seeking a bitta privacy for their walk? Even if he was, she shouldn't read anything into it. They both knew this was to be a professional conversation, but if anyone saw them together they might get the wrong impression.

They chatted easily as they went; about the nice weather, Therese and Jimmy's upcoming wedding, Christine's new boyfriend. Hard to believe the girl had turned seventeen and was walking out with a fella! Already, Kathleen was getting too old for a match. *Spinster, spinster.* Reminding herself that the spinsters in the days before the mills were highly-skilled women who made so much money out of spinning that they didn't need to marry, she walked on. They crossed the road then, and entered the Falls Park, even though neither of them had suggested it out loud. *Our minds are in harmony.* It was a nice thought.

It was Holy Week, with lots of different ceremonies at St John's church, so she would see plenty of Liam this week anyway. But this? This was special. The park was beautiful; gentle paths through lush lawns and groves, and the trees in their fancy spring clothes, leaves bright and fresh, new blossoms exploding, and daffodils nodding by their feet. The beauties of nature, a fine spring day, and Liam by her side.

'Therese and Jimmy are gettin' their keys tomorrow,' he offered. The pair had arranged to rent a nice wee house in the Whiterock Estate, and would be cleaning and tidying it over the next few days in the run-up to the wedding. Liam's expression was mixed, suggesting that he was pleased for them, yet . . .

'Are you sad at her leaving the house next week?'

'Aye. Everything's changing.'

'I know. But she's happy, so . . .'

'She is. And I wouldn't want her to be stuck living with us like an old maid. I'm glad she and Jimmy are getting married. And he's doing fairly well as a brickie so they should be all right for money.'

Kathleen winced.

'What? Have I annoyed you?' His brow was creased. 'What did I say?'

'Old maid. Sorry, it's just me.'

He eyed her dubiously. 'Your Bronagh could marry yet. It does happen, you know.'

*It wasn't Bronagh I was thinking of.* She shook her head. 'In theory it does.'

He looked away. 'I heard you're doin' a line with Johnny McQuillan.'

'Not any more.'

His head whipped round, and the intensity of it all was too much for her. 'Anyway.' Her tone was brisk. 'Air raid planning.'

'Aye. What if there's a woman that goes into labour?'

'I've been thinking about this since you mentioned it. Talked to Peggy Sheridan about it too. The thing is, women's bodies are smart. Labour only really gets going when women feel safe and relaxed – very unlikely if there's an air raid. So there's probably only a small chance of a woman going into labour properly during an emergency. And even if she's in early labour it'll all stop once she gets annoyed. I've seen it happen when there's trouble in the street outside a woman's house. Once she hears it and stiffens up, the contractions slow right down and can end up stopping. Peggy says it happens in the hospital a lot when women get disturbed.'

'Well that's good!' He shook his head in wonder. 'I suppose nature would have to have a way – women could be in natural disasters, wars, anything!'

'Houl' on, though. There's more.' She took a breath. 'If the baby wants out then it'll come out eventually. Labour will usually only pause for a few hours, a day at most. And if the woman is too far on it won't be able to stop even if the house is comin' down around her.'

'I see. So what should we do, if we hear of a woman in that situation?'

'The best thing would probably be to get her to the hospital. The Royal has a maternity hospital now.'

'Right. So she's a casualty, but a different kind of casualty.'

'Aye.' He was looking at her – one of *those* looks – and her heart was thundering. They had stopped beneath an apple tree, and a gentle breeze was sending white blossom drifting to the ground like snowflakes.

'You're amazing, Kathleen!' His voice was low, his gaze intent. 'That's exactly the information I needed.'

'Here, steady on!' She tried to give a light laugh, but could hear a tremor in her voice. 'I'll end up with notions about meself if you keep saying things like that!' *God, keep saying things like that!*

'I'm glad to know you, Kathleen Gallagher.'

There was a pause, and then his face was bending closer to hers, and – *Oh, God, is he wantin' to kiss me?* Time seemed to stand still as she realised this was really going to happen. She lifted her face towards his. *Liam! Liam Flynn!*

'And you *should* have notions,' he was murmuring, 'for I have a few notions meself . . .'

Their lips touched, feather-light and fleeting. They touched, touched, and touched again. And then – then the kiss deepened, and Kathleen was lost. His arms were around her, and hers were sliding round his back, and his warmth was against her. God, this was even better than she remembered! Her eyes were closed, and now their tongues were dancing a slow reel of sensation. How long the kiss lasted, she had no idea, for time was meaningless.

They parted then, to look into each other's eyes. Kathleen's heart was pounding, she could feel her pulse throbbing, and her knees felt so weak it was as though the bones had softened. Who knew that was actually a real thing?

Had she felt like this at sixteen, when he'd last kissed her? She could dimly recall the impact of it, but not the detail. The sensation of his lips, his tongue, his warm, firm body . . . Back then, she had probably seemed too young for him. Now, though. Now she was a young woman and he a young man, and there was nothing to stop them—

*Jesus!* How could she have forgotten the most important fact about her? Her expression must have changed, for his went from bemused wonder to confusion.

'What? What's wrong, Kathleen?'

'I—Liam!' Sorrow and longing rose within her. 'I can't! I shouldn't!'

'Why not?' His eyes widened. 'Is it about Johnny McQuillan?'

'Johnny . . .?' For a moment, she couldn't work out who he was talking about. 'No, we only walked out for a few weeks there. I've never had a proper boyfriend, as you probably know. And I've only ever kissed a few fellas.'

'How many have you kissed twice?' His eyes held divilment. 'And I don't mean twice in the same session, if you know what I mean . . .' He kissed her again, and this time his kiss was hard and demanding. She met his passion with her own, desire rising within her – a hunger that she had not known even existed. This time when they parted they were both breathless.

'Jaysus, Kathleen!' His voice cracked. 'Have you magic in you or something? I've had many's a kiss, but that has never happened to me before.'

'Me neither.' She took a slow breath, in. . .out. 'And I've only kissed a few fellas on more than one separate occasion, which is the information you were fishing for.' She was trembling from head to toe, and his arms tightened about her.

'You all right?' She nodded. 'That was really something, Kathleen Gallagher. Hidden arts, you have.'

She was frowning, as his use of her surname reminded her that she didn't really have a surname. Or a father.

'There's things you don't know about me, Liam.'

'What's that supposed to mean? I know an awful lot about you. Sure, you're never out of our house!'

'Aye, but you know the old sayin'. *Ní mar a shíltear a bhítear.' All is not what it seems.* 'I should tell you—'

She stopped. Liam had kissed her, but she shouldn't assume he wanted her to be his girl. If she told him her big secret would they both be scundered and would she always regret slabbering to him? 'That's true. I'm never out of there.' She tried to laugh it off. This was probably just a kiss to him. Nothing more.

His eyes narrowed, and she realised she had stiffened. Instantly he let her go; clearly he was too much the gentleman to ignore the signal.

'I'm serious. I want to know what's annoying you.' He was using 'annoyed' in the local sense, which meant upset rather than angry. Somehow, he could tell. *Because he knows me.*

'Are you, though?' she asked. 'Serious, I mean. Serious about' – she gesticulated vaguely –'this?'

'What "this" do you mean?' He leaned closer. 'Oh, do you mean *this*?' His lips brushed hers – the slightest of touches, giving her every opportunity to move away.

Moving away would be the sensible thing to do. The wise thing. The prudent thing. And so Kathleen claimed his lips with hers, slanting to angle her mouth just right. This time, it was she who pulled him close, and he responded with the same passion from a moment ago.

*God, this is amazing!* The half-formed thought encouraged her to make a memory of the moment, and so she tried to note everything she could about the sensation of his tongue in her mouth, their two tongues dancing, his hands stroking her back . . .

This time when they stopped she rested her head against his strong chest, drinking in the delicious scent of him, feeling the warmth of his skin and the distant thumping of his heart through his cotton shirt. Closing her eyes, she slid her arms down to his waist, noting how wonderfully his body narrowed from the muscular breadth of his chest and shoulders to the slimness of his hips. *He is perfect.*

His arms were still around her, holding her close, his hands gently stroking her back. Now he rested his chin on her head, and now he moved his upper body to press a small kiss on her head. And all the while, white petals danced about them.

If ever there had been a better moment in her life, Kathleen could not recall it. She was in the arms of the man she loved, and even if it was all about to end, she would never, ever forget.

# 32

Liam was in dreamland. Finally he had Kathleen in his arms, and those kisses – *my God!* Never had he experienced anything like it, and he had kissed a fair few girls in his time. These were more than kisses, because they were fuelled by more than his body's needs. *This is Kathleen!* Dimly he realised that he would never again kiss anyone but her, but the thought filled him only with joy.

Ever since Da had died and he had had to grow up too soon, his life had felt full of burdens, as though he were carrying darkness within him. *Kathleen brings light everywhere she goes.* And she was in his arms, no one else's. How lucky he was, how blessed! Momentarily he allowed himself to think about the kiss they'd shared one magical snowy night, a long time ago. The hints had been there even then, but he'd had to ignore them. They had both needed to grow up, and he had to be sure she was coming to him as an equal, not a green girl with a notion on her best friend's brother.

*There's things you don't know about me.* What could she be referring to? She had asked him if he was serious, and he sensed he needed to answer that question before she would tell him what was on her mind. Leaning back, he bent to kiss her cheek, her ear, her cheek again. She looked up, her expression one of joy, and his heart literally seemed to swell in his chest. But there were greater things at stake than him simply claiming another kiss.

'Kathleen.'

'Mm-hmm?'

'Yes,' he said, and she looked confused, as if struggling to understand what he was saying yes to. 'To answer your earlier question, yes, I'm serious. About you. I'm cracked on you, Kathleen. Do you not know that?'

'You are?'

He nodded. 'And I'm hoping you like me too. Enough to . . .' He swallowed, aware of his own nerves. So much hinged on this conversation. 'Enough to be my girl.' There was no response. Her eyes were wide, but she seemed frozen. *Is this a shock to her?* 'Kathleen, I'm more serious about this than I've ever been about anything.' Her eyes clung to his, but she didn't speak. Her expression suggested some sort of inner turmoil, but what?

'Let's sit and talk.' He indicated the summer seat a little way ahead, and they walked towards it hand in hand. *God, I can't wait to do this in public, and let everyone know that I've managed to catch the best girl in West Belfast!* If he in fact had.

They sat, and she very deliberately withdrew her hand, her expression closed.

Cold fear made his insides clench. *What the fuck is happening?* Never would he make a girl feel uncomfortable by pursuing her against her wishes. But he *knew* Kathleen, and he knew she liked him. Or were his instincts wrong? Had he wished for this so long and so deeply that he was imagining things? *But no.* Her reaction to their kisses . . .

*All I can do right now is be patient, and listen.* His mouth dry, he waited for her to speak.

'I have to tell you the truth, but I want you to promise you'll never share this with another living soul.'

'Of course. I swear to God.' *What is this?*

She nodded, then took a breath. He could see she was suffering, and he so wanted to take her hand or put an arm around her, but she had chosen to sit close but not touching. He had to respect that. Besides, he couldn't think straight when he was touching her, and this was important. He needed his wits about him.

'I'm not who you think I am. I'm not good enough for you, or for any respectable fella. Because I'm not respectable myself.'

He couldn't help it; a bark of laughter escaped him. 'Not respectable? Jaysus, Kathleen, what are you on about? Your ones is one of the most respected families in Beechmount, and you're an absolute lady. What do you mean, not respectable?'

'I'm illegitimate.' Her tone was harsh, and he sensed a little of the emotion behind her words. 'My parents are not really my parents.'

'What? What?' His mind was working furiously. *Adopted? But—* 'But you're the image of your Bronagh. Aye, and your da too.'

She shook her head slowly, eyes closed briefly, then she looked him straight in the eye. 'He's not my da. He's my granda. Bronagh is the one who gave birth to me.'

Instantly it all made sense. A wave of shock ran through him. *Bronagh is her real mammy.*

'Bronagh.' Twenty-one years ago, Bronagh Gallagher had become pregnant. The child had been raised as

Kathleen's sister, which wasn't that uncommon. What was a little surprising was that it had happened to a Gallagher. In his (albeit limited) experience, the girls who signalled they'd be up for. . .er, more *action* often seemed to be unhappy, troubled girls from unhappy, troubled families. Not like the Gallaghers. The Gallaghers were . . . *respectable.*

And as a respectable lad, he had always avoided those other girls. Not because they were willing to do things with boys, or because he judged them for it, but because he had enough on his plate without taking on someone who might well cause havoc for himself and his own family.

She was looking at him, her face twisted with anxiety.

'Yes. The person I was told was my sister is actually my mother.'

'And you're angry about it.' He shook his head in bemusement. 'When did you find out?'

'February.'

'This year?'

She nodded. 'I needed my birth certificate for the advanced first aid.'

'Do they know that you know the truth?'

She nodded. 'They do now.' She grimaced. 'Bit of a row in our house over dinner there now.'

He nodded sympathetically. 'I can imagine!'

'Please don't let on you know! Don't tell anybody!'

'I swear. I'll tell nobody.' He eyed her curiously. 'Who all knows?'

'I *hope*, nobody. I was born in Dublin while Mammy and Bronagh were down there, supposedly working.'

'Were you, now?' He whistled. 'This is some story!'

'I know! Shocking.' Her expression closed. 'So now you understand why I can't be your girl.'

'No.' She seemed to crumple, so he hurried to explain. 'No, I don't understand. Why, exactly, can you not be my girl?'

Her brow furrowed. 'I'm after telling you. I'm illegitimate. I'm not respectable.'

'What has that got to do with anything?' He would have to handle this carefully, he knew. 'The news about your birth must have come as a shock to you. You don't hear stories like that every day. But it doesn't change who you are as a person. As I said a minute ago, you're a *lady*, Kathleen Gallagher.'

'But Gallagher isn't even my right name! I don't know who my father was. Bronagh only ever had the one boyfriend, but he wasn't from here. I don't know his surname.'

'Well, if he left Bronagh in the lurch like that, would you even *want* his surname?' She shook her head. 'Well, then. Gallagher is a good name. And you're entitled to use it. It's on your birth certificate, right?'

'Well yeah, but—'

'But nothin'. In some countries a girl takes her mammy's surname anyway.'

'Is that right?'

'Aye.' He hoped she wouldn't question him further on this as his knowledge was limited. *Iceland, maybe.*

'So you don't mind?' She looked hopeful, and small, and his heart turned over at the desperation he saw in her eyes.

Daringly, he took her hand. 'Not in the slightest! We're a good match, you and me.' He smiled. 'Both lacking a father!'

'Aye, well at least yours is just dead!' She clapped her free hand to her mouth. 'God, I'm sorry, Liam. I didn't mean—'

He was chuckling. 'I know what you meant. Now, seriously, are you going to be my girl, Kathleen Gallagher?'

'I would love that.' She sent him a shy smile, and his heart soared. And then they were reaching for one another, and his heart was pounding at the sheer big-ness of the moment.

Kathleen Gallagher was his girl, and for a brief moment all was well in the world.

# 33

*Easter Tuesday, 15 April 1941*

> On Easter Sunday, Pope Pius XII broadcast a message asking listeners to pray for peace. He also called for an end to attacks against civilian targets. On Easter Monday sirens sounded briefly in Belfast as a Nazi reconnaissance plane was spotted over the city.

Therese Flynn and Jimmy McKeown were married on a cloudy Easter Tuesday in 1941. The two families were well known in the area, and as they emerged from St John's there was a fair crowd to salute them and their guests. Yesterday being Easter Monday, and twenty-five years since the Easter Rising, every man, woman, and child that Kathleen had seen that day had worn a badge depicting the Easter Lily, the symbol devised by Cumann na mBan – the league of women rebels – in 1926 to commemorate those who had lost their lives in the Rising.

Commemorative events had been banned, of course, and all day the police tenders had patrolled the Falls – particularly the area around Milltown Cemetery, in case the people of the area had wished to gather to remember those who had died in the Rising. It had given the preparations for Therese and Jimmy's wedding day an extra poignancy, particularly with this new threat of Nazi bombers hanging over everyone.

Therese looked beautiful in her wedding suit, a high-waisted green rayon dress with matching coat that Mrs Doherty the local dressmaker had made for her. Her shoes had been dyed to match, and the whole outfit was finished off with fine nylon stockings, delicate gloves, and a stylish felt hat worn at a cheeky angle.

Kathleen hugged her friend outside the chapel. 'You look wonderful! Congratulations, Mrs McKeown!'

'Mrs McKeown!' Therese beamed back at her. 'I'm Mrs McKeown!'

'It's a long time since that first dance in the hall here!'

'It is. And now the same spot is for the wedding breakfast!' All the Flynn women, along with Kathleen and Bronagh and a few of the neighbours, had tidied up the hall yesterday, moving all the beds and emergency equipment into the bottom end of the long hall, then laying out tables and chairs at the top for the breakfast. Even now, various neighbours and cousins would be heading to the hall to get the tea on.

'Congratulations, Jimmy!' Kathleen pressed a kiss to his cheek. 'You've a fine wife there!'

'I have, and well I know it!' Jimmy looked handsome in his suit and fedora, and Kathleen was delighted for the both of them. Deliberately, she went round every one of the Flynns, congratulating them and complimenting them. Which meant that when she and Liam finally came together, people would be less likely to think anything of it.

'Well, Liam.'

'Kathleen! You look stunning!'

'Thank you!' Her eyes were devouring him – the suit, the hat, the warm look in his eyes . . . They had decided to keep their relationship a secret for a few days, so they wouldn't take the shine off Therese and Jimmy, but soon everyone would know they were going with each other. For now, though, there was something decidedly exciting about the fact that only they knew.

He kissed her cheek and she felt herself flush. God, what was this fire that flared up within her every time he was near? He had always been something of an obsession with her, but since their talk and kisses in the park a few days ago, she had been living in some kind of dreamland. They had met secretly every day – sometimes only for a few minutes – but had managed to kiss each time. *Liam. Only Liam.* He was the last thing on her mind when she closed her eyes to sleep, and her first thought on waking up.

*And he is all mine!* Astonishingly, Liam genuinely didn't seem to care that much about the fact she was Bronagh's child, and the natural daughter of who-knew-whom? Briefly, her mind drifted to the identity of her mysterious father, but she dismissed the thought. The man had treated Bronagh appallingly; he didn't deserve a moment of her time.

'Hello, Liam.' The voice, sickly sweet and coy, made Kathleen's gut twist in reaction. *I know that voice!*

'Sadie.' Liam's tone was flat. 'I didn't expect you here today.'

'Well, of course I wanted to come. Me and Therese are friends, after all.'

Kathleen held her face very still. *I don't think Therese would see it that way.*

'And you and I are friends too, Liam, aren't we? After everything we meant to each other . . .' She sent him a winsome smile.

*Oh God!* Kathleen was feeling desperately uncomfortable. The whole thing was so awkward. *I have to get away!*

Glancing around, she spotted Peggy Sheridan and her big, handsome husband, and was about to make her excuses when a look from Liam stopped her. *Does he want me to stay?*

'Are you keeping well, Sadie?' His tone was flat.

'I am. Well, I am and I'm not, if you know what I mean?'

Kathleen cleared her throat. 'Hello, Sadie.'

'Kathleen.' The girl nodded, glancing at Kathleen's outfit, and Kathleen was absurdly glad of her new clothes, made from fabric Mammy had been hoarding for years. All the Gallaghers had been invited to the wedding, given their long friendship with the Flynns, and Mammy had somehow managed not only to pay for their new clothes to be made, but had even ordered three plain hats, which they had made over with dyed feathers and cloth flowers. Kathleen felt very pretty today – and she wasn't about to let Sadie O'Kane spoil things. 'How are you?'

'I'm great thanks, Sadie. They got a lovely day for it, didn't they?'

'They did – no rain again. We've been lucky this Easter.'

'Hopefully it'll be cloudy this evening,' said Liam, glancing at the sky. 'The moon is about three quarters full these nights and will still be fairly full for the next few nights.'

Kathleen shuddered. In the midst of joy – her own, and Therese's – the threat of an air raid was higher than ever.

'Well, as long as we have big strong air raid wardens to look after us, we'll be all right!' Sadie's hand was on Liam's upper arm, tracing the muscles there as though the two of them had never broken up.

'How's Barney doing?' Liam had stepped back a little, making Sadie drop her hand.

She tossed her head. 'How should I know? Turns out he's a bit of an eejit.' She sighed dramatically. 'Sometimes you don't appreciate what you have until it's gone.'

Her meaning could not have been plainer, and Kathleen almost gasped aloud. *She wants him back!* Then the insecurity kicked in. He was with Sadie for a long time. Maybe he wanted her back. *Am I in the way?*

'Do you know what I mean, Liam?' Sadie sent a quick glance in Kathleen's direction before refocusing on Liam. 'Besides, I don't even know yet if. . .' – leaning forward she whispered in his ear – 'if I'm pregnant or not.'

Vaguely Kathleen was aware that Sadie had deliberately whispered loudly enough for her to hear, but the shock of Sadie's words – and their implication – had her wheeling away already. 'Excuse me.'

Without even looking in their direction, she turned, making her way across to Peggy and Dan, shock rippling through her at what had just happened. The two women hugged, and complimented each other; Peggy was wearing a light floral maternity dress with white shoes and gloves, and looked radiant. She and her husband were heading off to Dublin on the train, with plans to travel on to Wicklow tomorrow.

'Dan's off this week, so we're going to a place called Enniskerry for a few days,' she confided. 'It's really special to me and Dan – we went there once when we were courting, and this'll be our first time back.' She sent Kathleen a puzzled look. 'But what's happening with you, Kathleen? You look . . . different, somehow. Are you all right?'

Kathleen pretended to be puzzled. 'Different how?' *God, please don't let her see how destroyed I am!*

'I dunno.' She thought for a minute. 'Distant, I think. You're sort of not really *there*.'

'Am I? Hardly surprising, I suppose. That bloody raid last week really unsettled me. Still, it's finally Therese's wedding day, which is great. We have to focus on the good things, right?'

'We do.' Peggy looked serious. 'Let's hope the Luftwaffe doesn't come back.'

'Are you staying for the breakfast?' Kathleen's voice sounded fairly normal to her own ear. But this was Peggy, who had a near-miraculous skill in tuning in to people's feelings.

'Sadly, no. Our train goes soon, so we better head to the station.' The look she exchanged with her husband was one that Kathleen now recognised. It spoke of togetherness, and anticipation, and shared secrets, and it was exactly like the looks that she and Liam had been sharing these past few days, when they thought no one was looking.

Had she really had nearly a week of bliss, before Sadie had brought it all crashing down? *God, is she expecting Liam's child?* And for pregnancy even to be a possibility, it meant the two of them had been doing things together . . . things that a girl should only do with her husband – or the man she fully expected to be her husband. Oh, sometimes couples got carried away. Handy-women knew *exactly* what the consequences were. At the very least, a respectable girl like Sadie would not have let Liam . . . No, not unless she was certain they would marry.

'Let's go, everybody!' Jimmy and his brother were indicating that the wedding party should make their way into the hall next door, and people were beginning to move.

Glancing round, Kathleen saw Bronagh and her parents were heading inside. If she wanted to sit with them, she'd better hurry up. And she needed to sit with them, well away from the eyes of the bride's brother. Bidding Peggy and Dan a brief farewell, she turned, seeing the back of Liam's head as he went to speak to Seány. Sadie was already heading out the gate, thankfully. And she had not seen how he had reacted to Sadie's shocking words. Now—

'Kathleen! Kathleen!' It was wee Alice, running towards her. Kathleen crouched to receive her, and the little girl flung herself into Kathleen's arms. 'I seen the wedding people!'

'Did you? Isn't that class?' She straightened, retaining Alice's hand. 'Well, Mrs McGowan. Hello, Cora.'

After the exchange of greetings and cooing over the babies – both tied to their mothers with Belfast shawls as usual – Kathleen turned her attention back to Alice, who had much to say about weddings, and dresses, and special breakfasts.

'And did you know there's to be cake today?'

Alice's eyes widened. 'Real cake? Woooooow. Yous are so lucky!'

'I know!' It had been over a year since Kathleen had had cake. 'We really are. Right, I have to go in. I'll see you tomorrow, Alice, all right?'

'Tomorrow? Why?'

Kathleen tapped Alice's little nose with a gentle finger. 'Wait and see.'

Making her way inside, she saw that the happy couple were already seated at the 'top table', accompanied by their witnesses, Jimmy's parents, and Mrs Flynn. Liam was also there, and Kathleen had a lump in her throat as she realised he was once again taking the place of his deceased father. When he had walked Therese down the aisle there had been a fair few of the congregation making subtle use of their handkerchiefs.

God, he was too good a man to do the dirty on a girlfriend. He would have to stand by Sadie, now that she had changed her mind and wanted him back. Because they had been doing things together. Even if she wasn't pregnant. If Sadie had been compromised then they were already as good as married.

There was soup then, and sandwiches, and speeches, and somehow, Kathleen survived it. Mr Flynn's absence was acknowledged by both the groom and the bride's brother, with comments that he would have loved seeing his Therese married. At some point during the speeches Kathleen calculated that Liam and Sadie had broken up six weeks ago. If the girl hadn't had a bleed in all that time then the chances were that she was indeed pregnant. She might not even be sure herself, for most girls were hopelessly ignorant about these things.

It was time for the cake. It was a decent-sized fruit cake, with icing, and Kathleen's mouth watered at the sight of it. Oh, her slice looked so tempting, sitting there on the plate in front of her! But she couldn't eat it. She didn't deserve it. No child should be born illegitimate; those who were had to take the censure of the community. Removing a spare, clean handkerchief she carefully wrapped the cake in it, then popped it in her handbag. *Tomorrow.*

'Are you not eating yours?' asked Bronagh, her mouth full of cake. 'It's delicious!'

Muttering something about saving it for later, Kathleen changed the subject. 'Weird to think it's twenty-five years since the Rising, and still the North is owned by the British.'

'Aye, bloody ridiculous. And them boys in Stormont aren't fit to run a bath, never mind six whole counties that they're pretending is a country!'

'Too right!'

'That time I was in Dublin with Mammy . . . you know?'

Kathleen nodded. *The time I was born.*

'It was 1920 and the War of Independence was in full swing. They were only after signing the Partition Act in London but it wasn't what people wanted – or not the people I spoke to anyway.'

'Where did yous live?'

Bronagh sent her a long look. 'For a couple of months I lived in' – her voice dropped – 'in one of them laundry places. That was where you were actually . . . you know—'

Kathleen gasped. 'My God!' *I was born in a feckin' Magdalene asylum?* Vaguely she recalled Mammy mentioning something, the day of the big row.

'Aye. They worked us hard, but I've never been afraid of hard work.' She shuddered. 'It was the other stuff. Penance and sin and punishment for our wrongdoing. That's what it was, seven days a week. Them nuns thought we were scum, so they did.'

'How did you get out?'

'Mammy. She came to see me after you were born, saw I was in a bad state. I had eaten hardly anything, and was jumping at my own shadow. I was bloody terrified!'

Kathleen swallowed. 'And you were only sixteen.'

'I turned seventeen while I was in there. Worst birthday I ever had. Anyway, Mammy took me out. Took the both of us out.' Her gaze turned to Mammy, currently laughing with Mrs Flynn about something. The two women were good friends. 'That's why I'll always be grateful to her. She acts tough, you know, but her heart is good.'

Kathleen felt tears prick her eyes. 'Aye.' A thought occurred to her. 'What would have happened to me – to your baby, if you'd stayed in there?'

Bronagh's lips tightened. 'The place was full of disease. We all slept in these big dorms, and if one girl got sick, everybody would catch it. A lot of the babies . . . died. Some of the mothers too. And the rest of the babbies were taken off their mothers and given up for adoption.'

Kathleen's jaw dropped. 'Jesus!' *Is that what might happen to Sadie, if Liam refuses to marry her?*

'Aye. I made a deal with Mammy that she would raise the child, and that I would never tell anybody the truth.'

Kathleen nodded slowly. 'The best thing, in the circumstances. I see that now.'

Bronagh sent her a long look. 'Thanks, Kathleen. I really am sorry.'

'It's all right.' And it was. Mammy and Bronagh had both done the best they could. Kathleen had had a good life – reared in a good family, with a decent house, enough food, and plenty of love.

And amazingly, Liam hadn't minded her origins. *God, was it because he and Sadie had already done it, and he wanted to have his way with me too?* Surely not. Yet everything she thought she had known about so-called respectable people had been turned on its head. Bronagh and her Michael. Cora and Tony. Liam and Sadie. She thought she knew Bronagh, but had not. Why should her previous assessment of Liam be valid? The world was upside-down, and her nerves along with it.

A couple of local musicians were now tuning their fiddles in the corner, and once everyone had eaten, a few sets got up for a dance. Bronagh dragged Kathleen up and together they stepped and swung their way through 'The Walls of Limerick', and all the while Kathleen was dying inside. Jimmy and Therese were dancing too, and once again Kathleen was reminded of the first time she'd seen them dance together, in this very hall, just after Kathleen's sixteenth birthday. Later that night, Liam had kissed her for the first time, and now . . . There should have been some sort of symmetry in it, some pattern that reinforced the rightness of it all. But it had all been destroyed by the revelation that Sadie and Liam had been intimate. A hardness came over her, forged in the months of cynicism since she had found her birth certificate. Other people took what pleasures they wanted, it seemed, leaving her eternally doomed to suffer. Well, not this time. *Not this feckin' time.*

Finally, he came to speak to her during one of the dances. And she was *so* ready. 'Well, Kathleen. Er . . . about Sadie . . .' He was frowning, at the same time searching her face. 'I want to reassure you. I have no notion of getting back with her.'

'Actually . . .' Kathleen knew that she couldn't have the temptation of him hanging over her. 'Actually, Liam, I've had second thoughts. I don't want to be your girlfriend after all.'

He paled. 'What? But why?'

She shrugged, realising that this was easy. Inside she was as cold as a bank of snow. 'I think you need to get back with Sadie. It's not right to leave her now she's changed her mind.'

'But I don't want Sadie. I want you.'

She shrugged. 'You can want away there. You still have to do the right thing, Liam.'

'What are you even talking about? I don't have to walk out with somebody I don't want! That would be madness.'

She was unmoved. Oh, she could see it all on his face – confusion, determination . . . None of it mattered. His duty was to the mother of his child. The woman he'd had *relations* with.

They stood there, simply looking at each other, just as Mrs McKenna was walking past. Her eyebrows headed skywards before, pointedly, she began singing the opening lines to another old song.

> *'I have often heard it said from me father and me mother*
> *That going to a wedding is the making of another . . .'*

Kathleen rolled her eyes, knowing the woman was commenting on the fact that she and Liam had been chatting intently in a corner. *Another wedding? I don't think so, but Liam will be married to Sadie before long.* 'I better go.'

'Wait! Kathleen!'

Ignoring him, she returned to their table, noticing Daddy was briefly alone. Deliberately she lingered, chatting with him about the lovely weather, the latest news from Europe – anything except last Wednesday's row. Indirectly, she wanted him to know that she was getting her head around it all. New information, new ideas could be hard to take in, but Kathleen was beginning to realise that things were never pure nor simple. There had been no good options for her family back then, and the path her family had chosen had been the best of them.

Liam would soon realise the same. He and Sadie had been together a long time – since August, in fact. She still remembered how it had hurt to hear that he had a girlfriend. There was no hurt now, though. No pain. No confusion. As she had always suspected, she was destined to be alone. The illegitimate daughter. The spinster.

'What is it, Kathleen?' Belatedly she realised she had been staring into space and had lost the track of their conversation. Daddy's brow was creased, and she hurried to reassure him. 'I was thinking about years ago, and how everybody did what was best in the end.'

He exhaled, relief apparent on his features. 'Aye. We all did the best we knew at the time.'

'I suppose that's all anybody can do.'

'Mr Gallagher! How are you?' It was Mrs Kelly, an elderly lady from Beechmount Street.

Rising, Kathleen gave up her chair, moving across to Therese and Jimmy. 'Well! Is it starting to sink in yet?'

'A wee bit.' The joy shining in Therese's eyes was mirrored in Jimmy's. 'We've to go shortly.'

'Aye.' The newlyweds were to spend two nights in a guest house in Greencastle on the shores of Belfast Lough, before taking up residence in their wee house in the Whiterock Estate. 'With this good weather the trains'll be packed.'

'We won't care.' The tenderness in Jimmy's eyes as he looked at his bride made Kathleen's heart turn over. Especially as it was *exactly* the way Liam had looked at her earlier this week. God, she had been *this close* to happiness.

Once the Happy Couple had left, to cheers and well-wishes ('Away and enjoy yourselves!' Mrs Flynn had called, to Therese's clear mortification), the atmosphere went a bit flat. Within the hour the guests had gone, and the hall had been re-made as a rest centre again. And all the while Kathleen kept well away from Liam.

'That's us now!' Mrs Flynn gave a satisfied nod. 'Right. I'm heading home to put my feet up. Back to work tomorrow!'

Kathleen left soon afterwards, heading away from home towards Milltown Cemetery. The park would be busy, given the good weather, and while there were always a few in the cemetery tidying up family graves, she would have peace there. It was genuinely the one place she could be alone. Unerringly she made her way to the Gallagher plot. Mammy's people were from the Short Strand and were buried in the Friar's Bush up Stranmillis, but Daddy's family were all here in Milltown. *I'll be buried here too, some day.* She shuddered, as a shadow passed over her. *Somebody just walked on my grave.*

A buzzing sound in her ears suddenly claimed her full attention – the unmistakable drone of an aircraft. Heart pounding, she searched the skies until she had found it. To the east, a lone aeroplane, flying lazily over the city.

*Luftwaffe.* Dread pooled coolly in her belly. *Probably reconnaissance. Same as yesterday.* Yes, there were worse things going on in the world than the troubles of a girl who had loved a boy, and lost him.

# PART V

# 34

*Tuesday, 15 April 1941*

> *The Belfast Emergency Plan included arrangements for dealing with up to two hundred deaths and ten thousand homeless. It was believed any raids would be small-scale and contained.*

*Dublin, 10.20 p.m.*

Captain Mick O'Hanlon, known as Micko to his colleagues, was completing his inspection in the Tara Street headquarters of the Dublin Fire Brigade when the noise started. The new shift had just begun, the previous crew had left for home, and it was part of Micko's job as captain to ensure his crews and equipment were well presented and ready for all eventualities.

Instantly he made for the window, his gaze angling skywards, but he could see nothing. The rumbling noise was distinctive – and increasing – so he swiftly made his way outside, ordering his crews to begin making their routine mechanical checks of the vehicles and equipment. The night was cloudy, but there was a small break in the clouds to the east. Looking up, he reeled in shock at the sight. Dozens of Nazi aircraft, all heading north. Dozens and dozens and dozens.

*My God!* There had to be more than a hundred . . . he stood transfixed as they kept coming, making their way through that small break in the clouds. A hundred and fifty . . . more . . . Must be nearly two hundred. And they were headed north to Belfast, to a place he'd only stayed in once, but which he had never forgotten. Belfast, where they made British warships, and British air force planes.

Belfast, where he'd loved a girl, once.

Hurrying inside, he lifted the phone to his boss. 'Major Comerford? O'Hanlon here. Yes, I seen them too. Right. Right, so.'

Hanging up, he reviewed the roster for tonight. Some good men were on duty, including Station Officer Ed Blake and Third Officer Gorman in Dorset Street. 'Ye may brace yourselves, lads,' he muttered to himself, 'for we might be needed this night.'

*10.40 p.m.*

Kathleen and Bronagh weren't long into bed when the sound they had dreaded began. *Air raid siren.* Kathleen had of course told the rest of her ones about the Nazi reconnaissance plane she had seen that afternoon. Combined with the raid last week, the clearing skies, and the near-full moon, they all knew it didn't bode well for their beloved city.

Daddy had then spent hours in the shelter, finishing the bench and table he was making, adding a mattress to the platform, and bringing out various supplies including a gas cooking ring and a kettle. Mammy had put together a box of food and drink including tea, bread, and empty milk bottles filled with water. There was even a chamber pot, in case it was too risky even to go to the outhouse, just a few feet away.

Grabbing their bags and taking the blankets from the bed with them, Kathleen and Bronagh hurried to the shelter to dress. Despite the space being cramped they managed, and once again hugged Mammy and Daddy before setting out into the night. *They're still my mammy and my daddy.* It didn't seem to matter that Bronagh was also her mother. *She's my sister, and my birth mother, and somehow it's all right.* A sort of sad acceptance had come over her. None of it was within her control. Not Bronagh. Not Liam. None of it. Her job – her only job – was to keep going with whatever time she had on this earth, and try to do the best she could.

Walking swiftly but carefully, the lamp correctly hooded, Kathleen sent a silent prayer to the skies. Her eyes followed, and she gasped. A flare was lighting up the night sky, illuminating what looked like dozens of planes flying in an ominous formation. Another flare followed, then another, making the city briefly as bright as day, and dimly she realised the Luftwaffe pilots would be using the light to orient themselves, and maybe to pinpoint the location of their key targets. The final death toll from last week's raid had been thirteen – and that had involved only a few planes. Tonight was going to be worse. Much worse. *Like Coventry. Like Swansea. Like London.*

First-aiders and ambulance volunteers were converging on the converted bus and the two ambulances parked beside it. Hurrying inside, Kathleen was immediately aware of an air of contained terror. Everyone had seen the planes. Making their way to station three, Kathleen and Bronagh began methodically laying out their supplies, exactly as they had the week before. There was a clock on the wall showing five to eleven. Hopefully most people were now in the shelters.

*Boom!* The sound of the first bomb was devastating. Somewhere, right now, someone may have died. *Boom! Boom! Boom!* The noise was deafening, as bombs began to rain down on the city. *BOOM!* A louder explosion, then – a bomb had fallen much nearer. Someone was crying at station four, but Kathleen couldn't look. It was time to stop thinking, stop feeling. If she was going to be any use to anyone, she had to focus on *doing*.

*11 p.m.*

The night sky was illuminated with white-bright flares – first a few, then a dozen. Liam hurried to the duty room, relieved to see a great turnout. He and his team emerged a few minutes later laden with a stirrup pump, a stretcher, ropes, axes, and buckets. There were also two blankets for each team.

Tonight they would be whatever they needed to be: doctor, fireman, rescuer . . . Before long they would be active in their allocated area, enforcing the blackout and encouraging people to get off the streets.

People were panicking everywhere – hardly surprising, given the noise of the bombs. The raid seemed to be concentrated in the city centre for now, but Liam knew that could change at any time. Apparently the Luftwaffe often began a raid by dropping high-explosive bombs designed to cause maximum damage, following these up with incendiary bombs. *Jesus!* Fleetingly, Liam thought about the fact that, if Ireland as a whole had gained her independence, his city would have come under Irish neutrality and been protected from the Nazis.

As ordered, he returned to the duty room after making his first rounds. Seymour was pale, but full of energy. 'Flynn! Report!'

'All wardens in place. Minor damage only.'

'Good.' He indicated the phone, a key tool in their role as conduits for communication. 'Latest report is an estimated hundred and eighty to two hundred planes. Brace yourself, Flynn. It's going to be a long night.'

'Yes, sir.' *Two hundred! God help us all!*

'Good man. Return to duty and report back each hour, or if there's any significant damage in the meantime!'

'Yes, sir.' Scribbling his written report as quickly as he could, Liam put it in the 'reports' tray then stepped back out into the night.

*Feck.* Even in the few minutes he'd been inside, things had got worse. Palls of smoke billowed to the north and east. The city centre, the docks – much of it was already ablaze. He dared not think of Seány, who had leapt into action as soon as the siren had sounded. Ambulance bells were now ringing, and fire tenders too, and all the time explosions continued, the screams of falling bombs adding to the cacophony. Hurrying back towards his area, Liam was forced to blow his whistle twice – both times at families hurrying along the road. 'Get under cover!' he ordered, adding the location of the nearest Anderson shelter. The first group explained they were heading for Clonard Monastery a couple of streets away, with the intention of hiding in the crypt. It had been announced at Mass, they said, that the crypt had been equipped with supplies in case it was needed.

The other group was stubbornly resistant. 'Not a chance!' the man said, his eyes wide in his pale face and a child on his shoulders. 'We're for the mountain – for Sliabh Dubh!' The woman beside him nodded, an infant peeping out of her tartan shawl. Beside them two young children half-ran, half walked.

Liam shook his head. While the Black Mountain was indeed less likely to be hit by bombs, trying to get there on foot would take ages, which meant the family would be exposing themselves to greater danger. 'You don't have time. Get under cover now!'

They ignored him, so he ran on. Turning back as another flare illuminated the scene, he saw they had continued their slow progress along the Falls. 'Feckin' eejits!' he muttered to himself, then noticed another family on the far side of the road, darting along fearfully.

Just as he saw them he heard the whistling scream of a falling bomb nearby. 'Take shelter!' he roared, throwing himself to the ground behind a line of oil drums. *Boom!* The blast was massive, making the ground shake and vibrate beneath him, and sending him sprawling over onto his back. Bits of debris pelted him – a large chunk that might have killed him bouncing off his steel helmet with a teeth-shaking thud.

Winded, he couldn't breathe for what seemed like an eternity. As he lay there, trying not to panic, he couldn't help but notice through the widening gap in the clouds hundreds of stars above, mercilessly beautiful in the vastness of the night. As he watched, bright blasts exploded in the sky, somewhere to the north. *Anti-aircraft missiles! We're fighting back!*

Thankfully within a minute or so he was taking air into his lungs, and soon afterwards he was on his feet again, turning back to inspect the blast damage. The family he had shouted to were all dead, every last one of them, their bodies blown to smithereens. Averting his eyes too late, he couldn't unsee the dreadful sight. His stomach heaved, and a moment later he was vomiting right there on the street.

A strange metallic groaning sound drew his attention. Wiping his mouth with the back of his hand he turned towards it. The row of shops opposite him had shuddered in the blast, the walls now bowing ominously, and that dreadful sound indicated a collapse was imminent. Unhesitatingly he ran towards it. *Families live above all them shops.*

'Anybody in here?' he shouted through the open door of the butcher's, hearing an answering call from the stairwell. 'Yous need to get out now,' he bellowed. 'Building is about to collapse. Move!'

From under the stairs they emerged: father, mother, children, and an elderly lady.

'Quickly!' he urged, hearing that ominous groaning sound again, and they hurried towards him.

'Take her!' the mother said, thrusting an infant into his arms then assisting the old lady behind her. Grabbing the small boy by the shoulder, Liam dragged him out to the middle of the road, whirling around as a cacophony behind him told him the building was collapsing. Dust and debris bellowed towards him, lit by another flare, and he clapped a hand on the boy's mouth and nose, at the same time pressing the baby to his chest with the other hand. Miraculously, from the dust emerged both parents, alive, holding up the granny, one on each side.

'Keep going!' he roared, knowing there was more to follow. He led the way across the street with the wee ones, sending a wary eye over the facing buildings as another flare briefly illuminated the scene. Sure enough a massive clatter ensued: a further collapse in the terraced buildings behind them. *I hope to God there's nobody else in there.*

More debris flew everywhere, tiny bits of masonry pebbling down on them. The infant was screaming by this stage, while the little boy was silent – probably terrified.

'It's all right, childer,' the mother managed, as she reached them. Taking the baby, she crouched to hug the boy, leaving her husband to support the old lady. Blood was now pouring down the father's face. *Head wound.* Information from the first aid training came to him. *Might be serious. Full assessment needed. Could be superficial. Head wounds often bleed profusely even when small.*

'You need to bring them all to the medical bus to be checked over,' he told the father. 'Down by the chapel. Now go! Quick as you can!'

Putting his whistle to his mouth he blew for assistance. Once. Twice. Three times. At the same time he was crossing back over to the collapsed shops.

'Hello!' he called. 'Anybody in there?'

'Help!' came an answering cry. 'Help us!'

'Where are you?' He found he was slightly deaf – probably from the terrible noise of the blast and collapse. It should ease in a minute, he knew, but right now locating the sound of the voice was difficult.

'Under the stairs.' It was a man's voice. 'McGuigan's!'

McGuigan's was the last shop in the row, he knew. It was a corner shop selling groceries, cigarettes, and newspapers. The shop was gone, unrecognisable amid the tumble of debris.

'Jesus Christ!' It was Matt Darcy, and Liam's relief at seeing him was enormous. 'What have we got?'

'Somebody trapped in McGuigan's.' He raised his voice. 'How many of you?'

'Three!' came the reply. There was a pause. 'They won't wake up. God, help us! Help us!'

Liam's heart sank. Whoever was with the man was either unconscious or dead. Hurrying to the end of the row, he whistled through his teeth. The gable wall was still standing, the top of the stairs briefly visible in the next flare. Everywhere else was one massive pile of rubble. Quickly they moved to the outer wall, which was leaning outwards and looked like it might fall on them at any minute.

'Push it from inside,' said Matt.

'Aye.' They both had the same idea. No point trying to rescue people only for more rubble to fall on them all. Moving carefully in the dim downward light of their hooded ARW lamps, Liam and Matt made their way up the pile of rubble towards the stairs. Testing every step, they slid a couple of times, but thankfully managed not to destabilise the entire pile of bricks, roof tiles, and rafters. Soon they were level with the top of the wall and ready to push loose bricks outwards. After shouting a warning they set to work, swiftly bringing down most of the unstable wall. Only then were they able to return to what had been the ground floor, and begin removing the rubble near where the man and his companions had hidden. Working swiftly and carefully, and talking calmly to the man throughout, they gradually managed to unearth the small cubbyhole. As Liam had feared, the man was the only one alive, his wife and son having been part-crushed by debris.

'Don't look!' he told the man, but it was too late. He had seen the horror, and began screaming hoarsely.

All the while the sound of bombs and more bombs continued, and now there was another blast wave from a bomb that must be fairly close. Once again Liam flew off his feet, landing with a grunt a couple of yards away. The noise of moving rubble and collapsing roof trusses surrounded him, as the rubble beneath him shifted and moved. *Is this the end?*

Somehow, he was still alive, and unharmed. The noise subsided and instinctively he turned to look for Matt, but he had dropped his lamp and could see nothing.

Cautiously he rose, shaking his head to try to rid himself of the ringing sound in his ears. A glimmer of light to his right indicated the location of the lamp and so he crawled towards it, feeling the rubble shift and slip beneath him as he went. Finally he closed his hand around the handle, lifting the lamp to survey the scene.

*My God.* There had been a further collapse; the stairs, cubbyhole, and what remained of the building was now entirely engulfed in masonry.

'Matt! Matt!' He was rewarded by a groaning sound ahead, and made his way to his friend.

'Matt! You all right?'

'I've been better,' was the reply, and Liam shook his head in acknowledgement of the older man's attempt at humour. Swiftly he assessed the man by feel, sight, and the sound of Matt yelping when Liam pressed his left leg.

'Right. Broken leg, a few cuts. Not too bad.' He blew his whistle again – three blasts – and within minutes one of his wardens arrived.

'Matt Darcy,' he explained. 'Left femur broken. Needs a full assessment. Get the stretcher men out here.'

'Straight away, Liam.'

Knowing he was needed elsewhere, Liam took a minute to find the other lamp and set it by Matt's side. Then, bracing himself, he made his way to the approximate location of the cubbyhole.

'Hello?' he called. 'Anybody there?'

This time there was no reply, and looking at the scene Liam knew there was no way the man could have survived the second wave. *Maybe it's for the best*, he thought, recalling the man's reaction to the sight of the broken bodies of his loved ones. They would have to be dug out in the morning, he knew, but for now the priority had to be finding those who could be saved.

Straightening, he walked carefully across the rubble. There was work to be done.

# 35

*Wednesday, 16 April 1941, midnight*

> On the night of the Easter Raid, the Ulster Hall on Bedford Street was hosting a Céilídhe mhór na Cásca – *a grand Easter céilí*. When the sirens sounded, the star of the show, Delia Murphy, carried on performing, telling the audience to sing along with her, and 'defy the Germans to do their worst'. Amid the noise, the tremor of nearby bombs, and the flickering lights, she sang on until the raid ended.
>
> Fifteen-year-old Seán McKenna, an Irish dancer from Clogher, County Tyrone was in the audience. An ARP volunteer, he left the hall at the start of the raid, heading for his post in Unity Street, singing as he went.

'Report, Mr Flynn!' The look in Seymour's eyes was the same look that Liam was seeing everywhere – a kind of determination mixed with bewilderment.

'Family of five dead outside these shops.' He indicated the location on Seymour's wall map. 'Three dead in McGuigan's shop. May be more under the rubble. This entire terrace has collapsed. Debris on the main road and side road, but both still passable. No smell of gas. I wasn't able to get them out.' His voice cracked, and he coughed to cover it, then felt Seymour's hand rest briefly on his shoulder.

'You did your best, son. What else?'

As Liam continued with his report he was conscious of an air of unreality about the whole thing. He was no safer here in Seymour's duty room than he was anywhere else, yet here was procedure, and routine, and forms to fill out, and it felt like a temporary haven from the madness outside. Even though the things he was writing were dreadful, the act of doing so was strangely calming. Most of the damage so far was north of the Falls, with Beechmount and the southern end of the road currently escaping major bombardment. *God, and it's only midnight!*

*Dublin, 12.30 a.m.*

Micko had been keeping his ear to the ground – or, more accurately, to the phone. Rumours were flying about the attack on Belfast. Apparently Minister of Public Security MacDermott from the north had unofficially contacted Cardinal MacRory in Armagh to raise the possibility of assistance from southern fire crews, if he could get his colleagues in Stormont to agree to the request. According to Major Comerford, they could do nothing at present, and Taoiseach De Valera – conscious that any perceived breach of Ireland's neutrality could lead to a Nazi invasion – would have to approve any order.

*Politics.* Despite MacDermott's actions, most of the Unionist leaders in the north were determined to ignore the south at all costs, and would see it as a sign of weakness to ask Dublin for help. Meanwhile Dev would be aware that the Nazis had already invaded Belgium, Norway, and the Netherlands – all neutral countries – which might put him off agreeing to help. *Feckin' politics. Feckin' Nazis. Feckin' unionists. Feckin' partition.*

And in the meantime real people – fellow Irish men, women, and children – were dying up the road in Belfast. The phone rang again and he snatched it up.

'Tara Street. Captain O'Hanlon speaking.' He gripped the receiver tightly. 'Yes, Major. Will do, Major.'

He hung up, thinking for a moment. While there was no go-ahead yet, P.J. Hernon – the Dublin city manager – had told Major Comerford to 'be ready'.

*Right. We will be ready.* Opening his directory, Micko scanned the list. All the Dublin stations, naturally . . . Dun Laoghaire . . . Drogheda . . . Dundalk. Important to leave men and engines to cover their own towns, but surely those locations could all spare a tender and crew. Putting a finger under the first number, he began to dial.

*Belfast, 1.30 a.m.*

Kathleen glanced at the clock on the wall, astonished to find it was already half past one. The noise of fresh bombs was relentless. The Luftwaffe had dropped what seemed like hundreds of explosive devices already. Wiping the back of her hand across her brow, she prepared to receive the next casualty. Thankfully, they had been joined by a handful of qualified nurses and even two doctors – all unable to get to the Royal because of blocked roads, gas leaks, and fires. The medically qualified had dealt with all of the major traumas where intervention was possible, while the first-aiders were concentrating on assessments and minor injuries. The bodies of the deceased – for now – were in the yard, covered with tarps.

Bronagh was long gone – called to Sussex Street, where the wall of the York Street Mill had apparently collapsed, crushing the entire street. The dozens of living casualties were to be ferried to whatever hospital they could reach, but apparently more roads were becoming impassable every half hour. Even now, Bronagh could be driving straight into a blast, or a fire, or a gas explosion . . . But no point thinking about it. A bomb could equally land on the bus at any time.

'Who's next?' She turned to the line of people, beckoning forward a man covered in grey-green dust, who had clearly had a head injury. Bracing herself, she prepared to be calm and reassuring.

*Belfast, 2 a.m.*

'Damn it!' Seymour was pressing the phone connection buttons. 'Line's dead! Right! Flynn, I'll need you to go on foot to the command centre with our District report. Can you do that?'

'Of course.'

'Hang on a minute. Here.' Opening his expensive thermos flask, Seymour poured some tea into a cup. He handed it to Liam, who took a sip.

He couldn't help it; he had to close his eyes as the delicious hot liquid slid down his throat. Surely this was the best drink he had ever had?

A few minutes later he was away, heading northwards. St Peter's Cathedral was still standing, and he wondered if it would still be there by morning. Glancing upwards at the famous twin spires, he saw hordes of Nazi planes in the now-clear sky, then caught his breath in momentary shock. The anti-aircraft fire had stopped. *Why are we not fighting back?*

On he went, heading northwards on the Falls and towards the Shankill, stamping out three small fires on the way. For the larger ones he simply noted their location, knowing they were beyond his capabilities. At least he knew his way, having travelled to Seymour's office three times a week since February. Liam thought briefly of the basic filing systems he had developed for the office. He had taken on some of the ordering too. Such a shame he couldn't keep working there. And how far away it all was, he thought as he raced towards Percy Street. Invoices and orders and building supplies.

'Warden! Warden!'

The plea came from a young woman carrying a baby. 'Help me! Where do I go?'

'Of course!' He thought quickly. 'There's a public shelter up here.' Putting an arm around her in case she stumbled, he angled his lamp so they could both see the debris-strewn ground in front of them.

'What the hell is that?' With a shaky finger, the woman pointed to a small greenish parachute, drifting downwards over the rooftops a street or two away. It looked so innocent in the light of a flare, moving lazily towards the tightly packed terraced streets.

Liam knew exactly what it was. *Parachute mine.* The most powerful bomb at the Luftwaffe's disposal. 'Down!' he shouted, at the same time bending and pulling the woman forward. Once on the ground he angled himself to cover the mother and baby as best he could.

Just in time. The few short seconds while they lay like that felt like a hundred years. Liam had said more prayers tonight than he had said in his entire life.

*BOOM!* The mine exploded, sending debris flying towards them. Dozens of pebbles and shards of stones and roof tiles hit him, and Liam cried out with the pain. *Thank God for my steel helmet!* And thank God he was covering the mother and baby.

The blast wave that followed was even worse. It sucked with such energy that Liam felt how fragile every inch of his body was. He was momentarily near-deaf again, the sound of his own cries, distant and muffled. The baby was screaming, he realised. *Well of course it was.* At least it was still alive.

After a minute he was able to sit up. Reaching for one of the sorest spots on his face, his hand came away sticky. But blessed detachment was there, soothing him. The only thing that mattered now was getting the woman and child to the shelter.

He staggered a little when he rose, then reached out a hand to her. Thankfully she and the child were largely uninjured. Together they passed the place in the street where three or four houses had been entirely taken out by the blast. Through the gap Liam could see the same damage in the next street. *That was some feckin' explosion! If the wind had blown it our way . . .* But there was no point thinking about it. No point in even checking for survivors. No one could have survived that.

Finally they were in Percy Street, and the woman hugged him before descending into the public shelter. At the last she turned back.

'What's your name?'

'Flynn. Liam Flynn.' *A taig name.*

'I'm Mrs Corry.' She stroked the head of her baby, who was settling again. 'And this is Elizabeth. Thank you, Liam Flynn.'

*At least I did something useful.* Why the woman had been in the street hours after the raid began, he could only guess. Many had tried to shelter in their homes, and had later panicked and run outside. No one seemed to know what to do for the best. Briefly he thought of a tartan shawl and wondered if that family had made it to the Black Mountain. But when his thoughts began to turn to his own family, to his loved ones, to Kathleen, he resisted, knowing it could unman him.

Finally he reached District headquarters and presented Seymour's report, along with the new damage and fires he'd witnessed on his way there. They already knew about the parachute mine and had dispatched a rescue team to look for survivors. In return he heard about continued heavy bombardment, particularly in the docks, the city centre, and North Belfast. Many phone lines were now down, and the anti-aircraft guns had to be stopped for fear of hitting RAF planes, which it was hoped were on their way to assist. The old waterworks on the Antrim Road had been hit and many mains burst, and the city water pressure was reduced to 50 percent.

*Fuck!* His mind flicked to the firemen, trying their best. *Our Seány . . . No! Can't think about him!*

'Tell Seymour thank you. And keep reporting.'

'Yes, sir.'

Hurrying back in a southerly direction, he saw activity outside the Falls Baths, and paused to ask what was happening. 'They've made it a temporary mortuary,' a stretcher bearer said, exiting the building with an empty stretcher. 'The morgues are all full so they drained the swimming baths here and in Peter's Hill. St George's Market is a morgue too.'

*Jesus! So many dead already* . . . As he hurried on in the darkness accompanied by the screams of mines and booms of bombs, he pictured the enormous swimming pool he had enjoyed as a child. Death was everywhere, and his city was ablaze.

# 36

*Belfast, 2.15 a.m.*

*A parachute mine exploded in the vicinity of Victoria Barracks on Unity Street, killing many people and destroying a number of buildings. Among the dead was a fifteen-year-old Irish dancer from Clogher.*

*Despite the decision to stop firing anti-aircraft guns, the RAF did not come to assist in the defence of Belfast.*

*A call from Dublin to the Northern Ireland Minister of Public Security, John MacDermott, was answered by the minister's wife. Asked by an Irish official whether firemen from the south should travel north to assist, she replied, 'Tell them to come!'*

Kathleen could wait no longer. She was bursting for a wee, so with a muttered apology she left the bus hospital – for it had become a mini-hospital – for the first time, making for the toilets in the parish hall. The stench of noxious smoke hit her as soon as she stepped outside, and instinctively she put a hand over her mouth.

Walking the few yards up to the main road, she looked about her. The entire city of Belfast was alight, or so it seemed. The flames of a hundred, a thousand fires lit up the night sky, and the billowing smoke created patterns that blocked out the stars. The screams and booms of falling bombs continued. *Surely to God this nightmare must end soon.*

Nearby, fires were blazing, and as the light flared briefly she saw that some buildings had collapsed. *God help anybody who was in there!*

Her ablutions completed, she was crossing the yard back towards the bus when some stretcher bearers arrived. 'More casualties? Bring them straight in.'

'Ah, nothin' you can do for these ones, love. Hit by a blast on the way to the mountain road.' Carefully, the stretcher bearers set down their burdens – the bodies of a father, mother, and three children – alongside the rows of corpses in the yard. A dead infant, still tied to its mother with a tartan shawl, completed the family.

Kathleen picked up a fresh tarpaulin, unfolded it, and tenderly covered the family. She blessed herself, but knew that if she allowed herself to feel too much, she'd be no good to anybody. 'Right,' she said briskly, 'I'm going back in.'

Opening the door of the bus, she recoiled as the stench hit her. Blood, death, antiseptic, and fear. Some of the casualties had had toilet accidents because of the terror, and the unit stank of piss and shit. Trying not to gag, Kathleen made her way back to her station.

'Who's next?'

*Dublin, 2.30 a.m.*

'The chief is here!' One of Micko's men came rushing in from the hallway.

'Thanks.' *Finally.* He went to the main space, where the fire tenders were lined up expectantly. 'Ready for inspection!' Instantly everyone stood, ready to receive the chief officer of the Dublin Fire Brigade.

Major James Comerford, formerly an engineer in the Irish Army, had restructured the Irish Fire Services in recent years, and increased training on structural engineering issues in firefighting – helping firemen assess risks more accurately and thereby increasing safety. He was admired throughout the service, and there was absolute silence in the station as he addressed the gathered men. He confirmed that, while there had as yet been no official confirmation, it was highly likely they would be asked to send aid to Belfast.

Ireland's neutrality had to be honoured, and so no one could be paid if they chose to travel. They would go as volunteers, although they would be covered by insurance in the event of injury or death. No fire engine bells were to be rung as they travelled north, and they were to return before nightfall tomorrow, in case there was a further raid.

*So we've to help with the aftermath only.* Micko nodded inwardly. It made sense. Realistically it would be near dawn by the time they reached Belfast, by which time the Luftwaffe would have departed. No southern firefighter would be killed by a falling Nazi bomb, and therefore no grief-stricken family could release details that would compromise neutrality.

Glancing around the room at men from all the Dublin stations, Micko knew he would not be short of volunteers. He also knew for certain he would be among them.

*Belfast, 3 a.m.*

'Sir, quick!'

A young man in uniform had run into the duty room, panting with effort. Liam, who had just delivered his latest report, felt his insides clench. *More disasters. What now?*

'Report!' Seymour spat out the word, and the man visibly straightened.

'Kenny Taylor, auxiliary fire volunteer. Parachute bomb on Percy Street – I seen it from Howard Street.' He swallowed. 'The roof of the public shelter has collapsed, sir.'

*Jesus, Mary, and Joseph!*

'Right.' Seymour remained outwardly calm, although his hand trembled as he made a note on his sheet. 'Taylor, alert the main command. Flynn, go you to Percy Street. Organise whoever's there. I'll send more help as I get it.'

'On my way.' Then Liam was racing out the door, blowing his whistle as he went. The noise attracted ordinary citizens as well as volunteers, everyone shouting about the Percy Street disaster, and to Liam's astonishment many men began to emerge from their hiding places to help, as soon as they had heard what had happened.

In the light of his lamp, what he could see was grim. The main blast had been a fair bit away, but had caused the concrete roof of the shelter to collapse onto those inside. *Mrs Corry. Baby Elizabeth.* He had taken them there, thinking they'd be safe.

Already there were men trying to lift what they could out of the way. The silence was eerie – no calls for help, nothing. *Are they all dead? All of them?*

He blew his whistle again. 'Everyone stop for a minute. Now, silence! Anybody need help in the shelter?'

Then they heard it – a male voice, coming from the top left corner. Liam pointed. 'There.'

The men were already moving, forming a living chain. 'Those pieces are too big,' one grunted. 'We're not gonna be able to lift them.'

'Go to Seymour's yard and take equipment from there.' The yard was close by, and the ropes, chains, and wheelbarrows would be invaluable. Seymour wouldn't mind, Liam was certain of it.

Women and children had also begun emerging from nearby houses – from whatever hiding places they had been using – clearly frightened by the bomb landing so close.

'Where do we send them?' a man asked. There was a pause as everyone looked at Liam for solutions. Then it came to him – a comment made hours ago.

'Clonard Monastery! There's a crypt that's been kitted out as a shelter!'

'But we're Protestant,' a woman replied dubiously.

'You think they'll care about that? You think anybody cares about them things tonight?'

They went, and more joined them. All night Liam had seen priests and ministers, nuns and brothers of all denominations around West, helping in first aid posts or assisting with bringing people to shelter. None of them had asked what religion a person was before coming to their aid. *As it should be. As it always feckin' should be.*

Miraculously, people were also still coming forward with offers of help. Others turned into gaping bystanders, which, though understandable, was frustrating as they might have made a difference.

Liam's role had changed from *doing* to *coordinating*, and strangely, everyone seemed to follow his orders as though he wasn't simply a young fella from Beechmount. There was work to be done everywhere, and once the bodies of young Mrs Corry and her baby had been pulled from the wreckage of the Percy Street shelter he had excused himself, reporting to Seymour – including telling him about the equipment from his yard currently being used in the rescue efforts.

'Ah, never worry about that, lad. Any survivors?'

'A few. Some badly injured. Probably thirty dead in the shelter.'

'Aye.' Seymour eyed him keenly. 'How are you holding up?'

Liam shrugged. 'I'm still standing.' *How come I'm alive, when so many have died?*

*Belfast, 4 a.m.*

Seymour had told them all to gather for a major group report at four, and the little room was filled with ARWs. Liam had made his latest report on arrival, astonished by the calm clarity in it. It was as though he had shut himself away. In a sense, Liam Flynn no longer existed. Only the air raid warden was real. There was a hidden reserve inside him, it seemed, and he had found it tonight.

'Thanks, Liam. The fires are the biggest problem now. The bombing is easing – most of the enemy are away, thank the Lord. But some of them fires could rage for days.'

Liam's mind flicked to Seány. 'And we don't have enough firemen. Or engines.'

'No. But Liverpool and Glasgow are sending some.'

Liam's jaw dropped. 'Liverpool? Feckin' *Glasgow*? And how long is that gonna take?'

'They responded instantly to the Stormont government's appeal for help. They're apparently sending hundreds of men, and around fifty appliances each. The Admiralty is organising their transport.'

Liam could not believe what he was hearing. 'Are you feckin' serious? Those *fuckers* in Stormont' – Seymour winced at his choice of words, but he carried on, unrepentant – 'did *nothing* to prepare for this, and then they have the *cheek* to look to their friends in feckin' Britain, sending fire engines to dawdle across the Irish Sea! There's Irishmen just down the road who will be itchin' to help, but they need to be *asked!*'

'I know, I know. Though the Free State is neutral, don't forget.'

'If I know my fellow Irishmen, they won't give a fuck about neutrality once they hear what's happening!'

Seymour was right about one thing, though. The heavy explosive bombs had eased; in this later part of the night the remaining Luftwaffe pilots were mostly dropping 'kilo bombs' – the lighter incendiaries. Whereas buildings hit directly by larger bombs tended to be destroyed in an instant, the incendiaries set off thousands of tiny fires; though less dramatic, these smaller bombs were no less devastating.

There was a banging at the door. Seymour had begun formally speaking to them all, but Liam moved towards the door to the hallway. A loud voice was shouting – something about *Newsome*. Liam froze. Wasn't that Seymour's daughter's name?

'Sir,' he managed, and Seymour's eyes met his. 'Newsome.'

Seymour swallowed. 'Go and find out, Flynn. Thank you.'

As Seymour continued his briefing, Liam allowed himself to be impressed by the man's fortitude. All of them – every last man – had had to ignore the possibility that their own families would be affected.

A young man was outside, looking agitated and glancing fearfully at the sky. 'What is it?'

'It's Mrs Newsome! George Seymour's daughter. Is he here?'

'He is.' God, had tragedy come to Seymour's door? Liam felt sick. After everything the man had done for the community . . . 'What's happened to her?'

'Her baby's coming, but the roads are blocked and no ambulances can get up or down.'

'How did you manage?'

'Motorbike.' The man looked distressed. 'Look, I'm only a neighbour – I know nothin' about these things. But Mrs Seymour was very definite. She says something's wrong and she needs help.'

Liam's heart sank. *Something's wrong. Roads blocked.* He nodded. Despite her rejecting him earlier, he knew he had to call upon the best person he knew. And before anything was even sorted between them.

'I think I can organise some help. Can I borrow the motorbike?'

'Of course!'

'Right. Come with me.' Opening the door carefully, he led the man inside. 'Are you free to give a hand here for a while?'

'I will, surely.'

'Good man.'

'What's your name?'

'Charlie. Charlie Bannon.'

'Well, Charlie, welcome to the district warden's team.'

They stepped on in, where Seymour was still speaking. His gaze fixed on Liam. 'Report!' he demanded, as he had done multiple times since the siren had first sounded last night. It seemed like a year.

Liam spoke carefully. 'This is Charlie Bannon, a neighbour of a lady called Mrs Newsome. Her baby's coming but she can't get to the hospital. Road is blocked.'

Seymour looked frozen. For the first time all night, his well-organised mind seemed incapable of making a plan. Liam took a breath, then continued. 'I know a brilliant handywoman – Kathleen Gallagher. I plan to use Mr Bannon's motorbike to take her up to the house.'

Seymour's face cleared. 'Good plan. Well, Charlie.'

'Mr Seymour.'

They were both being very discreet. Seymour wouldn't want the entire team knowing his business; he needed to maintain his leadership armour a little longer.

Less than five minutes later, with directions in his head and a brief lesson on working the motorbike, Liam was on his way to the first aid bus.

*Belfast, 4.15 a.m.*

'Corporal Gallagher!' Belatedly realising she was being called, Kathleen looked towards the door, where the sergeant was standing with— Her heart leapt. *Liam!* With a murmured word to the doctor she had been assisting as he stitched a head wound on a middle-aged lady, she rose, making her way towards them through a press of people.

God, the last time she had seen Liam, Sadie had been there, and— *No.* She must not allow herself to think of it. She had to be strong.

'Sir?'

'You are required to assist a woman in labour. Warden Flynn will take you.'

'Yes, sir.' She looked at Liam, careful to keep her expression blank. 'Let me get my bag.'

It was still dark outside, and the air stank of dust and chemicals, a pall of yellowish smoke hanging in the air. The booming of explosions was now almost unnoticeable, its impact dulled to background noise by relentless familiarity. Yes, bombs were still falling. But for now, Kathleen was still standing.

'Where are we going?'

'Isadore Avenue, near the Springfield Dam.' He tapped the side of his head. 'I have the directions. We'll have to go up the Whiterock way.'

She grimaced. 'God, that's a quare walk!'

'Ah, but we aren't walking.' He pointed to a shiny motorbike parked on the street, its light angled down. 'Your carriage awaits, my lady!'

Her jaw dropped. A *motorcycle*? 'Oh, holy God, where did you get that?'

'It belongs to Seymour's neighbour. He's the one that came to ask for help.'

'Right, so.' It was so odd, to be idly conversing with him like this, while bombs were falling, while she still had not fully felt the realisation that he could never be hers. *Don't think about it – any of it!* A woman needed her. That was all that mattered.

'Have I to sit behind you?'

'That's right. Here, let me get on first.'

A moment later she was on, her handywoman bag hooked over one arm, her hooded lamp on the other. Unsure what to do, she placed her hands lightly on his sides, feeling the warmth of his back against her front. She couldn't enjoy the sensation, though. This was Liam – the man who she had broken with a hundred years ago, before the bombing. *Was it really only yesterday?*

Once more she focused her mind on more practical matters. There was a serious risk of falling off, since she had never been on a motorcycle before and had no idea what to do. It also quickly became apparent that Liam was still learning how to drive the thing, so there was a strong possibility they would *both* fall off at some point. In addition, just to complicate matters their route was littered with debris, craters, and collapsed buildings. In places the gap was so narrow there would be no way for a car or ambulance to get through.

At one point it was so bad they had to get off and walk, pushing the motorcycle carefully through the obstacles. Liam sent her a sideways glance. 'Kathleen,' he began, his expression sombre, and her heart leapt. *God, not now!*

She swallowed. 'This isn't a good time for serious conversations, Liam. We both have work to do.'

He grimaced. 'Aye, and we might be killed stone dead any minute. Well, I'm not going to my grave without asking you this.'

She braced herself, for she knew *exactly* what he was going to talk about.

Carefully he wheeled the motorbike through a pile of rubble, lifting it up at one stage so the wheels didn't catch, while her heart pounded at the realisation they were about to share another difficult discussion.

'Right,' he declared, 'here's my question. Why did you tell me that I should get back with Sadie?'

She shrugged, hoping her heart could remain hard, and distant, and uncaring. 'Because that's what I think.'

'You said it's the right thing to do? Why? Because *she's* changed *her* mind?' His expression was grim, his mouth a hard line. 'Cos I don't think that's a good enough reason, Kathleen, and I'm disappointed that you would even try something so flimsy. If you don't want to be with me you should bloody be honest about it and say so!'

Anger rose within her. 'Don't you dare put this on me, Liam Flynn! I'm so feckin' sick of everybody takin' me for granted and thinkin' I'll just go along with things. Well, I'm done with that!'

'Go along with what?' He looked genuinely confused.

'Be your girlfriend while you abandon Sadie even though she's expecting!' The words exploded from her, and he flinched in the shockwave.

'Expecting?' He shook his head as if bewildered. 'But she's not exp—' His face cleared. '*Oh!* You heard what she said to me!'

She nodded, going ahead of him through a narrow gap between piles of bricks and wood. 'I did.'

'And you think I'm the sort of lad that would do that to a girl? Get her up the stick and walk away?' His tone was harsh, his face twisted in the half-light. Never had she seen him so angry.

She met fire with fire. 'Well, what the hell am I supposed to think? She said she's pregnant, or *might* be pregnant. That means . . .' Her voice tailed off.

He stopped to look at her. 'What? What does it mean, Kathleen?'

She tossed her head in defiance. 'It means that when you were together, yous . . . yous did things. Otherwise pregnancy wouldn't even be a possibility.' She glared back, the injustice of it all roiling within her. She had been so close to happiness, but what he had done with Sadie had changed everything.

'Tell me this,' he said in a deceptively casual tone, 'have you ever known Sadie to tell lies?'

'I—' New possibilities were flying through her mind. 'She *lied*?' Astonishment and bewilderment held her stock-still. In the distance, two more explosions sounded.

He nodded grimly. 'And until this minute, I had no idea why. But now I know.' Shaking his head, he walked on, and Kathleen hastened after him. 'She is a quare piece of work, that one. Thank God I'm away from her.'

'What? Why? Why did she lie?' Kathleen couldn't think clearly. *Sadie lied.*

'Come on, Kathleen!' He was still angry. 'You're smart. Work it out.'

She thought about it. Sadie's hand on Liam's arm. The look she had sent Kathleen. The loud whisper . . .

The penny dropped. 'She *wanted* me to hear her. She feckin' did it to wind me up!'

'Aye.' His tone was calmer. 'To keep us apart. And it worked, it seems.' His brow was furrowed. 'How could you think that of me, Kathleen? Me an' her never got up to anything serious!'

Regret pierced her like a knife. 'Ah, Liam. I'm sorry. I— Cora, and our Bronagh, and then Sadie . . . I wondered if I was the only virgin in West, and if the rules I believed in were only for me!' She closed her eyes. 'It shook me to the core. I thought you and Sadie . . . that everyone was at it, and that I was the only eejit in the parish.'

'Not a bit of it,' he said simply. 'Me and Sadie never did anything like that. So unless the Angel Gabriel is involved, she can't be pregnant. And she feckin' knows it.' They had reached the corner of the Whiterock Road. 'Looks to be clear. Let's hop on.' He stilled. 'Wheesht!'

She listened. The city was eerily silent, with only a single explosion in the distance. 'Is it easing?'

'I think it is!' He glanced at the sky. 'Fewer planes, too. Once they've no bombs left they go away.'

Relief flooded through Kathleen. Belfast was ablaze, with perhaps thousands still trapped in damaged buildings, but if the bombing was easing at least the rescue efforts could properly begin. They hugged, then kissed fervently, the motorcycle beside them tipping over, momentarily forgotten. *The bombing is stopped, and me and Liam are back together!*

But there was no time; a woman in labour needed her. With one last kiss Liam turned away to straddle the motorcycle, then carefully Kathleen slid on behind him. As she placed her hands on his sides, he covered her right hand with his left, squeezing it. Then, turning his head, he pressed a quick kiss to her cheek, making her insides warm with a delicious new sensation. In response, she slid her arms fully around his waist, leaning into him. 'I'm sorry for doubting you, Liam.'

'Aye, well next time ask me before you go flying away off, will you?'

*Next time.* 'So you'll forgive me?'

'On one condition.' He twisted back to look at her again. 'What's that?'

'That you be my girlfriend and stay with me this time.'

Her lips curved into a smile. 'Done!'

*Dublin, 4.35 a.m.*

*Finally!* The telegram was brief, but it was official. Stormont had asked for help, and De Valera had agreed to it.

'Let's go, lads!' Micko lifted the phone one last time.

'Dun Laoghaire fire station. Sub-officer Whelan speaking.'

'Whelan, it's O'Hanlon here. We have the green light. See you in Belfast.'

Within minutes they were away, the crew clinging to the outside of the tender as best they could for the long drive ahead.

Six tenders were coming from Dublin – the Dorset Street lads had set off ahead of them – along with one from Dun Laoghaire, one from Drogheda, and one from Dundalk. In all, around seventy men had volunteered, and Micko had never been prouder to be a fire officer.

It was always a bad idea to think too much about what you were heading into, so Micko kept his thoughts away from the death and destruction they were racing towards. Instead he allowed his thoughts to drift to that carefree spring he had spent in Belfast at the age of sixteen. That had been a happy time – albeit frustrating, for the War of Independence had been raging and his two older brothers had refused to let him sign up to fight until his seventeenth birthday.

Like a halfwit he had then been injured almost immediately, spending weeks in Jervis Street hospital. Once recovered he had joined another flying column only to be captured and imprisoned. By the time he had written to his Belfast girlfriend from prison some months had passed.

*No wonder she never replied*, he thought now, trying once again to see things from her perspective. He had vanished from her life, and she would no doubt have thought he was only after the one thing, and that once he had got it he was away . . .

He shook his head. *I was an eejit*, he acknowledged. He had loved Bronagh deeply, with all the fervour of a sixteen-year-old, but had felt like a coward letting his brothers fight for Irish freedom while he went for long walks in the Falls Park and on the Black Mountain with the girl he had adored.

He could picture her yet, though the image was hazy. Fair hair, deep blue eyes, divine figure . . . She had been like a Hollywood star – apart from the fact her blonde hair was natural, not from a bottle. She'd be thirty-seven now, the same as himself. Probably married with a lock of childer.

His mind drifted again, as it had hundreds of times over the years, to their parting. It had been May, and the *cloigíní gorma* – the bluebells – had been swarming all over the mountain. She had begged him to take care, and to come back to her, alive. He had promised to do so, and had broken that promise. Or she had, perhaps.

After there was no answer to his first letter he had sent a second, in case the postal service had messed up or the warders had deliberately lost his letter. But when she didn't reply to that one either he had accepted her choice. Maybe she'd had a new fella by then. As one of the best-looking girls in West Belfast back then she could have had her pick of the lads. *Aye, that was probably it.*

# 37

*Belfast, 4.50 a.m.*

*The Ulster Hall was still standing, the crowds inside safe. Once the bombing stopped they emerged and made their way home amid the smoke, the fires, and the dust.*

Up the Whiterock Road they went, and now she was getting the hang of it Kathleen was thrilled by the feeling of wrapping her arms around Liam. *My Liam!* Turning right at the bottom of the Mountain Loney, Liam shouted to some of the people heading up the mountain, curious about where they were going.

'Away to look for clean water up here – springs, like,' was the answer. 'Apparently you're not to drink the tap water.'

Well the area *was* called the Springfield Road. 'Molly's Well is up there,' Kathleen murmured. 'It has the healing plants all round it.'

'We used to all go up there when we were wee – picking blackberries, remember?' Liam turned slightly to speak to her. She squeezed him tight to indicate that, yes, she remembered, and then they were off again.

Once they passed the brickworks, Kathleen's focus turned to the houses. There were some fine big houses on this part of the Springfield, and she nodded knowingly as Liam pulled in to Isadore Avenue, stopping outside the first house. Middle-class women often chose to have their babies in hospital, and so she was rarely called to houses like this for a birth. She vaguely recognised the street, though. She had supported a family through the final illness and death of their grandfather, a little further down.

This was a mixed area, and she recalled the family telling her at the time there were RUC officers living there alongside well-to-do nationalists. She shrugged inwardly. There were some RUC officers who claimed to support a united Ireland, insisting they were only in the police as a professional career. Tonight everyone was helping everyone else. Tomorrow the old divisions would no doubt be back in play.

'I'll wait here a minute,' Liam offered, as she slid off, her handywoman bag and her lamp still safely over her arms. Then she paused. The all-clear was sounding, and she reckoned it was the best noise she had ever heard.

'The all-clear!' They hugged, relief flooding through Kathleen, and his lips found hers for the sweetest of kisses. She straightened, sending him a wide smile. In the midst of the Belfast Blitz she had found a miracle, and she was once again Liam Flynn's girlfriend. And another miracle – they had both survived the bombing.

But there was more work to be done. Walking up the path, she lifted her lamp and eyed the house in the pre-dawn light. It was substantial, made of Belfast brick with a bay window and an actual front garden. The main front door was open, revealing a vestibule with a white inner half-glazed door surrounded by fancy stained glass. The vestibule floor was finished with beautiful Victorian tiles, and a carved umbrella stand stood to the right.

Reminding herself she was friends with both the Clarkes and the Sheridans and had been in houses like these before, she pressed the doorbell.

No response. Were they in the house? Or should she go round to the back to their shelter?

Knowing whoever was with the woman in labour was unlikely to leave her simply because a doorbell had rung, Kathleen opened the inner door and called out.

'Hello? Mrs Newsome? Mrs Seymour?'

This did the trick, as after a moment she heard a door open upstairs. A middle-aged woman then appeared, the lamp in her hand revealing a flushed face and an air of anxiety about her. As she hurried down the wide staircase Kathleen stepped back, not wishing to appear rude.

'Mrs Seymour?' The woman nodded, and Kathleen gave what she hoped was a reassuring smile. 'I understand your daughter, Mrs Newsome, is in labour. I've been sent to help.'

'Oh, thank goodness!' Mrs Seymour was eyeing Kathleen's uniform. 'Are you a midwife? Or a nurse?'

'I'm an advanced first-aider – Corporal, St John Ambulance. And a handywoman.'

Mrs Seymour's face fell. 'Well, I suppose you'll have to do. Come with me.'

'One moment.'

Turning, Kathleen waved to Liam to indicate she was staying. He waved back, then started up the motorcycle.

Kathleen entered the house, her lamp raised, trying not to gape at the riches she saw everywhere. There were paintings on the wall – actual *paintings*, not simply prints of the Sacred Heart or the Pope. *Just like in Mrs Clarke's*. Beneath her feet was a carpet so deep her feet and ankles could *feel* the difference.

'What a beautiful home you have, Mrs Seymour,' she offered, as they climbed the stairs, hoping to find a connection with the woman.

Mrs Seymour sniffed. 'Thank you. Though the back windows all blew in at some point last night. All the rooms on that side of the house are full of dust.'

'That's terrible,' Kathleen offered. *She has little to worry about*, she thought, briefly allowing herself to recall some of the victims she'd treated, the bodies lined up in the yard beside the first aid bus.

Then, *No, I am being unfair.* Mrs Seymour's preoccupation with her own worries – including her daughter – was entirely understandable.

'Lily is in here.' She opened the door to a front bedroom, and instantly warm candlelight poured onto Kathleen's face. There was a large bed on the left, and in it, flat on her back and moaning, was a heavily pregnant young woman.

'Now then, Lily, here's the . . . nurse to help you.' Kathleen heard the pause, but ignored it. Most people called her 'nurse'. 'We were out in the shelter most of the night, but the raid seemed to be easing so I brought her in.'

Kathleen nodded. 'Hello, Mrs Newsome, how are you? My name's Kathleen.'

'Go away and leave me to die!' Mrs Newsome replied piteously.

Mrs Seymour tutted. 'I can do nothing with her, Nurse.' Turning to her daughter, she admonished. 'Less of that nonsense, now, Lily. D'ye hear me? You've a child to be born.'

'I can't,' her daughter moaned. 'I've told you, I can't. Oh, why can I not go to the hospital and let them cut it out of me?'

'Because the roads are blocked,' Mrs Seymour replied crossly. 'I've told you a hundred times.'

*Right. Tricky.* Moving round to the far side of the bed, Kathleen laid a hand on the young woman's shoulder. 'Is it all right if I help you, Mrs Newsome?'

'Lily. Call me Lily. I don't wanna be Mrs anything today! I just wanna be a wee girl with none of this going on!'

'I know, I know. Lily, then. Can you tell me where it hurts?'

'Everywhere!' She put a hand on her swollen tummy. 'Here, mostly. But my back is in agony every time it – oh, no, here we go!'

Her abdomen tightened, and Kathleen took her hand, speaking softly to her as she was overcome by the pain. Once it eased, she said, 'Well done, Lily. You'll never have to go through that particular pain again.'

'What do you mean?' Opening her eyes, Lily looked at her suspiciously.

'There's a certain amount of contractions needed to get the baby out. Once each one has passed, it's marked off the list. Done.'

Lily nodded thoughtfully. 'I get that. But how many? How long will it take?'

'How long is a piece of string?' Kathleen countered. 'There are things you can do that might help it to happen sooner, though.'

'Like what?'

'Do you mind if I feel your tummy first?'

Lily agreed, and Kathleen felt the bump with practised hands. 'Excellent. Baby is in a good position, head down. Not sure what way it's facing, though. It could be back-to-back.'

'What's that mean? Is it bad?'

'No, it's fairly common. It might be why your back pain is so strong, though. If the baby's spine is against yours, that can hurt.'

'Yes! That makes sense.' She began to cry. 'Why do bad things always happen to me?'

'Now, now. I have a suggestion.'

'What?' Lily's tone was flat as she reached for a handkerchief from the pretty little bedside table.

'If you flip over so you're on your hands and knees, that might take the pressure off your back.'

'Anything is better than this. But my mother said—'

'I'd prefer her to be on her back,' said Mrs Seymour firmly. 'That's the way I gave birth, both times. The correct way. That's the way they do it in the hospitals.'

'I'm sure that worked for you, Mrs Seymour,' Kathleen offered diplomatically. 'But if the baby is in the occiput posterior position then hands and knees is the recommended procedure.' Deliberately Kathleen used the medical jargon she'd picked up in Peggy's text book.

Intimidation via Latin worked well on this occasion. 'Ah, of course, of course,' said Mrs Seymour, an air of knowingness about her. 'Now,' her tone turned brisk, 'do you need me to get you anything?'

'Some hot water please, if you can. The town gas is off though, so—'

'Never fear, I have a bottle gas stove out in the shelter. My husband thinks of everything. He's the District leader of all the air raid wardens in this whole area, you know!'

'Impressive!'

'He is.' She turned. 'Right. Hot water.'

'And clean towels too, if possible. And a bucket.'

'A bucket? Whatever for? We have enamel chamber pots in this house, even though we have a plumbed-in bathroom,' she added proudly.

'Plumbed in? That's amazing. Er – can you bring a bucket as well as a chamber pot, though?'

'Yes, if you insist.'

*I do.* But she was gone, and Kathleen had – thankfully – suppressed her final comment.

Turning her attention back to the princess in the bed, Kathleen helped her flip on to her hands and knees – the young woman protesting throughout.

It had already been a long night, and now this. Still, Kathleen would manage. Somehow.

★ ★ ★

Liam went straight back to the duty room, assuring Seymour that the handywoman was now in his house. The borrowed motorcycle was returned to Charlie, who departed with an air of great relief.

'Thank the good Lord for that!' Seymour said, with fervour. 'I appreciate you fetching her, son.' He pressed a hand to Liam's shoulder briefly, and Liam felt something powerful well up inside him – a feeling he hadn't experienced since the age of fourteen.

'So,' Seymour continued, in a lighter tone, 'who is this handywoman?'

'Er . . . she's called Kathleen Gallagher. She's from Beechmount, like me, and she's a really good handywoman. Advanced first-aider too. She's a corporal in St John

Ambulance now – one of the four who got full marks after the basic first aid course.' *I'm talking too much.* He could feel his face flushing, and saw Seymour looking at him curiously.

'And is she a *young* woman, this Kathleen Gallagher?'

Liam nodded, feeling uncomfortable. Seymour was way too astute.

'Liam Flynn.' There was humour in Seymour's eye. 'I remember only one other occasion I saw you blush like this. It was when I asked if you were walking out with someone.' He looked at Liam expectantly.

Liam opened his mouth to deflect Seymour's curiosity, then thought better of it. After everything they'd gone through together, he could not dissemble with this man.

'Aye, well, yes,' he admitted, a grin breaking out. 'Kathleen is now my girlfriend – but nobody knows yet.'

'Is she special, this girl?'

'She is, aye.' There was a lump in his throat.

'Good lad, Liam,' was Seymour's comment. 'Good lad.'

# 38

*Newry 6 a.m.*

The fire tenders were nearly at Newry, and the border was approaching. The lads had been singing most of the way up the road to keep themselves awake, although the cold night air helped with that too. As it was still fairly dark, the northern blackout rules would apply, but unfortunately the southern fire service vehicles hadn't had their headlights adapted. Leaning in, Micko spoke to the driver, Jack Conroy.

'You'll need to turn the headlights off once we pass Killeen.'

'Ah, right, boss. Hadn't thought about that.' He slowed the vehicle as the customs signs were coming into view. Micko gaped in astonishment. The customs men from both sides of the line had formed something like a guard of honour, saluting the fire engine as it passed.

*Jaysus!* Swallowing against the unexpected lump in his throat, Micko saw a motorcyclist pulling in alongside them, the rider clad in the leather coat and peaked cap of a northern customs officer. 'Follow my light!' he shouted, and Conroy did exactly that, his speed increasing as he used the red rear light of the motorbike to guide him.

Through Newry they went – the town peacefully sleeping – then Banbridge, Dromore, Hillsborough . . . By the time they reached Lisburn they could clearly see the fires on the horizon. Bracing himself, Micko's firefighter brain began to kick in as they finally reached the outskirts of the city.

★ ★ ★

'That's it. Well done, Lily. You're doing brilliant.'

Thankfully, being on all fours (plus having her mother leave the room) had made a dramatic difference. Lily was now pushing, and had been doing so for a good forty-five minutes. Her labour must have been slowly progressing throughout the raid. *Poor girl. She must have been terrified.*

'I can see the head! You're doing it!'

Lily was pushing with great energy, and gravity was helping. Kneeling up, she was hugging the headboard – Kathleen had, with some effort, pulled the bed slightly away from the wall to make it easier for Lily.

Mrs Seymour had brought all the items Kathleen had asked for, and Kathleen had gently suggested the woman rest a while. She had agreed, saying she was going to take to the settee, for she hadn't had a wink of sleep all night. At that stage there had been no sign that a baby might be imminent, so off she'd gone.

Rummaging among the pile of pristine, expensive-looking towels, Kathleen found two that were a little less new looking – these had been washed many times, and as a result were much softer. Placing one carefully between Lily's knees on the bed, she fleetingly wondered if Mrs Seymour had thought to cover the mattress with a rubber sheet. She shrugged inwardly. The Seymours had plenty of money. They would likely simply buy a new mattress.

'Aaaahhh!' Lily's deep groans momentarily became a squeal, as the head finally emerged.

'Well done, Lily, the head's out.' She half hugged the other girl from behind. 'You're doing fantastic!'

Lily nodded, her focus on the brief respite between pains.

'That's it . . . good deep breaths,' Kathleen told her, glad the girl had remained calm. The head had made its slow quarter turn, and so she said encouragingly, 'Who knows, maybe the shoulders will come with the next few pains?'

This proved to be the case, and the familiar sound of slither-pop accompanied the baby as it landed squarely on the towel.

'Congratulations, you're a mother!' she announced. 'You did it!'

'I did? The baby's out?' Lily sounded astonished.

'It is! Now, move this leg . . . that's it, slide round . . . now you can pick your baby up.'

'Oh! It's a wee girl! I did it!'

On cue the baby began to cry. 'Shall I get your mammy to come up?'

'Yes please! I can't believe it!'

Mrs Seymour was delighted, and held the baby while Kathleen helped Lily with the afterbirth, which went in the bucket. The child latched on soon afterwards – Mrs Seymour giving sensible advice to her daughter, to Kathleen's relief. *At least Granny won't sabotage the feeding!*

*Belfast, 6.45 a.m.*

Dawn had come, and finally, *finally*, the Luftwaffe had all gone. The bombing had eased sometime around half four when he and Kathleen had been together, and eventually it had stopped completely. That all-clear had been the best sound he had ever heard – except perhaps for Kathleen's words as she agreed to become his girl.

Liam had hardly had the chance to breathe all night, never mind to notice the changes in the raid. Now though, walking through his own beloved Beechmount in the morning light, making his rounds for what seemed like the hundredth time, he took a moment to pause, and realise that somehow, he had survived. With trepidation he made his way to his own house, glancing anxiously up and down the street. While there was clear blast damage – the street littered with broken glass, roof tiles, and bits of masonry – there had been no direct hits here, and he could see no trace of fires burning.

Silently he walked through the empty living room to the kitchen, marvelling at the kettle, the tea towel – the evidence of yesterday's ordinary life. *Where is everyone?* His gut twisted in fear. Opening the back door he braced himself, but the shelter looked intact.

'Hello?' He called, his heart leaping as he heard his mother's answer.

'Is that our Liam?' Mammy's voice. 'Oh holy God, Liam's still alive!'

Then the wee door opened, and there she was. There were tears, and hugs. Mammy and the girls had had a tough night, full of fear and cold and physical discomforts, but right now relief was paramount.

'What about our Seány?'

Liam shrugged. 'No word. They're busy still – loads of fires.'

'Desprit. Hopefully our Therese and Jimmy are safe up in Greencastle too. Are we all right to come out? The planes have gone? We heard the all-clear but were too afraid to believe it.'

'Yeah, they're gone. For now anyway.' He straightened. 'Do you need anything?'

'No, we're grand, son.' Mammy kissed his cheek. 'So proud of you.'

Feeling ten foot tall, he made his way back outside, checking on a few of his neighbours before making his way round the area, and eventually to Kathleen's street. Mr and Mrs Gallagher were just emerging from their house, both in good spirits, and offering to volunteer with the rescue efforts.

'There's loads of injured and homeless in our parish hall,' he told them, inwardly marvelling at the fact he hoped to become part of their family.

'Right. We'll head over there,' Mr Gallagher declared. 'Any word of our Bronagh or Kathleen?'

His pulse leapt at the sound of her name, but he knew not to give away any secrets yet. 'Kathleen's with a woman in labour up on the Springfield, but I haven't seen Bronagh all night.' Abruptly his heart sank, as reality began reasserting itself, now the immediate danger from the Blitz had passed. The Gallaghers probably wouldn't want a man with no prospects for Kathleen. He certainly wouldn't have wanted that for Therese. He swallowed. 'I'm heading to the ambulance station next, so I'll walk down there with you.'

'Thanks, Liam.'

Walking down the slight hill into the yard outside the parish hall, he saw ominous rows of tarp-covered bodies, and ambulance volunteers taking them away, one and two at a time. Although very few bombs had hit this part of the city, this yard, designated as 'The Falls Road Ambulance Station', had become a receiving point for some of the dead. Bronagh was there, and he spoke to her briefly after she and her parents had hugged. Like everyone who had been in the thick of it all night she was covered in dust, and clearly exhausted.

'All right, Bronagh?' he asked softly.

'Who— ah, Liam!' Her face cleared. 'Glad you're all right. I saw your Seány about a half an hour ago. Crackin' jokes he was, lifting everybody's spirits.'

Relief flooded through him. 'He's a good lad.'

'He is. Did you hear about the Percy Street shelter?'

'I did. Desperate.' *Mrs Corry. Baby Elizabeth.*

'We should leave, you know. All of us.'

'Leave?'

'The Luftwaffe will be back. Are we really gonna just sit around and wait for them?'

The notion was shocking. Leave Belfast? The only home he'd ever known? *No!*

'Next one there, Bronagh!' a man shouted, and Bronagh made her way back to her ambulance, lifting a hand in farewell.

About to enter the first aid bus, instead Liam followed Mr and Mrs Gallagher into the parish hall. Visiting the men's toilets, he washed his face and hands as best he could, replacing his dented helmet and attaching the strap. *That helmet saved my life so many times last night.* Somehow, he had managed to survive with nothing worse than a few cuts and bruises. Was there some sort of meaning in that?

The main hall was busy. Liam took a report from the lead volunteers; the homeless would be told to gather here, and Liam knew the wardens and the Women's Voluntary Service would have to try to find shelter for all of them

*The Irish Midwife at War*

by nightfall. A tough ask, with many thousands of homes destroyed.

Matt Darcy was there too, his leg splinted. He and Liam exchanged a few words then Liam headed back outside, seeing that the sky was still dawn-pink and beautiful, despite the billowing yellow smoke. Walking straight across the yard he kept his eyes on the sky, the bus – anywhere but the tarpaulins. Going inside, he received a report from the St John Ambulance officer, noting the details of casualties and of supplies needed. There was no sign of Kathleen, who of course would likely still be attending Seymour's daughter. Bidding them a 'Cheerio!' he headed outside and up the wee hill. As he turned into the road, a voice hailed him.

'Liam!'

He turned, his heart warming at the sight before him. 'Kathleen!'

# 39

Kathleen's heart skipped. Having cleaned up, she had left Lily and her mother safely with the baby, then set off on the long walk back towards home. The Gallagher house and shelter were both empty, but the items from the shelter had already been tidied away, so she knew that Mammy and Daddy were probably safe. After washing and using the outhouse she had headed to the first aid station, knowing she would be needed. There was no time for sleep, no time even to *think* about the things she had seen and done since last night. She hadn't expected, however, to see the man she loved quite so soon.

Uncaring who was watching, she went to him. They clung to one another for a long, long moment – desperation and love and relief flooding Kathleen's body and mind. She closed her eyes, exhaling away some of the terror within her. Although it had only been a few hours since their motorcycle ride, anything might have happened to him. There were fires and gas explosions and bombs still detonating. *Liam is here. He is safe. I am safe.*

'You're still alive! Thank God!' she managed, drawing back to look at his beloved face. 'I'd have feckin' killed you if you'd died on me!'

He gave a twisted smile at her attempt at humour. 'How's Mrs Newsome?'

'She's fine. A wee girl. Can you let Mr Seymour know?'

'I will, aye.' He grinned at the news, then sobered. 'Kathleen. I have to say this.'

'What?' Concern ran through her as she saw the intent on his face. *Whatever this is, it's serious.*

He took a breath. 'I love you. That's it. I love you, Kathleen Gallagher.'

A huge smile split her face as joy rose within her. Fleetingly, she questioned in her mind whether he meant it. Maybe it was the terror and the drama and the relief at having survived the night . . . But no. She knew he was telling the truth.

'I love you too, Liam.' And she did. With every part of her. With everything that she was and was not and would ever be.

His lips met hers – reverently, softly. The kiss lasted only seconds then he was gone, promising they would speak properly later.

She watched him go, her heart full and her mind all confusion. *Did that really just happen?*

Yes. Yes, it had. Smiling, she turned to the first aid bus, pushing open the door.

*Belfast, 9 a.m.*

The southern firemen were directed initially to Chichester Street, where they were received with cheers from hollow-eyed, dust-covered fire officers. This echoed the crowds who had cheered them once daylight had come to the towns south of Belfast.

Once they had reached Dunmurry they had started to encounter evacuees – hundreds of people walking or driving whatever way they could, desperate to flee the city. Micko had seen ponies and traps, motor-cars, donkeys, and even wheelbarrows being used to carry the aged or infirm. Small children were either tied to their mothers or held on the shoulders of the menfolk. They had moved to the sides of the road to allow the fire tenders to pass, some blessing themselves as they were reminded of their reasons for running from their homes.

As the Belfast crew began their briefing, a door briefly opened into an inner office, and Micko was shocked to see a glimpse of a man in the uniform of a senior officer cowering under a large table, tears running down his cheeks. *Jaysus! How bad a night did they have?*

Most of the tenders were then immediately dispatched to the key areas: the docks, East Belfast, the city centre. A couple were sent to the north of the city, where apparently a massive mill was on fire. During the conversations, Micko had volunteered his own tender for one particular zone; the Crumlin Road in north-West Belfast. It was as close as he could get to West.

'There are currently around sixty significant fires,' the men were told, 'as well as hundreds of smaller ones. Our local firemen are exhausted, so can you relieve them at each of the major incidents indicated?'

This they were glad to do, and Micko's crew were astonished to find when they got to their first incident that a mobile canteen arrived soon afterwards, with tea and hot food for both the Belfast and Dublin firefighters. They soon settled in, taking turns to manage the massive fire in the linen factory while their comrades rested. They had been supplied with brass adapters, as many of the southern hoses were of a different diameter to those in the north. *Belfast*, thought Micko at one point. *I'm actually in Belfast.* The notion was too bizarre to contemplate, so he shook his head and got on with his job.

*Belfast, 9.45 a.m.*

After telling Seymour the good news about the baby, Liam was dispatched to help with a complicated rescue at a collapsed house in one of the wee streets north of the Falls. Apparently a group of rescuers had been there for ages, and the call had gone out for more assistance.

'Seány! I'd heard you'd made it!' His brother was there, looking exhausted but hale. Liam punched him lightly on the arm, and Seány grinned.

'Ach, it's hard to kill a bad thing!'

'No fires to put out?'

'Hundreds. But the water pressure is shite, and the Dublin lads have taken over the biggest incidents.'

Liam's eyes widened. 'Firemen from Dublin?'

'Aye. Dundalk and Drogheda too, I heard. About six or seven fire engines.'

Liam whistled through his teeth. 'Good stuff. I did wonder if the boys on the hill would let their hatred for all things Irish get in the way of common sense.'

'Common sense! I dunno about that!' Seány snorted. 'They made a complete hames of Belfast's defences, as we now know. Here, give us a hand, will ya?'

As Liam got stuck in, joining the chain of men removing chunks of masonry and then an old roof truss, he abruptly realised whose house it was.

'Is this the McGowans'?' he asked, his heart sinking. All night long it had been so much harder when he knew the people.

'Aye. The mother and two children under the stairs. Still alive, thank God.'

Glancing to the road, Liam saw the rest of the McGowan children standing forlornly by the ruins of their home. Looking again, he saw Mr McGowan was among those trying to get through the rubble.

'We're making good progress, though,' Seány continued. 'Should have them out soon.'

Seány was right. Within less than half an hour they had managed to clear a space around the little pocket where Mrs McGowan was hiding. They got the child out first, and Liam made a point of taking her himself. He had seen her holding Kathleen's hand outside the chapel after Therese's wedding . . . yesterday. Immediately after the Sadie thing.

Had it really been only yesterday? He shook his head. 'What's your name?' he asked gently, walking carefully over the rubble towards the street.

'Alice,' the child replied. She seemed dazed – hardly surprising. He settled her properly on his hip and she cried out in pain.

'I'm sorry, Alice.' Gently he lifted her away, holding her carefully. 'Where does it hurt?'

'My leg,' she declared solemnly. 'And my tummy. And my arm.' She glanced down, and he saw that her knitted cardigan was torn, revealing a deep gash on her arm.

'Oh, no! I think we should get Kathleen to put a bandage on that to make it better.'

She brightened. 'Kathleen? *My* Kathleen?' She eyed him suspiciously. 'How do you know Kathleen?'

*I'm going to marry Kathleen.* Almost, he said the words aloud, before realising how inappropriate they would be.

Strange how he had spent months avoiding the topic of marriage with Sadie, yet was already certain that Kathleen was the woman with whom he wanted to spend the rest of his life. And he had told Kathleen he loved her earlier – words he had never said to Sadie. Not once.

And while he had no idea how he was supposed to afford to get married, how he was supposed to look after two households, whether the Gallaghers would even want him to marry her, he now realised he didn't care. Not in the slightest. He was going to marry the girl he loved and *then* figure it out.

There was a shout from the rescuers, and he turned briefly to see that Mrs McGowan had been freed. Her baby was tied to her via a dust-covered shawl, and briefly he thought of other mothers, other babies he'd seen during this long, long night. A moment later they were all together on the debris-strewn street.

'Mammy!' The rest of the McGowan clan surrounded her. They had apparently sheltered in the nearby public shelter with their father during the worst of the raid, but for some reason Mrs McGowan had chosen to stay in her home with the two youngest. *Madness!* Realising the direction of his thoughts, Liam shook his head. Many people had survived under their stairs, while Mrs Corry and the others who'd trusted in the public shelter had paid for it with their lives. Who was he to say what anyone should do for the best?

Handing Alice over to her big sister (Cora, he remembered), he told her the child needed first aid. 'Aye, I'll take her. God, I was so worried!'

'I'm sure.' These were the moments he had to hang on to. The McGowans. Matt. The family who had got out of the butcher's shop in time. *Kathleen, and the future they would make together.*

He needed to see his love again. 'I'm headed that way. I'll go with you.'

'Thanks. Come on, Ma. First aid.'

'I'm grand,' said Mrs McGowan shakily. 'Honest to God.'

'Sure how could you be grand, with God-knows-what fallin' on you, then stuck in a cubbyhole for hours?' Cora was taking charge. 'Da, you take the rest of the children to Granny's house. We'll see you later. Come on, Ma.'

'How long was it since the house collapsed?' Liam asked Mrs McGowan.

'Haven't a clue, love.'

'About six hours,' one of the rescuers declared. 'Took us ages cos we had to move that lot first.' He indicated the pile of bricks, tiles, and other debris to their right.

'Six hours?' Mrs McGowan looked shocked. 'Felt like a hundred.'

'I'm with you there,' Liam said. 'Yesterday seems like it was ten years ago.'

'So are we goin', then? Can you walk all right, Ma?'

Cora set Alice down and the child tried to take a step. 'Ow! My leg!' Her hands flew out as if she was light-headed, and Liam swiftly bent to steady her.

'Right. Liam, can you carry her? Thank you.'

Off they went, a strange little procession: Cora and Mrs McGowan with their babies, Liam carefully carrying Alice. *I'm going to see Kathleen again soon!*

★ ★ ★

Belfast's water pressure was still dangerously low – too low to be any feckin' use to Micko and his men. The southern crews offered to pump water from the River Lagan into the water tanks. All the southern tenders had inbuilt pumps, unlike the northern ones which varied, and Micko's crews were much in demand.

'Where next?' he asked, and was directed to another fire in the same sector of the city.

Off they went, taking directions at every street corner from the air raid wardens and other volunteers. The fire was persistent, and it took an hour and nearly the full tank to put it out. There had been casualties too and eventually a couple of ambulances appeared. The first swung neatly into a narrow space amid the debris, the female driver jumping down lightly and nimbly. Something about her was familiar, so Micko took a closer look. Since arriving in Belfast a couple of hours ago he'd imagined seeing her everywhere, but it was never her. This time, though . . .

He walked closer as she opened the two rear doors, and the stretcher men ran up with two casualties she was to take to some or other hospital. She turned, her face filthy with dust and her hair stuck to her head. And still he could see her beauty.

'Bronagh?'

She froze, a shocked expression on her pretty features.

'Michael.' Her tone was flat, as she looked him up and down. 'You're a fireman now?'

'Captain in the Dublin Fire Brigade,' he replied, hearing the pride in his own voice. *I made something of myself, Bronagh.*

'Well, la-dee-dah,' she replied dismissively, turning to the stretcher bearers. 'Yes, on the left there.' She turned her attention to her casualties. 'What have we got?'

As the stretcher men listed the known injuries while depositing two injured people inside the ambulance, he waited. *Surely she'll speak to me again?*

But no. Without even glancing in his direction she closed the doors, then went round to the cab and hopped in. A moment later she had reversed out and was on her way.

★ ★ ★

Before long Liam was at the chapel with the McGowans, and both Mrs McGowan and Cora reacted in shock to the line of bodies in the yard, blessing themselves and commenting again how lucky they were. Little did they know that these were only the most recent casualties, although they'd all seen the horror of bodies simply lying in the street, along with hordes of dead animals – cats, dogs, horses, poultry, and even pigs. It was a waking nightmare.

It was now full daylight. Astonishing how good it felt to know the planes were gone – for now. Deliberately, Liam ignored the fact the sky was still full of yellowish smoke, giving the morning an eerie half-light. The planes were gone, that was the main thing.

Outside the ambulance bus there was a queue of casualties, which the McGowans resignedly joined. Everyone was simply glad to have survived the night, and strangely, there was an air of fevered exhilaration from some of those waiting to be seen. Liam could understand it, even though he couldn't share it. There were tears too; everywhere he looked he could see people crying, their tears tracking down dust-covered faces.

Some of the ladies from the Women's Voluntary Service were there, giving out cups of clean water and bits of bread.

Liam took a share, the water tasting like nectar on his dry throat. They handed out clean nappies too, and the women set about changing their babies, spreading their shawls right there on the ground.

Setting little Alice carefully down, Liam straightened. 'You could be here a while.' *I should do another round and report to Seymour.* He couldn't justify half an hour of idleness waiting to see his girlfriend – not when there was so much still to be done.

'That's all right, Liam. We'll be grand. Oh, Alice!' The child was being sick on the ground, and both women bent to comfort her.

'Is that blood? Jesus!' Mrs McGowan's voice sounded panicked.

*Do something.* 'Here, I'll take her on in.' He lifted the little girl carefully from the ground.

'Ah, thanks, Liam. The poor chile must have a stomach full of bits or something.' Mrs McGowan leaned forward to kiss her. 'Now, you go on in to Kathleen, and she'll make it better. All right?'

'All right, Ma.'

There were moments when wearing an ARW uniform helped, and this was one of them. No one protested as Liam walked straight to the top of the line carrying the injured child. Some even exclaimed at the cut on her arm, which had started bleeding sluggishly again. If they noticed fresh blood around the child's mouth, they didn't comment.

'Kathleen! Can you see this one next?'

Kathleen looked up from her current task – putting a sling on a man's arm. Immediately Liam was transported back to the first aid classes, and how he had felt when Kathleen was

## The Irish Midwife at War

practising on him. *I was an eejit!* He should have realised back then that she was the girl for him. The truth was he kinda had, but . . . oh, thank God all the complications were done with!

'Alice!' She looked back to the man. 'There, that's you all sorted. Try to keep it in the sling.'

'Thanks, love.' The man vacated the seat and Liam slid in, settling Alice on his knee. Kathleen gave him a brief look – love blazing from her eyes – then turned her attention to Alice. Her gaze rested momentarily on Alice's mouth, then swept over the child.

'Oh, I see you have a cut on your arm there, Alice. Where else does it hurt?'

Alice was gazing at Kathleen in adoration. Liam understood that.

'My leg. And my tummy.'

Kathleen was feeling her way down the child's limbs, at the same time asking Liam how long it had been since the incident that had caused the injuries.

'At least six hours. Probably nearer seven at this point.'

'Ow!' The child cried out when Kathleen touched her left leg, above the knee. 'Ah, I'm sorry, darling,' Kathleen murmured. 'Now, can I check your tummy?'

Alice nodded, and Kathleen carefully lifted the child's dress, ready to press the little abdomen and ribcage. Her hands hovered, then stopped, and Liam saw her expression change.

'Doctor!' She had turned her head to call out. 'Doctor, over here!'

Her tone alerted a man over at station one, and he immediately approached.

'Report!' He sounded like Seymour.

'Alice McGowan, aged three. Injuries sustained over six hours ago. Skin is clammy. Breathing rapid. Abdomen distended with severe bruising around the navel.'

'Any vomiting?' This was addressed to Liam.

'Yeah, there now. Blood in it.'

The doctor looked grim, his hands and eyes busy assessing little Alice.

'Also possible fracture of left femur and a cut on the left arm.'

He shook his head, and Kathleen gasped. Abruptly, Liam realised what was happening. *No! Not that! Not this wee one!*

'Next of kin?' He looked at Liam.

'Her mother and sister are outside.' He felt dazed. Alice was one of the survivors, one of the *good* stories from the raid. How could this be right?

'Bring them in. All we can do is make her comfortable. Nurse!'

Yes, Doctor?' A middle-aged woman approached, her brow creased as she saw the child.

'Alice, aged three. Terminal internal bleeding. How much morphine do we have left?'

The nurse looked stricken. 'Enough for this.'

'Right. Bring the mother and sister in. There's a bed free in the corner there.'

He and the nurse bustled off – probably to fetch the morphine. Liam looked at Kathleen, as the child relaxed against him. 'What's going on?'

'Nothing can be done,' she said, her eyes filled with sorrow. She shook her head. 'She'll be comfortable, and she'll have people she knows around her.'

## The Irish Midwife at War

*Jesus!* More death, and this time it was coming slowly. 'I'll get them in.'

For a moment, as he was passing Alice to Kathleen, he rested his cheek against hers. Then they were gone, Kathleen speaking in a reassuring tone about a lovely bed for Alice.

Liam made his way outside and down the queue. Of all the tasks he'd had to perform this night, surely this was the hardest.

'Liam!' They were both smiling at him, a hint of anxiety in their greetings. 'How is she?'

He simply stood there, unable to speak, watching their smiles fade as they read his expression. 'What? What is it?'

*Come on, Liam!* he admonished himself. He put a hand on Mrs McGowan's arm. 'Alice has internal bleeding,' he said gently. 'I'm so, so sorry.'

'No! Nooooo!' Mrs McGowan's wailing pierced the heart of everyone who heard it.

'She's dead?' Cora's voice was a thready half-whisper, barely audible over her mother's keening, but he saw the words form on her lips.

He spoke to the younger woman. 'Not yet. They're going to give her morphine for the pain. Yous can go in.'

Surely there was nothing in the world like a mother's grief? Mrs McGowan was wild-eyed and distraught, and he had to steady her as they made their way inside. Kathleen was waiting, and she spoke to Mrs McGowan, helping her contain her sorrow before taking her across to the bed in the corner of the bus.

Liam stood watching for a moment, then turned away. He could do nothing more for them here, but Mr McGowan needed to be informed.

*Belfast, 11 a.m.*

'Ah, we have it now lads! That's it!' Finally, Micko and his team had brought a large fire in North Belfast under control. The roof of the building had fallen a couple of hours ago, but thankfully the warning sounds had ensured no one was near when it collapsed in on itself. To Micko's right, rescue efforts were still going on in Sussex Street and Vere Street, where an earlier part-collapse of one of the massive side walls of the York Street Mill had engulfed both streets. The loss of life was shockin', so it was.

'Right! Keep your hoses trained on the smoking wood in case it reignites.' He directed this at the local voluntary firemen. The mains water pressure was pathetic, but should be enough for that task.

He called his crew. 'Back to the Lagan to refill!' Off they went, the route to the river taking three times as long as it should, for many of the roads were impassable. Craters, debris, and unexploded bombs were everywhere.

Jumping on to the side of the tender, he clung on as they navigated the smoke-filled streets of Belfast. The devastated city bore no resemblance to his memories, and Bronagh's hardness had contained nothing of the love they'd once shared. *And I'm a feckin' eejit who never grew up!* He hadn't had time for girls for many years, what with fighting a war, surviving prison, fighting again, and then trying to adjust to what passed for a normal life in the Irish Free State of twenty-six counties. Once he had got a start in the fire service things were better, but he couldn't handle the dances and céilís, and working in an all-male environment meant he'd had few opportunities to meet women.

His jaw tightened. And all the while, his heart had apparently been hanging on to memories of a fair-haired beauty from Belfast, as though she was some sort of ideal. He snorted. She had been *rude* today, and there was no need for it. It was *her* that had decided not to write back to *him*, not the other way round! Surely to God after more than twenty years the girl could at least have been civil?

As they painstakingly made their way to the river, he thought of all the things he wanted to say to her, the questions he wanted to ask. It was as though an entire world had been buried inside him. It had now erupted from its prison, and it would not be contained. Would he ever get the opportunity again? He was in Belfast for the first time in over twenty years. He might never be back.

They had arrived. As he went through the routine of setting up the pump, he put Bronagh from his mind in order to concentrate. God knows he had told his men often enough over the years about the importance of keeping your mind on your work. Distraction was dangerous.

'Look! Look!' The boys were pointing to the sky, and Micko followed their gaze. There, high above, were two Nazi reconnaissance planes. *Jesus, Mary, and Joseph and Holy Saint Patrick!* The sick feeling that came over Micko was like nothing he had ever experienced – and he had fought in both the War of Independence and on the antitreaty side in the civil war. But there was something so heinous, so merciless about what the Luftwaffe had done to Belfast . . . it was levels of evil not seen in Ireland since Britain took the food out of the country during the Great Hunger.

And Bronagh still lived here. Ruthlessly he turned his mind away from Bronagh, from the Nazis, from all of it. *I'm here to do a job.*

# 40

*Belfast, 1p.m.*

> *Around 900 people were killed in the Easter Raid on Belfast, with fifty thousand homes destroyed. Mass graves were dug in both Milltown and the City Cemetery to bury those who could not be identified.*

Seymour had started two lists – one for the dead, one for the injured. Grimly, Liam checked the Percy Street list, adding Mrs Corry and her baby, Elizabeth, and stubbornly refusing to add little Alice McGowan. She wasn't expected to live, but when he'd seen her last, she had been alive.

Astonishingly, the *Belfast Telegraph* was out, and contained statements from Stormont ministers about last night's devastation. There were photographs too, but Liam averted his eyes from those, for they were far too real.

All the wardens had been told to gather for a big meeting at one o'clock, and the duty room was filled with people and sombre talk. Those stationed there these past few hours had been spending their time receiving reports on who was dead and who alive, and answering a steady stream of queries from the public, anxious about missing relatives. Two of the wardens had died during the night: John O'Toole from the

Falls and Samuel Bell from the Shankill, killed side by side by a gas explosion on the Crumlin Road.

'Right, lads!' Seymour called them to order, efficiently going through the next set of tasks. Fifty-nine rescue teams were now active at all the major incidents and in the streets which had suffered the most damage, including Percy Street, Lincoln Avenue, and Sussex Street, with bodies being ferried to the Falls Road Baths, the Peter's Hill Baths, and the city centre market by the army and navy.

'The forces have taken over bringing people to the mortuaries,' Seymour confirmed, tactfully glossing over the gruesome reality. 'Our focus now shifts to the survivors. Thousands are leaving the city. Some trains and buses are running, and apparently most people don't even care about their destination – they just want out.'

'Can't say I blame them,' muttered one man, but Seymour ignored him.

'Many thousands will likely to choose to stay, and they will need all manner of practical assistance. Water supplies are an issue, and everyone on the Antrim side of the river is still being advised to boil their water until we can verify that there's been no contamination from the sewage system.'

'Boil water? With what? There's no town gas!'

Seymour shrugged. 'Tank gas, I suppose, if they have it. But the last thing we want is an outbreak of typhoid fever.'

Liam shuddered. The Nazi attack could claim many more victims yet.

'Power has been restored to most duty rooms and government posts. Telephone lines in north and west are currently working reasonably well, but remain down in the east.

Thankfully the power station in the harbour wasn't hit – a bloody miracle.'

*The harbour.* Liam had been trying not to think about Therese and Jimmy, the only people he had not yet heard from. Someone had mentioned that Greencastle up on Belfast Lough had been hard hit. He didn't dare to think about what that meant.

★ ★ ★

Alice McGowan, aged three, died around one o'clock, her parents and sister by her side. She had drifted into unconsciousness free of pain, free of cares and worries and fears. *A good death.* The handywoman in Kathleen appreciated it. The child's body, wrapped in a blanket, was taken away by her father, who looked like he had been hit by a motor-car.

'We have a coffin for her,' he told his wife. 'Mr Kane insisted.'

'That's good of him.' Mrs McGowan was in the dead-eyed disbelief stage.

'We'll do the wake at my house,' said Cora firmly. Hard to remember the girl was only sixteen, and had been through all kinds of changes this year. Maturity, or being forced to grow up too soon? *Both*, thought Kathleen, her mind flicking to fourteen-year-old Liam.

Resolutely, Kathleen resisted leaving her post and following them to offer support. Their home was gone, their darling too. But she had work to do here, and would have to call back up to Mrs Newsome later – a long walk. The queue was steady, more casualties arriving all the time. *I am needed here.* 'Right. Who's next?'

*2.30 p.m.*

Liam was still in the duty room, helping Seymour with the floods of reports that had to be collated.

'Hello?' Another member of the public, no doubt, seeking information on a missing loved one. Wearily, Liam turned to greet them, his jaw dropping as he saw who was there.

'Therese! Jimmy!' They looked tired and dusty, and Therese had a bandage on her head. He hugged them both. 'So glad to see you safe!'

'Aye well, it was hairy at times,' said Jimmy, grimacing. 'Greencastle was hit bad.'

'How bad?' Seymour chimed in – always seeking more information. Liam introduced them all and then Jimmy replied, detailing how the guesthouse they were staying in had taken a near-direct hit from a heavy bomb. 'I could tell by the shape of the walls and by the noise that we had no time to get out. We managed to get downstairs and dived under the table just as the first floor collapsed down on us.'

'And the table held?'

'Aye, thank God. It was a close thing, though.'

'What happened here?' Liam pointed to Therese's bandage.

'Ach, some flying bits hit me as it was all caving in. Bled like blazes but it was only a wee cut in the end.'

*Head wounds often bleed profusely even when small.* Vaguely Liam remembered thinking that thought somewhere near the start of last night's nightmare.

Seymour was eyeing Jimmy curiously. 'You mentioned you could tell by the shape of the walls that they were gonna go. Are you a builder?'

'Brickie,' said Jimmy proudly.

'And you're from where?'

'From the Falls. Why?'

'Then you would know other brickies in that part of the world? And sparks and that too?'

'I would, aye. Any that made it through last night. Why?'

'Very soon – within days, I'd guess – the government will start firing money at builders and tradesmen to begin repairing all this damage. Building new houses too. I intend to bid for the biggest contracts – and that means employing people from "both sides", as it were.'

Jimmy cast a dubious eye in Liam's direction.

'Mr Seymour is sound,' he offered, confirming the man was neither sectarian nor bigoted, and Jimmy's expression cleared.

'Gimme a shout, then, if you have anything.'

'Oh, I definitely will, Jimmy. Write down your details for me. Here.' As Seymour and Jimmy busied themselves, Liam took the chance to hug Therese again.

'Is our ones all safe?' she asked. 'Like, I'd have thought you'd have told me already if they weren't, but you seem . . .' She eyed him closely, a puzzled expression on her face. 'You seem strangely calm. *Contented*, I'd say. What's going on?'

He grinned. 'To answer your first question, yes they're all grand. Even our Seány!'

She exhaled in relief. 'Thank God for that! And Jimmy's family?'

'As far as I know, they're all doing well. Oh, and I'm not aware of any direct hits in the Whiterock Estate, so the worst you might have to deal with in your new house is broken windows and dust.'

'So go on then. Tell me.'

'Tell you what?'

'What has you looking so . . . I dunno . . . *smug*?'

'Smug? Interesting word. I could actually use that word to describe you and Jimmy . . .'

'Aye, but we're just married. You're not—' She broke off, her expression aghast. 'Don't tell me you got back with that cow Sadie!'

Jimmy and Seymour had returned, and were following the conversation with great interest.

'God, no!'

'He has got a girlfriend, though,' Seymour announced, laughing a little. 'Can you not tell from that stupid grin on his face?'

'A girlfriend?' Therese almost squeaked the word. 'Who?'

Now it was Jimmy's turn to jump in. 'Kathleen Gallagher, I reckon.'

'What? *Kathleen*?'

'Aye,' Jimmy was watching him closely. 'The two of them have been cracked on each other this long time.'

'They have?' Therese looked astonished. 'Kathleen and our Liam?'

'Aye, and if you hadn't been so caught up in wedding plans you'd have seen it too!'

She looked astounded. 'Is he right? Is it true?'

Liam nodded, and she squealed and hugged him again. 'This is perfect! You know, I've often wondered . . . but then I thought I was imagining things . . . and then, stupid Sadie . . . but now everything's perfect!'

'Perfect?' he laughed. 'Just look at the cut of us all!'

'Perfect,' she affirmed. 'We all survived, and our wee house is all right, and Jimmy's gonna have loads of work, and you're gonna marry Kathleen. *Perfect.*'

'Whoa!' He reacted as he was supposed to at the mention of marriage. 'Don't be runnin' away with yourself, now!'

'You better bloody marry her!' She wagged a finger at him, then grinned at his carefully blank expression. 'Fine. I'll leave you two to sort it out yourselves.'

'Thank you,' he offered neutrally.

'Oh, you're impossible!' She kissed his cheek, then grabbed her husband by the arm. 'Let's go, Jimmy. Is Mammy at home?'

Liam shook his head. 'Not sure. She and the girls were going to help at the parish centre once they'd had a bit of breakfast, I think.'

'Right. We'll head that way, then. See yous later. Nice to meet you, Mr Seymour!'

Liam watched them go, stifling a sigh. He was happy for Jimmy. Truly he was. But once again the prison of his own responsibilities had held him back. He had no trade, no way to make money even in the upcoming building boom. And some of the mills had been destroyed – casualties of Nazi bombs. No doubt there would be even more competition for mill work. His earlier determination to marry Kathleen regardless now met the cold light of day, and he cursed himself for wavering.

Might he be able to get labouring work with a demolition or building company perhaps? Maybe Jimmy could get him in with Seymour's foreman in that role, for he certainly couldn't ask Seymour for work himself. The man might feel beholden to him, so it wouldn't be right.

Once again his thoughts turned to Kathleen. What the hell could he offer her as a husband? He had no trade, no qualifications. Being an air raid warden was terrifyingly fulfilling, but when the war ended – as it surely would – that role would be gone. Plus it was entirely voluntary, and would never put food on the table, nor money in the rent tin.

'All right, Flynn?' Seymour was eyeing him closely.

'All fine, sir. Completely fine.'

A couple of other ARWs arrived, and Seymour began giving them instructions. Once done, he turned to Liam.

'Right. I'm going to head up the road. McCrea, you're in charge. Flynn, come with me.'

Liam was slightly mystified. To his knowledge, all night Seymour hadn't left his post for longer than he needed for the outhouse. 'Yes, sir.'

★ ★ ★

Kathleen was exhausted. It was an odd feeling, the need for sleep. As she had kept going the whole way through the night and morning, even when others had had brief naps, she had had no sleep since the night before last, and it was finally hitting her. Some of the volunteers had been emotionally overcome by it all, and cowered under tables during the last hours of the raid, shaking uncontrollably. Kathleen had been too exhausted by then even to feel fear.

'Go home,' the sergeant told her, and finally she had given in.

'I'll be back once I've had a few hours' break.'

'Take your time, love. You've been a wee star, so you have.'

At the wake for little Alice McGowan – held in the house of her married sister Cora – people were struck by the poignancy of the simple white coffin, and the angelic looking child laid within. Kathleen said a few prayers, helped for half an hour or so, and managed to slip unnoticed into the coffin a little treat from her bag, wrapped in a napkin.

'This is for you, Alice. Enjoy it!'

Stepping outside into April sunshine, she felt momentarily disoriented. So much was going on within her – Alice, and Lily, and the blur of faces and bodies she had supported all night. Still, she had seen Bronagh a few times, and had seen Mammy and Daddy earlier. She had had confirmation that all the other Gallaghers were safe and well. And she had seen Liam too. And he had told her he loved her.

Yes, maybe she could go a wee while longer without sleep. Straightening her shoulders, she set off for the Springfield Road.

# 41

Lily was awake, her bedroom smelling of childbirth and baby and carbolic soap. Kathleen had cleaned the whole room earlier. Baby was awake and Lily was elated, grinning in relief and joy. Kathleen sat with her quietly, listening as the new mother talked about the labour and birth. Most women needed to do that afterwards, she knew. The baby cried for a feed, and for a moment Kathleen swore she heard little Alice in the echo. Mrs Seymour came to join them, then, chipping in with her own comments and recollections.

Lily was just about done when a male voice sounded downstairs. 'Hello? I'm home!'

'My husband!' beamed Mrs Seymour, who went hurrying downstairs.

'How are you feeling now?' Kathleen asked Lily gently.

'I'm sore, and tired, but so, so proud of myself.' Lily's smile was genuine. 'I'm hungry too – but I suppose everybody is today.'

'Probably.' Kathleen certainly was. She literally couldn't remember the last time she had eaten.

'Thank you, Kathleen. I couldn't have done it without you.'

'Ah, you'd have been fine.'

Lily sent her a serious look. 'I really wouldn't, you know. I was panicking more and more inside. My poor mother didn't know what to do with me.' She took Kathleen's hand. 'Seriously. Thank you.'

Kathleen smiled. 'No problem.'

'Can we come in?' Mrs Seymour was on the landing.

'Yes!' Lily called, and Kathleen made for the corner, trying to look small and inconspicuous as Mr Seymour met his grand-daughter for the first time.

Today of all days such a special moment had even more impact, and Kathleen found that tears were streaming down her cheeks.

'I couldn't have done it without Kathleen,' Lily said after the initial exclamations, and Mr Seymour turned to look at her.

She knew him of course. *The district warden. The builder from the Shankill. Liam's boss.* She remembered him from those times she'd seen him at meetings in the parish centre, but today he looked different somehow. Softer. More vulnerable. Everyone had been shaken by the events of the past night and day, and Mr Seymour had now topped it by welcoming what Lily had told her was his first grandchild. In truth all Kathleen could see right now was a proud, relieved grandfather.

'Miss Gallagher, thank you.' How did he know her surname? *Liam must have told him.*

'No problem at all, Mr Seymour.' Her voice cracked.

'Now,' he said, all businesslike. 'A local baker popped in to the duty room with a gift; a couple of fresh loaves, baked an hour ago – so I took one home. We still have butter in the pantry, so I suggest we all have a little tea party.'

Mrs Seymour clapped her hands. 'I'll make tea!' She disappeared, leaving her husband to sit staring at the baby adoringly, and tell his daughter how wonderful she was. Leaving them to have some privacy, Kathleen slipped out, intending to visit the bathroom and perhaps help Mrs Seymour. Her stomach growled at the notion of food, but she could not be certain they intended to include her.

After making use of the fancy indoor bathroom (and ignoring the broken window and the dust), Kathleen made her way downstairs, heading for the back of the house, where she found the kitchen. Mrs Seymour was there, cutting bread and setting out a stack of clean plates, knives, cups, and saucers.

'Oh, hello, Kathleen,' she remarked warmly. 'Thankfully all the stuff in the cupboards isn't damaged. Look at that, though!' She indicated the window, of which there was very little left. The sink and floor was littered with broken glass like the bathroom above it, and Kathleen immediately looked around for a brush. There was one leaning in the corner, so she fetched it, making a comment about how awful the night had been.

Mrs Seymour was watching her, but didn't comment on Kathleen's instinct to assist. Instead she paused what she was doing, saying, 'Kathleen? There's something I'd like to say to you.' She took a breath. 'I was sceptical, especially as you're so young. But . . .' She shrugged. 'You handled her so well. You really know your work too. I appreciate it. And so does my husband.'

'Ah, that's the job. But thank you.'

'Right. Now, for some tea.'

Mr Seymour appeared in the doorway. 'Let's have it in the front room. We can bring some up to our Lily if she doesn't want to come down.'

Mrs Seymour looked at Kathleen, who shook her head. 'She's better staying in bed now. And she'll need someone with her tonight.'

'That'll be me,' Mrs Seymour said firmly. 'I'll sleep in the big bed with her. George, you'll be on the settee in the living room until we can get the windows in the back bedrooms sorted.' She made up two trays, one for herself and Lily, the other for Mr Seymour to carry through to the living room, Strangely, it was set for three.

'Follow me!' said Mr Seymour, leading the way to the well-appointed living-room. But it was not the beautifully crafted furniture or the marble fireplace that caught Kathleen's eye. It was the man sitting precariously on the edge of one of the fancy settees, looking deeply uncomfortable.

'Liam!'

His smile lit up his face. 'Mr Seymour insisted.'

'I did.' The man set the tray down on a low table, then pulled it towards the two settees. You deserve this treat just as much as me, Liam. Besides, with the main road clear now, I intend to give you both a lift home. It's the least I can do.'

And so, in the middle of drama and devastation, Kathleen sat down to what had to be the strangest tea of her life. Freshly-baked bread and pale yellow butter washed down with hot tea was always delicious. But when you hadn't eaten in nearly twenty-four hours, it was magical.

Mr Seymour cleared his throat. 'Now seems as good a time as any for this. Liam, I have a proposition for you.'

'A proposition?'

'Aye. I meant what I said to young Jimmy earlier. It's gonna take years to rebuild Belfast after last night's Blitz. They reckon near fifty thousand houses are gone. Plus all the businesses. Shops, pubs, churches . . . you name it, they'll all have to be rebuilt. McLaughlin and Harvey might think they're gonna get all the contracts, but I intend to win a good few.'

He looked Liam in the eye. 'I need a right-hand man alongside me. I'll do the deals and price the jobs, and you'll coordinate the office. Orders, invoices, wages, putting crews together for jobs . . . I'll need brickies and sparks and plumbers and hokers and roofers from the Falls as well as the Shankill, for there'll be more work than I've ever seen. I've a notion to step back a bit in a few years too, what with the grandchild arriving and all. I'm sayin' I need a . . . I suppose you'd call it a general manager. I need a man who's hungry to succeed, like I was. A man who's both smart and trustworthy.' He paused, still eyeing Liam keenly. 'Are you that man, Liam Flynn?'

\* \* \*

Micko had made up his mind. It was late afternoon and fairly soon, he reckoned, the Dublin brigades would be told to make their way back to Dublin so they'd be well clear of Belfast by nightfall. And he'd have missed his one chance to ask certain questions of a certain person.

'Where are the ambulance stations in West Belfast?' he asked a local volunteer.

'There's a few,' said the man. 'All the hospitals, obviously.'

'The community ones, then. Where the volunteers are posted.' He had seen Bronagh's uniform. *Volunteer Ambulance Driver*.

The Shankill, the Falls—'

'That one. Falls Road. Where is it, exactly?'

'St John's Parish Centre. Past the Whiterock junction. On the left.'

'Great. Can I borrow one of these?' There were a few bicycles stacked against the wall, for use by various volunteers.

'Aye, work away!'

'Thanks.' They were currently outside the Falls Baths, where military personnel were still carrying in the dead. *Life is precarious. We have to live before we die.*

'Lads,' he addressed his crew. 'Get some rest and food if ye can. I'll meet ye back here in an hour.'

Mounting the bike, he headed off towards the Whiterock part of the Falls.

* * *

Kathleen could barely breathe. *Is this really happening?*

Liam's brow was furrowed. 'I'm honoured, Mr Seymour. I have a question, though.'

'Fire ahead.' Mr Seymour leaned back, his attention entirely focused on Liam. Kathleen felt as though time was almost standing still. This was momentous.

'Where would I be based?'

Seymour's eyes widened. 'And here I thought you were gonna ask me about wages!' he sobered. 'In all seriousness, I was thinking about this even before the raid. There's a parcel of land I have my eye on near the brickworks. Everybody knows this is a more mixed area. There's people from all backgrounds working in the mills up here. I'll still use the Shankill yard for some storage. But I'll be moving the office to the new site. And I want you to run it. I'll get the jobs, you keep everything running well. How does that sound?'

'That sounds . . .' Liam's jaw was working; he was clearly struggling to speak. 'It sounds amazing.'

Great stuff!' Seymour rubbed his hands together. 'I plan to start a new company for this work. I'll keep going with the work round the Shankill via my father's company, but anything outside of that will be me and you. How does forty per cent ownership and the name Seymour and Flynn sound?'

Liam spluttered. 'Feckin' amazin'!'

'You can pay me a single pound for your shares. It's your brain I want, not money. And don't worry. I know you'll need a wage to tide you over while we're building it all up.' He named a figure that had Kathleen's jaw dropping. It was equivalent to about three months labouring in the mills – and Liam would be getting it every month!

'Will that do you? Every week, I mean?'

*Every week?* Kathleen met Liam's gaze. His eyes were wild with astonished joy.

'It's more than enough, and very generous of you, sir.'

'I know good people when I meet them, that's all. That salary is similar to mine, and perfectly reasonable. I won't do you wrong.' He stuck out a hand and Liam shook it. 'Now, we'll need to meet properly. Make plans. But for now, I'll run you both home.' He winked at Liam. 'I guess this means you can go ahead with other plans now.' He turned to Kathleen. 'I near forgot! Your handywoman fee, Miss Gallagher. How much do I owe you?'

'Not a thing,' Kathleen declared. 'Honestly, I don't need to be paid today.' Today was different. Today was special. And heartbreaking. And joyful.

Nevertheless he insisted, pressing coins into her hand that were about four times the amount she normally charged. 'My wife tells me you performed miracles with our Lily the day. So you and Liam here are well met. Right!' he added briskly. 'Let's go! I'm gonna take yous both all the way to Beechmount.'

In the event he was foiled by an uncleared heap of debris near the bottom of the Whiterock.

'It's grand,' said Liam. 'We can walk from here. Thank you.'

They climbed out, Liam and Mr Seymour agreeing to meet the next day to begin making plans. They watched while Seymour turned and drove back up the hill, then gave one another their full attention. No one was around so they kissed, and kissed, and kissed again.

They leaned back then to smile, and exclaim, and talk excitedly. 'Does he mean it, though?' Kathleen asked. 'I mean, is he all talk?'

'No, I don't think so. He loves making deals and getting contracts, but hates the office work. Which is surprising, because as district warden he's all over the details.'

'It seems too good to be true.' Kathleen was scared to believe in it, yet somewhere deep inside, she knew it was real.

'Like you.' He kissed her again, then pulled back, smiling. 'You do know what this means?'

'What?'

'It means we can marry as soon as we want.'

'Liam Flynn! Are you seriously asking me to marry you here and now, and me covered in dust and totally exhausted and looking shite?'

He grinned. 'Aye. Sorry about that. And you look beautiful.' He bit his lip, then straightened, taking a deep breath.

'Kathleen Gallagher,' he announced, in a serious voice, his expression solemn. 'Will you marry me?'

'Oh, I will! I will!' Flinging her arms around him, she sought his lips with her own, and there followed an entirely satisfying kiss.

'We'll have to tell your ones.'

'Aye.' She giggled, happiness coursing through her. 'And they don't even know we're together, so talk of marriage will seem awful quick to them.' She thought for a moment. 'Except for Bronagh. She's known for a long time how I feel about you.'

'My ones already know – well, Therese knows, which means all my ones will find out soon!' They began walking towards the parish centre, where it was likely they would find multiple Gallaghers and Flynns. He told her about Therese and Jimmy, and how delighted Therese had been, and she told him she'd had notions about him for as long as she could remember.

Turning off the Falls Road to the entrance to the parish hall and church, Kathleen saw that the tarp-covered bodies had all been taken away. Liam squeezed her hand. He had seen it too. As they went down the incline, Kathleen saw Bronagh walking towards her ambulance. She seemed to be restocking it, for the back doors were open and she was carrying a box of what looked like bandages and dressings towards it.

'Bronagh!'

She turned, her face lighting up – and then a curious thing happened. All the colour seemed to drain from her, as she gazed at someone or something behind Kathleen and Liam. Half-turning, Kathleen could see nothing to account for it.

There were a couple of people hurrying past in the direction of St James's, and a man in some sort of uniform on a bicycle, but there was nothing unusual in any of that.

At exactly the same time, the door to the parish hall opened and Mammy and Daddy emerged, saying goodbyes to someone inside. 'Aye. We better go – our Bronagh's waiting on us,' Mammy was saying. Kathleen couldn't stop thinking of her as 'mammy' and now reckoned she didn't have to.

'Better get a few hours' sleep in case it happens again!' Daddy added, ever the worrier. It was so lovely to see them, to know they were well, to enjoy the anticipation of them hearing her and Liam's news – but what on earth was wrong with Bronagh?

She turned back to look towards the ambulance. Bronagh had closed her eyes, as if in despair, and was muttering, 'This is a feckin' nightmare!' *But why?*

'Bronagh!' The man on the bicycle was dismounting, walking towards her. *He knows our Bronagh?*

'Bronagh,' he repeated, and she went to turn away. 'Ah, here. Don't run away again. I only want to talk to you.' He had a thick Dublin accent, Kathleen noted, as she and Liam approached. *What the hell is this?*

'I have nothing to say to you, Michael.'

Now it was Kathleen's turn to feel shocked. *Michael? Dublin Michael?* Abruptly, a wave of anger flooded through her. Was this the man who had condemned Bronagh to a life of loneliness? The man who had abandoned her after having his way with her? The man who—

Dropping Liam's hand, she stomped towards the pair. 'Is this Michael, Bronagh? *The* Michael?'

*The Irish Midwife at War*

Bronagh nodded, her eyes filled with pain.

'You fecker!' Kathleen slapped the man hard across the face, causing him to freeze in shock.

'Kathleen!' Mammy and Daddy both looked outraged. 'What the hell do you think you're doing?'

'This is the callous bastard that got Bronagh pregnant and dumped her! This is Michael, my *father*!'

Her words dropped into a sudden silence, as their meaning spread silently around the group.

Liam was the first to react, coming up to stand behind Kathleen and put his two hands on her shoulders. She was shaking from head to toe. *Liam's there to steady me.* His warmth was welcome, and his calmness. Kathleen's anger began to go from white-hot to something more contained.

'P-pregnant?' Michael managed. 'You were *pregnant*?'

'Yes, I was pregnant!' Bronagh spat. 'Not that you cared, running off to play at soldiers!'

'No! Bronagh, Bronagh! I wrote to you! Twice! You never replied!'

'No, you didn't! I never heard from you again! I—' Bronagh stopped, then slowly looked across to where her parents stood stock-still. 'Mammy?'

'You said he was married!' Mammy looked distraught. 'The last thing I wanted was for you to keep seeing him!'

'You destroyed the letters.' Bronagh's tone was flat.

'I burned them. I never opened them. I thought I was doing the right thing.'

Bronagh, pale and somehow *absent*, looked thoughtful at this. 'No, you were. If my boyfriend really had been married the last thing a pregnant sixteen-year-old should be doing is getting letters from him. It's my fault for lying.' She turned back to Michael. 'It seems I've been thinking badly of you all these years without good reason. I apologise.'

'Jaysus, Bronagh! I had no idea! If I'd known—'

'But you *should* have known!' There was still enough anger in Kathleen to accuse him once more. 'What sort of lad has his way with a girl and never thinks to check on her afterwards? She could have ended up in that Magdalene place for years!'

His jaw dropped. 'You were in one of them places, Bronagh?'

She nodded. 'In Dublin. But Mammy took me and the baby out when she saw how bad it was.'

He shook his head. 'I'm so, so sorry.' He glanced towards Kathleen. 'And you're right. I should have thought of it. There's no excuse.'

Their eyes met for a long moment. *He's my father!* Hysteria began bubbling within her so, deliberately, she engaged her brain. He was good-looking, this Michael, with a strong figure and a well-put-together face. Was there a similarity in the eyes? Kathleen had always thought she had the Gallagher eyes. Now, she wasn't so sure. The uniform had a crest. Dublin Fire Brigade. *So.*

'We need to talk. Properly.' Michael gestured vaguely about him. 'Walk with me?'

Bronagh thought for a minute, then turned and closed the doors of her ambulance. 'Let's go.'

As they went to pass her and Liam, Kathleen's eyes locked with Bronagh's, and abruptly, Bronagh pulled her aside for a hug.

'I'm sorry,' she muttered. 'This is a feckin' mess.'

*The Irish Midwife at War*

Kathleen's mind was working furiously. 'But it has possibilities,' she replied in a low tone. 'Find out if he's married!' she hissed into her ear.

Bronagh laughed. 'You're mad, Kathleen. Totally mad!' She glanced behind her. 'You and Liam?'

'We're together. He knows everything.' She grinned. 'He loves me!'

'Oh my God, that's amazing!' Bronagh hugged her again. 'Do Mammy and Daddy know?'

'Not yet. Though they might work it out any minute now!'

They parted, and Michael stepped towards them. 'What's your name?' he asked, his voice cracking and his gaze locked on her. He looked like a man in shock.

'Kathleen.'

His eyes flew to Bronagh's. 'You named her Kathleen?'

She nodded, then explained, 'We talked one day about our favourite names. Kathleen for a girl. Rory for a boy.'

Michael shook his head slowly. 'We did. But I never thought—' He straightened. 'This changes everything.'

'It kinda does,' Bronagh agreed calmly. 'See yous later!' She half lifted a hand towards Kathleen and Liam, Mammy and Daddy.

Michael picked up the bike and they walked away together, talking all the while.

'Well!' Mammy was the first to recover. 'I didn't expect that today, that's for sure and certain.' Her eyes narrowed. 'And is there something you've to tell us, Kathleen?' Her gaze was on Kathleen's shoulders, and Liam's hands resting there.

That was Liam's cue. He squeezed her shoulders, then stepped to the side. 'Mr Gallagher.'

'Yes?'

'The circumstances are a bit . . . unusual, to say the least, but could I possibly have a moment of your time?'

Daddy's eyes lit up as he looked from Liam to Kathleen and back again. 'It would be a pleasure, Liam.' Off they went, strolling around the yard like it was a hundred years ago, their expressions serious.

\* \* \*

Micko was gripping the handlebars so tightly his knuckles were white. He felt dazed, almost drunk. Bronagh had chosen to walk on his right, the bike between them. He shook his head slightly. The bike, aye, and years of hurt and misunderstandings.

'I could never understand why you didn't write to me. I kept waiting, hoping . . .' She was silent, her face pale, her expression closed.

'I was the same.' He swallowed. 'I am truly sorry, Bronagh. If I'd known—'

She shrugged. 'No matter. It all worked out in the end.'

'Worked out?' In his mind there flashed an image of his tidy flat in Dublin, and the loneliness that awaited him at the end of every shift. 'Not for me it didn't!'

She stopped, eyes blazing. 'For you? Oh, is this about *you*? You'll have to excuse me for forgetting for one second that this entire' – she waved her hands about – 'this . . . this *mess* was all about *you*.'

He winced. 'I suppose I deserved that.' His empty life was as nothing to what she must have experienced. 'Will you tell me about it? How soon did you realise you were expecting?'

Silence hung between them. He held his breath, feeling as though everything hinged on this exact moment.

'Let's cross here,' she said, breaking his gaze.

Bewildered, he looked about him. They had turned left when they left the church, and opposite was a cemetery. The sounds of digging came to his ears. Families would already be preparing for the funerals. So many dead. *Is she taking me to the cemetery?*

But no. Bronagh walked straight past the cemetery entrance, instead taking him through a narrow gateway a little further down. A path ahead wound its way through mature trees, green swards, and wide open spaces. 'Is this the Falls Park?' She nodded, and he whistled through his teeth. 'I remember it!' They had met here, many times.

'So you're a fireman.' It didn't sound like a question, but he treated it like one. God, why was she being so . . . so contained? Surely she should be raging, and thumping him, and shouting at her mother?

'I am. After the civil war I joined up. It was that or the army, and I'd had enough of fighting and killing.'

'And what about your brothers?'

'Pat died very soon after I left here. The Black and Tans got him.'

'Oh. I'm sorry to hear that.'

'Aye.' There was a pause. 'Our Barry works for the Corporation. He's married and they have six children.'

'Kathleen has cousins,' she murmured. 'This is so odd.' Turning, she sent him a piercing glance. 'And what about you?'

'What do you mean?' He was terrified of putting his foot in it. Ordering men about a fire scene was inadequate preparation for fraught conversations with someone you had once loved.

'Has Kathleen any half-brothers or -sisters? Have you a family yourself?'

'I never married. How about you?'

She shook her head, and abruptly his heart was pounding in his chest.

'Why did you not marry?' she enquired – the very question he was dying to ask her, yet couldn't.

He shrugged. 'I was wounded in Dublin and they put me in Jervis Street hospital. I then was caught and imprisoned, like a feckin' eejit.' Her jaw dropped, but he shook his head. 'Freeing Ireland is all very well until you're stuck in a cell for months.' He grimaced. 'I wrote to you, then wrote *again* in case the post had lost the first one. When you didn't reply I . . .' Shrugging his shoulders, he made light of the agonies he had felt. 'Pride, I suppose. I was a buck eejit, and found it hard to forget about you. I had really thought that what we had was, you know, *real.*'

Her brow was furrowed; she was thinking deeply. Seeing her expression, his insides got strangely twisted up – even more twisted than they had been since she brushed him off earlier. 'I recognise that look,' he blurted out. 'You look like Bronagh.'

She arched an eyebrow. 'I am Bronagh.'

'Aye. I meant, you know, *my* Bronagh.'

Her eyes widened, then she dropped her gaze. For a few moments the only sound was the hiss and click of the bicycle, and the birdsong in the trees all around them. The smell of smoke was fainter here too – almost as though nature had placed a blanket of safety over them.

'It took me ages to realise I might be expecting,' she began, and his heart lifted. *She is telling me about it!* A tiny step forwards, but he'd take it.

★ ★ ★

Mammy was looking at Liam and Daddy as they walked together around the yard between the church and the first aid bus. Kathleen could almost see the moment when her brain finally worked out what was happening.

'Are you— Is Liam Flynn— Are yous like . . .?'

For once, Mammy was lost for words.

'He proposed!'

'Ah, Kathleen, I'm delighted for you! He's a lovely lad!' Mammy hugged her, then frowned. 'We'll have to see about getting him more work, though. I wonder if they'll be taking on more hands at our place after this?'

Kathleen laughed. *Ah, Mammy, always ambitious!* 'Well, there may be no need!'

'Why's that?'

Linking her arm through Mammy's, Kathleen began promenading her around the yard in the opposite direction. 'Liam is after being offered a new job. A very good job. Just wait till you hear all the details!'

They had reached halfway, and Liam and Daddy were almost upon them. Liam winked at her as they passed, and Kathleen grinned back. Despite enduring the toughest twenty-four hours of her life, somehow she had ended up in a place where her entire being was filled with happiness. How it had happened, she could barely figure out. But it had happened, and she could only be grateful.

Above her head, a thrush flew by, coming to rest in a nearby tree and singing her little heart out. In the midst of war, of death, of sorrow and destruction, still there was joy.

\* \* \*

Micko was shook. Having now heard the entire story of Bronagh's ordeal – including the fact she had not been allowed to be a mammy to her own child – he was even more rocked. The notion of himself as a father was so new, and impossible, and life-changing that his mind simply could not cope with it. Dimly he knew he wanted to be a proper father to Kathleen from now on – if she would allow it. But that was for another day. Today his job was to take the first steps towards building trust with Bronagh. They had spent ages in the park before heading back along the Falls to the Baths, where his men were based.

'Micko!' Jack Conroy was there to greet him. 'They've asked if we can stay the night. Too many fires for them to handle.'

Micko thought about this. While their orders had been to come home before dark, they were all volunteers. 'Do the lads want to stay?'

'We do. Every one of us.'

'Right so.' He nodded, adopting his captain's voice. 'Ready up. Back on duty in five minutes.'

'Yes, sir!'

He turned to Bronagh. 'Can we talk again?'

She gave him a level look for a moment, then nodded. God, twenty years of hurt would take some undoing. But at least she was willing to talk.

They arranged to meet again in a few hours – their meeting place the Dunville Park beside the Royal Victoria Hospital. As he took his place on the tender beside his men, he reflected that he hadn't had a feeling like this – anticipation, excitement, hope – since he was last in Belfast over twenty years ago. His world had changed irrevocably, and not in a bad way. No, not at all.

# 42

*Friday, 18 April 1941*

> *Three days after the raid, the Belfast clear-up was well underway, amid unexploded bombs and fires still burning. Food was distributed at rest centres, bodies had been cleared from the streets and graves had been dug. More than two hundred thousand evacuees had left the city.*

Dunville Park was surprisingly quiet, Micko realised. It was teatime, and most people would be sitting down to eat. Food, however, was the last thing on Micko's mind. He had found Bronagh again, and she was single. That was enough to give him hope – hope that would have seemed impossible only a few days ago. Oh, he knew that he'd have to tread carefully, but there was no doubt in his mind about what he wanted.

These past few days he and Bronagh had spent every possible waking moment together when they were not actively on duty – walking, talking, or not talking, just being in each other's company. He'd seen her at work, seen how efficient and impressive and caring she was. He'd heard all about the awful time she'd had in the Magdalene laundry in Dublin, and *God*! It had made his blood boil. He'd seen her wit and her humour and her intelligence – qualities that he had not fully appreciated as a sixteen-year-old as much in love with her face and her figure as with her own self.

Not that he didn't notice those things now; his longing for her was twenty years in the making. But he saw so much more now. The tales she'd told him showed him how strong she'd had to be, all these years. *Jaysus!* Not to be able to acknowledge your own child! It didn't bear thinking about.

And here she was, walking towards him, making his heart soar and his pulse race. Was there a softening in her eyes? They both knew he was finally to leave Belfast within the hour, so his heart was torn between delight at seeing her, and soreness at the impending goodbye.

'Have you eaten?' she asked, without preamble, and he shook his head. The Tara Street crew had ended up staying for three days along with the other southern crews, catching sleep when they could and being fed at random times. Now, finally, fire crews from the Clyde and the Mersey had landed, and the Dublin lads had been stood down.

At her frown, he clarified, 'Apparently the people of Newry are making ready for us. We've to stop there for showers and food and rest. The Hibernian Club on the Mall,' he recited, having memorised the details in the past hour.

She nodded. 'That's very good of them. People are very grateful.'

He shrugged. 'That's not why we did it.'

'Oh, I know.' There was a silence. 'Michael, there's something I'd like to say.'

He eyed her warily, nodding, and she took a breath. 'A few days ago, I asked you why you never married, and you gave me your reasons, but it included . . . you mentioned that you thought what we had back then was . . . was . . .'

Her voice tailed off, but he had already worked out what she was trying to say. Daringly, he took her hand, and she let him. 'It was *real*. I never married, Bronagh, because of you. Because I never met any woman who even came *close* to you.'

Joy lit her eyes, and it was all he could do not to kiss her right there and then. But she wanted to speak. And he wanted to hear it.

'I . . . Michael, I never married either.' Her eyes held his. 'Because of you.' It was almost a whisper.

'Bronagh!' Then she was in his arms and his lips were on hers and all was well with the world.

*10.30 p.m.*

Liam was walking Kathleen home in the darkness, as he had done on one snowy New Year. This time, though, he held a hooded lamp, and the buildings around them were entirely blacked out. His free hand was in hers, where it belonged.

'Isn't it strange?' she began, and he glanced at her in the starlight. 'We're in the middle of a war. Belfast has been blitzed, and yet all I can feel is happiness.' She frowned. 'I hope Bronagh is all right. I wouldn't want him to hurt her again.'

'Michael.'

'What?'

'You avoid saying his name. I've noticed.'

She sighed. 'I'm afraid to trust him. For Bronagh's sake, and my own. It's all so new, and so bloody confusing.'

'I know, love. But I have high hopes for Michael O'Hanlon. I think he's been wronged too.'

'By Mammy. She's so interfering! If she'd only given Bronagh the letters.' She shook her head. 'I know, I know. We can't change the past. And thank God she was interfering enough to take our Bronagh out of that feckin' Magdalene laundry!'

He squeezed her hand. 'If Bronagh can forgive him, then you will too. I know you will. But you're right about everything being so strange. In the past week, my whole life has changed. I'm going to be Seymour's business partner, and you and I are getting married.'

'Married!' she breathed. 'It's a dream come true, Liam. I love you so much!'

'And I love you, my Kathleen.' They stopped, and he bent his head to kiss her, and in his mind snowflakes fell gently about them.

# 43

*March 1942*

The people of Belfast had held their funerals and begun repairing their streets and rebuilding houses. Rebuilding their lives would take much, much longer. Money was made available straight away for the most urgent repairs, and a new building company from West Belfast called Seymour and Flynn won a sizeable number of contracts.

The death toll from the Easter Raid ended up at around nine hundred, with thousands more injured, the biggest loss of life in a single night of the Blitz outside of London.

As the weeks and months went by, people began to believe again in their safety, and life began to feel more normal – or as normal as was possible given the rationing, and the blackouts, and the dreadful news every day on the radio and in the papers.

The Gallagher family celebrated not one but two weddings in the year that followed. Firstly, Kathleen married Liam Flynn from over the road – a popular match among the community. The young couple moved straight into a fancy house on the Springfield Road which it was rumoured they had *bought*, not rented, for young Liam was doing very well for himself as general manager in a building company, and his business partner had apparently stood as guarantor for the house loan.

The second wedding was in the early spring, and involved the eldest Gallagher girl, Bronagh – who was known to be nearly forty – marrying one of the Dublin firemen who had helped during the Easter Blitz. It was all terribly romantic, people said, as the bride and groom left to take the train to a new life together in Dublin.

Liam and Kathleen gave them a ride to the station, and then Kathleen stood hugging Bronagh until it was time for her to go.

'I'm so happy for you, Bronagh!' she declared. 'Turns out Michael isn't an eejit after all!'

Bronagh grinned. 'He's the best. I feel so lucky that we found each other again.'

'The bloody Blitz was good for something!'

'It was.' Happiness was radiating out of her, and Kathleen's heart warmed at the sight. She stole a glance at Michael, who was currently chatting easily with Liam. The two men got on well – a good thing, for Michael was now Liam's unofficial father-in-law. From having no father for years, Liam now had two – Daddy and Michael. Or three, for George Seymour seemed to think of Liam as the son he never had.

Kathleen got on well with Michael too, though she found it hard at times to truly understand he was her father. He was a nice person whom she was slowly getting to know. But he was Bronagh's choice, and so long as he was good to Bronagh, Kathleen knew she would eventually forgive him.

'I'm going to miss you, Bronagh.'

Bronagh hugged her again. 'And I'll miss you. But sure we'll be up and down from Dublin all the time, like we said.'

'Definitely!' Kathleen fished in her handbag – a proper fancy handbag. Liam had bought it for her as a Christmas present last year and she still got a thrill every time she used it. 'I have something for you.'

'Ach, Kathleen, you don't have to give me anything.'

'No, I do. I have to give you this.' She handed it to her: a small package wrapped in tissue paper.

'A handkerchief! Thank you!'

'I embroidered it myself.'

'It's embroidered? Let me see. I—' She stopped, seeing the pattern Kathleen had so painstakingly created – the word 'Mammy' surrounded by hearts and flowers.

'God, Kathleen!' There was another hug, and this time the two of them rocked together.

'Time to go.' Michael was there, looking at his watch.

'Yes, of course.' Bronagh planted a final smacker of a kiss on Kathleen's cheek, then turned away to take Michael's hand. Kathleen watched them as they made their way to the train and climbed aboard, Bronagh waving at the last minute. Then they were gone.

'Ach, are you crying, love?' Liam put an arm around her, and now pressed a kiss on her cheek.

'I'm really happy for her! I am! Truly!'

He smiled. 'I know you are – and it's all right to be sad at the same time.'

'I literally shared a bed with her from birth. It's hard to explain how close we've always been.'

'And now you share our bed with me, and from tonight Bronagh will be sharing hers with Michael.' He sent her a humorous look. 'Is that not a good thing?'

'It is! Of course it is!' Grabbing his beloved face with two gloved hands, she pressed her lips to his. 'In fact, since we both have the day off . . .?'

'Mrs Flynn! Shocking! You want to go to bed at' – he checked his watch – 'three o'clock in the afternoon?'

She affected a yawn as they began walking through central station. 'I'm very tired, you see. Must be all the work me and Bronagh were doing all week to prepare for the wedding breakfast.' Once outside they made for their shiny blue 1938 Hillman Minx motor car. 'Or maybe it's something else?'

He opened the door and held it while she slid inside, marvelling anew at the fancy leather seats.

'Something else like. . .' He sent her a look she knew well – one full of heat and promise.

'Yes. That.' Her breath was suddenly ragged. She and Liam had enjoyed months of sharing a bed, and her passion for him remained as strong as ever. 'Or . . .' she slid a hand to her abdomen, which was currently still flat.

He caught his breath. 'You're expecting?'

She nodded, eyes filling with fresh tears. 'I—' But his mouth was on hers, and his arms were around her, and for a long moment neither of them spoke.

'I love you, Mrs Flynn.'

'And I love you, Liam. My husband.' They shared a smile. 'Let's go home.'

# ACKNOWLEDGEMENTS

After writing *The Irish Midwife*, I knew that I wanted to stay in the world of handywomen, many of whom chose not to become certified midwives. I also knew that the story would be set during World War Two in Belfast. I was shocked to learn about the devastating events of the Belfast Blitz, and am indebted to books by Brian Barton and James Doherty in particular in ensuring that details in *The Irish Midwife at War* are as accurate as I can manage. I am again grateful to Dr Patricia Gillen, midwife, for checking the pregnancy and birth aspects of the book. Any factual errors are mine entirely.

The team at Hodder & Stoughton are superstars; I am so thankful to be working with such a passionate and dedicated group of professionals. In particular I want to highlight three women who have supported me every step of the way. Lucy Stewart, my editor, has nurtured, supported, and guided my work on these books since the day we first met. She is a warm and lovely editor and a fierce advocate all in one. She is also the RNA Editor of the Year – a fitting tribute to a phenomenal woman. Kallie Townsend, publicity manager, and Charlea Charlton, marketing manager, are unstintingly supportive and relentlessly unflappable when it comes to promoting and marketing my books. Nothing is too much trouble and everything is managed calmly and professionally. I have truly hit the publishing jackpot with Hodder.

My co-agents, Anna at Abner Stein and Liz at McIntosh & Otis, have guided me through exciting opportunities and career changes with patience and expertise; I am so grateful for your wisdom and professional skills.

Huge thanks to Waterstones Craigavon for hosting the launch of *The Irish Midwife* – Connor and Nathan are an absolute credit to the company.

Thanks also to my friends Val Troy, an effortlessly witty and funny woman, who expertly chaired our Q&A sessions at literary festivals, and Linda McEvoy, who connected me with the Laois Leaves Festival and is a fabulous cheerleader for my work, and to the rest of my RNA Irish Chapter friends including Lynne, Suzie, Karen, Karin, Karina, Debbie, Sylvia, Sharon, Fiona, Sheena, and Ruth.

To the team at the Tyrone Guthrie Centre for the gift of the Annaghmakerrig magic which helped me write like a demon while I was there (hmmm . . . how do demons write?), and to Eoghan Smith for friendship, walks, and dinnertime chat.

Thanks too, to my colleagues and friends in the Romantic Novelists' Association, and particularly to Saoirse, Katie, Ali, and Lucy. I am grateful for all of the tremendous work done by the RNA Directors, management team, and volunteers. It is a privilege to be the current chair of this wonderful organisation, and to be part of this community of writers supporting writers.

My own online communities include my two Facebook groups, so I must give a shout out to all the lovely members of Tinley's Tattlers (for writers) and Sagas and Sweethearts (for readers). Thank you for sharing this journey with me.

Finally, I have to thank my family. My husband Andrew who reads all my books even though romance wouldn't be his usual choice of genre, and the *clann*: Danny, Aoife, Maeve, Becca, Sam, and of course our wee Clodagh. Love you all.

# Reading Group Questions

1. The book begins on a hopeful, innocent note, with Kathleen's first kiss, amidst the wider context of the Great Depression and then the war. Do you think moments of hope get the characters through their toughest moments? How does this relate to your life?
2. Kathleen sees being a handywoman as a more interesting, less dangerous alternative to working in the mill. In what ways is she proven right? How is she proven wrong?
3. Were you familiar with the 'Belfast Blitz' before you started reading? Is this a period of Irish history you have previously been taught about?
4. Were you surprised by the societal attitudes towards sex and marriage portrayed in the book? Or is this what you expected of the time period?
5. How is Liam's relationship with Sadie different to his relationship with Kathleen? Do you agree with his reasons for not going out with Kathleen after their first kiss? How did the tough living conditions and limited opportunities of the time affect Liam's approach to marriage?
6. Kathleen must deal with lots of dangerous situations in the ambulance service, putting her life at risk for her community. How do you think you would cope in her position? Were you impressed by how she handled it?
7. The women that Kathleen looks after form a close bond with her. How do you think the book depicts the importance of community, especially between women?
8. How did you feel after finishing the book? Were you happy with how it ended?